THE BLOOD ROAD

Stuart MacBride is the No.1 *Sunday Times* bestselling author of the Logan McRae and Ash Henderson novels. He's also published standalones, novellas and short stories, as well as a children's picture book.

Stuart lives in the northeast of Scotland with his wife Fiona, cats Grendel, Gherkin, Onion, and Beetroot, some hens, horses, and a vast collection of assorted weeds.

For more information visit StuartMacBride.com
f Facebook.com/stuartmacbridebooks
@StuartMacBride

By Stuart MacBride

The Logan McRae Novels
Cold Granite
Dying Light
Broken Skin
Flesh House
Blind Eye
Dark Blood
Shatter the Bones
Close to the Bone
22 Dead Little Bodies
The Missing and the Dead
In the Cold Dark Ground
Now We Are Dead
The Blood Road

The Oldcastle Novels
Birthdays for the Dead
A Song for the Dying
A Dark so Deadly

Other Works
Sawbones (a novella)
12 Days of Winter (short stories)
Partners in Crime (two Logan and Steel short stories)
The 45% Hangover (a Logan and Steel novella)
The Completely Wholesome Adventures of Skeleton Bob
(a picture book)

Writing as Stuart B. MacBride
Halfhead

STUART MACBRIDE

THE BLOOD ROAD

HarperCollins*Publishers*

The quotation 'Heav'n has no rage...' is from William Congreve's *The Mourning Bride*, published in 1697.

This book contains public sector information licensed under the Open Government Licence v3.0. – specifically section 4.3.1 of the Criminal Justice (Scotland) Act 2016.

HarperCollins*Publishers*
1 London Bridge Street,
London SE1 9GF

www.harpercollins.co.uk

Published by HarperCollins*Publishers* 2018
18 19 20 21 22 LSC 10 9 8 7 6 5 4 3 2 1

Set in Meridien by Palimpsest Book Production Limited, Falkirk, Stirlingshire

Printed and bound in the United States of America by LSC Communications

For more information visit: www.harpercollins.co.uk/green

In loving memory of Peggy Reid,
a friend to cats, arranger of flowers,
and producer of the *best* cheese straws known to man.
1937–2017

Without Whom

As always I received help from a lot of people while I was writing this book, so I'd like to take this opportunity to thank: Sergeant Bruce Crawford, star of Skye and screen, who answers *far* more daft questions than anyone should ever have to, as does Professor Dave Barclay and the magnificent Professor Lorna Dawson; Christine Gordon, Geoff Marston, Lynda McGuigan, and Michael Strachan, who were a massive help with research (for a different story); Fiona Culbert, who helped with Social Work questions; ex-Detective Superintendent Nick Brackin, for 'the shed'; Sarah Hodgson, Jane Johnson, Julia Wisdom, Jaime Frost, Anna Derkacz, Isabel Coburn, Charlie Redmayne, Roger Cazalet, Kate Elton, Hannah Gamon, Sarah Shea, Louis Patel, Damon Greeney, Finn Cotton, Anne O'Brien, Marie Goldie, the DC Bishopbriggs Super Squad, and everyone at HarperCollins, for doing such a stonking job; Phil Patterson and the team at Marjacq Scripts, for keeping my numerous cats in cat food; and let's not forget Danielle Smith, Kim Fraser (née McLeod), and Andrew McManus, all of whom raised money for some very good causes in order to inspire fictionalised characters in this book.

Of course, writers, like *me*, wouldn't be here without people like *you* (yes, YOU – the person reading this book), booksellers, and bookshops too. You're all magnificent!

And saving the best for last – as always – Fiona and Grendel.

0

Duncan's eyes snapped open and he grabbed the steering wheel, snatching the car away from the edge of the road. The head-lights glittered back from the rain-slicked tarmac, sweeping past drystane dykes and hollow trees.

Don't fall asleep.

Don't pass out.

LIVE!

Madre de Dios, it hurt… Fire and ice, spreading deep inside his stomach, burning and freezing its way through his spine, squeezing his chest, making every breath a searing rip of barbed wire on raw flesh.

The wipers screeched back and forth across the windscreen – marking time with the thumping blood in his ears – the blowers bellowing cold air into his face.

He switched on the radio, turning it up to drown them out.

A cheesy voice blared from the speakers: *'…continues for missing three-year-old Ellie Morton. You're listening to* Late Night Smoothness *on Radio Garioch, helping you through the wee small hours on a dreich Friday morning…'*

Duncan blinked. Bared his teeth. Hissed out a breath as the car swerved again. Wrestled it back from the brink. Wiped a hand across his clammy forehead.

'We've got Sally's O.M.G. it's Early! *show coming up at four, but first, let's slow things down a bit with David Thaw and "Stones".'*

His left hand glistened – dark and sticky.

He clenched it over the burning ache in his side again. Pressing it into the damp fabric. Blood dripping from his fingers as he blinked...

Teresa walks across the town square, brown hair teased out by the warm wind. Little Marco gazes up from her arms, worshipping her for the goddess she is. The sky is blue as a saltire flag, the church golden in the summer sun.

Duncan wraps an arm around her shoulders and pulls her in for a kiss – warm and smoky from her mother's *estofado de pollo*.

She cups a hand to his cheek and smiles at him. *'Te quiero mucho, Carlos.'*

He beams back at her. *'Te quiero mucho, Teresa!'* And he does. He loves her with every beating fibre of his heart.

The car lurched right, heading for the drystane dyke.

Duncan dragged it back. Tightened his right hand on the steering wheel. Hissed out a barbed-wire breath. Shook his head. Blinked again...

— mice (and other vermin) —

1

Drizzle misted down from a clay sky. It sat like a damp lid over a drab grey field at the base of a drab grey hill. The rising sun slipped between the two, washing a semi-naked oak tree with fire and blood.

Which was appropriate.

A brown Ford Focus was wrapped around its trunk, the bonnet crumpled, the windscreen spiderwebbed with cracks. A body slumped forward in the driver's seat. Still and pale.

Crime-scene tape twitched and growled in the breeze, yellow-and-black like an angry wasp, as a handful of scene examiners in the full SOC kit picked their way around the wreck. The flurry and flash of photography and fingerprint powder. The smell of diesel and rotting leaves.

Logan pulled the hood of his own suit into place, the white Tyvek crackling like crumpled paper as he zipped the thing up with squeaky nitrile gloves. He stretched his chin out of the way, keeping his neck clear of the zip's teeth. 'Still don't see what I'm doing here, Doreen.'

Detective Sergeant Taylor wriggled into her suit with all the grace of someone's plump aunty doing the slosh at a family wedding. The hood hid her greying bob, the rest of it covering an outfit that could best be described as 'Cardigan-chic'. If you were feeling generous. She pointed at the crumpled Ford. 'You'll find out.'

Typical – milking every minute of it.

They slipped on their facemasks then she led the way down the slope to the tape cordon, holding it up for him to duck under.

Logan did. 'Only, RTCs aren't usually a Professional Standards kind of thing.'

She turned and waved a hand at the hill. 'Local postie was on his way to work, sees skidmarks on the road up there, looks down the hill and sees the crashed car. Calls one-oh-one.'

A pair of tyre tracks slithered and writhed their way down the yellowing grass to the Ford Focus's remains. How the driver had managed to keep the thing from rolling was a mystery.

'See, we're more of an "investigating complaints made against police officers when they've been naughty" deal.'

'Traffic get here at six fifteen, tramp down the hill and discover our driver.'

Logan peered in through the passenger window.

The man behind the wheel was big as a bear, hanging forward against his seatbelt, the first rays of morning a dull gleam on his bald head. His broad face, slack and pale – even with the heavy tan. Eyes open. Mouth like a bullet wound in that massive thicket of beard. Definitely dead.

'Still not seeing it, Doreen.'

She gestured him over to the driver's side. 'Course it *looks* like accidental death, till they open the driver's door and what do they find?'

Logan stepped around the driver's open door… And stopped.

Blood pooled in the footwell, made deep-red streaks down the upholstery. Following it upwards led to a sagging hole in the driver's shirt. So dark in there it was almost black.

'Oooh…' Logan hissed in a breath. 'Stab wound?'

'Probably. So they call it in and we all scramble out here like good little soldiers. Body's searched: no ID.'

'Give the hire company a call. They wouldn't let him have the car without ID.'

She turned and stared at him. 'Yes, thank you Brain of Britain, we did *actually* think of that. Car was booked out by one Carlos Guerrero y Prieto.'

'There you go: mystery solved.' Logan stuck his hands on his hips. 'Now, make with the big reveal, Doreen: why – am – I – here?'

Little creases appeared at the sides of her eyes. She was smiling at him behind her mask. Dragging it out.

'Seriously, I'm going to turn around and walk away if—'

'While we were waiting on Trans-Buchan Automotive Rentals to get their finger out and stop moaning about data protection, someone had the bright idea of taking the deceased's fingerprints with one of the wee live scan machines. We got a hit from the database. Dramatic pause...'

The only sounds were the clack-and-whine of crime-scene photography as she waggled her eyebrows at him.

'Were you always this annoying? Because I don't remember you being this annoying.'

She rolled her eyes. 'I'm surprised you don't recognise him. OK, so he's lost a bit of weight and shaved his head, and the Grizzly Adams beard and tan are new, but it's still him.'

'Doreen...'

'Carlos Guerrero y Prieto's *real* name is Duncan Bell, AKA: Ding-Dong, late Detective Inspector of this parish.'

Logan *stared*.

The hairy hands dangling at the end of those bear-like arms. The rounded shoulders. The heavy eyebrows. Take off the beard. Add a bit more hair. Put him in an ill-fitting suit?

'But ... he's dead. And I don't mean "just now" dead – we buried him *two years* ago.'

Doreen nodded, radiating smugness. 'And *that's* why we called you.'

The duty undertakers lifted their shiny grey coffin, slipping and sliding in the damp grass. Two of the scene examiners broke off from collecting samples and grabbed a handle each, helping them carry it away from the crashed Ford.

Logan unzipped his suit a bit, letting the trapped heat out, and shifted his grip on his phone. 'We'll need a DNA match to be a hundred percent, but they've done the live scan on his fingerprints five times now and it always comes up as DI Bell.'

'*I see…*' Superintendent Doig made sooking noises for a bit. When he came back, his voice was gentle, a tad indulgent. '*But, you see, it* can't *be him, Logan. We buried him. I was at his funeral. I gave a speech. People were very moved.*'

'You tripped over the podium and knocked one of the floral displays flying.'

'*Yes, well. … I don't think we need to dwell on every little aspect of the service.*'

'If it *is* DI Bell, he's been lying low somewhere sunny. Going by the tan and new name, maybe Spain?'

'*Why would Ding-Dong fake his own death?*'

'And having faked his own death, why come back two years later? Why now?'

One of the examiners wandered up and pulled down her facemask, revealing a mouthful of squint teeth framed with soft pink lipstick. 'Inspector McRae? You might wanna come see this.'

'Hold on a sec, Boss, something's come up.' Logan pressed the phone against his chest and followed the crinkly-white oversuited figure to the crashed Ford's boot.

A shovel and a pickaxe lay partially unwrapped from their black plastic bin-bag parcels – metal blades clean and glittering in the dull light.

She nodded at them. 'Bit suspicious, right? Why's he carting a pick and shovel about?'

Logan inched forwards, sniffing. There was a strange toilety scent – like green urinal cakes undercut by something darker. 'Can you smell that?'

'Smell what?'

'Air freshener.'

She leaned in too, sniffing. 'Oh… Yeah, I'm getting it now. Sort of pine and lavender? I love those wee plug-in—'

'Get the pick and shovel tested. He's been digging something up, or burying it, I want to know what and where.'

The other scene examiner sauntered over, hands in his pockets, glancing up at the hill. 'Aye, aye. We've got an audience.'

A scruffy Fiat hatchback lurked at the side of the road above, not far from where the crashed car's tyres scored their way down the mud and grass. Someone stood next to it peering through a pair of binoculars. Auburn curls made a halo around her head, tucked out of the way behind her ears. A linen suit that looked as if she'd slept in it. But she wasn't looking at them, she was following the duty undertakers and the coffin.

'Bloody press.' The examiner with the pink lipstick, howked, then spat. 'It'll be telephoto lenses in a minute.'

Logan went back to his phone. 'Boss? DCI Hardie's running the MIT, any chance you can have a word? Think we need to be involved on this one.'

'Urgh… More *paperwork, just what we need. All right, I'll see what I can do.'*

He hung up before Doig launched into his 'bye, bye' routine and stood there. Watching the figure up on the road. Frowned. Then turned away and poked at the screen of his phone, scrolling through his list of contacts. Set it ringing.

The woman with the curly hair pulled out her phone, juggling it and the binoculars, then a wary voice – laced with that Inverness Monarch-of-the-Glen twang – sounded in Logan's ear. *'Hello?'*

'Detective Sergeant Chalmers? It's Inspector McRae. Hi. Just checking that you're remembering our appointment this lunchtime: twelve noon.'

'What? Yes. Definitely remembering it. Couldn't be more excited.'

Yeah, bet she was.

'Only you've missed the last three appointments and I'm beginning to think you're avoiding me.'

'Nooo. Definitely not. Well, I'd better get back to it, got lots of door-to-doors to do. So—'

'You're on the Ellie Morton investigation, aren't you?'

The woman was still following the duty undertakers with her binoculars. They struggled up the hill with the coffin, fighting against the slope and wet grass. One missed step and they'd be presiding over a deeply embarrassing and unprofessional toboggan run.

'Yup. Like I said, we're—'

'Any leads? Three-year-old girl goes missing, her parents must be frantic.'

'We're working our way through Tillydrone as I speak. Nothing so far.'

'Tillydrone?'

'Yup, going to be here all morning... Ah, damn it. Actually, now I think about it, I'll probably be stuck here all afternoon too. Sorry. Can we reschedule our thing for later in the week?'

'You're in Tillydrone?'

'Yup.'

'That's odd... Because I'm standing in a field a couple of miles West of Inverurie, and I could swear I'm looking right at you.' He waved up the hill at her. 'Can you see me waving?'

'Shite...' Chalmers ducked behind her car. 'No, definitely in Tillydrone. Must be someone else. Er... I've got to go. The DI needs me. Bye.'

The line went dead. She'd hung up on him.

Those auburn curls appeared for a brief moment as she scrambled into her car, then the engine burst into life and the hatchback roared away. Disappeared around the corner.

Subtle. Really subtle.

Logan shook his head. 'Unbelievable.'

Something rocky thumped out of the Audi's speakers as it wound its way back down the road towards Aberdeen. Past fields of brown-grey soil, and fields of drooping grass, and fields of miserable sheep, and fields flooded with thick pewter lochans. On a good day, the view would have been lovely, but under the ashen sky and never-ending rain?

This was why people emigrated.

The music died, replaced by the car's default ringtone.

Logan pressed the button and picked up. 'Hello?'

'Guv? It's me.' Me: AKA Detective Sergeant Simon Occasion-ally-Useful-When-Not-Being-A-Pain-In-The-Backside Rennie.

Sounding as if he was in the middle of chewing a toffee or something. *'I've been down to records and picked up all of DI Bell's old case files. Where do you want me to start?'*

'How about the investigation into his suicide?'

'Ah. No. One of DCI Hardie's minions already checked it out of the archives.'

Sod.

'OK. In that case: start with the most recent file you've got and work your way backwards.'

'Two years, living it up on the sunny Costa del Somewhere and DI Bell comes home to dreich old Aberdeenshire? See if it was me? No chance.'

'He had a pick and shovel in the boot of his car.'

'Buried treasure?'

A tractor rumbled past, going the other way, its massive rear wheels kicking up a mountain of filthy spray.

Logan stuck on the wipers. 'My money's on *unburied*. You don't come back from the dead to bury something in the middle of nowhere. You come back to dig it up.'

'Ah: got you. He buries whatever it is, fakes his own death, then sods off to the Med. Two years later he thinks it's safe to pop over and dig it up again.'

'That or whatever he buried isn't safe any more and he has to retrieve it before someone else does.'

'Hmm...' Rennie's voice went all muffled, then came back again. *'OK: I'll have a look for bank jobs, or jewellery heists in the case files. Something expensive and unsolved. Something worth staging your own funeral for.'*

'And find out who he was working with. See if we can't rattle some cages.'

A knot of TV people had set up outside Divisional Headquarters, all their cameras trained on the small group of protestors marching round and round in the rain. There were only about a dozen of them, but what they lacked in numbers they made up for with enthusiasm – waving placards with 'JUSTICE FOR ELLIE!', or 'SHAME ON THE POLICE!', or 'FIND ELLIE NOW!'

11

on them. Nearly every single board had a photo of Ellie Morton: her grinning moon-shaped face surrounded by blonde curls, big green eyes crinkled up at whatever had tickled her.

Logan slowed the Audi as he drove by. Someone in a tweed jacket was doing a piece to camera, serious-faced as she probably told the world what a useless bunch of tossers Police Scotland were. Oh why hadn't they found Ellie Morton yet? What about the poor family? Why did no one care?

As if.

The Audi bumped up the lumpy tarmac and into the rear podium car park. Pulled into the slot marked 'RESERVED FOR PROFESSIONAL STANDARDS'. Some wag had graffitied a Grim Reaper on the wall beneath the sign. And, to be fair, it actually wasn't a bad likeness of Superintendent Doig. Always nice to be appreciated by your colleagues...

Logan stuck his hat on his head, climbed out, and hurried across to the double doors, swerving to avoid the puddles. Along a breeze-block corridor and into the stairwell. Taking the steps two at a time.

A couple of uniformed PCs wandered downwards, chatting and smiling.

They flattened themselves against the wall as Logan approached, all talk silenced, both smiles turned into a sort of pained rictus.

The spotty one forced a little wave. 'Inspector.'

Logan had made it as far as the third-floor landing when his phone dinged at him. Text message.

He pulled it out and frowned at the screen.

The caller ID came up as 'HORRIBLE STEEL!' and his shoulders sagged a bit. 'What do *you* want, you wrinkly monster?'

He opened the message:

Come on, you know you want to.

Nope. Logan thumbed out a reply as he marched past the lifts:

12

Told you – I'm busy. Ask someone else.

He pushed through the doors and into a bland corridor that came with a faint whiff of paint fumes and Pot Noodle.

A tiny clump of support officers were sharing a joke, laughing it up.

Then one of them spotted Logan, prompting nudges and a sudden frightened silence.

Logan nodded at them as he passed, then knocked on the door with a white plastic plaque on it: 'DETECTIVE CHIEF INSPECTOR STEPHEN HARDIE'.

A tired voice muffled out from inside. *'Come.'*

Logan opened the door.

Hardie's office was all kitted out for efficiency, organisation, and achievement: six whiteboards covered in notes about various ongoing cases, the same number of filing cabinets, a computer that looked as if it wasn't designed to run on coal or hamster power. A portrait of the Queen hung on the wall along with a collection of framed citations and a few photos of the man himself shaking hands with various local bigwigs. Everything you needed for investigatory success.

Sadly, it didn't seem to be working.

Hardie was perched on the edge of his desk, feet not quite reaching the ground. A short middle-aged man with little round glasses. Dark hair swept back from a high forehead. A frown on his face as he flipped through a sheaf of paperwork.

He wasn't the only occupant, though. A skeletal man with thinning hair was stooped by one of the whiteboards, printing things onto it in smudgy green marker pen.

And number three was chewing on a biro as she scanned the contents of her clipboard. Her jowls wobbling as she shook her head. 'Pfff... Already got requests coming in from Radio Scotland and Channel 4 News. How the hell did they get hold of it so quickly?'

Hardie looked up from his papers and grimaced at Logan. 'Ah, Inspector McRae. I would say "to what do we owe the pleasure?" but it seldom is.'

Number Three sniffed. 'Only positive is they don't know who our victim was.'

Number Two held up his pen. 'Yet, George. They don't know *yet*.'

George sighed. 'True.'

Logan leaned against the door frame. 'I take it Superintendent Doig's been in touch?'

'Urgh.' Hardie thumped his paperwork down. 'You know this is going to be a complete turd tornado. Soon as they find out we've got a murdered cop who faked his own death, it won't just be a couple of TV crews out there. It'll be *all* of them.'

'Did you ever hear rumours about DI Bell? Backhanders, evidence going missing, corruption?'

'Ding-Dong? Don't be daft.' Hardie folded his arms. 'Now: we need to coordinate our investigations. PSD and MIT.'

'Honest police officers don't run off to Spain and lie low while everyone back home thinks they're dead.'

'You can have a couple of officers to assist with your inquiries.' Hardie pointed at his jowly sidekick. 'George will sort that out.'

She smiled at Logan. 'Don't worry, I won't lump you with the neeps.'

'Should think not. And I could do with a copy of the investigation into DI Bell's so-called suicide, too.'

'I think Charlie's got that one.'

Sidekick number two nodded. 'I'll drop it off.'

Logan wandered over to the whiteboards and stood there, head on one side, running his eyes down all the open cases.

Hardie was trying on his authoritative voice: 'My MIT will be focusing on catching whoever stabbed Ding-Dong. You can look into … his *disappearance*.'

Logan stayed where he was. 'You're running the search for Ellie Morton?'

'I expect you to share any and *all* findings with my team. You report to me first.'

Aye, right. 'And Superintendent Doig agreed to that? Doesn't sound like him. I'd probably better check, you know: in case there's been a misunderstanding.'

A harrumphing noise from Hardie. Busted.

Logan gave him a smile. 'Ellie's been missing for, what: four days?'

DS Scott tapped his pen on the whiteboard. 'DI Fraser's working that one. My money's on the stepdad. Got form for indecent exposure when he was young. Once a pervert...'

A nod. 'I'll give Fraser a shout.'

Hardie harrumphed again. 'If I can drag you back to the topic for a *brief* moment, Inspector: DI Bell's files. Where are they?'

'DS Rennie's going through them.' Logan turned and pulled on a smile. 'You wanted us to look into the historic side of things, remember? Bell's disappearance?'

A puzzled look. 'But I only just told you that.'

Logan's smile grew. 'See: we're *already* acting like a well-oiled machine.'

2

The canteen was virtually deserted. Well, except for Baked Tattie Ted, in his green-and-brown tabard, worrying away at the deep-fat frier while Logan plucked a tin of Irn-Bru from the chiller cabinet.

Logan pinned his phone between ear and shoulder while he went digging in his pocket for some change. 'Anything?'

The sound of rustling paper and creaking cardboard came from the earpiece, followed by a distracted-sounding Rennie. *'Nada, zilch, zip, bugger-and-indeed-all. Not that screams "lots of money went missing!" anyway.'*

Two fifties, a ten and a couple of pennies. They jingled in Logan's palm as he walked to the counter. 'Of course it *might* not be about an old case. Maybe his personal life was what made him up sticks and disappear?'

A groan. *'Please don't tell me I'm wading through all this stuff for nothing!'*

The canteen door thumped open and in strutted a woman made up like something off the cosmetics counter at Debenhams. Jane McGrath: in a smart trouser suit, perfect hair, folder under one arm, phone to her ear, and a smile on her face. 'That's right, yes. ... Completely.'

She waved at him and helped herself to a cheese-and-pickle sandwich and a can of Coke. Tucked a packet of salt-and-vinegar under her arm. 'That's right. ... Uh-huh. ... Yes. I *know*, it's terrible. Truly terrible.' She pinned the phone to her chest and her smile blossomed into an evil grin – mouthing the words at Logan: 'Isn't it great?' Then back to the phone. 'It's a miracle their injuries weren't even more serious. I don't need to tell you how many police officers are hurt in the line of duty every year. ... Yes. ... Yes, that's right.'

Rennie whinged in his ear. *'Guv? You still there? I said, tell me I'm not—'*

'Don't be daft, Simon: it's not for nothing if you *find* something. And see if you can text me a list of DI Bell's sidekicks.'

'Hold on...' The sound of rustling papers. *'OK. Let me see... Here we go. Most recent one was Detective Sergeant Rose Savage. God that's a great police name, isn't it? Sounds like something off a crime thriller.* Detective Sergeant Rose Savage!'

Jane dumped her sandwich, Coke, and crisps on the countertop. 'I'll talk to the hospital, but I'm pretty sure we can get you in for a ten-minute interview: "brave bobbies suffer broken bones chasing cowardly criminal!" ... Yes, I thought so. ... OK. ... OK. Thanks. Bye.' She hung up and sagged, head back, beaming at the ceiling tiles. 'Ha!'

'Find out where this Sergeant Savage works now and text me.'

'Guv.'

Logan put his phone away as Jane launched into a little happy dance.

'Guess who just got all that crap about us being rubbish off the front page. Go on, I'll bet you can't.'

Logan frowned. 'Hospital?'

'Two uniforms were chasing down a burglar last night, he wheeches through some back gardens then up and over a shed. They clamber after him and CRASH! Pair of them go straight through the shed roof.'

'Ooh... Painful.'

'One broken arm, one broken leg. Which was lucky.'

She had a point. 'Especially given the amount of pointy things people keep in sheds. Shears, axes, forks, rakes, bill hooks—'

'What?' She pulled her chin in, top lip curled. 'No, I mean:

lucky they got hurt in the line of duty. Newspapers love a good injured copper story.' That kicked off another bout of happy dancing.

Logan paid for his Irn-Bru. 'Working in Media Liaison's really changed you, hasn't it?'

'And with any luck they'll have a couple of good bruises as well. That always plays well splashed across the front page.' She turned and danced away.

Logan shook his head. 'Why do we have to keep hiring weirdos? What's wrong with normal—'

His phone dinged at him and he dug it out again.

A text message from 'IDIOT RENNIE':

> Sargent ROSE SAVAGE!!! (crim fiter 2 the
> stars) wrks out the Mastrick staton. On
> duty nw. U wan me 2 get hr 2 com in??

Talking of weirdos...

Logan typed out a reply:

> No, I'll go to her. She's less likely to do a
> runner if it's a surprise. And stop texting
> like a schoolgirl from the 1990s: you've got
> a smartphone, you idiot!

North Anderson Drive slid by the car's windows, high-rise buildings looming up ahead on the right, their façades darkened by rain. A couple of saggy-looking people slouched through the downpour, dragging a miserable spaniel on the end of an extendable leash.

'...heightened police presence in Edinburgh this weekend as protestors are expected to descend on the World Trade Organization Ministerial Conference...'

He took the next left, past rows of tiny orangey-brown houses and terraces of pebble-dashed beige.

'...avoid the area as travel chaos is extremely likely until Tuesday. Local news now, and the Aberdeen Examiner has its sights set on a

Guinness World Record next week as it hosts the world's largest ever stovies-eating contest...'

Three teenaged girls hung about on a small patch of grass, sheltering beneath the trees to share what was quite possibly a joint. Passing it back and forth, holding the smoke in their lungs and pulling faces.

Logan slowed the Audi and wound down the passenger window. Waving at them. "Ello, 'ello, 'ello, what's all this then?'

'Scarper!'

They bolted in three different directions, their hand-rolled 'cigarette' spiralling away into the wet grass.

Logan grinned and wound his window back up again.

And people said community policing was a waste of time.

'...and I'm sorry to say that it looks like this rain's going to stay with us for the next few days as low pressure pushes in from the Atlantic...'

He turned down the next side street, past more tiny terraces, and right on to Arnage Drive in time to see one of the scarpering teenagers barrel out from the side of another grey-beige row. She scuttered to a halt in the middle of the road and stood there with her mouth hanging open, before turning and sprinting back the way she'd come. Arms and legs pumping like an Olympian.

Ah, teenagers, the gift that kept on giving.

He pulled into the car park behind the little shopping centre, designed more for delivery vans and lorries than members of the public. The front side might have been OK, but the back was a miserable slab of brick and barred windows on the bottom and air-conditioning units and greying UPVC on top. All the charm of a used corn plaster.

A handful of hatchbacks littered the spaces between the bins, but Logan parked next to the lone patrol car. Hopped out into the rain.

It pattered on the brim of his peaked cap as he hurried across to the station's rear door, unlocked it, and let himself in.

The corridor walls were covered in scuff marks, a pile of Method Of Entry kit heaped up beneath the whiteboard for people to sign out the patrol cars, a notice not to let someone called Grimy Gordon into the station, because last time he puked in Sergeant Norton's boots.

'Hello?'

No reply, just a phone ringing somewhere in the building's bowels.

The reception area was empty, a 'CLOSED' sign hanging on the front door. No one in the locker room. No one in the back office.

Might as well make himself comfortable, then.

The station break room was bland and institutional, with an air of depression that wasn't exactly lifted by the display of 'GET WELL SOON!' cards pinned to the noticeboard, almost covering the slew of official memos and motivational posters. A window would have helped lift the gloom a bit, instead the only illumination came from one of those economy lightbulbs that looked like a radioactive pretzel. A dented mini-fridge, food-spattered microwave, and battered kettle populated the tiny kitchen area.

Logan dumped his teabag in the bin and stirred in a glug of semi-skimmed from a carton with a 'STOP STEALING MY MILK YOU THIEVING BASTARDS!!!' Post-it note on it.

He sat back down at the rickety table and poked out a text message on his phone:

As it's Friday, how about Chinese for tea?
Bottle of wine. Bit of sexy business...?

SEND.

It dinged straight back.

TS TARA:

Make it pizza & you've got a deal.

Excellent. Now all he needed was—

A strangled scream echoed down the corridor and in through the open break-room door.

Logan put his tea down and poked his head out.

'Stop bloody struggling!' The sergeant was missing her hat, teeth bared and stained pink – presumably from the split bottom lip. Hair pulled up in a bun. Arms wrapped around the throat of a whippet-thin man in filthy trainers and a tracksuit that was more dirt than fabric. Both hands cuffed behind his back. Struggling in the narrow corridor.

A PC staggered about at the far end, by the front door, one hand clamped over his nose as blood bubbled between his fingers and fell onto his high-viz jacket. 'Unnnngghh...'

All three of them: drenched, soggy, and dripping.

Captain Tracksuit lashed his head to the side, broken brown teeth snapping inches from the sergeant's face.

She flinched. 'Calm down, you wee shite!'

He didn't. 'AAAAAAAAAAAARGH!' Bellowing it out in an onslaught of foul fishy breath. It went with the bitter-onion stink of BO.

Logan pointed. 'You need a hand?'

The sergeant grimaced at him. 'Thanks, sir, but I think we've got this. So if you don't mind—'

Captain Tracksuit McStinky shoulder-slammed her against the wall, hard enough to make the whiteboard jitter and pens clatter to the floor. 'GETOFFME, GETOFFME, GETOFFME!'

'You sure you don't want a hand?'

'*Quite* sure.'

McStinky spun away and she snatched a handful of his manky tracksuit. It ripped along the zip, exposing a swathe of bruised xylophone ribs. Then he lunged, jerking his forehead forward like a battering ram.

She barely managed to turn her face away – his head smashed into her cheek instead of her nose. She stumbled.

'Because it's no trouble, really.'

McStinky kept on spinning, both hands still cuffed behind his back. 'I never touched him! It was them! IT WAS THEM!' Dance-hopping back a couple of paces then surging closer to bury one of those filthy trainers in her ribs. Then did it again.

'Aaaaargh! OK! OK!'

Logan stepped out of the break room and grabbed the chunk

21

of plastic that joined both sides of McStinky's handcuffs and yanked it upwards like he was opening a car boot.

McStinky screamed as his arms tried to pop out of their sockets. He pitched forward onto the floor, legs thrashing. Bellowing out foul breaths as Logan kept up the pressure. Leaning into it a bit. Up close, the BO had a distinct blue-cheesiness to it and a hint of mouldy sausages too.

The sergeant scrambled backwards until she was sitting up against the corridor wall. Spat out a glob of scarlet.

McStinky roared. 'DON'T LET THEM EAT ME!'

The PC with the bloody nose staggered over and threw himself across McStinky's legs, struggling a set of limb restraints into place. 'Hold still!'

Logan held out his hand to the other officer. 'Let me guess: Sergeant Savage? Logan McRae. I need to talk to you about DI Bell.'

Logan leaned against the corridor wall, mug of tea warm against his chest. The station's rear door was wide open, giving a lovely view of PC Broken Nose and Sergeant Savage 'assisting' McStinky into the back of the patrol car parked next to Logan's Audi.

Rain bounced off the cars' roofs, sparked up from the wet tarmac, hissed against the world like a billion angry cats.

Ding.

He pulled out his phone and groaned.

HORRIBLE Steel:

> Come on, it's only one night. One wee
> teeny weeny night.

A quick reply:

> I'm busy.

Sergeant Savage slammed the patrol car's door shut, then lurched into the station again. Wiped the rain from her face. Scowled. 'God, I *love* Fridays.'

Logan nodded at the car. 'He's nice.'

McStinky thrashed against his seatbelt, screaming – muffled to near silence by the closed car door – while PC Broken Nose stuck two fingers up to the window.

Savage peeled off her high-viz jacket. 'You wanted to talk about DI Bell.'

'Don't you want to take your friend straight to the cells?'

'Jittery Dave? Nah, he's off his face. They won't let us book him in till they know he won't OD or choke on his own vomit. And the hospital won't take him: not while he's violent. So he can sit there and chill out for a bit. Smithy'll keep an eye on him.' She prodded at her split lip and winced. There was blood on her fingertip. 'Why the sudden interest in Ding-Dong?'

'You hear what happened this morning?'

'Been chasing Jittery Dave since I got on shift. I've run a sodding marathon already today – never mind Mo Farah, we should put a couple of druggies in for the next Olympics.'

'OK.' Logan led the way back into the break room. 'You were Bell's sidekick.'

She bristled a bit. 'I *worked* with him, yes.'

'How was he as a boss?'

'Good. Yeah. Fair. Didn't hog all the credit. Actually *listened*.'

Logan stuck the kettle on and dug a clean mug from the cupboard. 'What about his state of mind?'

'He blew his brains out in a caravan. What do *you* think?'

Teabag. 'I think someone wouldn't do that without a very good reason. What was his?'

She looked away. Shrugged. 'The last case we worked on. It was ... *tough* for him.'

'Tough how?'

'Ding-Dong... Look: Aiden MacAuley was three when he was abducted. He was out with his dad, in the woods near their house. Fred Marshall attacked them. Killed the father, abducted Aiden.'

'Fred Marshall?'

'And we couldn't lay a finger on him. We know he did it – he boasted about the attack to a friend of his down the pub.

23

Told him all the grisly details about bashing Kenneth MacAuley's brains out with a rock. Never said what happened to the kid, though. So we dragged Marshall in and grilled him. Again and again and again. But in the end, we didn't have a *single* bit of evidence to pin on him.'

The kettle rattled to a boil and Logan drowned the teabag.

Savage prodded at her split lip again. 'Course, we couldn't tell Aiden's mother any of that. We're banging our heads against the Crown Office, but far as she's concerned it looks like we're doing sod-all to find her son and catch the guy who killed her husband.'

'So what happened with Fred Marshall?'

'It really weighed on Ding-Dong. We were a *good* team, you know? And now he can't get it out of his head: he can't sleep, he's stressed all the time...' Another shrug. 'Then Ding-Dong's whole personality changes. He's jumpy, nervous, irritable. Shouting at you for no reason.'

She stared at the tabletop. Shook her head.

Somewhere in the station, that phone started ringing again.

'He... He came to my house ... about two in the morning. Told me I was to look after his wife. That I had to protect her from the press and the rest of the vermin. And that was the last time I saw him.' Savage cleared her throat. 'Until I had to ID his body in the mortuary.'

She shook her head. Blinked. Wiped at her eyes. Huffed out a breath. 'Anyway... Nothing we can do about it now, is there?'

'You ID'd the body?'

'What was left of it. According to the IB, he rigged the caravan to burn before sticking a shotgun in his mouth. The whole thing went up like a firelighter.' Deep breath. 'The smell was... Yeah.'

Logan let the silence stretch.

The station phone went quiet for a couple of seconds, then launched into its monotonous cry for attention again.

Savage shook her head. 'Couldn't get any usable DNA off the remains – you know what it's like when you cook every-thing.' She shuddered. 'Had to do it from his possessions: rings, watch, wallet. But we had his car at the scene, the suicide notes, what was left of his dad's shotgun; even managed to lift some of Ding-Dong's prints off the caravan...' Savage's eyes narrowed. 'You still haven't explained: why the sudden interest?'

Logan fished out the teabag and sloshed in a glug of milk. Added two sugars and stirred. 'Did you ever think he was involved in something? Maybe got in over his head?'

'Ding-Dong? No. He was a good cop. Most honest guy I've ever worked with.'

'Hmmm...' He handed her the mug of hot sweet tea. 'I *might* have some bad news for you.'

3

Logan stepped into the Major Investigation Team office and closed the door behind him.

Chief Superintendent Big Tony Campbell prowled the line of electronic whiteboards at the front of the room like a horror-film monster: big and bald, bushy black eyebrows scowling over small dark eyes. He barely fit into his police-issue black T-shirt, his bare arms forested with salt-and-pepper fur.

Hardie didn't look much happier, perched on the edge of someone's desk in one of the cubicles that lined the other three walls, enclosing the meeting table in the middle. 'Honestly, if you've got any suggestions I'm all ears.'

Big Tony jabbed a hand at the windows. 'Well he must've been staying somewhere!'

'I've got teams out canvassing every hotel and B-and-B in the area. Media Liaison are putting together "Have you seen this man?" posters. There's another team at Aberdeen Airport going through the CCTV and every passenger manifest for the last two weeks. What else can I do?'

Logan knocked on a cubicle wall. 'Not interrupting anything, am I?'

A harrumph from Big Tony, then, 'Inspector McRae, *please* tell me you've got something.'

'We're pursuing several lines of inquiry at the moment.'

'Wonderful. So *you've* got sod-all too.'

'Early days, sir. Early days.'

Big Tony lumbered over to the window, peering down at the gathered TV people and protestors below. 'Look at them, grubbing about, sneering at us, doing their snide pieces to camera about how NE Division couldn't find a fart in a sleeping bag.'

Logan stuck his hands in his pockets. 'I want to get someone exhumed.'

'Ellie Morton's mother's giving a press conference at twelve. No points for guessing what *her* main theme will be. She's...' Big Tony frowned. 'Wait, what? You want to exhume someone? Who?'

'Don't know yet.'

Hardie sniffed. 'How can you not know who you're going to exhume?'

'We buried DI Bell two years ago, remember? Only he wasn't really dead: he faked the whole thing. So who *did* we bury?'

Big Tony's eyes widened as it sank in. 'Oh for... CHRIST'S SAKE!' He booted the nearest wastepaper basket, sending it flying, crumpled-up sheets of paper and sweetie wrappers exploding out like cheap confetti.

Hardie covered his head with his hands and groaned. 'Not *again*.'

'Why did no one think of this till now? What the fffffff...' Big Tony screwed up his face, marched over to the dented bin and booted it away again. It clattered off a filing cabinet. 'Aaaaargh!'

'Now...' Hardie peeked out between his fingers. 'To be fair, there's been a lot going on and—'

'So let's get this straight: not only do we have the PR disaster of DI Bell faking his own death then turning up stabbed in a crashed car, now we've got to investigate him for *murder* as well? We buried him with full police honours!'

Logan nodded. 'So I can dig up whoever-it-is?'

'The media are going to *love* this...' Big Tony sagged. 'Our beloved bosses at Tulliallan are already pulling on their hobnail boots to give my arse a kicking. When *this* hits... Argh!' He gave the wastepaper basket one last whack and stormed from

27

the room, flinging his arms about like a man on fire. 'Dig him up. Dig them all up! Every single last bloody one of them!'

The door slammed shut.

Hardie stared at it for a moment. 'I would really like to make it clear that *none* of this is my fault.'

'I know how you feel.' Logan settled back against the meeting table. 'Speaking of which: have you heard of someone called Fred Marshall?'

A frown. 'Possibly. Probably... I think so. Wasn't he one of those rent-a-thug-have-baseball-bat-will-travel types? Why?'

'Just wondering.'

The office they'd given him wasn't exactly huge: lined with half a dozen manky old desks, a couple of scuffed whiteboards, and a collection of swivel chairs that looked as if they'd fallen off the back of a lorry. And then been driven over. Twice. Everything looked shabby and used, especially the carpet.

Logan sat back in one of the creaky chairs, phone to his ear, case file open on the scarred desktop in front of him. Frowning at the pathologist's report on what was left of whoever it was they'd buried in DI Duncan Bell's grave. 'According to this, cause of death was indeterminable, but *likely* to be due to the extensive shotgun wound to the cranium.'

On the other end of the phone, Rennie gave a little sarcastic laugh. *'"Likely"? Thought it took half of Ding-Dong's head off!'*

'Turns out DI Bell had stashed about fifteen litres of petrol about the caravan, set fire to the place, then tried to gargle his dad's shotgun.' Logan turned the page. A crime-scene photo popped and crackled with reds and blacks and pinks. Like a *Texas Chainsaw Massacre*-themed barbecue. 'Urgh... What was left of the remains isn't pretty.' He turned the page, hiding the image. 'Do me a favour: run a PNC check on a Fred Marshall, IC-One male, thug for hire.'

'Hold on, have to excavate my keyboard.' The sound of rustling paperwork. *'Fred Marshall. Fred Marshall... Why does that sound familiar?'*

'Prime suspect in the Aiden MacAuley case.'

'*Ah*, that *Fred Marshall. Here we go. Clickity, clickity … Fred Marshall.*' A low whistle came down the earpiece. '*Well he does seem like every girl's dream date. Five counts of threats and extortion, four aggravated assaults, three possessions with intent, two thefts from a lockfast place, one arson, and a partridge in a pear tree.*'

'And where's Prince Charming now?'

The clatter of computer keys went on and on and on and on…

'Rennie? You still there?'

'*Going digging.*'

'You better not be searching for porn on the office computers. This isn't the Houses of Parliament.'

'*Moi? Never. Well, maybe that once… Right – I've got nothing for Fred Albert Marshall for … call it twenty-six months.*'

Sounded unlikely.

'Nothing at all?'

'*Not so much as a parking ticket. Hang on, I'll check Twitter and Facebook…*' More clattering. '*Nothing. Nada. His last status update was going from "in a relationship" to "it's complicated" and his last post … here we go: a picture of a monkey peeing into its own mouth with the caption "Police Scotland's finest". Two years and two months ago.*'

Logan nodded. Frowned at the wall for a bit. Two and a bit years. So Fred Marshall was definitely a contender for 'Most Likely To Have Been Buried In A Police Officer's Grave'.

'*Guv?*'

'Yeah, I need you to get me everything you can about Fred Marshall: dental records, hospital X-rays, everything.'

'*And do you want that before or* after *the other four million things you've asked me to do?*'

'Thanks, Simon.' He hung up, and had *almost* got the phone back in his pocket when it dinged at him.

HORRIBLE Steel:

> Stop being such a dick. They're your kids
> too – wouldn't kill you to babysit the little
> monsters now and then!

29

He thumbed out a reply.

> I'm not being a dick, I'm busy. I have
> plans. And I babysat them two nights ago,
> you ungrateful lump.

Logan closed the case file.
Ding:

> OK: you can bring Ginger McHotpants with
> you as long as you don't leave dirty
> heterosexual stains on the couch again.

Reply:

> That was hummus and you know it. And
> I'm busy. Find someone else.

And with any luck, that would be that.

Logan called up the inter-department contact list on his steam-powered computer. 'Right: exhumation.'

'OK. Thanks. Bye.' Logan hung up and pocketed his phone. Swaggered over to the whiteboard and put a big red tick next to the words 'EXHUMATION REQUEST'.

The other whiteboard was covered in maps; post-mortem photos; photos of a burned-out caravan in a clearing somewhere; and photos of a large, hairy, middle-aged man. DI Duncan Bell. Heavy, rounded shoulders, a thick pelt of hair on his head, more hair escaping from the neck of his shirt. Skin like boiled tripe.

Logan dumped the pen back in the tray beneath the whiteboard and grabbed his fleece. Pushed through into the corridor.

A couple of support staff were gossiping outside the stationery cupboard. Both of them shrank back as he passed, their voices dropped to hushed whispers.

He nodded and kept going.

So what if they were all terrified of him. Wasn't *his* fault, was it? Just because he worked for Professional Standards now, that didn't make him a monster. Not often anyway.

The stairwell echoed with the sound of laughter, coming from one of the landings above.

Logan headed downward, digging out his car keys with one hand and... Stopped.

DI Fraser came marching up the stairs – late twenties, not that tall, in a black denim shirt-dress. Black leather jacket. Long red hair with a pair of sunglasses perched on the top. *Massive* handbag. She was trailing a pair of plainclothes officers. One, a small wrinkly woman in a wrinkly suit. Hair like someone had run over Albert Einstein with a ride-on lawn mower. The other, a thin short-arse in the full Police Scotland ninja-black uniform, with a ginger buzz-cut and a pointy nose. Detective Sergeant Steel and Police Constable Quirrel. North East Division's answer to Blackadder and Baldrick.

All three froze as soon as they saw Logan, making a strange mini-me tableau there on the stairs.

He gave them a smile. 'Ah, Kim, I was on my way to see you.'

DI Fraser narrowed her eyes. 'Were you now?'

He nodded at her miniature friends. 'Roberta, Tufty.'

Tufty beamed back. 'Hi, Sarge. I mean, *Inspector*. Sorry, force of habit.'

Steel made a cross with her fingers, as if she was trying to ward off vampires, and hissed at him like an angry cat.

'OK...' He turned back to Fraser instead. 'You're running the Ellie Morton case. Can we have a word?'

'I'm a bit busy trying to track down a missing three-year-old.'

Logan stayed where he was. Saying nothing.

She rolled her eyes and slumped. 'Urgh... Go on then.'

'Somewhere a bit more private?'

Fraser snapped her fingers. 'Tufty: one tea, so milky it's borderline offensive; two coffees, one with sugar, one black. Roberta: go chase up the media office about that appeal.'

Tufty scurried away, but Steel lingered.

'*Now*, Roberta.'

Another hiss, and Steel stomped off back down the stairs.

'And stop hissing at people!' Fraser grimaced at Logan. 'Sorry about that.'

'She's upset because I won't babysit tonight.' He lowered his voice. 'What's happening with Ellie Morton?'

'Why?'

'You put in a complaint about DS Chalmers.'

'Ah.' Pink flushed Fraser's cheeks. She cleared her throat. 'Maybe we *should* talk about this in private.'

Photos covered Fraser's office walls. Most were family gatherings, but pride of place went to a big portrait of a black Labrador by the name of Maggie, going by the plaque mounted on the frame.

Fraser dumped her huge handbag on the desk and settled into the chair behind it. 'Ellie Morton went missing Monday morning. The mother leaves her alone in the back garden and nips to the shops for a pack of fags and four tins of own-brand lager. It's a Co-op at the end of the street: so a five-minute trip, tops. She stops to talk to a friend on the way back, which means Ellie – and I can't stress this strongly enough – a *three-year-old girl* was left unsupervised for approximately twenty, twenty-five minutes.'

Logan leaned against the short row of filing cabinets. 'Forensics?'

'Nothing useful. No fingerprints, no footprints, no sign of fibres or a struggle. Garden backs onto a path that sees a fair bit of traffic.' Fraser dug her iPhone out of The Gargantuan Handbag Of Doom and fiddled with it. 'You know what it's like with child abduction cases: if you don't get a major break in the first twenty-four hours...' Was she Tweeting? 'No one saw Ellie run away, no one saw someone take her. We've got a few reports of a red car, or maybe a blue one, estate and-slash-or hatchback in the vicinity, but that's it.'

'And DS Chalmers?'

A hard sigh. 'I thought she'd turned herself around, I really did. Yes, she's always been ambitious, driven, but... I don't know.' Fraser put her phone down. 'I ask her to go interview someone, she doesn't do it. I tell her to do door-to-doors, she never shows up. I *order* her to help search the neighbourhood sheds and garages, she goes AWOL.'

No surprises there, then.

'Where is she now?'

'Tillydrone: breaking the stepfather's alibi. Or at least she's *supposed* to be. God knows, half the time.'

Logan softened his voice. 'What happens when you talk to her about it?'

'Might as well paint a penguin on your willy and call it Antarctica. She's sorry; she'll change; she's going through a rough time right now.' Fraser reached into her desk drawer and produced a blue folder. Thumped it on the desk. 'I documented every infraction, every meeting, and every outcome.'

'You should've come to me earlier.'

'I know, I know. But ... sometimes they just need a slap on the wrist. Getting your lot involved isn't...' She went back to fiddling with her phone again. 'They're still my people.'

'Professional Standards aren't here to screw people, Kim. We're here to help.' Logan picked up the folder and stuck it under his arm. 'Do you still want her in your team?'

Fraser kept her eyes on her phone's screen. 'I... We're looking for a wee girl, Inspector McRae. We can't afford to lose this time.' She finally looked up. 'And loyalty has to go both ways.'

Why did everything require nine million forms to be completed in triplicate? Couldn't go for a pee in the police without a Three-Sixty-Nine B, two corroborating witnesses, and a—

Logan's phone dinged.

HORRIBLE STEEL:

> Look, how about a compromise? You
> babysit J&N tonight and I'll look after
> Cthulhu if you want to take Ginger
> McHotpants on a dirty weekend later.

Reply:

> No. And stop calling her "Ginger
> McHotpants"!

He'd barely hit 'SEND' when the office door thumped open and Steel slouched in. The phone in her pocket chirruped as she settled on the edge of his desk.

'That better be you texting me back in the positive, Laz.'

Logan put his phone down, sat forwards in his seat, steepled his fingers, and stared at her. 'Ah, Detective Sergeant Steel, I wanted a *word* with you.'

'If the word's no' "I'd be delighted to babysit" I don't want to hear it.'

'DS Lorna Chalmers: tell me about her.'

A shrug. 'Magnificent breasts, so-so arse. But overall? I'd still ride her like a broken donkey.'

Oh God, there was an image.

'No! What's she like to work with?'

'Aye, because I'm going to clype on one of my team to you sneaky Professional Standards scumbags.'

'Scumbags?'

'With all due blah, blah, blah, etcetera. Now what about that babysitting?'

He folded his arms. 'I'm busy.'

'No you're no'. You have all the social life of a garden gnome.'

'Yes I *am*. But maybe if you scratched my back...?' Leaving it hanging.

'Lorna Chalmers is a pain in the hoop,' Steel stood, 'but I'm still no' clyping on her.'

Interesting.

'But you admit there's something to clype about?'

'I'm admitting sod-all.' She stuck her chin out. 'And if you didn't want to babysit your own kids you shouldn't have got my wife pregnant.'

'Not this *again*.' He pointed at the door. 'Away with you. Out. Go. Depart. Before I do you for insubordinating a superior officer.'

'Pfff…' She flounced out, nose in the air, leaving the office door hanging open. Then her hand appeared in the doorway, did a wee mime turny flourish, then flashed two fingers and flipped him the Vs before disappearing.

'You're supposed to be a grown-up!'

No reply.

'Typical.' Logan checked his watch: 12:10. Oops… Should've been back at Bucksburn for that meeting with Chalmers ten minutes ago. Assuming she'd bothered to turn up this time. He pulled out his phone and called Rennie. 'Have I got any visitors?'

A strange, wet, slurping noise came down the line, followed by a muffled, *'Have you noticed that no one visiting ever brings us biscuits?'*

'Are you eating something?'

Another slurp. *'… No?'*

'Visitors, Simon. Specifically, DS Lorna Chalmers: we've got a twelve o'clock scheduled.'

'But it's ten past.'

'I know. That's why I'm—'

'Ah, I get it. You're making her stew in her own guilty gravy for a bit. Ratchet up the tension.'

'No. I got caught up with these—'

'Hold on.' One more slurp, then a scrunching sound – the background noises changing as Rennie wandered off somewhere. *'Nope: no sign of her in reception. Well, not unless she's hiding under the coffee table.'*

'Damn it.' Of course she wasn't there. When did she ever turn up? 'What about Fred Marshall?'

'His doctor and dentist won't give me anything without warrants, so I asked the Warrant Fairy for some and do you know what she said?'

Logan groaned.

'That's right, she said, "Naughty DS Rennie! You know you can't have a warrant to seize people's medical records without probable cause. Bad DS Rennie! Back in your box!"'

'Then get me a last known address. And stop eating whatever it is you're eating: it sounds obscene.'

'*Nothing obscene about Pot Noodles.*' Rennie gave his noodles an extra-loud slurp. '*You know, when you asked me to come be a plainclothes gruntmonkey for you at Professional Standards I thought that was a playful euphemism for "valued colleague and important member of the team".*'

'Diddums. Now be a good gruntmonkey and text me that address.'

4

Laughter and voices filled the station canteen as a collection of about two dozen uniforms, plainclothes, and support staff gorged on lunch. They filled all the tables but one. The one Logan sat at, all on his own, Billy Nae Mates in the middle of his own private bubble.

Good job he had a dirty-big plate of macaroni cheese and chips to console him.

He helped himself to a forkful of soft cheesy goodness as the phone in his other hand rang and rang and rang and—

'This is Lorna Chalmers' voicemail. Leave a message.' Curt and to the point.

'DS Chalmers, it's Inspector McRae. Again. We had an appointment this afternoon. Please call me back.' He hung up. 'Not that you will, because you haven't the last three bloody times.'

Logan balanced another gobbet of macaroni, on the end of a crisp golden chip. Crunching as he scowled at his phone. 'Fine, there's more than one way to skin a snake.' He picked another name from his contacts and set it ringing.

'Ahoy-hoy?' What sounded like rain hissed in the background.

'Tufty? It's Logan. I need a favour.'

There was a small pause, then, *'Aunty Jane, how you doing?'*

More macaroni, chewing around the words, 'Have you fallen on your head again?'

'No, no. I'm at work, though, so I can't talk for long.'

'Steel's there, isn't she?'

'That's right, the party's tonight, isn't it? Don't know if I can make it though, depends on the case.'

'Fine.' Logan shook another dash of vinegar into the puddle of cheese sauce. 'DS Lorna Chalmers didn't show for her appointment. You're on the same team: where is she?'

'Ah… Don't really know. I could find out though, if you like?'

Then Steel's voice blared out in the middle distance. *'Come on, Tufty, you gimp-flavoured spudhammer, make with the chicken curry pies! I'm starving here.'*

'Text me.'

'Will do. OK, got to go. It's—'

'Aren't you going to tell your aunty you love her, before you hang up, Tufty? How very rude.'

A groan crawled out of the earpiece. *'OK, Aunty Jane. Love you. Bye.'*

'Should think so too.'

He ended the call and dug back into his macaroni again. Cheesy vinegary crunchy potatoey goodness.

Over by the canteen counter, the lone figure of DI Kim Fraser peeled away from the till and wandered into the middle of the room. Clearly looking for a seat. But everything was taken, except for Logan's table. Even then she kept looking.

Logan slid one of the chairs out with his foot. 'It's OK, I don't bite.'

She stood there, staring at him for a beat, then settled into the proffered seat. The heady smell of spices wafted up from her plate – heaped with Friday's curry special: chicken madras, rice, vegetable pakora, and naan bread, according to the board on the wall.

Logan gave her a wee shrug. 'After all, no one wants to sit with either of us.'

'People want to sit with me. Why wouldn't people want to sit with me?'

'People look at me, all they see is Professional Standards. People look at *you* and they see fast-tracked graduate-scheme "tosspot".' He held up a hand. 'Not what *I* see, it's what *they* see. We've got guys who've been on the job for twenty years and they still haven't made it as far as sergeant. You're, what, twenty-six?'

A blush darkened her cheeks. 'Twenty-*nine*.'

'And already a detective inspector. Some people feel threatened by that.'

'Hmmph...' Fraser crunched down one of the veggie pakora. 'I take it you saw Ellie's mum's press conference.'

'How can you eat that when there's perfectly good macaroni cheese and chips on offer?'

'How is it our fault? Tell me that!'

'And if you go near my chips I *will* stab you with a fork.'

'She's the one abandoned her three-year-old daughter in the back garden to nip out for booze and fags! If she'd been a halfway decent parent, Ellie wouldn't have been snatched.'

Logan put down his fork and looked at her. Silent.

Fraser groaned. 'All right, all right: I know. But still... That doesn't make it *our* fault.'

'Imagine if you were her. Would you want to admit you were responsible? How would you live with yourself?'

'Yeah, maybe.' Fraser chewed on her curry for a bit. 'And I'm not a "tosspot", thank you very much. I had to do a *law degree* to get on the fast-track programme. You try it if you think it's so easy.'

'Whoever took Ellie, it has to be someone who knows the area, right?'

'Back garden's got a path behind it. Anyone walking past would see Ellie'd been left on her own.'

Logan scooped a chip through the cheese sauce. 'You run a check on sex offenders living nearby?'

'And not just Tillydrone. We did Hayton, Hilton, Sandilands, Powis, and Ashgrove too. Interviewed the lot of them. Checked alibis. Nothing.'

Over in the corner someone launched into 'Happy Birthday to You'. One by one the other tables took it up and belted it out. The only ones not joining in were Logan and Fraser.

39

She dug into her curry again. 'Of course the smart money is on the stepfather, but he interviews clean.'

'Alibi?'

'Playing video games, drinking Special Brew, and smoking dope at a friend's house.'

'Sounds like an excellent role model.'

'Tell you, Inspector, I've scraped things off the bottom of my shoe with more—'

The song reached a deafening climax, complete with operatic wobbling harmonies and a hearty round of applause with extra cheering.

Fraser shrugged when it was quiet again. 'Five to one, when Ellie's body turns up, her stepdad's DNA is all over her.'

'*If* her body turns up.'

'Yeah. If.' She jabbed a pakora with her fork and gesticulated with it. 'Course, if we can break his alibi it's a different story. Assuming DS Chalmers has bothered her backside to even try. And before you say anything: I know. I should've sent someone else. She's had enough last chances.'

Logan put his fork down. 'Why didn't you come to me sooner?'

'Because… When you were in CID, would you have shopped one of your team to the Rubber Heelers? Of course not. No one…' She cleared her throat. Ate her pakora. 'Bad example. But the rest of us wouldn't. Not unless there was no other option.'

'There wasn't. And I did it for the same reason you are. Sometimes people don't leave us any choice.'

His phone dinged, a new message filling the screen.

TUFTY:

It is I, SUPERTUFTY! Scourge of naughty people! A tiny birdy tells me the GPS on DS Chalmers's Airwave puts her at/near Huge Gay Bill's Bar & Grill, Northfield.

Logan polished off the last glistening tubes of macaroni and stood. 'Now if you'll excuse me, I'm off to the pub.'

*   *   *

The building was set back from the road – an oversized mock Northeast farmhouse, long and low, with white walls, gable ends, a grey slate roof, and dormer windows. The Scottish vernacular charm was somewhat undermined by the big neon sign towering over the entrance in shades of yellow and green: 'HUGE GAY BILL'S BAR & GRILL!' It steamed and fizzed in the drizzle.

Only two vehicles sat in the large car park, a gleaming Land Rover Discovery and a mud-spattered Fiat. *Chalmers'* Fiat. Logan parked two spaces down. Clambered out and hurried into the pub.

Inside, the place had a soulless, unloved feel. Like an abandoned Wetherspoons. A soulless mix of polished wood and psychedelic carpet. Lots of small round tables with chairs. Menus everywhere.

Something romantic oozed out of the jukebox.

The only two people in here were slow dancing in front of it – all wrapped up in each other – one a large, white-haired woman, the other a Victoria Wood look-alike. Oblivious to everything else.

Logan went across to the vacant bar and rapped his knuckles on the wood. 'Shop!'

A grunt preceded a huge, broad-shouldered man who looked like the answer to the question, 'What do you get if you cross a cage fighter with a gorilla?' The lump of gristle clinging onto the middle of his face barely qualified as a nose. Somehow, the pristine-white shirt and dark-blue tie made him seem even more dangerous. He nodded at Logan. 'Inspector.'

'Bill. How's Josh?'

Bill bared his teeth – teeny, like Tic Tacs. 'Joshua is a scum-sucking arsehole.' He grabbed a bottle of Bell's whisky and shoved it into an empty optics slot, gripping the thing so tight his knuckles were white. 'Why do I have to keep giving my heart to arseholes?' Trembling, face darkening. 'Tell me that. Go on!'

'Don't look at me, my track record's not much better.' Logan counted them off on his fingers. 'One emotionally distant

41

pathologist with intimacy issues; one PC with violent tendencies; a self-harming, Identification Bureau tech, tattoo addict in a coma; and a Trading Standards officer.'

Bill folded his massive arms. 'What's wrong with her?'

Good question.

Logan shrugged. 'Don't know yet. Early days.' He pulled a photo from his police fleece and placed it on the bar. Lorna Chalmers. 'Her car's parked outside.'

'The scabby Fiat?' Bill picked up the photo and squinted at it. 'This your Trading Standards woman?'

'No: colleague. I'm worried about her.'

'Hmph... Well, suppose *someone* should be. State of her.' He dumped the photo back down again and jerked his head to the side. 'Ladies.'

'Thanks.' Logan had to detour around the slow dancers in front of the jukebox; they didn't even look up.

Bill's voice boomed out after him. 'And take it from me, the crazy ones might be great in bed, but they'll screw you over every time! Every – single – time.'

He had a point.

Logan pushed through the grey door marked 'Pour Femme' and into something off of a film set. Dark grey slate tiles, a plush red chaise longue against one wall, individual mirrors in heavy gilt frames above the marble sinks.

A lone figure was hunched over one of the sinks – DS Chalmers. She held her mass of auburn curls back with one hand as she spat something frothy and pink into the marble bowl. Her other hand clutched at her ribs. Holding them in as she washed her face. Grunting and groaning.

Logan settled onto the chaise longue. 'Having fun?'

She flinched, whipping around with a strangled scream, fists up. Ready.

He held his hands in the air. 'Whoa. Calm.'

Chalmers lowered her fists, voice all muffled and lispy. 'Inspector McRae. Oh joy.' Either she'd fallen under a bus, or someone had given her a serious going-over. Scrapes darkened her cheeks, chin, and forehead. The first flush of bruises beginning to spread around them. Face damp where she'd washed the blood off. Or most of it anyway.

Logan pointed. 'Want to tell me who did that?'

'It's nothing.'

'You were out breaking Russell Morton's alibi, so it was either him or his mates.'

'I *said* it's nothing. Leave it.'

The awkward silence grew. Then Chalmers turned her back on him and splashed another handful of water on her battered face. Winced. Prodded at her gums.

A tooth clattered into the marble sink.

'You've been married, what, three years? If it wasn't Russell Morton...?'

She froze. 'Leave Brian out of this.'

'There are people out there you can talk to. Domestic abuse isn't—'

'Christ, you don't listen, do you? It *wasn't* Brian. It wasn't anyone.'

'Ah...' Logan nodded. 'The first rule of Fight Club.'

More silence.

Chalmers dabbed at the scrape beneath her right eye. 'And you shouldn't be here.'

'Huge Gay Bill's? Bill and I go way back. One of his ex-boyfriends broke into his mum's house while she was in hospital and cleaned her out. Bill got his hands on him. Was going to rip the guy's arms and legs off, till I talked him down. He's always had terrible taste in men.'

She limped over to the driers and patted at her face, ignoring him as they roared at her.

Logan stretched out on the chaise longue, making himself comfortable. 'You've been avoiding me.'

She tucked in her torn shirt. 'Are they firing me?'

'I'm not your enemy, Lorna.'

'Could've fooled me.'

'I'm here to help. We can—'

'Then keep them off my back, OK?' She limped back to the mirror and took out a small make-up kit. 'Tell them everything's

43

fine. I've apologised and promise to be a good little girl from now on.'

Logan sighed. 'It doesn't work like that. You've been disappearing when you're meant to be on the job. Ducking assignments. Not doing what DI Fraser tells you.'

'DI Fraser's an idiot.'

'No she isn't. And you know what? Even if she was, right now she's your *superior* idiot and if she tells you to go interview someone you actually have to go interview them.'

A wodge of foundation got slathered on, covering up the scrapes and bruises. Wincing as she did her best to blend it in. You could still tell, though.

Eventually she stood back and stared at the result. Grimaced. 'It'll do.' Her make-up clattered into the bag again. 'Russell Morton's alibi's sound. He was where he said he was, *when* he said he was. I spoke to the guy who delivered one fourteen-inch four seasons with extra anchovies, one mushroom feast, a spicy American, two garlic breads, and three six-packs of Peroni.'

'A lot of food.'

'Morton paid him from a big roll of cash. Ten-quid tip, too.'

'Flashy.'

'Especially for someone on the dole.' She examined herself in the mirror again. 'So you can tell *DI Kim Fraser* I've been doing my job. Did it yesterday before she even asked. Just because I'm not grubbing around her feet, begging for titbits like those idiot sidekicks of hers, doesn't mean I'm slacking.'

'No one's asking you to grub about, Lorna, but this is the *police*. You have to follow procedure. The chain of command's there for a reason!'

She stared at him from the mirror, face blank. 'Are we done, Inspector?'

'Have you forgotten what happened with the Agnes Garfield case? You could've *died*. You very nearly got me and PC Sim killed! All because you couldn't stand the thought of sharing the glory.' Logan stood. 'Police Scotland doesn't need lone wolves, Lorna. That's not how this works!'

Nothing back. Not even a flicker.

Then, 'If it's all right with you, I'd like to have a wee now. Or do you want to follow me in there as well?' She turned and barged into one of the cubicles. Slammed the door. Clacked the latch.

Logan knocked on the cubicle door. 'They're going to suspend you. Is that what you want?'

The sound of piddling hissed out from inside. Accompanied by what might have been muffled sobs...

Great. That went well.

Bill shook his head. '...so Shoogly Dave says, "Wasnae me, it was like that when I found it." And he's staggering about the stock room surrounded by two thousand...' Bill pointed over Logan's shoulder. 'Your friend's back.'

Logan turned and there was Chalmers, coming out of the ladies. Grimacing as she saw them.

He went back to his cappuccino, watching her in the mirror behind the bar as she marched over.

She stopped right behind him. Put on what was probably meant to be a reasonable voice. 'You *can't* let them take this away from me. Do you have any idea what I've sacrificed for this job? Not just the hours: I barely *see* Brian. I've put every-thing on hold for this. *Everything.*'

'We all make sacrifices, it's part of—'

'Oh that's easy for *you* to say, isn't it? You didn't even have to have your own kids, did you? You farmed them out to someone else!'

'That's not—'

'If you really want to help, keep Fraser off my back for a couple of days.' A frown. 'Better make it three.'

Funny.

He took a sip of warm milky coffee. 'Twenty-four hours.'

She gave him a pained smile in the mirror. 'No, it *has* to be seventy-two. I need—'

'It's not an offer, it's the cliché.' Putting on an American accent for, '"Ya gotta give me twenty-four hours to crack the

45

case, Lieutenant."' Then back to normal again. 'And no. If you've got information that might save Ellie Morton, you tell me or you tell DI Fraser. You do *not* keep it secret so you can grab the glory. A wee girl's life is at stake!'

'I *know* what's at stake!'

Logan thumped his mug down. 'Then grow up and stop playing Sam Sodding Spade!'

She glared at his reflection in the mirror. Turned. And marched out the front door.

Logan shouted after her. 'I mean it, Lorna, this isn't a game!'

The door slammed shut.

Bill stared at it. 'Told you – great in the sack, but they'll screw you over every time.'

5

Patronising, holier-than-thou, big-eared, *wanker*. Lorna stared through the windscreen at Huge Gay Bill's Bar and Grill, teeth bared. Blood fizzing in her ears as the rain battered down and—

A boot thuds against the small of her back, another one into her shoulder. Lorna curls up tighter, arms wrapped around her head as the pair of bastards lay into her. First it was shoving. Then fists. Now boots.

Two against one.

'Aaaargh!' She bites it down. Don't scream. Don't give them the *satisfaction*.

More kicks, on her arms and legs. One to the kidneys that erupts around her torso like it's full of angry wasps. Another to the hand covering her face and the world tastes of rust and hot batteries.

Lorna coughs and splutters out a spattering of bright scarlet.

And the beating stops.

She can hear them backing away. Panting.

Then Danners leans in close, her breath warm on Lorna's skin. 'Take a telling, you two-faced *bitch*. Next time we won't be so polite.'

There's the scuffing of feet on tarmac and she flinches, waiting for the blows to start again... But they don't. Instead the sound of a Portakabin door slamming booms out into the rain.

She risks a look.

They've gone.

They've *gone*. She almost laughs, but her ribs hurt too much. So instead she struggles up to her knees, setting the wasps off again, then to her feet. Lurching across the car park to her little Fiat. Fumbling her keys from her pocket with fingers that are already starting to swell and stiffen. Unlocks the door and does her best not to fall inside.

Rows and rows of Northfield tenements drone by the car window, bricks and harling stained by the downpour. *Everything* aches.

Lorna's mobile phone buzzes in her pocket, then launches into Radiohead's 'The Bends'. She pulls it out with one aching hand and squints at the screen: 'BRIAN'.

Sod off, Brian.

She hits 'IGNORE' and keeps on driving.

Should get him a ringtone of his own. Something good. Then at least she can *enjoy* ignoring his calls.

The car park's nearly empty as she pulls up outside Huge Gay Bill's Bar And Grill. Turns the engine off. Sniffs. Blinks. Wipes a sore hand across her damp eyes.

Sits there and cries for a while.

Her phone goes into 'The Bends' again, the word 'BRIAN' filling the screen like a corpse. She hits 'IGNORE' *again*. Sags. Then grits her teeth and winces her way out of the car.

Locks it and lurches across the rain-puddled tarmac and in through the front door. Straight across the revolting carpet.

Huge Gay Bill looks up from stacking the fridge with alcopops and stares at her. 'Dear God, are you OK? Do you need me to call a—'

'NO!' Storming right past him and into the ladies.

It's all very fancy and fashionable in here, but the only thing that matters are the mirrors and the sinks. She grips the marble with blood-smeared swollen fingers and stares at the animal in the glass. Her left eye's beginning to puff up – a thin purple line underneath it promising to blossom into a full-on shiner over the next couple of days. More scrapes and lumps on her cheek and forehead. A swollen bottom lip.

Her jacket's torn at the shoulder and scraped through at the elbow – straight through the shirt too, all the way down to a raw patch of skin flecked with grit that starts stinging as soon as she sees it.

She turns on the taps and fills the sink with warm water. Splashes it on her face. Working her tongue along her bottom jaw. Flinching as it finds a rough bit of gum and a tooth that won't sit still when she touches it.

How could it all go wrong? She's been doing so well, and now *this*?

It isn't fair...

The woman in the mirror blurs. Lorna drags in a serrated breath that tastes of blood. What does it matter if she cries in here? Isn't as if there's anyone to see it. Why shouldn't she cry if she wants to?

She splashes her face with water again.

It's a setback, that's all. Nothing she can't handle.

Bright red drips into the water, turning it pink.

Nothing she can't handle.

Just breathe deep and calm down.

Stop shaking.

She folds forward and tries. And tries. And tries.

Then the door clunks behind her. And when she looks up – there, in the mirror, is Inspector Logan Bloody McRae. Because today isn't enough of a crapfest.

Lorna glowered up at the neon sign above Huge Gay Bill's, closed her eyes, and dragged in a deep breath. 'AAAAAAAAA AAAAAAAAAAAAAAAAAAAAAAAAAARGH!'

Turned the key in the ignition, wrenched the car into gear, hauled the steering wheel around, and drove for the exit.

'The Bends' jarred out of her phone and when she checked the screen, there it was: 'BRIAN'. Again.

'LEAVE ME ALONE!'

Lorna stabbed 'IGNORE' and tossed the phone on the passenger seat.

It was time to stop feeling sorry for herself and *do* something about it.

Lorna pulled up at the kerb opposite the house and frowned. There was a car in the driveway – a new-looking Mini Cooper, *parked* on *her* driveway. Brian's precious midlife-crisis Alfa Romeo was right outside the house, two wheels up on the pavement.

Thought he was meant to be at work today?

She winced her way out of the car and limped across the road. Ignoring the rain.

The Mini had to be new – the number plate was that year's. Metallic red, with a white roof. A child seat in the back, about the right size for a toddler.

Why park here? Why not park in front of someone else's nasty little matchbox house on the nasty little matchbox street with its nasty little matchbox people? Bland three-up two-downs with built-in garages that no one ever parked their car in, because they were too small. Putting fake stonework around the windows and edges, didn't make it any less like an undiscovered circle of Dante's Inferno. Where dreams went to be punished.

She huddled under the porch, pulled out her keys, and unlocked her front door.

Stepped inside.

The sound of a kids' TV show jangled out of the open living room door, cheerful idiots singing a stupid song:

'Now Doris had a friend called Morris, he was a tyrannosaurus,
He had teeny tiny arms and couldn't brush his teeth,'

A new coat had joined the fleeces and waterproofs behind the front door: pale pink, checked, feminine and fitted. Not hers. The material was soft between her fingers, and it smelled of … sandalwood and roses?

'His breath was vile, he had no style, his cavities: an awful trial,
So Doris asked a stegosaurus how they could fix his smile,'

50

Lorna looked around the open living room door.

A toddler was imprisoned in front of the TV in a collapsible travel-playpen thing. Jiggling and gurgling in time with the song, beaming up at a bunch of *really* crap puppets, and a pair of morons dressed in overalls.

'And he said,
 We haven't invented soap, so that's why we're all smelly,
 There's no toothpaste, it's a disgrace, that's why we can't eat jelly,'

Lorna eased the door closed and limped down the short hall to the kitchen – small, cluttered, but no one there. Maybe...

A creak came from somewhere overhead.

She stood at the bottom of the stairs. Listening.

The only noise was the muffled song in the living room.

She climbed up to the landing.

Stopped with one hand on the bannister as all the air hissed out of her lungs. Staring.

Brian's bedroom door was ajar.

Oh God...

A mousey blonde lay spreadeagled on the double bed, naked, one arm thrown over her eyes, nipples brown and swollen like Ferrero Rocher. Biting her bottom lip and moaning, because Brian – Brian who was supposed to be in meetings all day – was on his knees at the foot of the bed, going down on her. Chubby little Brian, with his hairy arse and bald bit at the back of his head. And this ... *woman* had her hand hooked behind his ear. Guiding him as she squirmed and moaned.

Lorna turned and walked downstairs. Across the hall and through the door to the tiny garage that they'd lined with cheap metal modular shelving units, because neither of their cars would fit in here. Packing the place with all the things that wouldn't fit in the kitchen or any of the other rooms. Bleach, scouring pads, boxes of lightbulbs and oatmeal and dishwasher tablets. The food processor and the bread machine they never used, the skis for the skiing holidays they never went on, old sporting equipment from her university days – back when she used to have *dreams*! Before she buried them away, out here in suburbia, with the domestic detritus of a marriage that had died years ago, leaving nothing but this rotting corpse behind.

She hauled a hockey stick from the rack of sports kit. Old and dusty and solid. Perfect.

Lorna marched to the garage door and twisted the mechanism, pulling the whole thing up-and-over. The springs and hinges squealed – probably the first time it'd been opened since they moved in. She kept going, down the driveway and across the road to her manky little Fiat. No midlife-crisis sports car for her. No baby for her. No promotion for her.

Nothing – but – *crap*.

She yanked open the back door and hurled the hockey stick into the footwell.

Stood there, staring at it.

Then Danners leans in close, her breath warm on Lorna's skin. 'Take a telling, you two-faced bitch. *Next time we won't be so polite.'*

Not any more.

Lorna grabbed the hockey stick again, turned, and stomped back across the road to the brand-new Mini Cooper, with its shiny red body and its jaunty white roof. She swung the stick like a sledgehammer, right into the windscreen, sending cracks spidering out from the centre as the impact juddered up her arm and the car alarm screeched. Hazard lights flashing as she battered the hockey stick into the glass again. One more go and the whole windscreen sagged inwards.

Good enough.

Lorna went back to her Fiat, tossed the stick inside. Slammed the door. Got in the front and drove off.

Grinding her teeth, gums aching, the taste of blood in her mouth, hands tight on the steering wheel.

'Take a telling, you two-faced bitch. *Next time we won't be so polite.'*

Yes, well: two could play at that game.

'Ready or not, here I come!'

6

Superintendent Doig placed a bag of currants on his desk and followed it up with one of candied peel. Then one of dates. Making sure they stood in a straight line, as if they were on parade. 'Now, you see, Logan, the trick is to get your fruit in to soak *early*.' A tall man with a big forehead surrounded by closely cropped hair. The wee bald patch at the crown glowing with fine little hairs, deep creases around his eyes as he smiled and added a packet of suet to his fruity soldiers. Doig frowned at a bit of fluff on his black police T-shirt. 'Tsk...' He picked it off and dropped it into the bin – a rectangular one, presumably because it was easier to align with the desk.

Everything in its proper place: the photo of a British Blue cat on his desk, precisely lined up with keyboard, pen holder, monitor, and notepad; the framed commendation from the Chief Constable *exactly* equidistant between the filing cabinets and the whiteboard; the perfect crease in his trousers, the perfect shine on his superintendent's pips, the perfect mirror gloss of his boots.

His smile faltered when he looked at Logan slumped there in one of the visitors' chairs. 'Is something wrong?'

Logan rubbed his face with both hands. 'Urgh...'

'A Christmas cake can be a tricky thing, Logan. It's important to follow proper procedure.'

'One: it's October. Two: I'm not "Urgh"ing about your cake,

I *like* cake, I'm "Urgh"ing about Detective Sergeant Lorna Sodding Chalmers.'

'Ah, I see. Well … I'm sure you did your best.' A bag of dried cherries joined the ranks. 'Now, as I was saying: it's important to get your cake prepared in plenty of time so you can feed it. You want your cake nice and moist and boozy.'

'I hate to do it, but I'm going to have to recommend disciplinary action.'

'I like a mixture of brandy and whisky. Sherry's too … trifley for me.' Sultanas appeared next.

'She'd *clearly* been in a fight today, but denied the whole thing. Lied right to my face. We didn't even get onto what she was doing at the crash site this morning.'

'And of course, it has to be black treacle.' The tin joined the growing battalion.

'I got Rennie to go digging. There's no sign she ever worked with DI Bell. So why was she at the crash site?'

Superintendent Doig looked up from his troops. 'And how is Simon getting on?'

'Rennie?' Logan pulled his chin in. 'Why?'

'I know he's only on temporary loan from CID, but if he's fitting in, perhaps we should make it permanent?'

'Yeah… Anyway: about DS Chalmers—'

'I do *love* Christmas, don't you?' Doig went back to smiling at his packets of fruit.

'Allan, can we focus on my problems for a minute?'

'People think it's a bit odd, a grown man obsessed by Christmas, but when you're adopted you know how important human kindness is. Everyone needs a bit of hope.'

Logan sat up. 'Are you saying I *shouldn't* recommend disciplinary action?'

'Oh God, no. If DS Chalmers really *is* sitting on intel that could save Ellie Morton she needs a short sharp shock, not mollycoddling.' Next up: a packet of ground almonds. 'What's happening with DI Bell?'

'Early days, Guv. Early days.'

'Hmm…' Doig blinked what had to be the longest eyelashes

known to man. 'I know it's petty of me, Logan, but it'd be nice if Professional Standards discovered something useful *before* DCI Hardie and his troops.'

'Whatever Chalmers knows, it probably won't save Ellie Morton. A three-year-old girl, missing for four days with no ransom note? Chances are she's already dead.'

'Well, you might as well get it over with, then.'

Logan groaned, pulled out his phone and scrolled through his contacts. Selected 'DS Lorna Chalmers' and listened to it ring. And ring. And ring. And—

'This is Lorna Chalmers' voicemail. Leave a message.'

He hung up. 'No answer. Shock horror. She's been avoiding me for days.'

'You're a fine one to talk. Chief Superintendent Napier used to say that getting hold of you was like trying to catch oiled eels in a barrel of slippery socks.' A bag of demerara sugar took up position at the rear of the column.

Logan pulled over Doig's desk phone, knocking over a couple of soldiers – much to their commander's distress – and dialled Chalmers' number. Listened to it ring again. 'Come on... Pick up the damn—'

'Who's this?'

'DS Chalmers, it's Inspector McRae.'

The response was muttered, but still clearly audible. *'Oh for God's sake...'* There was a pause, filled with what sounded like engine noises. *'What do you want? I'm busy.'*

'They want to suspend you, Lorna, but I've talked them into giving you one last chance.'

Doig raised an eyebrow at that.

OK, so it was *maybe* a bit of artistic licence. Still worth a go, though. 'Go into the office right now and tell DI Fraser what you know, or suspect, or whatever it is you're chasing about Ellie Morton.'

'Is that it?'

'Work with me; I'm trying to help you here!'

The contempt virtually dripped from the earpiece. *'Remind me to send you a thank you card and a medal.'* Another pause. *'Now, if you're finished being beneficent and condescending, I've got work to do.'*

God's sake, she was impossible.

'Lorna, don't be...' Logan stared at the phone. 'She's hung up.'

Superintendent Doig shrugged. 'Some people just don't want to be helped.'

Lorna turned off the main road, into the little industrial estate, ignoring the five miles an hour speed limit as she roared past the line of warehouses. Slamming on her brakes so the Fiat slithered to a halt outside one of the Portakabins at the far end of the car park.

A big sign decorated the front wall: 'AberRAD INVESTIGATION SERVICES LTD. ~ FAST, EFFICIENT, & DISCREET' with a ram's head above it for a logo.

She climbed out into the rain and nothing hurt any more, adrenaline singing through her veins. She slammed the car door, pulled the hockey stick from the back seat and strode over there. Rolling her shoulders. Loosening up. Getting ready.

She swung the stick, smashing its head into the glass panel that made up the top half of the Portakabin's door, shattering it, sending the 'COME ON IN, WE'RE OPEN!' sign flying.

Yes. This was more like it.

Lorna backed away, cricking her neck from side to side, feet planted shoulder-width apart, stick at the ready. Took a deep breath 'COME ON THEN! LET'S SEE HOW BRAVE YOU ARE NOW!'

The door opened.

Logan tucked the packet of Penguin biscuits under his arm, picked up the two mugs of tea, and wandered out into the PSD office. They'd taken over half of the floor, stuck a couple of offices down one side, a reception area, put in a cupboard-sized kitchen, and left the rest open plan. Divided up by the ubiquitous Police Scotland cubicles.

A poster adorned one wall – a kitten climbing out of an old boot, beneath the slogan, 'GO GET 'EM, TIGER!'

Someone definitely go-getting-'em was Shona. Logan nodded at her as he passed, keeping his mouth shut. Because if you said *anything* to her she'd drag you into her ongoing battle with the office printer. She was belting it with a packet of Post-it notes, teeth gritted, her brown fringe flopping with every blow – exposing the toast-rack wrinkles that crossed her forehead.

She gave it another thwack. 'Print both sides, you useless pile of junk!'

Brandon was on the phone, one foot up on his return unit, rocking his chair from side to side. '...only, and here's the problem, I don't think that was a wise thing to say to a member of the public, do you, Constable?' He looked over at Logan's mugs and raised two massive hairy eyebrows. Hopeful.

Logan kept on going.

The eyebrows fell again. 'Because, Constable, when you tell someone to *"bleep"* off *"bleeping"* filming you on their *"bleep-bleeping"* mobile phone and stuff it up their *"bleeping bleephole"*, they tend to make formal complaints!'

Rennie's cubicle lurked in the corner, mostly hidden by a wall of file boxes, archive crates, stacks of paperwork, and a faint miasma of beef-and-tomato. Its occupant sat hunched over, tongue poking out the side of his mouth as he traced a finger through a document and typed with his other hand.

Logan stuck one of the mugs on Rennie's desk. 'Milk, two sugars.'

A beaming smile. 'Ooh, ta.' Slurp. 'And does one spy biscuits?'

'One does, but only if one has actually discovered something useful.'

'Oh.' He poked at the papers spread across his desk. 'I've been through all of DI Bell's cases for the last ten years. Nothing with missing evidence. No gold bullion, or jewellery, or non-sequentially numbered banknotes, or works of art. If he was digging up loot I've no idea where it came from.'

'What about forensics? They get anything off the car, or the pick and shovel?'

'Tried chasing them up this morning: they laughed at me.

Apparently we're not the only case they're working on.' Rennie dug into his stacks of paper and came out with a 'HAVE YOU SEEN THIS MAN?' poster. He handed it over. 'Media Department released that at lunchtime.' Someone had done an e-fit picture of DI Bell, looking like he had when they found his body in his crashed car this morning. Only less dead. Above the e-fit, in big block capitals, was, 'CARLOS GUERRERO Y PRIETO AKA: DUNCAN BELL'.

Logan frowned at the poster. 'Please tell me someone's been to see his next of kin?'

'Dunno, Guv.'

'How much do you want to bet?' He pulled out his phone and called Hardie. It rang for a bit, then crackled.

Hardie's voice had a strange hollow echo to it, the words broken and fuzzy. *'Inspector McRae?'*

'DI Bell: has anyone delivered the death message yet?'

'What? I can barely hear you. Hold on...' A couple of thumps. A click. Some rustling. Then, *'Urgh... Are you there?'*

'I said, has anyone delivered the death message to DI Bell's next of kin?'

'Reception's terrible *in the mortuary.'*

'Only I'm pretty sure his wife's still alive. He's got grown-up kids too: boy and a girl.'

'Inspector McRae, did you drag me out of Ding-Dong's post mortem for a sodding reason, because—'

'And if we're going to plaster the Northeast in posters with his face on them and "have you seen this man?", they're probably going to notice.'

A moment's silence, broken only by what *might* have been a muffled swear word.

Logan took a sip of tea. 'Would be nice if she heard it from us, before the press find out and go after her.'

'All right, all right.' Then a sigh. *'I'll get a Family Liaison Officer sorted.'*

'Thanks.'

'Professor McAllister says Bell probably bled to death as a result of the stab wound to his right side. Straight through his ascending colon

and severed a chunk of his small intestine. Wasn't a whole heap of fun watching her remove that lot.' Hardie huffed out a breath. *'Anyway: knife went in deep enough to nick the common iliac vein, if that means anything to you? The hilt left a narrow rectangular bruise on the skin too, so we're looking at a six-inch knife with a wide blade tapering to a point. Maybe a kitchen knife.'*

Wow.

'Isobel said all that? Used to be you couldn't prise a diagnosis out of her without a crowbar and two weeks' notice.'

'Not that it helps.'

'No, I don't suppose it does.'

'Anyway, better get back to it. Still got the urogenital block to dissect.' What sounded like a shudder. *'Always a favourite.'* And Hardie was gone.

Logan hung up and stared out of the window.

Cars and lorries and trucks and buses crawled their way along the dual carriageway outside Bucksburn station. Backed-up westbound by the roadworks and roundabout, eastbound by the traffic lights and potholes.

Kitchen knife. So probably untraceable, unless they already had a suspect and something to match the stab wound with. Which they didn't. And that—

Rennie poked him. 'So, about those biscuits?'

Logan checked his watch. 16:30. Ah, why not. He opened the packet and tossed a Penguin onto the desk. 'Here. Got to keep your strength up: big day tomorrow. Interviews and an exhumation.'

'But … it's *Saturday* tomorrow! I've got to take Donna swimming, then we're off to KFC and ballet classes.'

A shrug. 'Ah well. I suppose we'll just have to cope without you.'

'No, but I want to come with!' Rennie stood, arms spread in true martyr style as he gestured at his piles of paper and boxes. 'All I ever do is go through files and stuff. I want to be out there, where the action is. Solving crimes!'

'Well we can't just put everything on hold for the *weekend*, Simon, I've got a JCB digger booked for half-nine tomorrow.'

'Argh...' He slumped back into his chair, hands over his face. 'Emma's going to kill me...'

'Then man-up and take your daughter swimming.' Logan pointed at the paperwork. 'And when you've finished whatever it is you're doing, you can pack up for the night. Whoever's buried in DI Bell's grave will still be dead on Monday.'

7

Rain sparkled in the Audi's headlights as he pulled into his driveway, illuminating the yellow bulk of the skip sitting on the weed-flecked lock-block. Logan parked in front of it and sat there.

Need to get that guttering fixed. And do something about the garden. Compared to the rest of the street it was a bit ... well, 'shabby' was probably being generous. Call it an overgrown jungle instead. The rattling spears of rosebay willowherb shook beside a rhododendron bush big enough to swallow a caravan. A couple of beech trees lurked in the gloom, dropping their pale-cream leaves in the tussocked grass.

Never owned *trees* before. Or rhododendrons. Or a garden, come to that.

Still, one thing at a time.

He climbed out and hurried up the drive, past the skip, to shelter under the porch.

Ivy wound its way around the granite pillars supporting the little roof, reaching out from a massive wodge of the stuff that choked the living room window and curled into the gutters, hiding the blockwork. That would have to go too.

He plipped the Audi's locks and let himself in.

'Cthulhu?'

Click – the bare lightbulb showered the hallway in cold white light.

Scuffed floorboards clunked beneath his feet, tiny tufts of fabric still sticking to the gripper rods where he'd torn the carpet up. Walls stripped to the bare plaster, white blobs of Polyfilla making it look like a child undergoing treatment for chicken pox.

Logan peeled off his Police Scotland fleece and hung it over the newel post at the foot of the stairs. Tried not to think too much about the patch of brand-new floorboards surrounding it.

At least the smell had gone.

More or less...

'Cthulhu? Daddy's home!'

He unbuttoned the flaps on his T-shirt and slid the epaulettes free on his way into the living room.

It was almost pitch-black in here, the yellow glow of the streetlights dimmed to a septic smear by the ivy outside.

Click – more chicken-pox walls, and bare floorboards.

But at least he was making a start. Rolls of fresh paper lay piled up on the floor, by the wallpaper table. Two stepladders with a scaffolding board slotted into the steps between them. Pots of paint. A couple of cheap camping chairs, a sofa that wouldn't have looked out of place in the skip on the driveway, and a decent-sized TV – even if it was propped up on breeze blocks.

'Cthulhu? Where the hell are you, you...' Logan smiled as she padded into the room. He squatted down and held out his hand.

She prooped and meeped her way across the floorboards, huge fluffy tail straight up, white bib and paws almost fluorescent in the harsh overhead light. Cobwebs sticking to her brown-and-grey stripes. Fur so soft it was like stroking smoke.

'How's Daddy's bestest girl?'

She did her little cat dance, treadling on the floor as she turned around him.

'Oh, you've been hunting *mouses*? Good girl! Did you catch any?'

She thumped her head into his thigh and purred.

'Well, that *is* exciting.' He scooped her up with a grunt, holding her upside down and rubbing her tummy as he wandered back through to the hall.

More purring.

'What? No, not really. It was a horrible day.'

Up the stairs and along the landing. More chicken pox. Probably have to replace a few of the floorboards here too.

'Someone abducted a little girl. Four days and there's still no ransom note.'

At least the master bedroom was finished: nice thick carpet, cheerful yellow walls, some framed photos above the double bed.

'I know, I know: if they didn't snatch her for ransom, then it's probably sexual, isn't it?' He lowered Cthulhu onto the bed and stripped off his Police Scotland T-shirt. The scar tissue crisscrossing his stomach shiny and pink. Might be an idea to invest in some of those warm-white lightbulbs instead? Something a bit less intense and guard-towery.

Cthulhu treadled on the duvet cover, making delighted noises.

'That's what I was thinking.' He changed out of his boots and police-issue trousers. 'Oh, *you* think she's been abducted to order? Could be. Amounts to the same thing, I suppose.'

A pair of paint-spattered jeans came out of the wardrobe.

'Or maybe someone abducted her to sell on? A little girl's got to be worth a fair bit on the open market. If you had somewhere to sell her.' He did up the buttons. Fastened his belt. Frowned. 'That's a very good point. Maybe it *is* the fabled northeast Livestock Mart...'

Cthulhu started in on a wash.

'Or maybe it's the obvious answer? The stepfather abused her, killed her, and hid the body somewhere.' An equally painty T-shirt joined the jeans. 'I knew you'd say that, but Chalmers interviewed him. His alibi's sound.'

Cthulhu washed her tummy in a barrage of shlurpy noises.

'True... I don't think I'd trust Lorna Chalmers either.' Logan perched on the end of the bed and pulled on a pair of painty trainers. 'Tara's coming over later for pizza. That'll be nice, won't it?'

One last shlurp and Cthulhu stopped washing and stared at him.

'What?'

More staring.

'Oh come on, not *this* again. There's nothing wrong with talking to your cat. People do it all the time.' He leaned over and kissed her on her fuzzy little head. 'And it's not as if you're actually answering *back*, is it? Only crazy people own talking cats.' Another frown. 'Which reminds me.'

Logan stood and wandered down the landing again, into the bathroom.

Still have to finish tiling those other two walls. Just because the shower was usable, didn't mean the room was done.

Blah, blah, blah.

He opened the medicine cabinet, took out the box of Aripiprazole and popped two small orange tablets out of their blister pack and onto his hand.

Cthulhu appeared in the cabinet's mirrored door as he shut it – following him into the bathroom and jumping up onto the toilet lid. More staring.

'I know: I'm taking them, see?'

He popped the pills in his mouth, washing them down with a full glass of water before the taste hit. Then turned and opened his mouth wide for Cthulhu to see.

'Look: all gone. So if Doctor Goulding asks, you can tell him I'm definitely taking my antipsychotics.'

She didn't move.

'Because I know you're in cahoots with him, that's why.'

A long slow blink of those big yellow-and-black eyes.

Logan sagged. 'I know. I love you too.' He blinked back at her. 'Now, do you want to help Daddy wallpaper the living room?'

She jumped down from the toilet and padded off towards the bedroom.

'Lazy sod!'

Ah well, she'd only make the wallpaper paste all hairy anyway.

* * *

Logan smoothed down the lining paper's edges with his brush, making the seam disappear. Might even get this wall finished tonight. Which would be—

His phone launched into its generic ringtone.

'Arrrgh! Leave me alone!'

But it kept on ringing.

He gave the lining paper one last flourish, then dumped the brush on the table and wiped his fingers clean on his painty T-shirt. 'Pfff... Almost finished as well.'

When he picked his phone off the couch, the words 'DS LORNA CHALMERS' glowed in the middle of the screen.

Interesting.

He prodded the 'ANSWER' button then stuck the thing on speakerphone. 'Hello?'

'Hello?'

Lorna sagged back in her seat. Outside, the North Sea boomed and crashed against the beach, the spray a grey smear in the night. Lights flickered in the gloom, small and distant – huge supply boats anchored down to wait out the storm. If only it could be that simple...

The tower blocks of Seaton rose up on the left, windows shining as normal people went about their normal evenings as they did every single day of their normal little lives.

When did she forget what that felt like?

Most of her ached. And what didn't ache, *hurt*. Stung. Burned.

'Hello? DS Chalmers? Are you there?'

She dragged in a breath, ribs squealing in protest at the movement. Her voice came out muffled and lisping. Weak. Pathetic. 'All I ever wanted to do was help.'

A sigh came from her phone's speaker. *'Then come in tomorrow and help. Ellie Morton might still be out there, alive.'*

She wiped her other hand across her eyes. Do *not* give him the satisfaction of hearing you cry! 'Why does it always have to be so hard?'

Headlights swept around the corner, getting closer, making her squint.

The woman in the rear-view mirror was a disaster: her face covered in scrapes and fledgling bruises. A black eye. Shirt collar ripped. Jacket too. Blood smeared around her nose and mouth.

Then the car was past and she was in darkness again.

'Because it's about people. Nothing about people is easy.' McRae put on one of those fake, gentle voices – pretending he cared about her. When he didn't. No one did. *'Come in, Lorna. We can find her. Together. We can save a wee girl's life.'*

Lorna swallowed. Blew out a breath. Blinked at the car's roof. 'I've got to go.'

'Lorna? Lorna, it's—'

She hung up. Put her phone on the passenger seat.

Fumbled a half-dozen painkillers into her palm, swallowing them with a mouthful of Ribena. Grimacing as they clawed their way down her throat. Chased them with another mouthful.

Lorna curled forward, till her forehead rested on the steering wheel, and let the tears come. Why did everyone hate her? Why did everything go wrong? Why wasn't—

Her phone burst into 'The Bends' and there was his name on the screen again: 'BRIAN'.

She stared at it. Snarled. Picked the thing up.

'AAAAAAAAAAAAAAAAAAAAAAAAAAAAAAAAAAAAAAAAAAARGH!' Then hurled it into the passenger footwell.

Enough!

She turned the key in the ignition, scrubbed a hand across her eyes, turned on the headlights, and pulled away from the kerb.

There was going to be a reckoning, and it was going to happen right *now*.

'Sure you don't want any wine?' Tara waggled the half-empty bottle again, making the tips of her long, dark-orange hair jiggle.

Logan gave her a pained smile. 'Sorry the kitchen's kind of a tip.'

That was gilding the jobbie a bit. The walls hadn't even made it as far as the chicken pox stage – instead seventies brown-and-green wallpaper lined the room, faded so much that the pattern looked more like mould than anything else. Dark shapes lurked around the edges where he'd ripped out all the kitchen units. Sockets and switches dangled from their wiring. All the skirting removed to reveal holes in the lathe and plaster. The whole thing topped off by the decorative sculptural presence of an electric cooker straight out of the *Flintstones* and a battered stainless-steel sink.

Tara settled back in one of the six nonmatching chairs arranged around the rickety kitchen table and looked at him over the top of her glass. Piercing blue eyes, a bit like a wolf's, surrounded by smokey make-up and freckles. Heart-shaped face with a strong jaw. And, let's face it, slightly out of his league. The unattainable goddess vibe was only undermined by the big red blob of sauce on her fitted white shirt.

She raised an eyebrow. 'Am I boring you?'

'No. No. Not at all.' He took another slice of pizza from his box. Shrugged. 'It's just … my day's been all errant cops and a missing child. It's not really … you know.'

Cthulhu jumped up onto the table and plonked herself down between Logan's ham-and-mushroom and Tara's vegan Giardiniera with prosciutto. Stuck a leg in the air and started washing her tail.

Tara took a sip of wine. 'Mine's been all lockups stuffed to the rafters with counterfeit vodka and cigarettes. So I think you probably win.'

He took a bite. 'Can't help wondering what happened to Ellie Morton. Maybe it's better if she *isn't* still alive.' He followed it with a mouthful of fizzy water. Stifled a burp. 'You ever heard of something called the "Livestock Mart"?'

'What, Thainstone?'

'No, not Thainstone. This one's highly illegal: supposed to be a place where you can buy and sell abducted children. Moves about the countryside so no one can find it unless they know where to look.'

'Yeah…' She lowered her glass. Curled her lip. 'Not really the kind of thing we deal with in Trading Standards.'

'Been rumours doing the rounds for years. Decades, probably. But no one's ever—'

Cthulhu sat bolt upright on the table, staring off into the corner of the room at a large hole gnawed through the lathe and plaster.

Logan scooted forward on his chair. 'Oh ho, here we go.'

Cthulhu thumped down from the table like a dropped washing machine and prowled across the kitchen floorboards. Hunting.

'Mice.' Another bite of ham-and-mushroom. 'Rotten wee sods have eaten half the wiring and nearly all the pipe insulation.'

'So let's get this straight: you invited me round to your vermin-infested house to eat takeaway pizza and talk about people *buying* and *selling* kids – and you think you're getting lucky tonight?'

He pointed at the bottle in front of her. 'There's more wine, if that helps?'

Tara shook her head. 'I'm a fool to myself.'

'Hopefully...' A grin. 'And what's a few mice between friends?'

Tara shuddered. 'I hate mice.'

Ellie hugged her knees to her chest and pulled the blankie tight. It wasn't easy, cos the man had tied her hands together with itchy rope. She sucked a breath in around the big red ball stuck in her mouth. And she couldn't even spit it out cos it was all buckled at the back of her head.

The buckle pulled at her hair whenever she leaned against the wall of the crate.

A wooden crate, made of bits of wood, with spaces between the bits of wood so she wouldn't stuffocate. And she could peer out, through the gaps, into the Scary Room that was all dark and smelled of dirt and nasty things and crying.

Dirty-orange light glowed through a manky-pants window, thick with spiders' webs and the shiny black lumps of dead flies. It was barely bright enough to see the edges of boxes and piles of stuff and dead bicycles hiding in the shadows. And the other crates...

Seven crates and her one made eight – same as the number of tentapoles on an octopus.

Mouses skitter-pattered across the dirt floor between them, on teeny pink feet, their eyes shiny as black marbles, teeny pink noses twitching, teeny pink ears swivelling.

One of them crept closer to Ellie's crate, sniffing, whiskers twitching.

It slid between two of the wooden bits, even though the gap was only big enough to poke a finger.

A tiny mousey, with its twitchy tail and its sniffy nose.

She held her breath as it stared at her, then inched towards what was left of her sammitch – just the crusts, because they were icky.

Soft and fluffy mousey.

Ellie tried to make a smile, but the big red ball in her mouth was all difficult, so she did gentle crooning noises instead. Grubby fingers reaching, reaching...

The mousey looked at her, pointy head on one side as her fingers got closer and closer.

Then she'd got him! She'd got the mousey! And he was all soft and fuzzy and warm and she would call him Whiskers and Whiskers would be her best—

Whiskers squeaked and sank his teeth into her thumb and it stung and it hurt and teeny drops of blood fell out of her thumb and she dropped Whiskers cos he'd *bitted* her!

Bad mousey!

She snatched her hand away and he tumbled to the floor, scampering back out through a gap in the wooden boards.

He bitted her...

Her thumb thumped and stung and throbbed and there was nobody to kiss it better.

Ellie slumped against the crate walls as big snottery sobs rattled out of her.

She only wanted a friend.

Everything was horrid and cold and unfair and her thumb hurt and SHE WANTED TO GO HOME!

And outside, in the Scary Room, someone else started crying

too – all muffled and sniffy. Then the other someone, till all three of them were snuffling in the darkness. Like little piggies, waiting to be turned into sausages.

— the widows' waltz —

8

The letterbox went *chlack*, and that morning's *Aberdeen Examiner* thumped onto the bare floorboards. Logan bent to pick it up, as the light on the papergirl's bike faded through the rippled glass.

He held his mug against his chest, its warmth seeping into the bare skin. Probably should have put on a bit more than jammie bottoms, but hey-ho.

A noise mumbled out from the bedroom upstairs.

Logan took a sip of coffee and unrolled the newspaper, heading back through into the living room.

The *Examiner*'s front page carried a big picture of DI Bell's crashed hire car, beneath the headline '"Suicide Cop" Faked Own Death'.

A grunt. '"By Colin Miller." Of course it is.'

Logan tossed the paper onto the couch and kept going to the open patio doors. Had another sip of coffee.

Twenty past seven and the sky was a dirty shade of charcoal, the first rumours of dawn catching at the horizon. A thin drizzle misted its way across the gloomy expanse of grass and weeds and bushes and trees. Going to be an absolute nightmare getting all that whipped in to shape. No point worrying about it now, though – had the house to do first.

He scratched at his checked jammie bottoms and yawned – a proper jaw-cracking one – then sagged. 'Pfff...'

Cthulhu sat right at the edge of the veranda, on a little stump of log, just out of reach of the rain. Logan wandered over and squatted beside her. Tried to ignore the popping sounds his knees made. Goosebumps rippled his bare arms as he rubbed the fur between her ears. Soft and warm. She *mrowped*.

'Don't start – I've taken my pills, OK? Did it first thing, so Tara wouldn't see.' He smiled. 'What makes you think that? Was it the sleeping together? Of *course* I like her.'

Cthulhu turned big dark eyes on him.

'Well, yes, I know she snores, but so do you.' More between-the-ear rubbing. 'That's very true, she *is* less of a nutjob than my usual.'

A stretch, then Cthulhu thumped down from her perch and sashayed back into the living room.

'Yes, OK. You're right: "so far".' Logan stood. 'But we can always—'

'Logan?'

He turned and there was Tara, wearing one of his old baggy hoodies. Bare legs poking out from underneath. Her hair was …*huge*. Haystack huge.

She yawned. Shuddered. 'Who are you talking to?'

'Cthulhu. She likes you.'

'Are you not cold?' Tara's finger was warm as it traced its way down his chest to the collection of twenty-three shiny lines that criss-crossed his stomach. 'This is a lot of scar tissue for one man.'

'I was dead for five minutes on the operating table, if that makes me sound windswept and interesting?'

'Makes you sound like a zombie. Or a vampire.' She narrowed her eyes and poked him with the finger instead. 'You better not be the sparkly kind!'

'So technically you've had sex with a dead person. You dirty necrophiliac pervert.'

She poked him again. Then stole his coffee, padding across the bare floorboards to where Cthulhu waited at the kitchen door – one paw up on the wood. Expectant.

Logan cleared his throat. 'I have to head off soon. Got an exhumation organised and a couple of widows to talk to. You can stay here and keep Cthulhu company if you like? There's a spare key by the kitchen door.'

She raised an eyebrow. 'Why, Inspector McRae, are you giving me a key to your house?'

'Lending. On the condition that you don't turn out to be a complete nutjob.'

A smile made little dimples in her cheeks. 'I promise nothing.'

Logan hurried through the rear entrance to Bucksburn station, shaking the rain from his peaked cap. No sign of anyone as he walked down the corridor, past closed office doors.

Water rippled the stairwell windows, distorting the romantic view of the station car park – almost empty – and the main bulk of the building itself. Two storeys of rectangular brown-and-grey blockwork, devoid of character or charm. Like a miserable primary school, only without the swings and roundabouts.

His phone dinged at him and he hauled it out.

HORRIBLE STEEL:

> Hope you're happy with yourself, McRae.
> We had to spend the night watching kids'
> TV instead of dinner and a shag! I WILL
> HAVE MY REVENGE!!!

He thumbed out a quick reply on his way up the stairs:

> Tough. I was busy.

His footsteps echoed back at him – *still* no sign of anyone – through the doors at the top and into another empty corridor. Ten to eight on a rainy Saturday morning and the place was like the *Mary Celeste*... At least that meant he might actually get some work done for a change, free from the distraction, whingeing, and general all-round pain-in-the-backside-ishness of his fellow officers.

Logan punched in the door-code and let himself into the Professional Standards office. Stopped. Suppressed a little groan.

So much for the *Mary Celeste*.

Rennie was slouched in his chair, surrounded by his file-box battlements, staring at the ceiling tiles as he swivelled left and right.

Logan stripped off his fleece and hung it on the coatrack. 'Thought you were taking Donna swimming?'

'Guv.' Rennie snapped upright.

'You're an idiot; it's Saturday morning. Go home.'

A frown. 'You didn't hear?'

Logan sank into his own chair and powered up his computer. 'Get the kettle on. And there better be some of those Penguins left.'

'Yeah, but...' Rennie grabbed a sheet of paper from his in-tray and hurried over. Held it out. 'It's DS Chalmers.'

He didn't bother suppressing this groan. 'What's she done now?'

Sobbing howled out of the living room in jagged painful stabs. He was just visible, through the open door, hunched up on the floor in the corner of the room slumped against a set of DVD racks. A slightly chubby man, going bald at the back, arms wrapped around himself. Face buried in his knees, shoulders shaking.

Logan eased the door shut.

A uniformed PC stood at the other end of the hall, talking into the Airwave handset attached to her shoulder. '...no, Sarge, no sign of forced entry I can see, but the SE haven't finished with the back garden yet.'

Past her, a patrol car sat at the kerb, its lights flickering blue and white in the rain.

Logan stepped through the plain door and into the garage again.

It probably hadn't been big enough to park an actual car in to start with – 'Executive Family Homes' being developer-speak for 'Tiny Rabbit-Hutch Houses You Can't Swing A Cat In' – but it *definitely* wasn't big enough now. Lorna Chalmers and her husband had filled the garage with metal shelving, leaving a four-foot-wide path down the middle. Tins of beans, soup, tomatoes, fruit, and sweetcorn. Semi-transparent boxes of crockery, others of spices, towels, clothes, cleaning products, and unidentifiable things. Various items of kitchen gadgetry, still in the original boxes. Cartons of washing powder, rice, macaroni-and-cheese mix, cereal... As if they'd tried to pack their lives away out here.

And Lorna Chalmers had finally succeeded.

She was halfway down the space between the shelving units, the toes of her socks grazing the concrete floor. Scuffing the fabric as her body turned in the draught that slipped in beneath the garage door. A thick electrical cord made a makeshift noose around her neck, the other end tied to the exposed rafters above. Arms slack by her sides. Eyes open. Mouth too. Face covered in scrapes and the faded remains of bruising on waxy yellow flesh.

The hard *clack* of a camera's flash caught a bluebottle as it landed on her bottom lip. Then wandered inside.

Definitely dead.

9

Logan leaned against the open doorway as a couple of scene examiners got Lorna Chalmers down. One hugged her around the middle while the other clambered up onto a chair, holding a pair of snips. Their white SOC suits rustled and crumpled.

Snips took hold of the electrical lead in her other hand. 'You ready?'

Hugs kept his head as far away from Chalmers' remains as possible without letting go. 'Gawd... Soon as you like, Shirley. She *reeks* of booze!'

A *click* and the body dropped, but didn't sag.

So still in the throes of rigor mortis, then.

Snips – Shirley – jumped down from the chair and helped her colleague wrestle Chalmers into a body bag. She zipped it up and backed off, waving a hand in front of her face. 'Pfff... You weren't kidding.'

Logan shook his head and turned away.

Shirley shouted after him. 'Hoy! You SIO then?'

'Nope.'

'You're Senior, you're an Officer, and you're Investigating. Sounds like SIO to me.'

Logan kept going. 'Yeah, nice try. But the answer's *still* no.'

Logan leaned his forehead against the bedroom window, breath making a foggy crescent on the glass.

Outside, the duty undertakers wheeled their shiny grey coffin down the driveway, then lifted it into the back of their shiny grey van. The name of the firm was picked out in discreet white letters, 'CORMACK & CALMAN ~ FUNERAL DIRECTORS' above the words 'PRIVATE AMBULANCE', but other than that there was nothing to indicate that Lorna Chalmers' remains were on the way to the mortuary.

What a bloody waste...

'Guv?'

'Mmm?' Logan turned, and there was Rennie waving at him from the bedroom doorway.

'I know you don't want to be SIO, but do you think ... maybe...?' He raised his eyebrows and mugged it up a bit.

'You want to be SIO?'

'Come on, Guv, got to be good practice, right?' Rennie shrugged. 'For the old CV? Even if it's only a suicide.'

'You know it's mostly paperwork, right?'

'And maybe people would say, "You remember that police officer who hanged herself? DS Rennie was the SIO on that. Did a bang-up job. Let's give him something exciting to be in charge of next time!"'

Logan puffed out a breath. 'I suppose I can ask. But no promises.'

Swear to God, the little sod did a wee jig. 'Cool biscuits!' Then stopped and pointed over his shoulder. 'Oh, and you might want to come see this.' He led the way across the hall and into a bathroom barely big enough for the bath, sink, and toilet that had been squeezed into it. Nearly every flat surface was littered with assorted shampoos and conditioners and body butter and talc and moisturisers. A small mountain of empty toilet-roll middles lay slumped against the loo brush.

Rennie opened the medicine cabinet above the sink, exposing a huge stash of pill tubs, boxes, and blister packs that all seemed to have Lorna Chalmers' name on them. He pulled out a white box with a pharmacist's label stuck to the front. 'Tranylcypromine sulphate: Emma was on this stuff after Donna was born, they're antidepressants. And so are these: Venlafaxine hydrochloride,

79

and Nortriptyline, and Moclobemide too. And yes, you should be impressed that I managed to pronounce all that.' He returned the first box to the cabinet, then pulled out another one and frowned at it. 'Not sure what Aripiprazole is though.'

Good old Aripiprazole, banishing visions of dead girlfriends and other assorted hallucinations for nearly two years now.

Logan took the packet off him. 'It's a second generation – or atypical – antipsychotic. Possible side effects include anxiety and suicidal thoughts.'

'Really?' Rennie raised an eyebrow. 'Oh. Right. Wow.'

Logan replaced the box and shut the mirrored door. Stepped out onto the landing again.

Rennie followed him. 'Her husband says there was a "sort of fight" yesterday. She stormed off, he didn't hear her come back. Look at this.' A smartphone appeared from Rennie's pocket and he held it out. A text message sat in the middle of the screen. 'Had his phone on to charge, so he didn't get her text till an hour ago. Came down and found her.'

Logan accepted the phone, reading the message out loud. '"I'm sorry. I just can't take it any more. I can't." Sent at ten thirty last night.' He scrolled down to the earlier text messages. 'Long time to be left hanging there.'

'I had a snoop round.' Rennie hooked a thumb over his shoulder at another small bedroom. 'Someone's definitely sleeping in this one: got loads of women's things in it. Lipsticks and jars of stuff. Women's underwear in the chest of drawers. Women's clothes in the wardrobe. No man things.'

A chain of yesterday's texts swept up onto the screen.

BRIAN:

I can't wait to see you today!

STEPH:

I miss the touch of your strong hands on my body! Searching and probing my most intimate secret places.

80

BRIAN:

> I miss the warmth of your tongue on my
> neck. The hot swell of your bosom against
> my bare chest.

STEPH:

> I miss your hardness deep inside me.
> Thrusting. Thrusting!

There was more of the same, each one more flowery than the last.

'God, it's like a bargain-basement Mills and Boon.' Logan stepped back into the master bedroom again. Slid the door to the fitted wardrobe all the way across.

It was full of men's clothes: no dresses, skirts, or high heels. Nothing feminine at all.

He pointed at the bedside cabinet. 'Have a squint in there.'

Rennie did. 'Man socks, man pants, man hankies. No lady things.'

Logan nodded. Slid the wardrobe door closed. 'Then I think it's time we had a word with the grieving husband.'

A tiny conservatory clung to the side of the tiny living room – its doors closed, trapping inside a small herd of clothes horses draped with washing.

Brian had moved himself to the couch, sitting there as if someone had rammed their hand down his throat and ripped out everything inside him. He kept his eyes on his knees, as Logan handed him a mug of tea.

'I'm sorry for your loss.'

He didn't look up. 'It's... I never...'

Logan put a bit of steel in his voice. 'Mr Chalmers, someone assaulted your wife yesterday. *Twice.* I want to know who.'

'I don't... I didn't see her. She went out before I got up and—'

'Would you say Lorna was happy at home?'

81

Oh, he looked up at that. 'What? I...' Pulled his chin in. 'Hey, no, wait – I didn't do that! I would *never* do that!'

'And yet Lorna texted you a suicide note at half ten last night, but you didn't call the police till after seven this morning.'

'No!' Looking from Logan to Rennie. Bottom lip trembling. 'I told your constable—'

'Constable?' Rennie folded his arms. 'I'm a detective *sergeant*.'

Brian blinked at the pair of them, getting smaller. 'Sorry. It... I was recharging my phone. I didn't check it till I got up!'

The central heating gurgled.

Rain pattered on the conservatory roof.

'I *didn't*!'

'Really?' Logan loomed over him. 'Are you expecting us to believe your *wife* was hanging there for *nine* hours and you didn't notice?'

Rennie put a hand on Logan's arm. 'Guv?'

'We didn't... She has her own bedroom. It's the antisocial hours. We decided it'd be better if we didn't wake each other up.'

'Who's Stephanie?'

Brian flinched as if he'd been slapped. 'I don't...'

'Don't you?' Logan held up the phone again, reading from the screen. '"The milk of your passion fizzes inside me like finest champagne." If that helps jog your memory?'

'Oh God.' Brian wrapped his hands around his head.

'You said there'd been "a sort of fight".'

'You don't know what it was like. She was never *here*. Not properly. Even when she was physically in the room, she was somewhere else. I was...' Deep breath. 'Stephanie is... I met her at work. She's the account manager. We... Her husband isn't there either. We were lonely.'

Logan stepped back. 'And Lorna found out you were having an affair.'

The heating gurgled. The rain fell.

Brian shrugged. 'Steph was here yesterday afternoon. We were in the bedroom when her car alarm went off. Someone had smashed the windscreen and the garage door was lying wide open. It's... It's not like Lorna and me had a sex life of our own, is it? We don't even sleep in the same *room* any more!' He ran a hand across his face. Bit his lip. 'I was going to ask Lorna for a divorce next week, once we'd got her birthday out of the way. It would've been Wednesday.'

And with that, Brian dissolved into tears again.

The garage looked strangely empty without Chalmers' body hanging there. Like a living room after the Christmas decorations had been taken down... Now the only sign that she'd ever been there were the scuff marks on the concrete floor – tiny tufts of fabric stuck to the rough surface where her socks had dragged across it.

Logan turned and stared at the shelving unit by the door. Chalmers' glasses sat on a shelf next to the dishwasher tablets. Her shoes were on the shelf below lined up side by side.

Rennie pointed at them. 'Why do people do that? Why take off your shoes and glasses before topping yourself?'

The glasses were cold to the touch. Surprisingly heavy. 'Suppose it's like getting ready for bed.'

'See if it was me? If I was crossing the great dark veil? I'd want to see where I was going.'

Logan put the glasses back on their shelf. 'Her husband's having an affair; she's about to be suspended; she's on antidepressants; she's sacrificed having a family for her career, but her career's going nowhere.'

'And I wouldn't want to tread in anything either.'

'She's getting into fights...'

Rennie nodded. 'Sounds like she had a proper, full-on, card-carrying meltdown.'

'Yup.' Logan walked out into the hall. No point wasting any more time here. Still had to figure out what Chalmers knew about Ellie Morton's disappearance. He opened the front door. Paused on the threshold. 'Do me a favour: soon as we hit the station, have a word with the CCTV team and see if they can place her car anywhere. Find out where she went yesterday. Maybe we can dig up who she spoke to.'

'Guv.'

Logan hurried down the driveway, shoulders hunched against the rain, Rennie trotting along behind him.

Pale faces gazed out at them from the surrounding houses. The nosy ghosts of suburbia, haunting the lives of their neighbours. Feeding on their tragedy.

He clambered into the PSD pool car and checked his watch. A little after nine. 'Probably got time to pick up coffee on the way to the cemetery. If we're quick.'

Rennie clunked his door shut and sat there, looking up at the house. 'Guv... Not being funny or anything, but back there, with the husband, was that not a bit ... *harsh*?'

'Good.'

'No, but what if he makes a complaint?'

'Brian Chalmers was screwing around on his wife. A wife he *knew* was on antidepressants. He was going to ask for a divorce the day after her birthday.' Logan fastened his seatbelt. 'So yes: I gave him a hard time. What do you think I should've given him, biscuits and a cuddle?'

Rennie started the car. 'Sure you weren't just punishing him because you feel guilty about what happened to her?'

Idiot.

'*I* didn't do anything.'

'So, let's get this straight,' Rennie turned, voice and face deadpan, 'being investigated by Professional Standards had nothing to do with her topping herself.'

The little sod *might* have a point.

'Oh ... shut up and drive.'

Hazlehead Cemetery stretched down towards the Westhill road. They'd made an effort to lay this bit of it out in long sweeping curves, but there was a lot of ground to fill. Space for thousands more bodies.

And soon, there would be space for one more.

A bright-yellow JCB sat by a bend in the road that wound through the middle of the cemetery – presumably so the hearses could deliver their passengers to their allotted spots.

The digger hunched over one of the graves. Like an expectant beast. Growling.

Logan and Rennie stood beneath a row of trees, on the very edge of the cemetery. Not that they provided a lot of shelter from the thick drifts of pewter-grey drizzle that coated everything with a sheen of cold and damp. But at least it was somewhere to drink their coffee.

Next to the JCB, three SOC-suited figures were busy erecting a Scene Examination tent – big enough to plonk over the grave when it was excavated.

Rennie sucked a breath in through his teeth. 'You ever had a shot on a digger? I'd love that. Gouging huge great clods out the surface of the earth... Oh, ho. Clap hands, here comes Charlie.'

A man in a brown suit and council-issue tie worried his way up the hearse road towards them, clutching his fluorescent-yellow waterproof jacket shut. Woolly hat jammed low over his ears, a scowl pulling his jowls into a disappointed-scrotum shape.

His glasses were all steamed up too. 'Closing the cemetery... I don't see why this couldn't have been done *last night!*'

Logan had another sip of lukewarm coffee. 'Health and safety.'

'There are people wanting to visit their loved ones and they expect the council to facilitate that. If you're a bereaved relative, what are you going to think about all this?'

Logan leaned over to one side, looking across the cemetery to the car park. Its only occupants were the PSD pool car, Scene Examination's grubby white Transit, the duty undertaker's discreet 'Private Ambulance', and the battered rattletrap Mr Scrotumface had arrived in. Other than that, the place was deserted. Logan stood up straight again. 'Please don't let us stop you comforting them. We'll let ourselves out.'

'Hmmph!' An imperious sniff, then he turned and marched off into the drizzle again, nose held high. Walking as if his buttocks were tightly clenched. Presumably to stop the stick from falling out.

Rennie sidled closer, keeping his voice down. 'Bet he's the kind of guy who can't get it up unless he's filled out a requisition in triplicate to boink his girlfriend.'

Logan's Airwave handset gave four bleeps. He answered it. 'McRae. Safe to talk.'

'Bet he's a riot in the bedroom too.' Rennie put on a droning nasal voice. 'Tonight, Jean, you'll observe that we're departing from our usual missionary position due to roadworks on the A944 outside Dobbies Garden Centre.'

Down by the JCB, one of the white-oversuited figures waved at them. Then her voice crackled out of the Airwave's speaker. *That's us ready.*

Logan pressed the button. 'Off you go then.'

'Instead we'll be attempting the "Reverse Cowgirl" in honour of John Gordon MP, the 178th Lord Provost of Aberdeen – 1705 to 1708.'

She turned and gave the digger driver a wave.

The great beast roared.

'And I know it'll cause you a great deal of sexual excitement, Jean, when I say that John Gordon was also the *185th* Lord Provost of Aberdeen. He served *two* nonconsecutive terms in office. Hmmm? Hmmm? Yes, I thought you'd like that.'

The digger's yellow arm reached forward, its claw digging deep into the turf, peeling it back to expose the dark-brown soil beneath.

'Now, enough foreplay, Jean. Let us commence with having "the sex" as per council regulation fifty-four, paragraph six, subsection—'

Logan hit him.

10

The JCB towered over the opened grave, glistening in the drizzle. Its claw thick with dark-brown earth.

Logan inched closer.

One of their three-person Scene Examination team peered down into the pit, hands on her knees. 'You ready?'

Her two colleagues hunched at the bottom of the hole, fiddling with thick tie-down straps. Then the bigger of the two stood and gave her the thumbs up, his white oversuit clarty with dirt.

She passed the signal on to the digger driver and the JCB's engine growled again – the arm lifting over the hole. A chain with a hook on the end of it dangled from the claw.

Clarty the Examiner reached up and fastened the straps onto the hook, before he and his filthy friend scrambled out of the grave.

'OK.' The scene examiner in the clean suit pointed a few graves down. 'If we can all retreat to a safe distance, please.' She ushered Logan and Rennie to step away from the hole, and all five of them gathered around a shiny black headstone – like a chunk of kitchen worktop with gold lettering on it: 'Now Annoying The Angels'.

She took off her facemask and raised her eyebrows at Logan. Shirley, from Chalmers' garage that morning. 'This your first exhumation?'

'Third.'

Rennie leaned against the headstone. 'I've never done one before. It's *kinda* like Burke and Hare, only with a JCB. And in daylight. And not Edinburgh. Or 1828.'

Everyone stared at him.

The tips of his ears went a darker shade of pink. 'Sorry.'

Shirley raised a hand to shoulder height and pointed at the sky. Then made small circles with her finger, the other hand held flat just beside it.

A deeper growl and the digger's arm went up, slow and steady.

She smiled at Logan. 'And, as if by magic...'

A mud-covered shape rose from the grave. It wasn't a standard wooden coffin – a chunk of dirt fell off exposing what looked like wickerwork. One of those trendy woven-from-sustainable-materials biodegradable jobs.

It cleared the lip of the grave and kept going ... five, maybe six foot into the air ... and that was when the bottom gave way. The remains cascaded down into the pit. Bones and chunks of stuff and plastic bags swollen with internal organs. Everything slithery and glistening and dark. As they spattered back into the earth, the stomach-clenching stench of rotten meat exploded out from the pit and everyone recoiled, coughing and gagging.

Rennie slapped both hands over his nose and mouth. 'Aw... *God*!'

Shirley hurled her facemask to the ground. 'Low-carbon-footprint, saving-the-planet, eco-friendly, recycling bollocks!'

A purple nitrile glove appeared over the lip of the grave, its fingers dark and slimy with mud. It dumped a chunk of ... was that a pelvis? It was. It was a pelvis, still partially encased in stinking...

Nope.

Logan backed away even further from the grave as a handful of finger bones joined the pile of yuck on the filthy tarpaulin they'd spread out beside the hole.

A muffled voice rose from the grave. *'Oh for... Urgh, I've stood in it!'*

'Yeah…' Shirley grimaced at Logan. 'This is going to take us a while.'

Logan patted her on the shoulder. 'It's *all* yours. Give us a shout when you've got everything back at the mortuary.'

'Will do.'

As he walked away, down the hearse road, Shirley's voice took on that irritating over-the-top enthusiastic tone kids'-TV-show presenters always used. 'Come on, guys, I *know* it's horrible, but we can do this!'

The reply from the grave was a bit more to the point: 'Sod off.'

Rennie started the pool car's engine. 'Let's *never* do that again. Exhumations are horrible.'

Logan fastened his seatbelt and waved at Mr Scrotumface from the Council. 'Look at him: standing there in his high-viz jacket and woolly hat, presiding over his empty car park like an impotent gnome.'

The man glowered back at them.

'Told you, he needs his bonking chits filled out in triplicate.' Rennie pulled out of the space. 'Back to the ranch?'

'No. We're off to see Bell's widow.'

He launched into song. 'The wonderful widow of Bell.'

'And if we're lucky, she'll be able to give you a brain.'

Aberdeen faded in the rear-view mirror as Rennie took the second exit and accelerated up the dual carriageway. Fields. Fields. And more fields. All of them a drab sodden green.

Logan's phone dinged in his hand.

TS TARA:

> Yuck! Cthulhu caught a mouse in the
> kitchen! It's still alive! She's torturing it!

Rennie overtook a mud-encrusted flatbed truck. 'You ever met Bell's wife before?'

'Barbara?' Back to thumbing out a reply on his phone. 'Only at the funeral.'

> Good. Serves the insulation & wire eating
> monsters right. Make sure you tell her
> she's a good girl!

Send.

'Babs was in the am-dram group DI Insch used to run. I saw her in that musical version of *Shaun of the Dead* they put on. She was the mother. Very convincing.'

'Hmm.'

Ding.

> Oh God she's eating it now!!!!

Rennie let out a long sigh. 'It's got to be hella weird, doesn't it? Your husband kills himself, only he doesn't really, and two years later someone else kills him again, but for the first time.'

Ding.

> It's like something off a horror movie!!!
> She's eating the brains! THE BRAINS!!!!

'I mean, put yourself in her shoes: he's been hiding away somewhere sunny all that time and she's been stuck here in Aberdeen with the drizzle and the cold, thinking he's dead.'

Ding.

> The only bits left are the tail, some
> revolting looking green kidney bean thing,
> & the bits of head she didn't eat! I'm
> going to barf!

Another sigh from the bleached-blond philosopher behind the wheel. 'That's the kind of thing that'll really screw you up.'

The housing estate could have been any new-build one in Aberdeenshire. Identical houses on an identical road with identical speedbumps and identical driveways. Tiny patches of

90

miserable soggy grass masquerading as lawns. Trees that would probably still look like twigs for years to come. Four-by-fours parked on bricked-over front gardens. Grey harling with fake-stone details.

Three houses down, the road was packed with outside broadcast vans and journalists' cars. No way through. A lone uniformed PC stood outside the front door, two down. Holding the mob at bay.

Rennie pulled into the kerb. 'Pffff... Maybe we should come back later, when they've all got bored and sodded off?'

'Don't be so damp.' Logan climbed out into the rain and strode along the pavement on the other side of the road, skirting the scabby Saabs and fusty Fiats parked half-on-half-off of it. Keeping his head down.

Didn't work though.

He'd barely made it level to the house when someone spotted his uniform and they all crowded in on him. Shouting over the top of each other.

A curly blonde weather-girl-made-good type forced her way to the front. Pekinese perky. A red-topped microphone in her hand. 'Inspector? Inspector, Anne Darlington, BBC: is it true you suspect DI Bell of murder?'

A ruddy-faced man who looked as if he'd fallen off the back of a tractor. Sounded like it too: 'Come on, min, oor readers have a right to know what's goin' oan here. Have you got a suspect yet or no'?'

An androgynous woman in a shabby suit and short-back-and-sides. Deep voice: 'Angela Parks, *Scottish Daily Post*: are you aware of the rumours that DI Bell was involved in people trafficking in Spain?'

A well-dressed short bloke with a bushy beard – like an Ewok off for a job interview at a bank. English accent: 'Phil Patterson, Sky News: why won't Police Scotland come clean about DI Bell's previous whereabouts? What are you hiding?'

Anne Darlington pushed past him. 'Police Scotland exhumed a body this morning – is that connected to this case?'

Angela Parks shoved her iPhone in Logan's face, a red

'RECORDING' icon glowing in the middle of the screen. 'Is it true that DI Bell was stabbed during a drug deal that went wrong?'

Logan kept his chin up and his face forwards, pushing through them, not slowing down. 'We are pursuing several lines of inquiry and I can't say any more than that at this juncture.'

Rennie struggled on at his shoulder. ''Scuse me. Pardon. Sorry. Oops. 'Scuse me...'

Anne Darlington pushed her microphone in front of Logan again. 'Was DI Bell under investigation at the time of his alleged death?'

'Fit's the deal, min? Fit lines of inquiry are ye followin'?'

Another eight feet and they reached the relative safety of the tiny porch – more an extension of the garage roof than anything else.

'Inspector, was it a drug deal gone wrong or not?'

The PC at the door opened it, shifting to one side so Logan and Rennie could squeeze past, hissing out the side of her mouth as they did. 'It's like a swarm of sodding leeches.' Then stepped forward with her arms extended, blocking the way. 'All right, you heard the Inspector: everyone away from the house. Let's give Mrs Bell some privacy.'

Anne Darlington stayed where she was. 'If you didn't bury DI Bell in that grave two years ago, who *did* you bury?'

Phil Patterson was right behind her. 'Was DI Bell involved in organised crime? Is that why—'

Rennie thumped the front door shut, cutting the rest of it off. 'Now I know how rock stars feel. Only without the ever-present threat of group sex and free drugs.'

The hallway was an antiseptic-white colour with a single family photo next to the light switch. DI Bell, his wife and their two children at the youngest's graduation ceremony. Everyone looking very proud and alive.

A door was open at the end of the hall, murmured voices coming from within.

Logan stepped into a gloomy little living room. The blinds were down, shutting out the rain and the media, but a standard lamp cast just enough light to see the dark patches on the walls where pictures must have hung for years, leaving nothing behind but the unfaded wallpaper and a capstone of dust. Most of the shelves were empty too, as if they'd had a clear-out recently. The only thing left was a single photo in a black frame: Mrs Bell and her husband. Her in a blue frock and him in his dress uniform, taken at some sort of official ceremony.

She was sitting on the couch now, by the electric fire, bottom jaw twitching as if she was trying to work something out from between her teeth. Eyes focused on the fake flames.

But Barbara Bell wasn't the only one in here.

Sitting in the armchair opposite was a wee hardman in a well-fitted suit. Broad shouldered with a good haircut, even if his head was going a bit threadbare on top. Colin Miller. A trio of gold chains glinted around his neck, signet rings on over his black-leather-gloved fingers. And standing behind him: an older lady in a safari-type waistcoat – its pockets bulging with photographic equipment. A huge Cannon DSLR hanging around her neck.

Last, but by all means least: a young male PC, face covered with a moonscape of pockmarks, sitting in the other armchair. He struggled to his feet. 'Inspector. I know this isn't—'

Logan pointed at Miller. 'Colin. Should you not be outside with the rest of your lovely Fourth Estate mates?'

A grin, followed by a Glaswegian accent so strong you could have stood on it. 'Laz, my man, you're lookin' well, but. We've been expressing our sympathy to poor Barbara here. Haven't we, Debbie?'

The photographer nodded, one side of her mouth clamped shut as if there were a fag poking out of it. 'Terrible shame.'

Logan stood in front of the couch. 'Mrs Bell?'

She didn't even look at him. Just made a shooing gesture, batting away an invisible fly. Saggy and defeated.

He nodded. 'Well, I'm sure everyone would like a nice cup of tea. Colin, why don't you lend a hand?' Then marched from the room, thumping Rennie on the way past. 'You too.'

*   *   *

Rennie filled the kettle at a Belfast sink that was far too big for the small kitchen. Colin Miller leaned back against the working surface, crossing his arms and smirking.

Logan gave him a loom. 'How the hell did you get in here?'

'Easy, Tiger.' He held up his hand in self-defence – some of the fingers stiff and twisted in his black leather gloves. 'That any way to talk to an old friend?'

'She's just discovered that her husband died. *Again*. Bad enough you splashed it all over the front page this morning – she doesn't need—'

'Speaking of suicides,' he dropped his voice to a conspiratorial stage whisper, 'a wee birdy tells us you've got another deid copper on your hands.'

'I mean it, Colin: leave Barbara Bell alone!'

'So did Lorna Chalmers *really* kill herself, or did she do a DI Ding-Dong Bell? Enquiring minds and all that.'

Logan backed off a step. 'Who told you about Lorna Chalmers?'

'Cos, see, it's no' hard to put two and two together, is it? Babs is sitting there in her gloomy wee living room and even she knows what's coming. Her beloved deid husband killed someone to take his place in the grave.'

'I'm going to count to three, then you either tell me who told you about Lorna Chalmers or I hurl you out of here on your arse.'

A grin slashed its way across Miller's face. 'That the quote you want me to use when this is all over the *Examiner*'s front page tomorrow? Cos I'm cool with that.'

The kettle rumbled to the boil and clicked off.

Silence.

Logan glowered at Miller. Miller grinned back at him.

Then Rennie broke the moment by hauling a bunch of mugs out of a cupboard and clattering them down by the kettle.

Miller shrugged. 'It's no' goin' all that well for Northeast Division, is it? You can't find Ellie Morton, DI Bell turns up not-dead-but-dead-again, and now DS Lorna Chalmers tops herself.' He tried on a casual, innocent voice: 'You were investigating her for something, weren't you?'

'DS Rennie, make sure one of those mugs has extra spit in it.'

'All right, all right. Easy, big man. Me and Debbie got all we need from Babs already. Was only hanging about to be nice to the poor dear. Keep her company and that.' Miller pushed himself upright. 'She's all yours.'

Logan settled back on the couch as Rennie laid out four mugs of milky tea on the coffee table.

The thump of a closing door came from the hall and Family Liaison Officer McCraterface stepped into the room again. 'That's them gone now.'

Logan smiled at Mrs Bell. 'Barbara, you didn't have to speak to them.'

She flexed her hands into fists. 'He lied to me.'

'Of course he did, he's a journalist.'

'He left a bloody suicide note!' Mrs Bell bared her teeth at the electric fire. 'I memorised it. I thought I'd done something. Two *bloody* years and I thought... I thought if only I'd *done* something. If only I'd noticed how depressed he was. If only I'd got him some help!' She picked up one of the mugs and hurled it at DI Bell's photo. Knocking it flying, the mug shattering. Tea exploded across the wall. 'And he wasn't even dead! He was living it up in the sunshine, drinking sangria and shagging some Spanish tart!'

Logan shook his head. 'Barbara, we don't know that.'

'Oh, we bloody well do! Mr Miller got someone to track down Duncan's new family in Villaferrueña.'

Wonderful. The wee sod never mentioned *that*.

Mrs Bell ground her fists into her lap. 'Duncan and his Spanish tart have a one-year-old son. I thought he was dead and he's been making bloody babies!' She snatched up another mug and hurled it to join the first. Another sharp-edged shattering and beige tea sprayed the wall.

Rennie grabbed his tea before it went flying too.

Logan took out his notebook. 'We need to ask you some questions about what happened two years ago.'

She was still scowling at the tea-drenched wallpaper. 'I boxed up all his *crap*. Did it last night, soon as they told me he hadn't really killed himself.' A sniff. She wiped at her eyes. Voice brittle. 'I've been keeping this house like some sort of bloody shrine. Like he'd magically come back from the dead and everything would be fine again. I'm such a bloody *idiot*.' Her whole face crumpled.

'Can you remember him talking about a case he was working on at the time? Maybe something that was preying on his mind?'

'Well, you know what? I'm happy he's dead. I'm *glad* someone stabbed him. I hope they get away with it!'

11

Logan was last in line, barely able to see over the top of his large cardboard box. At least it wasn't that heavy. He followed the FLO and Rennie out through the front door and into a lightning storm of camera flashes.

'Inspector? Anne Darlington, BBC.' Her blonde curls bounced as she fell into step, dragging a cameraman after her. 'Inspector: is it true you've uncovered the identity of the individual who died in that caravan two years ago?'

Logan shifted his box, turning it into a cardboard shield between himself and the rampaging hordes of the media. 'Please get out of the way.'

The Ewok man – Patterson? – jogged alongside as they hurried towards the pool car. 'Is this case linked to the recent suicide of Detective Sergeant Lorna Chalmers?'

The thin androgynous one hadn't gone away either. 'Angela Parks, *Scottish Daily Post*. Will there be a public inquiry into the handling of DI Bell's *alleged* suicide? Were you involved in the investigation?'

Rennie plipped the locks and they stuffed their boxes in the back of the car.

Anne Darlington tried to block Logan's way. 'Why won't Police Scotland respond to any of our questions, Inspector? What are you trying to hide?'

The teuchtery one shoved himself to the front of the scrum.

'Yer DS Chalmers was working on the Ellie Morton case – fit did she discover that led her to kill hersel'?'

The Family Liaison Officer put a hand against the teuchter's chest. 'Come on, back up please.'

Logan pushed around to the passenger side, Angela Parks close on his tail.

'Is the Ellie Morton case connected to the disappearance of Stephen MacGuire this morning?'

Anne Darlington grabbed at his arm, but he blocked her with the passenger door. 'Inspector, do you have an ID for the body, or don't you? It's a perfectly simple question: yes, or no?'

'It's an ongoing investigation.' And inside.

The Parks woman wasn't giving up. 'There's been a string of child abductions in the last two weeks, hasn't there? Are they linked to Ellie Morton?'

He hauled the door shut with a thump and snibbed the lock.

Rennie clambered in behind the wheel and started the engine. 'Gah... It's like something off *The Walking Dead*!'

Anne Darlington knocked on the window. Voice muffled by the glass. 'Yes, or no, Inspector?'

Logan fastened his seatbelt, talking to Rennie out the side of his mouth, so they couldn't film it. 'Drive. And if you accidentally run over three or four of the bastards on the way, that's fine with me.'

'Done.' But as soon as he put the car in gear, the horde backed away, cameras filming, flashguns flashing, recording Rennie's three-point turn for posterity. Then Darlington primped her hair and launched into a piece to camera.

Rennie grimaced, accelerating down the road. 'Well, *that* was fun.'

'Bloody Colin Bloody Miller!' Logan pulled out his phone and poked at the screen. Listened to it ring. 'Pick up, you rancid little...' A click. 'Colin? Why the hell didn't you tell me you'd tracked down DI Bell's Spanish family?'

Miller tutted a couple of times, then, *'You used to be a lot more polite on the phone.'*

'You should've told me he had another family in Villafff…
weren…'

'*Villaferrueña. It's a middle-of-nowhere teeny-wee village. Popula-
tion about a hundred and fifty? Boring. You'd love it.*'

'This is an ongoing investigation!'

'*Aye, and you can read all about it in tomorrow's* Aberdeen Examiner. *Now, if there's nothing else, I'm away to that nice butcher in
Rosemount to pick up some steaks for tea. You know how Isobel loves
a good slab of meat when she's been post-morteming all day, but.*'

'Colin!'

A laugh rattled down the phone. '*I know stuff you don't. If you
want to play quid pro quo at some point, you know where to find us.*'
Then the connection went dead. He'd hung up.

'Damn it.' Logan lowered his phone.

Rennie looked across the car at him. 'We could get a warrant?'

'Yes, because we've done such a *great* job of that recently.'
Logan shook his head. 'You know what? Not my case: not my
problem. DCI Hardie can deal with it.'

The identikit houses and identikit streets drifted past the car
windows as Rennie made for the dual carriageway again. 'Guv?
That reporter– the one who looks like a *really* thin bloke – she
said, "was the Ellie Morton case connected to Stephen MacGuire
going missing?"'

'And?'

'Who's Stephen MacGuire?'

Good point.

'No idea.' Logan pulled up a web browser on his phone and
thumbed in the name. Set it searching.

A link to the *Clydebank Herald and Post* website came up and
he followed it. Waiting for the page to load. 'Here we go.' The
headline 'FAMILY'S FEAR FOR MISSING STEPHEN' filled the screen.
Scrolling down revealed a photo of a small blond boy, smiling
a gap-toothed smile. Lots of freckles. A dark-purple birthmark
spread itself across one cheek and along the side of his nose.

'"Stephen MacGuire, brackets four, went missing from outside
his East Kilbride flat at half past eight this morning." Blah, blah,
blah. "'A wonderful little boy who lights up every room he walks

into,' said his distraught mother, Janice, brackets twenty-three."'

Rennie nodded. 'Any word of a stepdad?'

'No, but the mother's partner says, "Stephen would not just wander off, I am sure someone must have taken him."'

'There you go – it'll be him. The partner.'

'"We are desperate to get our beloved son home. Please, if you have any idea where Stephen is, get in touch with the authorities before it is too late." Why do newspapers have to make everyone sound like robots? "Before it is too late." Who talks like that?'

Another nod. 'It's *always* the mum's new bloke.'

Logan put his phone away. 'Don't see how a kid getting abducted in East Kilbride has anything to do with a wee girl snatched from Tillydrone.'

'All that "Stranger Danger" stuff is a waste of time. We'd be better off teaching kids to run away from their stepdads.'

'...appealing for any information on missing four-year-old, Stephen MacGuire. Stephen was last seen outside his home on Telford Road at eight thirty-two this morning...'

God, it was a lovely day. Not so nice back home with its wind and rain, of course, but out here? With the mighty Cairngorms rising on either side of the road, purpled with heather? The majestic Scottish sky a bright saphire blue? The sun shining down on natives and tourists alike? Who wouldn't love this?

'...distinctive port wine stain birthmark on his left cheek. Stephen was wearing blue jeans, a red sweatshirt with a panda on it, brown trainers, and a light-blue jacket...'

The sign went past on the left, 'Fàilte Don Ghàidhealtachd ~ Welcome To The Highlands' above a stylised illustration of the landscape, complete with trees and a shining loch.

Lee grinned as his trusty old beige Volvo grumbled past it at a sensible 58 miles per hour: some wag had added a wee Nessie to the loch. Had to love the *imagination* of these people.

'...morning. Police are keen to trace anyone who was in the area at the time, especially the drivers of a green Citroën Picasso and a grey Nissan Micra...'

An idiot in a BMW overtook him, even though there was *clearly* a coach-load of day-trippers coming the other way. Roaring past, then slamming on its brakes to screech back into the left lane. Idiot. It was people like that who caused accidents.

'...*following statement.*'

A rough woman's voice replaced the newsreader's more professional tones. '*While we can't rule out a connection with the disappearances of Ellie Morton in Aberdeen, and Lucy Hawkins in St Andrews, I have to say that it's very unlikely.*'

Aw, bless.

'*We have a considerable number of officers out searching the area as we speak, but I have to stress: if you saw Stephen MacGuire this morning, or have any idea where he is, I* urge *you to come forward and talk to us.*'

It was all rather sweet, really. Pointless, but sweet.

'*Stephen's family are obviously very distressed at this time, so if you have any information, please get in touch by calling one zero one. Help us bring Stephen home.*'

And the newsreader was back. '*Sport now and Aberdeen are looking to bring home three points from their Ibrox fixture this weekend. The Dons have been riding high since the start of the season and—*'

Lee switched the radio off.

A full-scale manhunt – well, full-scale *child*-hunt – was excellent news. Nothing like a bit of publicity to whet people's appetites.

He took his eyes off the road for a brief moment and looked in the rear-view mirror – at the pet carrier in the boot, partially covered by a tartan blanket. 'Did you hear that, Stephen? You're famous!'

A pair of watery green eyes blinked back at him through the pet carrier's grille door. Freckles and tears on the wee boy's pale cheeks. That distinctive port wine birthmark. The chunk of duct tape across his mouth.

'Isn't that exciting? All those policemen out looking for you? I bet they'll have your picture on the lunchtime news and everything.'

Stephen snivelled and cried.

Which was only to be expected. He'd had a pretty big day

after all: being bundled into a car boot by a woman he thought was his mum's friend, then sold on at a disused-petrol-station in the middle of a run-down industrial estate. It was probably *quite* overwhelming for a wee lad.

Still, that was no reason to mope, was it?

'How about a sing-song to pass the time? Come on then, all together now: A hundred green bottles, hanging on the wall,' belting it out, with a smile in his heart and his voice, 'A hundred green bottles, hanging on the wall, and if one green bottle, should accidentally fall, there'd be...?'

He glanced in the mirror again. Stephen stared back with his tear-stained cheeks and duct-tape gag.

'Oh, that's right. Sorry.' Lee shrugged. 'Never mind.' Deep breath: 'There'd be ninety-nine green bottles, hanging on the wall...'

'*But* how*?*' DCI Hardie's voice whined out of the phone, making him sound as if someone was slowly beating him to death with a haddock. '*How did they find out so quickly?*'

The Asda car park was getting busier as workers in Dyce's industrial estates and oil offices rolled up to buy something for lunch. At least it had stopped raining.

'No idea, but you know what the press are like. They don't have to go through official channels, they can just bribe people.' Logan hunched over the pool car's boot. Shifted his phone – freeing up his other hand to rummage about in one of the cardboard boxes from DI Bell's house. Well, ex-DI Bell's ex-house.

This one was nearly all clothes, suits and shirts and trousers, crumpled and mangled where they'd been rammed in.

'*And he was living in Verti...?*'

'Villaferrueña.' There were socks in here too. And Y-fronts. 'There's probably more info, but Miller's saving it for the front page tomorrow. Unless we've got something we can trade?'

'*I'll get on to the Spanish cops, see what they can dig up.*'

'The press are having a feeding frenzy outside Mrs Bell's house, by the way. And from the sound of things they've started making stuff up.' Some ties. A ten-pin bowling trophy sat at the very bottom of the box; the little man on top's head had been snapped clean off.

'Wonderful. Well, I've got a press conference starting in half an hour. Looking forward to that about as much as my last colonoscopy.'

Should probably go through all the jacket and trouser pockets too.

'When Rennie gets back, we're off to speak to Sally MacAuley. Bell was obsessed with her case, so maybe...?'

'But probably not.'

'Probably not.'

And talking of Rennie – he was bumbling his way out through the supermarket's main doors, pushing a small trolley with a wonky wheel. Not a care in the world.

Must be nice to be that divorced from reality.

Logan dipped into the box again. A handful of serial-killer thriller paperbacks with cheesy predictable titles on a 'DARK DEADLY DEATH BLOOD DEATHLY DYING' theme. 'While I've got you: you'll need a Senior Investigating Officer for the Chalmers suicide. Because she was a police officer?'

'Are you volunteering?'

'No. But what about DS Rennie?'

'As SIO?' A laugh barked out of the phone. 'I'd rather put drunken hyenas in charge of my granddaughter's third birthday party.'

'Yes, but he's done the training course; he's worked on several murders; he's not got himself suspended, demoted, or fired; and it's an open-and-shut suicide. Not even Beardie Beattie could screw this one up.'

'Hmmmm...'

Rennie made a massive detour around a puddle, trolley juddering and rattling away as if it was having a seizure. The idiot was grinning like this was the most fun he'd had in ages.

Maybe Hardie was right? Maybe making Rennie SIO was asking for—

'I can't believe I'm saying this, but OK. On the strict condition that he goes nowhere near the media and you supervise him the whole time. And I mean the whole time.'

Rennie arrived with his wobbly trolley. He pointed at the contents and waggled his eyebrows.

'Do we have a deal?'

Oh God... He was going to regret this, wasn't he?

'Fine. If that's what it takes.' Logan pointed at Rennie, mouthing the words in silence: 'You owe me!' Then back to the phone. 'Got to go. Good luck with the press conference.'

'We'll need it.' And Hardie was gone.

Logan put his phone away.

Rennie frowned. 'Owe you for what?'

'You're now *officially* SIO on Laura Chalmers' suicide.'

His eyes bugged and a wonky grin lopsided itself across his face. 'Woohoo!' He even did a little dance between the puddles, finishing with a half-arsed pirouette. Pointing at his purchases again. 'And to celebrate: one pack of spicy rotisserie chicken thighs, hot. One four-pack of white rolls. One squeezy bottle of mayonnaise. One bag of mixed salad. Bottle of Coke, bottle of Irn-Bru. Six jammy doughnuts for a pound. Luncheon is served.'

The pool car's engine pinged and ticked as it cooled, the bonnet dulled by a thin film of drizzle. From here the view was ... interesting: looking down, past a couple of fields to the massive concrete lumps of the new bridge over the River Don. The fabled Aberdeen Western Peripheral Route, rising from the earthworks slow and solid. A dark slash across the countryside, trapped beneath the dove-grey blanket of cloud. About forty years after they *should* have started building the damn thing. Back when the area was awash with oil money. Before the industry tanked.

Ah well, better late than never.

Rennie passed in front of the car again, pacing round it in the rain. Idiot.

The windows were getting foggy, so Logan wound his one down, letting in the distant roar of construction equipment and passing traffic.

Rennie did another lap. 'No, I'm not kidding, they made me SIO!' A pause, then his voice went all deadpan. 'Oh: ha, ha, ha. No, it *doesn't* stand for "Seriously Idiotic Onanist". Thank you, Sarah Millican.'

Logan poked away at his phone again:

> Did DS Chalmers say anything to you
> about any leads she was following about
> Ellie Morton's disappearance?

SEND.

'Senior Investigating Officer, Emma! They made me Senior Investigating Officer on the Laura Chalmers case. ... Yeah, it *is* a pretty big deal.'

Ding.

HORRIBLE STEEL:

> Nice try. I'm still not clyping on her. Or
> speaking to you.

'I guess they finally recognised all the great work I've been doing. ... Oh yeah.'

Logan frowned and picked out a reply:

> She's DEAD, Roberta. Whatever secrets she
> had aren't hers to keep any more.

SEND.

'Who's your daddy? ... Damn right I am.'

No reply from Steel.

Probably sulking. Or sodded off for a vape.

Some things never changed.

'OK, yeah. ... Love you, Fluffkins. ... OK, bye. ... Bye. ... Bye, bye.' Rennie blew a half-dozen kisses, then hung up. Turned to see Logan staring at him. 'What?'

'You've got a mayonnaise moustache.' Logan took another bite of chicken-thigh buttie – savoury and salty and spicy and creamy. Talking with his mouth full. 'And that's not a euphemism.'

'Ta.' Rennie wiped his face with a napkin, scrumpled it up and tossed it over his shoulder into the back of the car. 'So far we've had a suicide, a collapsed coffin, a baying mob of reporters, and I've got my first SIO gig.' He performed a little bum-wriggling dance in the driver's seat. 'Best day at work for *ages*.'

'When we get back to the Big Top, write up your report on Chalmers' suicide and submit it to the Procurator Fiscal. Then I want you to go through the boxes in the boot. See if you can find any of DI Bell's old notebooks in there. Maybe we'll get lucky for a change?'

Rennie peered across the car at the bag on Logan's lap. 'You wanting that bit of skin?'

'Nope.'

He grabbed the slab of chicken skin and wolfed it down. 'How come you always call him "DI Bell" now instead of "Ding-Dong"? Always used to call him "Ding-Dong".'

'Because you shouldn't use friendly nicknames for police officers who kill people.'

'Ah. Point.'

Outside, a crane lowered another chunk of grey onto the massive Lego set crossing the river. A handful of sheep skirted the chunk of flooded grass at the bottom of the field. The sound of chewing and slurping filled the car.

Rennie had another scoof of Coke. 'Yeah, but maybe he didn't mean to kill whoever it was we buried? Maybe it was, like, *a fight to the death*!'

'Then why use the body to fake your own suicide?'

'Convenience? Wasn't like anyone else was using it.' Another mouthful, bits of salad falling into his lap.

'And the person who attacked him coincidentally *happened* to be a good enough match for height and weight that everyone would be fooled?'

'Another point.' Rennie polished off his buttie and sooked his fingers clean. Checked his watch. 'Oops, nearly missed it!' He clicked on the car radio, stabbing the buttons until 'Northsound 1' appeared on the dial and a horrifically upbeat pop song belted out of the speakers.

Logan turned it down a bit. 'My money's still on Fred Marshall.'

Rennie dipped into the doughnut bag. 'Nah, can't be. I read his file: Marshall was six-two and built like a whippet. Ding... DI Bell was five-ten tops and built like a grizzly bear. No way you'd get them mixed up. Not even after a fire.'

The song on the radio faded out, replaced by a teuchter accent so thick it *had* to be fake. *'Ah, mighty me, another* Dougie's Lunchtime Listening Classic *there. Gets better every time I hear it! But it's one o'clock now and we ken fit that means: here's Claire with the news and weather. Aye, aye, Claire, fit like the day, quine?'*

Claire didn't even try to do the accent. *'Nae bad, Dougie. Commuter chaos came to Aberdeen this morning when a burst water main flooded the Denburn roundabout...'*

Logan frowned. 'Six foot two?'

'Well, probably a bit less once you took the top of his head off with a shotgun. But yeah, not the same body type at all.'

'Good job we didn't get those warrants then.'

'...for missing three-year-old Ellie Morton, local businesswoman Jerry Whyte has put up a five thousand pound reward for any information...'

Logan helped himself to a doughnut. 'Better go through all the missing person reports for the month DI Bell allegedly killed himself.'

'Assuming it was someone anyone would miss.'

A woman's voice thumped out of the radio, positive and confident. *'I'm glad to be in a position to help. And if we all chip in, I'm sure we can make a difference.'*

Then Claire was back. *'And we can go live now to Northeast Divisional Headquarters.'*

Rennie licked the granulated sugar from his lips. 'What if he offed a homeless person? Or a crim?'

'Thank you all for coming.' DCI Hardie didn't sound as if he meant that. *'I can confirm that the body of a man found in a crashed car yesterday morning was that of Duncan Bell, a former detective inspector with Police Scotland.'*

Logan's doughnut popped with sharp-sweet raspberry jam. 'Then we're screwed.' He caught the drip with a finger. 'They couldn't get any viable DNA the first time round, and I doubt we'll do any better. Bell didn't set fire to that caravan by accident, he knew it'd cook the remains and cover his tracks.'

'Mr Bell had been living in Spain under an assumed name, having apparently staged his own suicide two years ago.'

'Tooth pulp cavity?'

Logan shook his head. 'Blew them all out with a shotgun, remember?'

'...currently working with the Spanish authorities to establish his whereabouts during that time.'

'Maybe someone picked them up?'

'Maybe.'

'We are treating Mr Bell's death as murder and have set up a Major Investigation Team to look into his death.'

'But knowing our luck?' Logan washed the last chunk of doughnut down with a mouthful of Irn-Bru. Suppressed a belch. 'If Bell hadn't set fire to the caravan you could've just dug them out of the walls, but mixed in with all that burnt wreckage?'

'Anne Darlington, BBC: have you identified the body buried in DI Bell's grave?'

'Investigations are ongoing and I would urge anyone with information about Mr Bell's murder to get in touch.'

Rennie held out the doughnut bag. 'Better eat another one before I scoff the lot.'

'No, I'm good thanks.' Logan wiped his hands together, showering the footwell with sugar. 'Where's the MacAuley case file?'

'Back seat.'

'You haven't answered my question, DCI Hardie. Do you know who it is or not?'

Logan turned in his seat and picked up the file. Opened it and skimmed through the contents.

'As I said, investigations are ongoing. So—'

'Colin Miller, Aberdeen Examiner. Are you aware that DI Bell had returned to Aberdeenshire on at least three prior occasions?'

He flipped through to the end, then back again. 'Didn't she write a book, or something? Thought I remembered a book.'

Hardie cleared his throat. *'As I say, investigations are ongoing* and *if* you, *or anyone else, has* any *information they should get in touch.'*

'*Or you could buy a copy of tomorrow's* Aberdeen Examiner?'

'Yeah, there was definitely a book: I read it.' Rennie plucked another doughnut free. '*Cold Blood and Dark Granite.* Subtitled, "A Mother's hunt for her husband's killer and her missing child." Doesn't exactly trip off the tongue.'

'*I would strongly advise* against *withholding information from a murder investigation, Mr Miller.'*

Rennie bit into his doughnut, getting sugar all down his front. 'Pretty sure she co-wrote it with a retired *P-and-J* journalist. There's talk of a film, but you know what Hollywood's like.'

'*Tom Neville,* Dundee and Perthshire Advertiser: *are you* threatening *the press, DCI Hardie?'*

'*I'm asking for its* cooperation.'

Logan drummed his fingers against the paperwork. Frowning at it. His fingertips making little greasy circles. 'Three and a half years ago, someone kills Sally MacAuley's husband and abducts her three-year-old son. Eighteen months later, DI Bell kills someone and uses the body to fake his own death.'

'*Aye, tell you what: why don't you and me sit down after this and see if we can't help each other, but?'*

'Eighteen months.' Logan stopped drumming. 'A long time to let something fester... Guilty conscience?'

'*Angela Parks,* Scottish Daily Post: *there are rumours DI Bell was involved in a so-called "Livestock Mart" where children were bought and sold. Is this—'*

'*I'm not here to talk about rumours, Ms Parks.'*

Rennie crammed in about half his doughnut in one go. Mumbling through it. 'You don't think Bell killed Kenneth MacAuley and abducted the wee boy, do you?'

'*Philip Patterson, Sky News: DS Lorna Chalmers committed suicide last night, is it true she was under investigation for corruption?'*

'*No, it's not. Thank you all for your time. No more questions.'*

Logan closed the file. 'He was definitely running from something.'

12

About three or four miles past Rothienorman, Rennie pulled the car off the back road and onto a potholed strip of tarmac lined by ragged beech hedges and waterlogged fields. He slowed to a crawl, slaloming between the craters. Sheep watched them from the high ground, wool faded to ash-grey by the rain.

The windscreen wipers squealed. Thumped. Squealed. Thumped.

They took a right, through a farmyard with warning notices about livestock and gates and unsolicited callers and bewaring of the dogs. Past agricultural equipment and barns and outbuildings and a ramshackle farmhouse, then out the other side – onto a rough track with a solid Mohican of grass down the middle.

Another right, past a couple of cottages lurking in a block of trees, and up the hill. Fields full of reeds and docken.

A gorse bush scraped and screamed along the car's bodywork.

More trees. A tumble-down bothy with half its roof missing. Someone was standing in front of it, chopping logs. He stopped, axe over his shoulder, watching them pass.

Logan gave him a smile and a wave. Got nothing back.

Rennie sniffed. 'God, welcome to Banjo Country.'

Past a stack of big round bales, rotting and slumped in the rain.

'All together now: "Squeal piggy!" Diga-ding ding, ding, ding, ding, ding, ding...'

More trees. Getting thicker. Crowding the road.

They kept on going, right to the end of the track. A sagging gate blocked the way, wrapped in chicken wire and peppered with signs: 'BEWARE OF THE DOG!', 'PLEASE SHUT THE GATE!', 'NEIGHBOURHOOD WATCH AREA' and 'SKEMMELS-BRAE CROFT'.

A new-ish house sat about a hundred yards further on, just visible through the trees and tussocked grass. Two storeys high, pale pink harling darkened by moisture. Lurking in the woods. The only thing missing was a roof made of gingerbread and a small child cooking in the oven.

Rennie nodded towards it. 'You want to get the gate?'

'I'd love to, but...' Logan sucked a breath in through his teeth. 'Inspector, remember?'

'Gah...' Rennie climbed out into the rain. Hurried over and fiddled with the gate. Then hurried back to the car again. 'It's padlocked. But there's a car in the drive and a light's on.'

Great.

Logan grimaced at the downpour, tucked the case file under his fleece, pulled on his hat and high-viz jacket, then joined Rennie in the cold and damp. Branches loomed overhead, dark and oppressive. But at least they kept some of the rain off.

Rennie clambered over the gate and froze, arms out, shoulders hunched. 'Arrgh... Right in a puddle.'

Idiot.

Logan climbed over, making sure *not* to step in the dirty brown lake spreading on either side of the track's central ridge. He picked his way along the middle bit, past more trees, around a corner, and there was the house.

A big four-by-four sat outside it, along with a filthy blue-and-white horsebox. The light above the door glowed a septic yellow.

Not exactly welcoming.

They were about twenty foot from the house when barking exploded into the damp air.

Rennie froze, staring. 'Dear God, that's a *massive* dog.'

It looked more like a bear than a dog. About the same size

as a bear too, covered in thick black hair. Saggy eyes and jowls. Teeth the size of traffic cones. Well, maybe not *traffic* cones, but big enough. Thankfully it was shut into a kennel / run thing at the side of the house.

Beardog launched itself at the bars of its cage and they shook with a boom and a rattle.

Rennie gave a small tittering laugh. 'Nice doggy. Don't eat the lovely policemen...' He scrambled up the steps and sheltered beneath the small porch, casting worried glances at the massive scary animal as it fell silent.

Logan joined him. Rang the doorbell.

Rennie flinched as the barking started up again. 'What if she's not in?'

'Then we got wet for nothing. You should've phoned ahead.'

His bottom lip popped out. 'But you keep telling me off for doing that! They always find a way to sneak off, you said. You can't trust them, you said.'

'Yes, but I was talking about *police officers*, you total—'

A woman's silhouette appeared on the other side of the glass-panelled door, growing clearer the closer she came. Tall, with dark eyes and full lips, long brown hair falling over her shoulders. A hint of crow's-feet and what probably weren't laughter lines. A soft blue sweater and faded jeans. She didn't open the door. 'Who is...' Her eyes widened as she looked Logan up and down. 'Oh God. It's... I didn't...?'

'Mrs MacAuley? Can we come in and have a word, please? It's about your son and husband.'

She unlocked the door and threw it open. Stood there blinking at them. Voice half panicked, half hopeful. 'Have you found him? Have you found Aiden?'

'I'm sorry, no.'

Mrs MacAuley buried her head in her hands and cried.

Mrs MacAuley sat at the long wooden table, digging the nails of one hand into the palm of the other. 'I didn't... It's just when I saw you there in your uniform, I thought...' A small laugh rattled free, cold and bitter. 'But then I always do.'

The huge farmhouse kitchen was a deep red colour, a bit too womb-like to be cosy. Lots of wooden cabinets. A big AGA-style range cooker gurgling and thrumming away to itself. The kettle rattling to a boil as Rennie busied himself making three mugs of tea.

Logan pulled out a chair and sat across from Mrs MacAuley. 'You have a lovely home.'

Rennie pointed with a teabag. 'Shame about the shed, though.'

She frowned. 'Shed?'

A pair of patio doors led out from the kitchen into a big garden, bordered by a six-foot-high hedge, surrounded by woods.

'All burnt down.'

He was right. It must've been a fairly substantial one too, at least six-by-eight, but all that was left of it were a few burnt stubs where the walls used to be. Glistening and dark in the rain.

'Ah. No. That was years ago. Kids. I think.' She looked away. 'I keep meaning to get rid of it, but Ken built it and Aiden painted every single bit he could reach, even when we asked him not to.'

'Sorry. Didn't mean to upset—'

'Anyway,' Logan sat forward, 'we'd like to ask some questions about the investigation, if you're OK with that?'

She nodded.

'Good. Well, when—'

'Aiden had been a pain in the backside all morning, shouting and squealing and running about the house.' She picked at her palm again, digging at it with her fingernails. 'I was trying to do the ironing. He wasn't looking where he was going and he … he battered right into the ironing board. The whole thing went crashing down.' Voice getting more and more brittle. 'And I screamed at him. I...'

Rennie threw Logan a pained look as she wiped away a tear.

'I called him a "horrible little monster"; told him he was stupid and careless.' She looked up. Pleading. 'He could've *killed*

113

himself! The iron was red hot, what if it'd landed on his head? Or scarred him for life?' She lowered her eyes, nails gouging away at her palm. 'So Ken took him off to the shops. And I never saw Aiden again. I never saw either of them ever again.'

Logan put his hand on her arm. 'I'm sorry.'

'The last thing I said to my son was "You're a stupid, careless, horrible little boy."'

'You weren't to know.'

Deep breath. 'It's only fifteen minutes through the woods – there's a track takes you right into Rothienorman. They went out for milk and flour and eggs and they never came back.'

In the silence that followed, Rennie placed the mugs on the table.

Mrs MacAuley covered her face. Her whole body wracked by each juddering sob. 'They ... they were going ... to make pancakes ... to cheer ... to cheer me up. ... My husband ... died ... and my ... my little boy vanished ... because ... because of bloody pancakes!'

Rennie was outside on the patio, wandering across the paving slabs, phone clamped to his ear. 'Yeah. ... Yeah. ... No. Don't think so anyway.'

Logan stepped through the open patio doors, closing them behind him. 'We better give her a bit of space.' Up above, the clouds were nearly skimming the treetops. Rain drumming against Logan's peaked cap. He set off down the path towards the bottom of the garden. 'Come on.'

'Yeah. ... Will do. ... OK. Thanks.' Rennie hung up and hurried after him. 'Creepy Sheila says that's our exhumed remains all installed at the mortuary. Kickoff's at three.'

They passed the burned-out shed. Ivy crawled around the base. A drooping fern curling its way through the charcoaled wood in one corner.

Rennie scampered past, looking back towards the house. 'Nice place, isn't it? Very big and fancy. Be great to bring a kid up here. Donna would love it. All this space...'

A couple more sheds lurked in different corners of the garden, the undergrowth pressing in on all sides, windows greyed with dust and spiders' webs. One was almost completely consumed by a rampant thicket of ivy and brambles. The other shed's door barely clung on to its hinges, exposing the rusting hulk of a ride-on mower inside.

Nature was reclaiming most of the garden, all except the washing line and a child's play area: climbing frame, slide, and a pristine swingset. Slowly being battered into submission by the rain.

The path led to a gap in the hedge, then off away into the woods. Dark and cold and deep. A thick canopy of pine blocked out most of the rain. The drops hissed and clicked above them, joining the chorus of crunching twigs and rustling needles beneath their feet as they followed the path downhill.

Rennie stuck his hands in his pockets. 'I mean, did you see how big that back garden was? Ours is about the size of a facecloth.'

They passed the remains of what was probably a croft, now little more than tumbled-down ruins. Ominous bones in the gloom.

'And think of the games you could play in here! Charging about with a wooden sword.' He slashed the air with an imaginary one. 'Being dinosaurs.'

A clump of broom had invaded the path, crowding in from both sides so only a narrow gap remained. Logan pushed through it.

The pine gave way to beech – leaves drooping like scraps of skin waiting to drop – opening out into a clearing with a burn running through the middle of it. Someone had thrown together a makeshift bridge over the water with planks and chunks of stone. The sort of thing a child would build.

On the other side, a fusty grey teddy bear was cable-tied to a tree, along with some faded artificial flowers.

Rennie wandered out into the rain. 'Ooh... It's like something off Winnie-the-Pooh, isn't it?' He grabbed a twig. 'Wanna play Poohsticks?'

Logan reached into his jacket and pulled out the case file,

sheltering beneath a huge beech tree. He checked the crime-scene photographs, then pointed at the far side of the bridge. 'That's where they found Kenneth MacAuley.'

MacAuley lay on his side, one hand dangling in the burn, head reduced to red and purple mush. Logan held the picture out to Rennie.

'Urgh... That's *horrible*.' Backing away. Face curdled with disgust.

'Thought you'd read the case file? I told you to read the case file!'

'Yeah, but I didn't ogle the crime-scene photos, did I? I'm not a sickie weirdo.' A shudder. 'Urgh...'

'Imagine you're the killer: why are you here?'

'To bump off Kenneth MacAuley.'

Logan leaned back against the tree. 'Then why abduct Aiden?'

'Ah, OK. So either that was a bonus, or maybe *that's* why I'm here? It's an abduction gone wrong.'

'Then why the overkill? First blow to the head probably did the job, but you keep on going till there's nothing left above his neck but mince. Why?' Logan held up the photograph, moving it around until it overlaid the real scene. Kenneth MacAuley sprawled out with his hand in the water. 'What does that get you? Why do you do that?'

'Because I'm a freak?'

'Or maybe you know him and you can't stand him looking at you with those accusing dead eyes...' Logan lowered the photo and stared off into the woods. 'And what do you do with the wee boy afterwards?'

Rennie dropped his stick in the water and watched it float away.

Mrs MacAuley stood at the living room window, looking out at the dreich view. Shoulders slumped.

A pair of big leather sofas faced each other across a large wooden coffee table covered in dog-eared – and possibly dog-chewed – copies of *Horse and Hound*. An old upright piano in the corner, almost buried under framed photos of Sally, Kenneth,

116

and Aiden MacAuley. More on the walls. A shrine to the missing and the dead.

It was difficult to tell which Mrs MacAuley was. Probably more than a little bit of both.

Logan shifted on his sofa, the leather creaking beneath him. Rennie sat on the other one, notepad out, pen poised.

Mrs MacAuley wrapped her arms around herself, kept her face to the window. 'I'm sorry. I'm a bit...' She huffed out a breath. 'I've spent the last three and a half years trying to get my son back. And before you say anything: no, he's *not* dead. I know he's alive. I *know* it.'

'DI Bell was the Senior Investigating Officer.'

She flinched at his name.

Strange.

Logan tried again. 'Mrs MacAuley?'

'He was... I saw it on the news.'

'His colleagues say he was obsessed with Aiden's disappearance. With finding your husband's killer.'

Her chin went up. Back straight. 'I call the station every Monday. They tell me the investigation's still open, that you're still trying to find my little boy. But nothing ever happens. Nothing.'

'Did DI Bell come to see you before he ... didn't commit suicide?'

'When my father died, I sold his house. That's where I got the reward money from. Fifty thousand pounds after I'd paid off all his debts.' She made a strangled *hissing* noise. Then, 'Oh, there's plenty of people who want to get their hands on it. Liars and frauds pretending they know things. And then there's the *press*.' She pronounced that last word as if it was drenched in sick. 'Every time a child went missing, they'd be up here with their cameras and their microphones and their stupid insensitive questions. "How does it feel to lose a child, Mrs MacAuley?" "What would you like to say to the missing five-year-old's parents, Mrs MacAuley?" Till I started setting Tristan on them.' A smile – short and cruel. 'One of the benefits of having a very large dog. They stopped coming after that.'

117

'We're just trying to figure out what happened to DI Bell.'

She turned, face dark and creased. 'WHEN YOU SHOULD BE TRYING TO FIND MY SON!'

Outside, the dogbear started barking again.

Mrs MacAuley bared her teeth. 'Instead I had to hire private detectives. So when the timewasters and the greedy come after the reward at least I know *someone's* investigating it.'

'Now,' Logan held up a hand, 'I'm sure the inquiry team is—'

'Is anyone even working on the case any more?'

Good question.

'I'll look into that, I promise.'

She stared at him in silence for a bit, the colour in her cheeks faded to its usual grey, then she nodded. 'Duncan turned up on my doorstep at two o'clock one morning. He'd been drinking. He stood there in my kitchen crying and apologising, because he couldn't catch the piece of shit who killed Kenneth and took my boy.'

Now that *was* interesting.

Logan sat forward. 'You called him "Duncan"?'

She waved a hand – dismissive. Turned her back on them.

'Mrs MacAuley, were you and DI Bell...?'

'Duncan was ... complicated. He was the only one of you who cared. And I don't mean pretend "I'm sorry for your loss" cared, I mean *really* cared. And now he's dead.' She rested her forehead against the glass. Sighed. Her shoulders slumped even further. 'I think I'd like you to leave now.'

The pool car lurched and rumbled down the track, the dark woods swallowing Skemmelsbrae Croft in the rear-view mirror. No wonder Mrs MacAuley was a bit... Well, living there, given what had happened by that little shonky bridge, surrounded by those looming twisted trees.

Rennie clicked the radio on. More pop music. 'What do you think: were she and Ding-Dong at it?' A smile. 'Good for Ding-Dong if they were, she's milfalicious. I would, wouldn't you?'

'Don't be a sexist arsehole. Her husband's dead and her son's missing. Have a bit of respect.'

Pink rushed up Rennie's cheeks. 'Sorry, Guv.'

Logan turned the radio off again, pulled out his phone and dialled. 'Shona? Hi, It's Logan. Listen I need a favour.'

A disgusted sigh. Then, *'You* always *need a favour.'*

'I'm out and about at the moment – see if you can dig up whoever's SIO on the MacAuley investigation: murder and abduction.'

'What happened to your plainclothes gruntmonkey?'

'He's out and about too.'

'Pfff...' The sound of a keyboard receiving two-finger punishment clacked in the background. *'Right, here we go. ... Oh.'*

'Shona? I don't like the sound of that "oh", Shona.'

'Senior Investigating Officer is DCI Dean Gordon.'

Wonderful. Just sodding marvellous.

Logan screwed his eyes closed. 'Oh for God's sake.'

'Not my fault.'

'DCI Dean Gordon. The same DCI Dean Gordon who had a stroke three months ago and is now permanently off on the sick?'

'And I repeat: not *my fault.'*

As if Mrs MacAuley didn't feel let down enough already.

A sigh. 'Thanks, Shona.' Logan hung up and slumped in his seat.

Rennie pulled a face. 'Let me guess: complete and utter, *total* cocking disaster?'

'In a top hat.'

13

Logan's phone dinged at him again.

TS Tara:

> I was going to have a bath, but you don't
> have any bubble bath. HOW CAN YOU
> NOT HAVE ANY BUBBLE BATH YOU
> MONSTER?!?!

Rain battered against the pool car's roof, bounced off the bonnet, hammered the hatchbacks on either side. The Lidl they'd parked outside squatted in the downpour, a dreary grey bunker of a building with cheery posters in the windows.

Logan thumbed out a reply:

> Because I'm a man. The willy should have
> been a giveaway on that one. Are you
> staying for tea tonight?

Send.
Ding.

> I'll swap you. You bring home bubble bath
> & I'll cook something for dinner. No more
> pizzas and takeaways. Proper food for a
> change!

Now that sounded like an excellent idea.

The driver's door opened and Rennie thumped in behind the wheel. Sat there grimacing for a moment with his arms raised. Hair plastered flat to his head. Clothes darkened and dripping. 'Urgh...' He stuffed a couple of carrier bags into the rear foot-well. 'It's like *swimming* out there!'

A wee girl exploded from the Lidl's doors – couldn't have been much older than eight – a bottle of brandy clutched in both hands. Running for it.

Two seconds later, a lanky security guard appeared, sprinting after her, mouth moving as if he was shouting something.

Logan turned, watched the pair of them hurdle the low stone wall and race off down the Lang Stracht. 'I'm troubled, Simon.'

'Might as well have jumped in the River Don.' Wiping his face with his hands. 'Utterly soaked.'

'The timeline worries me.' He counted it off on his fingers. 'Aiden MacAuley is abducted and his dad is killed. DI Bell fancies Fred Marshall for it, but can't prove anything so Marshall is released without charge. Then Marshall vanishes off the face of the earth and Bell fakes his own death.'

'You still think Bell killed Marshall?'

'He killed whoever it was we buried, so why stop there? If you're planning on disappearing anyway, why *not* go for a bit of rough justice?'

Rennie wriggled his bum in his seat. 'I would like to announce that I'm damp right down to my pants here. There's going to be a whole lotta chafing going on.'

'What else did you dig up on Fred Marshall?'

'Forget trench foot, I'm going to get trench—'

'Rennie: concentrate! Fred Marshall.'

'OK, OK. Sheesh...' He pulled out his phone and poked at the screen. 'Emailed myself the details.' More poking. 'Here we go: Frederick Albert Marshall, AKA Freddy Marsh. Two kids, both under five. Different mothers, though. He's got a brother doing a nine-stretch in HMP Grampian for armed robbery and his sister's awaiting trial for attempted murder.'

'Bet family Christmases are fun.'

'His mum died of an overdose when he was eleven and his dad's not been arrested for *three whole years*. Which is something of a record for him. Burglaries, possession with intents, assaults … oh, and dear old dad's a registered sex offender too.'

The security guard came limping up the road again, one hand clutching his side, face a worrying shade of puce. No sign of the brandy or the little girl.

A bus rumbled by, drenching him with dirty road spray.

Rennie started the engine and cranked up the blowers. 'If we hurry, we can probably make the PM on Not-DI-Bell's burnt and stinky remains?'

'It'll be all poking about and tissue samples. Won't get anything useful out of the labs for weeks. *If* we're lucky.'

The security guard clambered over the low stone wall and into the car park. Then turned and shook his fist. Bested by an eight-year-old criminal mastermind. And a bus.

Hmmm…

Logan frowned. 'Has Fred Marshall still got a social worker?'

'Dunno, but I can find out?'

Laughter rang through the Bon Accord shopping centre – high-pitched and giggly – as Logan climbed the stairs. Then some screaming. Then more giggling.

He stepped onto the landing.

The upper floor was pretty crowded. Families. Feral children. Couples. Slouching teenagers. Young men and women with clipboards and collecting buckets. Lots and lots and lots of shops full of damp people.

Rennie topped the stairs and looked around, then pointed over at the food court. The usual collection of baked tattie / salad / things on a conveyor belt / fried chicken joints were arranged around the outside of the seating area. 'That's her there.'

Two women sat at a table over by the baked tattie place: one short, young-ish, with a short-back-and-sides haircut, a leather jacket that had seen better days, a pot of tea, and a raisin whirl; the other a sagging, knackered-looking figure in a burgundy cardigan, hunched over a latte and a sticky bun. Her brown hair had a thick grey line, right down the middle of it, face as pale as rice pudding. Not a make-up kind of person.

The pair of them had bags under their eyes you could fit a week's shopping in.

Logan walked over. 'Maureen Tait?'

The one in the scabby leather raised a hand. 'For my sins.' She nodded at her becardiganed companion. 'This is Mrs McCready, she was Fred Marshall's C-and-F worker when he was a juvenile. What she doesn't know about him ain't worth knowing. Isn't that right, Mags?'

Mrs McCready looked up from her milky coffee and pulled a sour face. 'Has he decided to grace us with his presence again, then? Freddie?'

Logan patted Rennie on the shoulder. 'I'll have a tea, thanks.' Then pulled out a chair and joined the pair of them as Rennie slumped off, muttering under his breath.

McCready sniffed. 'Well?'

'Thanks for agreeing to meet us. Especially as it's the weekend.'

Tait folded her arms, chin up. 'So come on then, what's he done? Where's he been?'

'You've not seen him for, what, two years?'

She hauled a massive handbag up onto the table and went a-rummaging – producing a large ring binder packed so tight it was on the verge of bursting. It thumped down next to the handbag, setting her crockery rattling. 'Freddie was ... *challenging*, but he never missed a single appointment.'

McCready nodded. 'Not since he first came to see me, when he was six.'

'And then, two years, two months ago: nothing. We went round his flat, but they hadn't seen him for a week.'

Logan raised an eyebrow. 'We?'

Tait dumped her handbag on the floor again. 'Yes "we". Margaret and me. And I know, *technically*, that Children-and-Families aren't supposed to maintain involvement in a service user's life once they've transitioned to supervision by the Criminal Justice team, but Fred Marshall needed ... *continuity*.' She looked at her colleague. 'Didn't he, Mags?'

'His father beat his mother so badly she ended up in a wheel-chair. She'd forgotten to put a bet on for him.' Mrs McCready tapped the huge file. 'Not that *she* was any sort of saint, but when she died it really messed Freddie up.'

'Must be hard losing your mum to an overdose.'

That got him a pitying look. 'She was in a wheelchair, Inspector, who do you think bought drugs for her? Can you imagine being eleven years old and feeling responsible for your mum's death?' A sigh. 'You know, I was probably the closest thing he had to a stable family relationship? When he was a teenager he'd go out and shoplift just so they'd catch him and he could see me again. How sad is that?'

Tait nodded. 'He was a very troubled young man.'

Rennie reappeared, complete with tray: two cups, two wee teapots, some wee tartan packets of something. 'I got us some shortbread. You're welcome.'

McCready picked at her sticky bun. 'And, of course, I told him he didn't have to get arrested, I'd be happy to see him anyway. As long as it was always somewhere *public*. Course he wanted to come stay with me – thought it would be the best thing in the whole world if I adopted him so we could see each other all the time. But...' The hole she'd worried in her bun got bigger. 'Freddie always had that sharp little core of violence in him, you could see it even when he was a wee boy. No way I was exposing my kids to that.' McCready frowned and ripped the chunk right off. Dunked it in her latte.

Tait tucked into her raisin whirl, flecks of pastry falling from her mouth as she spoke. 'Tell them about Jeffery Watkins. Go on, tell them.'

'Watkins was a wife-beating armed robber with a drink problem. His daughter, Nadia, was a client of mine. He didn't like that I recommended she be taken into care, so he broke my nose and my wrist. Freddie tracked him down and battered the living *hell* out of him. Freddie was thirteen, Watkins was twenty-six.'

Sounded lovely.

Logan poured himself some tea. 'Did Fred Marshall ever mention Aiden or Kenneth MacAuley?'

Rennie whipped out his notebook and pen. Poised and expectant.

Tait stared at him, face pinched, voice guarded. 'Was he *capable* of it? Possibly. Did he do it?' A shrug.

'What about DI Duncan Bell?'

'Oh, *he* was called all the names under the sun. Questioned Freddie at least five times about the killing and the abduction, even though there was absolutely no evidence. But you know what some police officers are like, they won't...' Tait stared at them. 'Wait, DI Bell? He's the one who faked his own death, isn't he? It was on the news. You exhumed...' She reached out and took her colleague's hand.

Mrs McCready shrank away from the table, eyes and mouth open wide. 'Oh God... It's him, isn't it? It's Freddie in that grave! That bastard, Bell, *killed* him!'

Logan held up his hands. 'We're running tests now, but we *don't* think it's Fred Marshall.'

She scraped her chair back and stood. 'THEN WHERE IS HE?'

People at the surrounding tables fell quiet. Everyone looking at them.

'That's what I'm trying to find out.' Voice soft and patient. 'We want to make sure he's safe, OK?'

Tait got to her feet and wrapped an arm around her colleague. 'Shhh... It's all right, Mags. I'm sure it isn't Freddie.'

'I've known him since he was a little boy.' She stayed where she was, trembling, the food-court lights sparkling in her wet eyes. 'I sang at his wedding...'

'Look, Mrs McCready, Mrs Tait, Fred had a reputation as a thug for hire.' Another placating gesture. 'I'm not saying he *was* one, I'm saying that was his reputation. Do you know who he worked for?'

Tait glanced at Rennie and his notebook again. 'Are you honestly expecting us to inform on a service user?'

'He's been missing for two and a bit years. You and I both know there's only three possibilities: he's gone straight, he did something so bad he had to do a runner—'

'Or he's dead.' Mrs McCready lowered herself back into her seat and sagged a bit further.

Tait put a hand on her shoulder. 'Freddie isn't a *bad* person, Inspector, he simply... Look: the last meeting we had he turned up with this lovely lady's watch for Mags. He'd won some cash on the horses and wanted to treat her. Had the receipt and everything. He was so *proud* of himself.'

Logan nodded. 'I still need to know who he was working for.'

'Freddie didn't have the opportunities you and I had. Yes, he could be difficult, but he was turning his life around. Getting married to Irene was the best thing he ever did.'

No point pushing it. Instead, Logan let the silence stretch. Sitting there, watching the pair of them.

A couple of wee kids thundered past: the girl in a dinosaur onesie with fairy wings and a tiara, chasing a boy dressed up like a Disney princess complete with wand.

Over in the distance someone dropped a cup or a plate and got a round of applause in reward.

Mrs McCready wiped at her eyes.

Maureen Tait fidgeted.

Logan just watched.

A ragged chorus of 'The Northern Lights Of Old Aberdeen' broke out in Yo! Sushi.

Tait groaned. 'All right, all right.' Then jabbed a finger at Rennie. 'But this is *strictly* off the record and if it comes up in court we'll deny the whole thing. Are we clear?'

Logan nodded. 'Agreed.'

'Aw...' But Rennie put his pen down anyway.

'All right.' She cleared her throat. 'He *might* have mentioned something about a broker who put work his way from time to time.'

'A broker?'

'Someone called "Jerry the Mole". And no, I don't know any more than that.' Tait picked up the big ring binder and jammed it into her massive handbag. 'Now if you'll excuse us, our co-worker's getting married next weekend, and we've a hen party to buy inflatable willies for.' She snapped out a hand and grabbed Logan and Rennie's packets of shortbread, stuffing them into her pocket as she flounced off. 'Come on, Mags.'

Mrs McCready nodded, then hauled herself to her feet and slouched off after her colleague.

Rennie watched them go, then reached across the table and helped himself to the half-eaten sticky bun and raisin whirl. 'Well: waste not, want not.'

The sounds of Divisional Headquarters thrummed along the corridor: voices, phones, laughter, the elliptical dubstep whump-whump-whump of a floor polisher.

'Oh for goodness' sake.' Logan let go and the door to his temporary office bounced off one of the desks crammed inside. Empty. Not a single minion to be seen. Nothing but furniture and carpet stains. So much for DCI Hardie and his we-need-to-coordinate-our-investigations speech.

Logan propelled Rennie inside with a little shove, pointing at one of the ancient computers. 'You, Gruntmonkey: go find Jerry the Mole.'

'Gah...' The boy idiot slouched over to the computer, popping on an Igor-from-Frankenstein voice. 'Yeth mathhhhhter.'

'And when you've done that: make sure you do your report for the PF. And if anyone asks, I'm off to kick DS Robertson's backside till I get my promised minions.'

He turned and marched down the corridor, up the stairs, and onto the MIT floor. Past posters and notices. Past a handful of plainclothes officers who scattered away from him like sparrows before a cat. And through into the MIT incident room.

Unlike *his* office, this one was full of minions. Officers on the phone, officers writing things up on the whiteboards, officers hammering away at their keyboards. Officers *doing* things.

Detective Sergeant Robertson sat on the edge of someone's desk, making notes on her clipboard as a Spacehopper-round PC with a Donald Trump tan talked to someone else on the phone. The reconstruction of DI Bell's face sat in the middle of his monitor.

PC Spacehopper nodded. 'Uh-huh. ... Uh-huh. ... OK. ... OK, yeah. Hold on...' He put his hand over the mouthpiece and turned to Robertson. 'It's a match. Definite. Manager says he checked in last Monday.'

She punched the air. 'Yes! Tell them we'll be right over.'

'Hello? Mr Murdoch? Don't touch anything, we're on our way.'

Robertson hopped down from the desk and took out her mobile phone. Froze as she saw Logan standing right there in front of her. Then pulled on an uncomfortable-looking smile. 'Inspector McRae.'

'George. You promised me some staff to chase stuff up. Where are they?'

'Ah. Yes.' Getting quicker with every word. 'Well, we thought ... that is, DCI *Hardie* thought, that as yours is a historical cold case investigation and we're hunting an active murderer, we would maybe release someone when there was more time?' Another go with the smile. 'Sir.'

Rotten bunch of...

Logan stared at her.

A shrug. 'Sorry?'

He turned and marched away.

Water gurgled in the downpipes around the back of Divisional Headquarters. Presumably run-off from the mortuary roof, because it had *actually* stopped raining for once.

A chunk of sunlight snuck through a gap in the clouds to turn this bit of tarmac and granite into a tiny grey suntrap. And, as was traditional in Aberdeen, someone was out enjoying it before it disappeared.

Sheila Dalrymple leaned against the mortuary wall, one long thin leg bent at the knee – its white welly resting against the blockwork, the other smeared with something dark-red-and-brown. She was dressed in her full Anatomical Pathology Technician get-up: blue scrubs, green plastic apron, and fetching grey hairnet. A steaming mug of something in one long-fingered hand, at the end of her long pale arm. Wide flat face turned to the sun.

Logan wandered over. 'Sheila.'

She didn't move, just stood there with her eyes closed. Sunning herself. 'If it's about that sponsorship money, I'm skint.'

'DI Bell's remains.'

A tiny snort. The words hard and bitter: 'Ah, the duplicitous Detective Inspector Bell. And are we here about the body you exhumed from his grave, or the one you pulled from his crashed car?'

'Are you feeling all right?'

'Because if you're here about that rotting pile of meat and bones, you're *crap* out of luck.'

'You don't sound all right.'

She cradled the mug against her chest. 'There are two hundred and six bones in an adult human body, not counting the thirty-two teeth. You know what we got out of that grave? One hundred and fifty-two. As the great man said: "The shotgun is an unforgiving mistress when it practises its art upon the human cranium."'

Sod.

Logan leaned against the wall next to her. 'Any luck with DNA?'

'You're kidding, right? When you take a body, blow its head off, burn everything, post-mortem what's left, then bury it in an eco-friendly grave for two years, what you end up with isn't exactly DNA viable. The *smell*, on the other hand...'

'Wonderful.'

She toasted him with her mug. 'Welcome to my world. If we had the teeth, then *maybe* we could have drilled something out of the tooth pulp cavity, assuming they weren't cooked too much. But guess what?'

'No teeth.'

'Once again, "the shotgun makes its mischief felt".' She pushed off the wall and squinted at him. 'And for future reference, see next year? When someone asks what to get me for my birthday? Assuming anyone sodding *remembers*. Tell them gudding about in rotting corpse bits isn't as much fun as they think!'

'Oh...' He pulled on a smile. 'Happy birthday.'

'Yeah, *now* you remember.' She stalked off, shaking her head. 'They're all the bloody same...'

14

Somewhere, off in the gloom, a radio belted out a cheery 'modern' song. Which, let's be honest, was a euphemism for 'crap'.

'Pfff...' He scuffed a foot along the concrete floor. 'Getting old, Logan.'

Yeah, but it *was* crap.

A large sign sat on the metal grille that separated the small reception area from the expanse of shelving, boxes, and crates: 'OFF-SITE EVIDENCE STORAGE FACILITY'. It lurked above a small whiteboard with 'THIS FACILITY HAS WORKED FOR 3 DAYS WITHOUT A LOST TIME ACCIDENT' on it.

They'd probably do better on that front if they fixed the lighting: no windows in here, so there was nothing but the striplights overhead and about a third of those were dead. Half of those still alive buzzed, blinked, and flickered into darkness – only to judder on again ten or fifteen seconds later. As if someone had tried setting up a Santa's grotto in hell.

Logan took a deep breath and made a loudhailer from his hands. 'COME ON, ELLEN, SOME OF US STILL HAVE CAREERS TO GET ON WITH!'

'Cheeky sod.' She came limping out from the depths of the storeroom. Small, but solid. The kind of person whose pint you *really* wouldn't want to spill. Dust greyed the front and arms of her Police Scotland T-shirt. Probably from the large cardboard box she was carrying. 'You're in luck.' Ellen shouldered open the gate and kicked it closed behind her. 'Normally suicide stuff gets cleared out after a couple of years.'

She thumped the box onto the productions desk and raised her eyebrows. 'Teeth?'

'Teeth.'

Ellen went digging in the box, laying evidence bags out in front of him. 'Teeth, teeth, teeth, teeth...' More bags. Then a couple of small cardboard boxes. Then some big bags. 'Let's see: we've got burned clothes, burned shoes, a burned shotgun, and a petrol container. Also burned. No teeth.'

'*Please* tell me they didn't leave them at the scene.'

'OK: "they didn't leave them at the scene".'

'Oh for God's sake...' He paced away to the other side of the reception area and back again. 'I've got a body lying in the mortuary and no idea who it belongs to. How am I supposed to find out, if there's no bloody evidence?'

She held up a finger. 'There's *evidence*, there's just no teeth.'

'Urgh...' Logan slumped forward, thunking his forehead gently against the grille.

The rustling of paperwork sounded behind him, then: 'That's odd. Looks like they *did* find some teeth, but they're not in the box. Did you try the mortuary? Might have sent them over there for analysis.'

'They swear blind they've never seen them.'

More rustling. 'According to this, the IB recovered Ding-Dong's prints off the shotgun and the shells inside it. His prints were on the caravan table's metal frame and the petrol containers and the caravan door handle too. No one else's prints were found.'

'That's sod-all use to me. I know DI Bell was there – he had to be, he set all this up. What I *need* to know is whose head he blew off!' The grille rattled as Logan boinged his head against it again. 'How could we bury the wrong bloody person?'

'To be fair, Ding-Dong left *two* suicide notes. The body was wearing his watch, wedding ring, signet ring, and a stainless-steel bracelet with his initials on it. It was all returned to his widow, by the way, in case you think we've lost them too. She also ID'd what was left of his clothes, his shoes, and the wallet they found on the passenger seat of his car. I mean, look at it.'

Logan turned.

Ellen held up a photograph. The skeletal remains of a caravan sagged over the blackened carcass of its contents – everything burned to small unrecognisable lumps. Everything except for the torso-sized chunk of charcoal caught on the metalwork that used to support the floor and the twisted chunks of arms and legs scorched all the way down to the bone in places. A Volkswagen Passat sat in the background, the paintwork on its bonnet blistered from the heat, front-left tyre flattened.

She shook her head. 'Not surprising they believed it was him, is it? I mean, no way you're getting DNA out of something burned *that* badly, right? And with all the documentation...'

Why did everything have to turn into a disaster?

Logan sighed and held out his hand. 'Let's see the wallet.'

She scribbled something onto a clipboard, spun it around on the desk so it was the right way up for him. 'Sign there. You need gloves?'

He scribbled his signature on the line and nodded. Snapped on the proffered gloves and opened the evidence bag: one black leather wallet, with pictures of Bell's children proudly displayed in two matching photo insets.

Logan laid the contents out in a line. Two credit cards and one debit. A bunch of slips of paper that had filled one segment of the wallet – receipts probably, their thermal ink all faded away by the heat. A condom lurked in its wrapper at the back of the wallet. And last but not least: three filthy five-pound notes. He added them to the line.

Ellen whistled. 'Fifteen quid and a condom? Naughty old Ding-Dong.'

'Better give me the suicide notes too.'

The off-site storage facility loomed over the pool car in all its miserable glory. A bland industrial building in a bland industrial

132

business park, sealed behind bland industrial chain-link fencing. Topped with exciting razor wire. Or at least, anyone trying to clamber over it would find it exciting – a DIY vasectomy courtesy of Police Scotland.

Above, the sky had taken on a disturbing burnt-toast look, spattering down fistfuls of rain that clattered against the car roof, fighting with the roar of the blowers.

Logan opened the big brown envelope and pulled out two A4 sheets in individual plastic wallets. Rested them against the pool car's steering wheel.

DI Bell's suicide notes. One to his children, one to his wife. Both handwritten in red biro on what was probably photocopier paper.

'If I Only Had a Brain' warbled up from Logan's mobile phone and he answered it, not even needing to check the caller ID. 'Simon?'

Rennie's voice bounded out like a Labrador. *'I have news, my liege!'*

'Did you know it was Sheila Dalrymple's birthday today?'

'Creepy Sheila? We should all chip in and get her a broomstick.' A pause. *'I know, I know. We're not allowed to say things like that in Professional Standards.'*

'No we're not.'

'Not even a little bit?'

'No.' Logan skimmed the letter to DI Bell's kids. 'Got my hands on Bell's suicide notes. He wants his children to know how proud he is of everything they've achieved and everything they're going to achieve. No mention of why he's allegedly topping himself.' Suicide note number two: '"My dearest Barbara, I'm sorry, but I'm so tired. I can't do this any more. I know I've not been the best husband for the last few months and I'm truly, truly sorry for that. You were always my soulmate and I want you to be happy, but all I do is make you miserable."'

'That's cheery. You want my exciting news?'

'"I really do love you, Barbara, I always have. Please don't hate me for doing this. Give my guitar to Bob and my AFC

133

collection to Gavin. I love you." Signed, "Duncan". Again, no reason why.'

'Jerry the Mole, AKA: Jerry Whyte with a "Y". She's real and I've got an address.'

Logan slipped note number two back into the envelope. 'Criminal record?'

'Not even in the system: clean as a pornstar's bumhole. Found her through a friend of a friend of a backdoor burglary specialist. And no, that's not a euphemism.'

'Address?'

'Ooh, do I get to come too?'

The wee sod was probably just trying to get out of doing some actual work for a change.

'Have you done your report for the Procurator Fiscal?'

'Done, spell-checked, and submitted. For I am the very model of a modern major SIO.' His voice took on a saccharine child-asking-for-a-toy-and-or-sweetie tone. *'So can I? Please? I promise I'll be ever so good!'*

Logan glanced at the suicide note to Bell's kids again. Then shrugged. 'What's the worst that can happen?'

The man behind the reception desk gave them the benefit of a perfect white smile. 'Give me a second and I'll see if Jerry's free.' He stood. Had to be at least six two, maybe even six four. Mid-fifties in a Breton top, jeans, designer stubble, and glasses, with a grey shark-fin haircut perched on the top.

It was a fairly plush reception room, with leather couches and prints by local artists on the walls. A fancy coffee machine and a water dispenser.

Mr Sharksfin opened the door behind his desk and poked his head through.

A woman's voice boomed out from the room. *'That sounds great, Lee. I think all we need to do now is…'* Then fell silent as Mr Sharksfin waved at her.

'Sorry to bother you, Jerry, but the police would like a word.'

'Have to call you later, Lee. Some people here I need to speak to. OK. Yeah. … Bye.'

Mr Sharksfin turned and beckoned to Logan and Rennie. 'She'll see you now.'

Logan stepped into a large office, overlooking the car park with its cordon of yet more chain link and the dreich day beyond. For some reason they'd clad the room in pine, like a sauna, then added huge rubber plants, a display cabinet full of awards and booze, rap-star furniture and a row of fancy wooden filing cabinets.

The company logo filled one entire wall – a cheery Westie in a red collar and the words 'WHYTEDUG FACILITATION SERVICES LTD. ~ YOU NAME IT, WE CAN HELP.'

That booming voice again: 'Gentlemen.' It belonged to the woman lounging on one of the matching white sofas that dominated the middle of the room, her bare feet on the coffee table. A crisp dress shirt with rolled-up sleeves, a bold red tie, and grey suit trousers. Stylish pixie cut, bleached the colour of bone. As if she was trying out for a Eurythmics tribute band. Moles peppered her face and arms – dozens and dozens of them. She placed a mobile phone facedown on the sofa beside her.

Mr Sharksfin wafted Logan and Rennie towards the other couch. 'Now, would anyone like a tea or coffee?'

Rennie opened his mouth, but Logan got in first: 'We're fine, thank you.'

Jerry Whyte stretched her arms out along the back of her sofa. 'Harvey: give Stevie Zee a bell, make sure that marquee's up and ready to go Wednesday for the run-through, yeah? Don't let him fob you off with "It'll all be up by Thursday." *Wednesday*.'

'Will do.' Mr Sharksfin strutted from the room, closing the door behind him.

A smile from the woman opposite. 'So, what can I do you for?'

That logo wasn't the only Westie in the room. The other one was a wheezy old thing, fur stained to a smoker's-yellow, snuffling and grunting its way around the coffee table. It made a beeline for Logan's trousers and gave them a damn good sniffing.

He reached down to scratch the dog's head, the fur slightly

sticky against his fingertips. 'What exactly do you do here, Mrs Whyte?'

A smile. 'It's Miss. And I help people accomplish things. I facilitate.' She pointed at the closed door. 'That marquee's for the *Aberdeen Examiner*. They're doing a world record bid – biggest ever stovies-eating competition – and we're pulling it all together for them. MC, catering, advertising, social media, the works.'

'So you're an event coordinator.'

She shrugged. 'Events, recruitment, mediation, logistics, PR, project management... You name it, we facilitate it.'

Of course she did.

Logan nudged Rennie with his foot.

And for once, the silly sod did what he'd been told. 'Did you do any facilitation for Fred Marshall?'

'Let's find out, shall we?' She stood and padded her bare feet over to the filing cabinets. Rummaged through one. 'Fred Marsh?'

Rennie shook his head. 'Marshall.'

'Marshall, Marshall, Marshall... Here we go.' She pulled out a file and opened it, flicking through the contents. 'Yup, placed him as a doorman at the Secret Service Gentlemen's Club for three months. Six-month stint as a security guard at Langstracht Business Park. Some more security work at maybe a dozen concerts? Couple of gigs as a courier during Oil Week.' She held a sheet of headed notepaper up, reading from it. '"Fred Marshall is a conscientious worker who gets on well with his fellow employees and isn't afraid of hard work. Would hire again."'

'I'm confused, ma'am.' Rennie scooted forward, giving her that idiotic Columbo look of his. 'You had him working as a *security* guard?'

The wee dog stopped sniffing Logan's trousers and lumbered over to Rennie. Squared up to him and barked. Twice. Then let loose a wee wheezy growl.

'You have to forgive Haggis, he's a devil when he's riled.' Whyte popped the file back in her cabinet. 'And if you're asking about Fred Marshall's criminal record: yes. We were fully aware of it when we placed him, as were *all* of his employers. Not everyone is prejudiced against people who've been through the criminal justice system, Inspector...?'

Chin up. 'Detective Sergeant Rennie.'

The smile turned more than a little condescending. 'I believe in rehabilitation, DS Rennie. We've got a number of ex-offenders on our books, ex-police-officers too, *and* serving ones. At W.F.S. we don't discriminate, we *facilitate*.'

'Frank Marshall was a thug for hire and you're the one who—'

Logan stamped on Rennie's foot.

'Ow!'

At that, Haggis stopped growling, turned his bum on Rennie, and scuffed his back feet through the carpet a couple of times. Then waddled over to the other couch and scrambled up onto it.

Rennie stared at Logan. 'What was that—'

Logan thumped him. 'When did you last hear from Fred Marshall, Miss Whyte?'

'Oh.' She dug her file out again and checked. 'According to this, he wanted to try a job in catering ... two and a bit years ago? We didn't have anything at the time, but when something came along we tried to get in touch. No answer.' A shrug. 'Sorry.'

'Does anyone else on your books know him?'

'No idea... But I can ask around, if you like?' She carried the file over to her desk and wrote something on a Post-it note. Stuck it on her monitor. 'I know Fred Marshall did some bad stuff in his time, but he was getting his life together. When you find him, tell him he's always got a place on our books.'

Logan nodded. 'Thank you. We'll be in touch.' He made for the door, but Rennie stayed where he was. Sitting there, head on one side. Logan pointed at him. 'Heel.'

Rennie didn't. 'You were on the radio today, weren't you, Miss Whyte? You put up a five grand reward for info about Ellie Morton.'

She shook her head. 'How could anyone do that to a wee girl? I've got a niece that age; see if anyone laid a finger on her…' Whyte gave herself a little shake. 'Anyway, we've got to pull together as a community, don't we?' She patted him on the shoulder. 'And you tell your mates at the station: bring Ellie home safe and there's a case of Glenlivet waiting for you.'

Rennie bustled over to the pool car, unlocking it and scrambling in out of the rain.

Logan paused, one hand on the door handle, looking up towards the building.

Jerry Whyte's office was on the first floor, and there she was: standing at the window, phone to her ear, smiling down at him. She even raised her hand and gave him a little wave.

He didn't wave back. Opened the door and got in the car.

Rennie reversed out of the space. 'Like we need bribing with whisky to find Ellie Morton. Not saying it wouldn't be a nice bonus, though.'

She was still standing there, watching them.

Logan fastened his seatbelt. 'Notice how everyone says Fred Marshall was a really great guy?'

'You thinking what I'm thinking?'

'Maybe.'

'Yeah, you are. You're thinking it's time to go visit Fred Marshall's last known address, shake the family tree and see how many dead bodies fall out.'

'Why are they all bigging him up? You've seen his criminal record, he was a violent thug.'

'Maybe he had one of those Scrooge-type epiphanies? Three ghosts, "Oh poor Tiny Tim!", and it's turkey-and-presents for everyone.' Rennie drove them out onto the main road and took a right at the roundabout, heading into town again. 'Or, *maybe* DI Bell got it wrong and Fred Marshall didn't have anything to do with Aidan MacAuley's abduction after all?'

'Don't know. It's all a bit … itchy. Like there's something we need to scratch till it bleeds.'

'Don't be revolting.'

'We just need to figure out who to scratch first.'

15

People didn't appreciate places like this enough. Nice places.
Family places. *Traditional* places. OK, so it was a little run-down,
but nothing a bit of elbow grease wouldn't fix. A grid of static
caravans followed the contours of the hill, overlooking a lovely
sandy beach. There was even a nice mown area at the far end
to park your Swift Challenger 460 – power point and water
hook-up included – with the other discerning touring-caravan
owners. A low building in the middle of the site for showers
and a wee shop that did a very nice sandwich and scone. Then
out across the emerald grass to the golden dunes and the
sapphire sea beyond. Well, the Moray Firth, anyway – the Black
Isle clearly visible through the afternoon haze.

Happy families played on the sand with kites and balls and
Frisbees and dogs – shrieks of children's laughter wafting up
the hill towards him on a deliciously salty offshore breeze. The
sun warm on his face and bare arms.

You wouldn't think it was October. No July day was ever
nicer than this.

Absolutely lovely.

'Lee?'

Oh, the tyranny of owning a mobile phone.

'I'm really in the middle of something...' He shifted on his
picnic bench, turning to keep them in sight.

The wee blond boy squealed with delight, face one big grin

as he hammered up and down the sand – a kite fluttering at the end of his string. His mum wasn't doing a great job of keeping up with him, but she was trying. Bless. Couldn't be easy, especially since she'd clearly not managed to lose all that baby weight yet. Her podgy arms and legs were sunburnt where they protruded from her shorts and 'I VOTED YES!' T-shirt.

'I've just had a visit from two police officers.'

Interesting.

'That's nice.'

The wee lad wasn't looking where he was going, lost his footing and went sprawling. Whoomp, right on his tummy. Little bare feet kicking at the air as if they hadn't realised he'd stopped running yet.

'At Whytedug Facilitation Services we're always happy to help the local authorities.'

'And did the nice officers want anything in particular?'

'Information on a young man I used to get work for.'

Mummy reached the wee lad and helped him up. Ruffled his hair. Laughed. Now *that* was good parenting. None of this, aw did poor liddle diddum hurt himsewf, nonsense.

'And this concerns me, because?'

'I think it's wise if we concentrate on our core projects at the moment. Best not take on anything else right now.'

The wee boy ran and squealed on the end of his kite's string again. Not a care in the world...

'Did you hear me? No more extra projects.'

'That'll leave us short stocked.'

'Nothing wrong with a bit of enforced scarcity. No one wants to go home empty-handed – it'll incentivise them to dig deep and bid high. And, more importantly, it reduces opportunities for ... unfortunate occurrences. Do you understand?'

Ah well.

Lee stood, gathered up his sandwich wrapper and the paper plate that came with his scone and popped them in the bin. Nothing worse than people who littered: it was *everyone's* countryside. 'Fine.'

He screwed the top on his thermos of tea, shook out the cup

and clicked it into place. Picked up his holdall from the picnic bench – familiar and heavy, reliable – then headed for the car. Also familiar, heavy, and reliable, in a forgettable shade of anonymous beige.

'Trust me, it's for the best.'

He hauled the tailgate up and chucked the holdall into the boot. The zip popped open a couple of inches, exposing two rolls of duct tape, some rope, a ball gag, and a couple of knives. Oops!

Lee zipped it up again. Then checked the tartan rug was still nice and snug over the pet carrier and its silent occupant. Of course there was a risk of overheating, but he *had* parked in the shade and opened the windows a—

'And listen: I also wanted to tell you that we've picked a venue for the company barbecue.'

About time!

Lee straightened up, grip tightening on the phone. 'Where?'

'A lovely little farm, out past Inverurie. I'll text you the details. Just make sure it's all set-up for Monday night.'

Well, that *was* excellent news. He put his mobile away. Smiled. It'd been far too long since the last one.

The Volvo's boot squealed as he closed it – have to get some WD-40 on that. And then another squeal *eeeeeeked* out behind him, only this one was due to delight, rather than a rusty hinge.

The wee blond boy burst over the brow of a dune, running through the spiky grass, hauling his saggy kite with him.

He thundered past the Volvo.

Lee's hand snapped out, grabbing hold of the wee boy's T-shirt – pulling him up short. Holding him there as Lee knelt beside him.

More rustling in the undergrowth and Mummy lurched over a different dune, pink-faced and puffing hard.

Lee waved to her, then gave the wee boy a tickle, making him wriggle and giggle.

Mummy staggered over. 'Urgh... Thanks, he's a proper little monster this one. Nought to sixty in three seconds!'

The little monster squirmed, beaming. 'I want ice cream!'

Lee gave her a wink. 'Not a problem.' Then ruffled the kid's hair. 'You have fun, Tiger.'

He let go and the wee boy took his mummy's hand.

The pair of them skipped off towards the low building and its shop, singing a happy song about dinosaurs and soap.

Lee smiled. 'Cute kid.'

Ah well.

He climbed in behind the wheel, pulled out of his parking space, and made for the exit. Sticking to the five-mile-an-hour speed limit. No point taking risks when there were small children running about.

The wee blond boy and his mum waved as he passed them, and Lee waved back. Then adjusted his rear-view mirror until the pet carrier filled it, draped in its jolly tartan rug.

'Looks like it's just you and me, Kiddo.'

Lee slowed at the junction, waited for a blue Nissan to rumble past, and turned onto the main road. Time for home.

Deep breath:

'Ninety-nine green bottles, hanging on the wall...'

— the mortuary songbook —

16

A bus rumbled past the pool car and Logan turned away from it, a finger in his other ear. Didn't make any difference to the noise, though – still couldn't hear the phone. 'Sorry? I didn't get that.'

Outside the car windows, George Street was a grey mass of grey buildings beneath the grey sky. A swathe of down-at-heel businesses lined the bit they'd parked in: bookies, charities, pawn shops, and a wee café with steamed-up windows.

A gust of wind slapped an empty crisp packet against the windscreen. It caught on the wipers and writhed there, crackling.

But at least it'd stopped raining. For now.

Superintendent Doig sighed and had another go. *'I said, "Well what is it in particular that's worrying you?"'*

'Don't know. It just feels … off.'

'Have you seen the opinion piece in today's paper?' Rustling sounds came down the phone, followed by, *'Listen to this. "It's about time Police Scotland admitted NE Division,"* brackets, *"formerly known as Grampian Police,"* close brackets, *"is incapable of finding little Ellie Morton and send in a team of more qualified officers instead."'* Another sigh. *'No wonder Hardie's got his Y-fronts in a knot.'*

'Why would DI Bell kill someone and fake his own death? Why not simply disappear?'

'Of course it's all that Colin Miller's fault. Stirring things up. Nothing he likes more than putting the shoe-leather into us poor souls.'

'He had to be panicking that something was going to come out. Some secret so bad that he'd be utterly screwed if anyone discovered it.'

'*I bet he was bottle-fed as a child. You can always tell.*'

On the other side of the road, Rennie emerged from the coffee shop – a paper bag in one hand and a cardboard carrier-thing in the other. It had two wax-paper cups in it. So at least he'd got that bit right.

'Only it *didn't* come out. So there he is, lying low in Spain, worrying at it like a loose filling.'

'*You want a bit of advice, Logan?*'

'Hiding away all that time, until now. What changed? Why come back *now*?'

'*The human heart is a dark and sticky animal, but nobody does anything without a reason. Your job is to figure out what that reason is.*'

Logan slumped in his seat and rolled his eyes. 'Yes, thanks for that, Boss. Very helpful.'

You could hear the smile in the rotten sod's voice. '*I thought so.*' And then he hung up.

Always nice when senior officers shared the fruits of their hard-won experience.

Not far up the road, a woman with a pushchair launched into a screaming row with an older man. The pair of them in tracksuits that looked as if they spent more time in the kebab shop than the gym. Flailing their arms around and yelling at each other, their words torn away by the wind, leaving nothing behind but the pain on their faces.

The driver's door opened and Rennie thumped in behind the wheel. He plucked one of the wax-paper cups from his carrier and passed it over. 'Iced Caramel Macchiato, with a shot of raspberry, and white chocolate sprinkles.'

Logan curled his lip and creaked the plastic lid off. Sniffed at it. Sort of sweet and bitter and fruity all at the same time. 'I asked for a coffee.'

'It's got coffee *in* it.' He held out the paper bag. 'Bought this for you from the charity shop.'

OK...

Inside was a paperback copy of *Cold Blood and Dark Granite*, by Sally MacAuley and someone billed as 'AWARD-WINNING JOURNALIST: BOB FINNEGAN'. The cover was a bit lurid – the Aberdeen skyline Photoshopped into a scene from Skemmel Woods, a close-up of that teddy bear cable-tied to the tree, and a head-and-shoulders of Aiden and Kenneth MacAuley. A bit tatty around the edges, the pages yellowing, spine cracked.

'Are you happy working with Professional Standards, Simon?'

'What?' A look of utter horror crawled its way across Rennie's face. 'But... But I bought you a coffee, and a book!'

'I'm not firing you, you halfwit, I'm asking if you're enjoying the job.'

Rennie's mouth clamped shut and his eyes narrowed. 'Why?'

'Superintendent Doig is thinking of offering you a permanent post. Well, two to three years, depending. Something to think about, anyway.'

A smile, then he reached across from the driver's seat. 'Guv...'

Logan batted his hands away. 'No hugging. I can still tell Doig you're a liability.'

Rennie beamed at him.

Urgh...

Logan opened *Cold Blood and Dark Granite*, flipping through to the shiny pages in the middle, where the photos were.

First up: a smiling family at Aiden's third birthday – party hats, cake, candles, and grins.

Then another pic of Aiden, sitting in the back garden, little face fixed in a serious frown as he played with a Dr Who action figure and a couple of Daleks.

Next up was a series of holiday snaps. Then one of Kenneth MacAuley lording it over a smoking barbecue in shorts and a T-shirt. Sausages and chicken blackening away.

And the next page: DI Bell, looking threadbare and knackered, directing a group of uniformed constables.

Opposite him was a black-and-white portrait of a middle-aged man with a hint of grey in his swept-back hair. A strong nose and jaw. The caption underneath was, 'RAYMOND HACKER – AberRAD INVESTIGATIONS.'

And last, but not least, some more pictures of the woods. The bridge. The stream. The tributes. Not a single crime-scene photograph to be seen.

Logan closed the book. 'Two options: we go see Fred Marshall's family, or we try our luck with Sally MacAuley's private investigators.'

Rennie dug a fifty-pence piece from his trouser pocket and held it up. 'Toss you for it.' Then his face contorted in a panto-mime wink. 'Oo-er missus!'

'I'm an inspector with *Professional Standards*, Detective Sergeant. And if you expect to join us, you're going to have to learn the difference between what *is* and is *not* acceptable. Professional Standards don't do "oo-er missus".'

His face sagged. 'Sorry, Guv.'

'We do "fnarr-fnarr".'

17

'...anything else?'

'No, that's good for me. Thanks, Brucie.' Logan stuck his phone back in his pocket.

Rennie took a left, parking outside a drab beige-and-white row of tenement flats in Hayton. Four storeys of rain-soaked brick and harling, punctuated by steamed-up windows and rusting satellite dishes. Eight flats to a communal door, three doors per block. An identical tenement faced it across the potholed parking area.

Why did council housing have to look so depressing? Why couldn't they build something *nice* for people to live in?

Tower blocks loomed behind the flats – big and grey, sticking up like the transistors on a circuit board – their upper floors scratching at the low grey sky.

The pool car's wipers clunked and groaned.

Rennie pulled a face. 'Well, this is ... lovely.'

'Intel's a bit out of date, but Brucie says Fred Marshall's last known associates were Liam Houghton, Valerie Fuller, Oscar Shearer, and Craig Simpson.'

'Urgh. Great. Crowbar Craig. Don't suppose we can call for backup, can we?'

Logan climbed out of the car, into the rain. Stuck his hat on his head as he hurried up the little path to the middle door. A crack in the downpipe sent a gout of water spraying across the harling, like a teeny waterfall. Or a slit wrist.

The intercom was broken, wires protruding from its battered casing, the names obliterated by a squirt of red paint that bled its way down the wall. He gave the door a quick shove – it swung open.

Rennie scurried up the path after him, shoulders hunched around his ears. 'What if they've got a dog? Or a sawn-off? Or a candlestick in the library?'

'Then I'll hide behind you.'

Inside, the stairwell was every bit as bleak and damp as the outside. Rainwater made lopsided puddles on the concrete floor. Or at least it *looked* like water.

Rennie's face curdled, nostrils flaring as he sniffed. 'Smells like a tramp's Y-fronts in here.'

Logan picked his way up the stairs. 'Top-floor flat.'

'And not a healthy tramp either. One who's been drinking anchovy smoothies and rubbing his crotch with mouldy onions.'

'Feel free to stop talking now.'

Around the landing and up another flight.

'And then peeing on the onion. Then eating it.'

Another flight. Another landing. Another questionable puddle.

'And then peeing out oniony piddle and rolling in it.'

'Will you shut up about piddling?'

The third-floor landing had all the charm of an abattoir, only without all the blood and dead animals. Instead the skeletal remains of a bicycle were chained to the metal balustrade, both wheels missing, the frame kicked and bashed into a twisted wreck. Two flats – one on either side.

Logan knocked on the door to number seven.

Rennie dropped his voice to a whisper. 'It's not too late to call for backup.'

Across the hall, what had to be an utterly *massive* dog barked and barked, thumping against the door, making it rattle.

'Oh God...' Rennie reached into his jacket and pulled out his extendable baton. 'I knew I should've taken Donna swimming this morning...'

Logan knocked again: three, loud and hard.

Another dog joined the cacophony, only this one high-pitched and whiny, coming from number seven.

Then a woman's voice. Small, thin, and wary. 'Who is it?'

He held his warrant card up to the spyhole. 'We need to talk about Fred Marshall.'

Irene Marshall's flat was spotless. OK, so the furniture and décor were a bit old-fashioned and dark, as if a pensioner lived there, but there wasn't a hint of dust anywhere.

A playpen sat in front of the TV, imprisoning a toddler in a tiger onesie who was busy banging the living hell out of some wooden blocks. His teddy bear cellmate was about three times bigger than him, eyes sparkling in the reflected light of a kids' show with the sound turned off.

Mrs Marshall sat on the brown corduroy couch. Late-twenties, dressed like a schoolteacher, hair cut into a curly brown bob. Big glasses. An ugly yappy miniature sausage dog in her lap. She fidgeted with its ears, eyes fixed on the rain-streaked window. 'No. Not for two years one month and twenty-seven days.' Deep breath. 'Something must have happened to him.'

Sitting on a throw-covered armchair, Rennie scribbled in his notebook. 'Happened to him...'

Logan leaned back against the sideboard. 'What about his friends? Liam Houghton, Valerie Fuller, Oscar—'

She sniffed. 'They weren't his *friends*, they were bad for him. Every time Freddie got into trouble, one of them was standing *right* behind him, egging him on. As soon as Freddie found out I was pregnant, that was it. He never spoke to any of them ever again. *Ever.*'

'Never spoke to them ever again...'

'So where do you think he went?'

'He loves me and he loves baby Jaime. He would never abandon us!' The dog whimpered and she hugged it, all four little legs poking out straight ahead. 'Shhh, Tyrion. Daddy loves you too.' She sniffed back another tear. 'He was going to catering college...'

'Going to catering college...'

'Thank you, Detective Sergeant, I think we can do without the echo chamber.'

Rennie blushed. 'Sorry, Guv.'

Idiot.

'Mrs Marshall, did Fred ever mention someone called Aiden or Kenneth MacAuley?'

She frowned, head on one side. 'He was ... that little boy who went missing, wasn't he? I remember, because the book came out when I was pregnant with Jaime. And I felt so sorry for that poor woman. If anything like that happened to Jaime I'd die. I would, I'd just die.'

The ugly dog whimpered again.

'Did Fred say anything that made you think—'

Her mobile phone dinged and buzzed, on the couch next to her. She ignored it.

Logan had another go. 'That made you think he was in trouble of some kind?'

'Other than you lot hounding him and blaming him for things he hadn't done?' She stood, holding the dog even tighter, its tail whapping against her stomach. 'I have to put Jaime down for his nap.'

Another ding-and-buzz from her phone. She glanced at it. Licked her lip. Stepped between it and Logan.

'We're trying to help, Irene. We're trying to get Fred back for you.'

Mrs Marshall's eyes flicked to the window. 'Please, I need to put baby Jaime to bed! He's tired.'

The prisoner went on battering his wooden blocks together.

'Don't you *want* Fred back?'

Her face flushed. 'OF COURSE I WANT HIM BACK! I MISS HIM LIKE I'D MISS A LEG, YOU...'

A rattle sounded in the hall, followed by the front door's creak. Then a man's voice, getting louder: *'Baby? Baby, I got them Oreos you like: peanut butter...'*

Logan turned.

He was big, broad, with tiny piggy eyes and a barbed-wire tattoo around his neck. Handlebar moustache and a chin tuft.

Hair shaved at the sides and swept back on top. Fancy-looking chunky watch on his wrist, gold sovereign rings on his fingers. A hessian bag-for-life covered in daisies in one hand and a mobile phone in the other.

'Well, well, well.' Logan reached for his handcuffs. 'If it isn't Crowbar Craig Simpson. How nice of you to...'

And Simpson was off, dropping the phone and legging it.

Rennie scrambled out of his chair and ran after him, Logan close on his tail.

Down the short hallway, and onto the landing.

Crowbar hammered down the stairs, taking them two at a time, arms out to keep him upright.

Bloody hell, he was *quick*. Throwing himself around the corners, bouncing off the walls, getting away.

Logan skidded around onto the first-floor landing. 'STOP! POLICE!'

And then Rennie grabbed hold of the bannister and vaulted it, clearing the gap between the flights of stairs – coat-tails flapping out behind him, like a cut-price Batman. Crashing down on top of Crowbar as he reached the bottom step.

They tumbled across the wet concrete floor in a tangle of arms and legs.

Grunting and hissing. Struggling.

A lurch to the left and Rennie was on top. 'Hold still, you wee—'

Crowbar roared. His fist snapped forward, right into Rennie's jaw, sending him rocking backwards.

And as Rennie thumped against the wall, Crowbar wrestled his way upright, lurching to the front door and yanking it open as Logan clattered down the last few steps and leapt.

BANG – Logan slammed into his back.

They burst out through the open door and thumped onto the rain-slicked path. Rolling over and over. Crowbar swinging his arms and legs. Grunting. Teeth bared. 'GERROFF OF ME!'

A fist whistled past Logan's nose.

He grabbed the wrist it was attached to, twisting it around the wrong way and leaning on it.

A flicker of lightning sparked the sky white for a moment, then thunder roared – a vast booming crackling howl. And the rain hammered down.

'GERROFF ME! I'LL KILL YOU!'

Logan twisted harder.

'AAAAAAAAAAAARGH!' Thrashing and writhing.

'Hold still!' Logan yanked Crowbar to the left, grabbed a handful of his *Peaky Blinders* haircut and forced his face into the grass at the side of the path.

'I AIN'T DONE NOTHING!' The words muffled by mud. 'GERROFF ME! YOU'RE BREAKING MY ARM!'

'I said, hold still!'

Rennie staggered out through the front door, clutching his jaw. 'Rotten sod...'

'Little help?'

'You're not meant to punch police officers in the face!' Rennie pulled out his cuffs and snapped one end onto Crowbar's wrist. Forcing it up behind his back so he could get the one Logan was holding as well. *Crrrrritch.* All nice and secure.

They stood, panting as Crowbar bellowed his rage out into the downpour.

Served him right.

Irene Marshall sat on the couch with her ugly little sausage dog, glaring up at them.

The middle of the tidy living room was almost completely taken up with Rennie and Crowbar Craig – still in handcuffs and all clarted in mud – dripping on the carpet.

Logan shook the rain from a trouser leg. Absolutely soaked right through. 'So that's why you were so keen to get rid of us.'

Mrs Marshall hugged her dog tighter. 'No comment.'

'What happened to "they weren't his friends, they were bad for him"?'

'Oh yes, because *you* know what it's like being a single mother living on benefits!'

Crowbar tightened. 'You leave her alone.'

Rennie patted him on the shoulder. 'Easy...'

'I have needs! OK? I'm flesh and blood and I have needs.' The ugly dog bared its teeth at Logan and growled. 'Shhh, Tyrion. Shhh...' Mrs Marshall turned her back on them. 'I have needs.'

The custody suite had that strange biscuity smell to it again, like stale digestives and vinegary BO. It went with the painted breeze-block walls, community engagement posters, and row of creaky plastic seating. It especially went with Sergeant Jeff Downie – standing behind the chest-high custody desk, ignoring his domain. Skin so pale it was nearly fluorescent, shining in the overhead strip lights. Hooded eyes. Almost no chin.

Gollum in a Police Scotland uniform.

He was reading that morning's *Aberdeen Examiner*. The one with the photo of DI Bell's crashed rental car and '"SUICIDE COP" FAKED OWN DEATH' headline.

Logan squelched over to the desk and knocked on the Formica top. 'Got a present for you.'

Downie looked up, sniffed, then actually smiled for a change. Beaming at Crowbar Craig. 'Ah, Mr Simpson! How *lovely* to see you again. You'll be pleased to hear that your usual suite is available. I'd recommend a spa treatment, but I see you've already had a mudbath. And what is that delightful *smell*?'

Crowbar glowered at him, jaw clenched shut.

'Now, how about we empty our pockets so I can sign it all in?'

Rennie dug through Crowbar's pockets, lining the contents up on the custody desk. 'Assorted keys, cash, a wallet, a bag of weed, rolling papers, some betting slips.' He patted Crowbar on the arm. 'Come on then, let's have those sovereign rings. That massive lump of a watch too.'

Between them they added his jewellery to the line.

Sergeant Downie picked up the watch and gave it a good hard squint. 'Ooh, now *that's* a swanky timepiece if ever I've seen one. Stolen?'

Crowbar shrugged. 'Knock-off, isn't it?'

'Story of my life.' Downie tried the wallet next, pulling out a credit card. 'What have we here? When did you become Agnes Deveron? Looking after it for a friend, are we?'

'No comment.'

Logan helped himself to Downie's copy of the *Aberdeen Examiner* and wandered off to the line of plastic chairs while Rennie got Crowbar booked in. The photo of DI Bell's crashed car with accompanying article by Colin Scumbag Miller.

He scrolled through the contacts on his phone and set it ringing.

It rang. And rang. And rang. And rang. And rang. And rang. And—

'Mortuary.'

'Sheila, I need to talk to Isobel.'

'My mistress is engaged in her profession and cares not for interruptions.'

'Your...? Why are you talking like that?'

'Talking like what?'

'Just get Isobel on the phone, OK?'

Her voice went a bit muffled, as if she was partially covering the mouthpiece. *'Inspector McRae craves your attention, Professor.'*

Isobel's voice was barely audible in the background. *'Urgh... Oh, all right then: put him on.'* And then she was up to full volume. *'If you're calling for DS Chalmers' post-mortem results, you're at least three hours too early.'*

Logan gave the *Aberdeen Examiner* a pointed rustle. 'I had a run-in with your husband today.'

'How nice for you. Now, if that's all, I'm busy. It's gone five and I'd like to get home before the children are all in bed.'

'He was in DI Bell's widow's house this morning, with a photographer. Says he *knows* what Bell's been up to for the last two years, but he's not going to tell us.'

'And?' All calm and unconcerned, as if it had nothing to do with her.

'He's withholding information from a murder investigation!'

She sighed. *'Inspector McRae, you know perfectly well that Colin's professional life and mine are completely separate. Do we have to go over this again?'*

'He—'

'He doesn't speak to me about his work and I don't speak to him about mine. *If you've got a problem with him, talk to him about it, not me.'*

'You could at least have a word with him and—'

'No.' She actually had the cheek to sound annoyed, as if this was somehow all Logan's fault. *'Now, is there anything else, or can I return to dissecting DS Chalmers' liver?'*

Pfff... There was no point arguing with her when she was like that. It only ever made things worse.

'How's it going?'

'We'll have to wait for the toxicology results, but going by the smell of her stomach contents, she'd consumed a lot *of alcohol.'*

'Dutch courage. She was on antidepressants too. Probably helped.'

Silence from the other end.

'Isobel?'

'Which antidepressants? Do you know which ones?'

'Erm...' Nope – Chalmers' medicine cabinet was a blur. Well, everything but the Aripiprazole, and that was an antipsychotic, not antidepressant. 'I can find out, if you like?'

'Thank you.'

One last go: 'And Isobel? Talk to Colin. *Please.'*

'No. Goodbye.' And she was gone.

'Great.' Ah well, no one could say he hadn't tried. Logan put his phone away and wandered over to the custody desk. Pointed at Crowbar Craig. 'Do you a deal, Craig. I'm soaked right through, and DS Rennie here needs a shower so he doesn't smell of stairwell-urine any more.'

Rennie folded his arms. 'I do not smell of...' He sniffed. Frowned. 'OK, now I'm getting it.'

'You tell us all about Fred Marshall and we'll forget about you assaulting a police officer and resisting arrest. One-time-only offer, you've got until I get dry and changed to make up your mind.'

Simpson scowled at him, mouth working on something, jaw muscles clenching... Then he hung his head. Groaned. Nodded. 'I hate Aberdeen...'

18

Rennie's voice oozed out through the closed door. *'...and it's a really big deal, right? They don't make just anyone Senior Investigating Officer, do they? So I said to him, I said, this isn't—'*

He went quiet when Logan opened the door and stepped inside. Rennie winked at Crowbar Craig. 'I'll tell you later.'

Someone must have given Interview Room Three a coat of paint recently, hiding its usual scent of desperation and cheesy feet beneath a magnolia-coloured chemical funk.

Crowbar sat in the chair opposite Rennie's, with his back to the window, fidgeting. Not making eye contact as Logan closed the door and sat down.

A thumbs up from Rennie. 'Ready when you are, Guv.'

'Go on then.'

He set the machinery recording again. 'Interview resumes at seventeen twenty-one, Inspector Logan McRae has entered the room.'

Logan dumped his folder on the table and settled back in his seat. Watching Crowbar. Letting the silence grow.

'Aye.' Crowbar fidgeted a bit more. Glanced up at the camera mounted in the corner of the room, where the walls joined the ceiling. 'Before we begin, I want to make it crystal: I *don't* shag my mates' wives.'

Rennie nodded. 'Well, except for, you know, shagging your mate's wife.'

'That's different. That's no' shagging, that's ...' his cheeks went all pink, 'making love.'

Rennie spluttered.

Logan was a bit more professional, but it wasn't easy hiding the smile. 'You wanted to tell us about Fred Marshall, Craig.'

'Aye. Long as we agree about the shagging thing, right?' He paused, eyebrows raised. And then, when no one said anything: 'Right. OK, so Freddie was going straight. Didn't want to do nothing any more. No robbing, no nicking cars, nothing. I tried... I mean, some *other* bloke tried to get him involved in a bit of protection racketing and he wouldn't even do that!' Crowbar inched forward in his seat, eyes shining. 'And I mean it was buttery as a fresh rowie: old fart shopkeepers with grand-kids. No *way* they'd put up a fight or go to the cops.'

'But he wouldn't do it.'

A shrug, arms out as if it were unbelievable. 'Told you: gone straight.'

Logan put on a full-throated panto voice. 'Oh – no – he didn't!'

'Aye, he *did*. And anyone says different is a lying bastard.'

'Really?' Logan opened the folder and pulled out a sheet of paper. 'Because I have here your statement to Detective Sergeant Rose Savage, two and a half years ago, where you claim that Fred Marshall told you he abducted Aiden MacAuley and murdered Aiden's father Kenneth.'

'Ah.' Crowbar looked away, cheeks darkening even more. 'No comment.'

'You see, it's hard to take you seriously when you say Fred Marshall was going straight with one breath and with the next you're telling us he's murdered someone.'

He slumped in his seat. 'Aaaaaargh...'

'In your own time.'

'Before we go any further I want it made crystal: I don't clype on people, right? Right.'

Rennie grinned at him. 'But...?'

'Yeah, he told me he killed the dad. Bashed his head in with a rock.' A shudder. 'He ... kept on going with it, you know?

Smashing and bashing till there's blood and brains and bits of skull and that *everywhere*.'

Logan leaned forward. 'Why?'

'Why? Said he must've recognised him or something. I dunno, do I?'

'Then why did he abduct Aiden MacAuley?'

'Some bloke offered him two grand for the kid.'

Silence.

Logan skimmed the statement again. 'Doesn't say anything about money *here*, Craig.'

'Yeah, I … must've forgot about that bit.'

'You *forgot* that your best mate was paid two thousand pounds to abduct a child and murder someone?'

He went back to fidgeting. 'I was doing a lot of coke then. Stuff gets muddled up.'

'Riiiiiiiiiiight. Course it does.' Logan tapped the tabletop. 'Who paid two thousand pounds for Aiden MacAuley?'

'I don't do coke no more, cos of Jaime. Can't be around a kid when you're on coke. Got to raise kids right, like.'

'Who – was – it?'

Barely a mumble, like a small child caught with a handful of biscuits: 'Don't remember.'

Of course he didn't.

The little red lights on the recording equipment blinked.

Outside, in the corridor, someone shouted something incomprehensible.

Rennie sneezed.

Crowbar *fidgeted*.

More incomprehensible shouting.

More fidgeting.

A lovely uncomfortable silence.

Logan finally broke it. 'You're a strange friend, Craig. First you rat out Fred Marshall; then, when he disappears, you move in on his wife and raise his kid.'

'When Jaime was born, Fred *said*, didn't he? If anything happened to him, I had to promise to look after them!' An embarrassed shrug. 'You know: doing my bit. As a mate.'

'Tell me, Craig, if I was to get a sample of Jaime's DNA would it match Fred Marshall's or yours?'

His face flushed red as a freshly popped zit. 'No comment.'

'Yeah, thought so.'

Hardie didn't look up from his paperwork as Logan slipped into his office.

'Have you got a minute, Chief Inspector?'

Hardie's shoulders slumped. 'Inspector McRae. Lucky me.'

'It's about the Kenneth and Aiden MacAuley investigation. We—'

'I'm going to stop you right there.' He held up a hand. 'Whatever it is: I don't care. Go tell the Senior Investigating Officer.'

Logan settled into one of Hardie's visitors' chairs. 'Don't think it would do much good. DCI Gordon's still going to be off on the sick.'

And at *that* Hardie looked up. 'Please tell me you're trying to be funny?'

Logan shook his head.

'Oh in the name of the hairy *Christ!*' He crumpled the form he'd been reading, then did the same with his face. 'Why the hell did I agree to do this job? I could've stayed where I was, banging up drug dealers, but no...'

'Look on the bright side: at least DCI Gordon had his stroke *before* you took over. Not your fault Truncheon Tom forgot to assign a new SIO.'

'Try telling our beloved leaders that.' Hardie stared at the ceiling tiles for a moment. Sagged even further. 'OK, OK, leave it with me. Gah...'

Logan let himself out.

Logan scuffed into his temporary office. Still no sign of any minions.

Rennie was there, though, with his feet up on his desk, hands behind his head. Whistling a cheery tune.

Logan dumped his fleece on the back of his chair and sat. 'Should you not be working?'

'Ten to six, Guv, shift's over, time to go home.' A grin. 'Or better yet: time to go out and celebrate! Three and a half *years* the MacAuley case has been going on, and who gets the first breakthrough? We do. Ka-ching!'

'Just because Crowbar Craig Simpson says something, doesn't make it true.'

Rennie held up a hand. 'Don't widdle on my parade, I'm having a moment.'

'You're having an idiot.' He pointed at Rennie's computer. 'Did you get an address for Sally MacAuley's private eyes yet?'

A Post-it was produced with a flourish. 'AberRAD Investigation Services Limited. Northfield Industrial Estate on Quarry Road. Open Wednesday to Sunday, ten till six thirty.'

Logan stood and grabbed his fleece again. 'Well don't sit there like a sack of neeps: get the car keys! If we hurry we might make it before they close.'

Rennie did a little wiggly dance in the driver's seat as the pool car drifted across Northfield – singing along with some horrible autotuned nonsense on the radio, in what, to be honest, was a perfectly passable light baritone. Didn't make it any less irritating, though. Especially as the whole thing was out of time with the groaning windscreen wipers:

'Cos I'm a deep-sea diver, and I'm searching for your love,
    Got the sharks down there beneath me and the boats soar up above...'

Logan hit him. 'I'm trying to read, here.' Then returned to his copy of *Cold Blood and Dark Granite*. According to Sally MacAuley, when the investigation stalled, they—'

'And the octopus, he knows me, cos his heart is lost like mine,
    But we're both sure we'll find it, if you'll only give us time...'

'Seriously, I've read this page three times now. Shut up, or I'll rip your ears off and make you eat them.'

A humph emanated from the boy idiot. 'Not my fault you don't like music.'

The car lumped and bumped its way across a potholed stretch of road and into a small industrial estate opposite the playground on Quarry Road. What looked like a builder's yard and a couple of warehouse-style buildings.

'That isn't music.' Logan clicked off the radio. 'It's a venereal disease with a tune.'

The pool car lurched to a halt in front of a cluster of Portakabins, in the corner furthest from the entrance, backed against the boundary wall and fence.

Rennie pulled on the handbrake. 'How do you want to play this?'

'I don't care as long as it doesn't involve you singing.'

'Good cop, bad cop? Maybe a bit of Columbo?' Rennie put on the voice. '"Ehhh... Just *one* more thing..."' Then back to normal. 'No?'

'I should've left you at the station.' Logan tapped the page he'd been over four times now. 'It says here that DI Bell was a regular visitor to Sally MacAuley's house.'

'Told you they were at it.' Rennie pointed at the Portakabins. 'Shall I see if anyone's in?' He didn't wait for an answer. Instead he climbed out of the car and strode over to the nearest one. A big sign was mounted on the side: 'AberRAD Investigation Services Ltd. ~ Fast, Efficient, & Discreet' in bright-red letters, beneath a stylised ram's head logo.

The Portakabin's front door must've had a glazed bit at one point, but now the glass was boarded over with chipboard. Rennie opened the door and ducked inside.

Logan flicked through to the photos again. Stopped at the one of DI Bell organising his team. 'What the hell were you involved in?'

No answer from the dead man in the photograph.

Rennie made a surprise reappearance, backwards – staggering to a halt on the tarmac as two figures bustled out of the AberRAD offices.

Number One: black biker jacket, black jeans, black trainers, and a bright-pink top. Long hair streaming out behind her as she surged forward, chin out, perfectly made-up face contorted into a snarl.

Number Two: a small burly bloke in blue jeans, with a brown

leather jacket on over a garish Hawaiian shirt. Not a lot of hair left on his head. Both hands curled into fists.

The pair of them advanced on Rennie, who, for some reason, had adopted a fighting stance.

'Oh for God's sake.' Logan closed his book and climbed out into the drizzle.

The woman shoved Rennie, sending him staggering away. 'You want some, do you? You *want* some?'

'I'm warning you, I'm a—'

'Aye, he wants some.' Her friend rolled his shoulders. 'Look at him, Danners, he wants some: *big* time.'

Wonderful.

Logan reached into the pool car and grabbed one of the collapsible batons.

Number One, 'Danners' shoved Rennie again. 'I'm going to tear you apart and feed what's left to my dog, little boy.'

Number Two grinned. 'Ooh, you're screwed now, sunshine!'

Logan slammed the car door. 'All right, that's enough.'

Number Two turned, arms out. Teeth bared. 'Get back in the car, Lugs, unless you want a spanking as well.'

Danners gave Rennie another shove. 'You're *mine*, sunshine!'

'You're not listening.' Logan clacked his extendable baton out to its full length. 'I *said*, that's enough!'

A grin spread across Number Two's face. 'Oh it – is – on!' Bouncing on the balls of his feet, cricking his head from one side to the other.

Then the Portakabin door thumped open again.

'Hoy!' Raymond Hacker stood on the top step, a mobile phone clamped to his chest. 'Will you idiots keep it down? I'm on the phone with a client.' He looked much the same as he did in Sally MacAuley's book. The swept-back hair was maybe a bit greyer at the sides, and the lines in his face a little deeper. But it was definitely him.

Number Two pointed at Rennie. 'This arsehole barged in like he owned the place.' He swung his arm around and jabbed the finger at Logan. 'And *this* arsehole's begging for a kicking.'

Logan looked down at his own clothes. 'You *can* see I'm

164

wearing a police uniform, right? You do know what "the police" is?'

Danners stepped in close to Rennie, looming over him, even though they were much the same height. 'This tiny strip of piss isn't wearing one.'

'I'm a police officer too!'

She curled her top lip. 'You *have* to be joking. No way they'd give something like you a warrant card.'

Rennie stuck his chest out. 'I'm Senior Investigating Officer on a very important case!'

'Oh aye?' Number Two raised an eyebrow. 'What kind of half-arsed case could you possibly... Ooh, I know: is it shoplifting?'

Danners poked Rennie. 'Overdue library books?'

'Someone's stealing the CID biscuits?'

Rennie stuck his nose in the air. 'It's the suicide of a *police officer*, thank you very much!'

'Ah...' Danners looked away. Cleared her throat. 'Sorry. Didn't know.'

Number Two shrugged. 'Yeah. Sorry.'

'Pair of halfwits.' Raymond Hacker shook his head. 'Now, if we're all quite finished playing British Bulldogs: Andy, get the kettle on. Danners, see if we've got any biscuits left in the tin.' Then Hacker stepped down from the Portakabin and held his business card out to Logan. 'Raymond Hacker, Inspector...?'

'McRae.'

'Sorry about that.' Hacker settled behind his desk. 'We had a couple of Soprano wannabes in last week, trying to tap us for protection money. Well, you saw what they did to the front door. Danielle and Andy are a bit ... disapproving about that kind of thing.'

It wasn't a huge office, but it took up about a quarter of the Portakabin, separated from the rest of it by a dividing wall and a glazed panel door. On the other side of the glass, Number Two, AKA: Andy, was busying himself with a kettle in a tiny kitchen area at the far end while Danners rummaged through a barricade of filing cabinets.

No filing cabinets for Hacker's office. Instead he had a couple of large pot plants, framed testimonials, and a photo of him shaking hands with the First Minister. A big digital camera, mounted on a tripod, overlooked the desk and visitors' chairs. A fish tank burbling away to itself, full of little fish in cheery colours.

'So, what can we do to help our brothers in blue?' Hacker gestured towards the chairs. 'Well, brothers in black now, I suppose.'

Logan sat. 'Are you still working for Mrs MacAuley?'

'Sally?' He seemed a bit surprised at the question. 'Yes. We're still looking for Aiden on her behalf.' He turned his chair and waved at the framed testimonials. 'Course our bread-and-butter's divorces. Cheating husbands, wayward wives – you know the drill. But we always keep an ear out for Aiden.'

'Any luck?'

A shrug. 'Rumours from time to time. Sightings everywhere from John o' Groats to Istanbul. But nothing solid.' Hacker sat back and squinted at him. 'Can I ask what this is about?'

'Did you have much to do with DI Duncan Bell?'

'Ding-Dong? God, now *there's* a blast from the past. Ding-Dong was my DI for about two years, before I left the force.'

Rennie took the other chair, notebook at the ready. 'You were Job?'

'Divisional Intelligence Office. But I never liked following other people's orders. That's why I left – to set up this place. Be my *own* boss.'

'Don't remember you...'

'DIO isn't meant to fraternise with other teams. Can't risk compromising sources.'

'Oh.' Rennie nodded. 'Yeah, suppose.'

Logan leaned forward. 'Did DI Bell ever talk to you about the MacAuley case?'

'I resigned from the force *long* before Aiden was abducted, but yeah. When Sally hired us I tried to get Ding-Dong to spill his beans loads of times. Only managed it once – think it was a couple of weeks before he topped himself. If I remember it right, he was sweating like a paedo in a nursery, acting all shifty.'

The fish tank gurgled.

Outside, in the office, a phone rang and Danners answered, the conversation too muted by the closed door to be audible.

Rennie shifted in his seat.

And Hacker just sat there. Completely unfazed by the silence.

Ah well, worth a try. 'And what did DI Bell say?'

'Word for word? Don't remember.' Hacker pulled a face, rocking his hands back and forth. 'Something about time and consequences and never getting any justice for poor wee Aiden. He was pretty cut up about it.'

There was a knock on the door and Andy appeared with a tea tray – three mugs, a plate of biscuits, and a one-pint plastic container of milk. 'Don't have any full-fat, so you'll have to make do with semi-skimmed.'

He put the tray on the desk and Rennie and Hacker helped themselves.

Logan left his where it was.

Andy thumped a hand down on Rennie's shoulder and squeezed. 'Sorry about earlier. Thought you guys were here to smash up the place, like. No hards, right?'

An uncomfortable smile. 'Yeah.'

'Andy?' Hacker plucked a chocolate Hobnob from the plate. 'Get on to Benny, will you? Make sure he's got our equipment ready for that surveillance on the Buchan job before we close.' A crunch of biscuit. Chewing as he turned back to Logan. 'You'd be surprised how much infidelity goes on at the weekends. People get two days off and they're at it like guinea pigs.'

Andy slipped from the room, closing the door behind him.

'What else did DI Bell say?'

Hacker polished off his Hobnob. 'If you're after something in particular, might as well save us both the time and get to the point.'

'Did he talk about suspects?'

A grin. 'And there it is! You want to know about Freddie Marshall.' He held up a chocolatey finger. 'Yes, Ding-Dong told me about Freddie. My opinion? Don't get me wrong, Freddie Marshall was an Olympic gold-medal-winning scumbag, but a killer?'

'Everyone keeps telling me what a great guy Marshall was. Family, friends, social worker...'

'A great guy? OK: pop quiz.' Hacker wheeled his seat forward. 'For ten points: who broke an old man's arm in three places because he wouldn't hand over his wife's purse?'

Sarcasm. Great.

'Is this really—'

Hacker made a harsh buzzing noise. 'Nope, it was Freddie Marshall. Ten points: who battered a fifteen-year-old boy so badly the kid's now confined to a wheelchair?'

'I get the—'

Another buzz. 'No. Freddie Marshall again. A bonus five if you can tell me who stabbed Limpy Steve Craigton three times in the guts over a twenty-quid wrap of heroin.'

Logan's hand drifted down to cover his own collection of scar tissue.

'I'm going to have to hurry you.'

Logan stared at him.

Hacker threw his arms in the air. 'No, the answer was *Freddie Marshall*! But thanks for playing.'

'Have you finished?'

Hacker picked up another biscuit, gesturing with it for emphasis. 'I asked around. I probed. I questioned. And you know what? The only thing pointing at Freddie was Crowbar Craig Simpson. No forensics, no witnesses. Nothing but Crowbar's word for it.' A bite sent crumbs tumbling down the front of his shirt. 'Did you know he's shacked up with Freddie's missus now? A more cynical man might draw a line connecting those two things. Still, all's fair, eh?'

'So Fred Marshall had nothing to do with Aiden's disappearance or Kenneth MacAuley's murder?'

'Why don't you *find* him and *ask* him?'

'You've worked for Sally MacAuley all these years, why haven't *you*?'

'Don't think we haven't tried.' Hacker pulled a face. 'Oh, the wee sod's still out there somewhere – probably Manchester or Birmingham, keeping his head down, eking out a living as a low-level drug dealer or enforcer – but he must've changed his appearance and got himself a new alias, because no one out there recognises his picture *or* his name. Or maybe he's slunk off to the continent?' Hacker pointed with what was left of his biscuit. 'You haven't touched your tea.'

Logan stayed where he was. 'If Fred Marshall didn't have anything to do with the MacAuleys, why did he vanish?'

'Well, if you were him, with *his* background, and your best mate's telling everyone you abducted a wee boy and killed that wee boy's dad, would you hang about waiting for the cops to fit you up?'

Ellie leaned her head back against the crate and rubbed the metal buckle thing across the bits of wood: *scrape, thump, scrape, thump, scrape, thump...* Then did the same going the other way: *scrape, thump, scrape, thump, scrape, thump...* Not that it did anything to undo the buckle, or loosen it, or get the big red rubber ball out of her mouth, but it made a noise. And that was something.

The trick was not to bite into the ball – that just made her jaw all achey – but to relax like Granny on the couch after Christmas dinner, with her mouth hanging open, teeth out, making noises like an angry piggy.

Scrape, thump, scrape, thump, scrape, thump...

The spotty boy was crying again, all muffled and sniffing, cos he had a big red rubber ball in his mouth too. Hunched up in his crate, cos he wasn't little like they were – he was a big boy with shiny-dotty-spots on his arms and chest. Ellie had seen them, because he only had jammie bottoms on. Cos he'd been naughty.

A warm gold-and-pink light dribbled through the dirty window, but the shadows were getting deeper and bluer. Stretching out behind all the stuff on the shelves and racks. Growing bigger and hungrier.

Someone, in one of the other crates, made an *eeeeeping* noise and Ellie scooted forward, pressing her eye to the gap. Over by the workbench, a teeny weenie hand wriggled between two of the wood bits, the fingers all reachy and dirty. Too far away.

The boy in the crate next to the hand turned away – Ellie could see the reflections in his eyes go out. *He* never ever cried. Never made a single sound. Just watched from the darkness of his wooden box. Like he wasn't really there.

Then those teeny reaching fingers went all floppy and the hand disappeared inside again. Before a new set of sniffling sobs clicked and hushed through the Scary Room.

Four of them and eight crates. That meant there was still—

The Horrible Song crackled out of the speakers up by the roof and the sniffy crying stopped like someone had thrown a tea towel over a budgie:

'Teddy bears and elephants went up the stairs to bed,
They'd had a lovely dinner of tomato soup and bread,'

The man was coming back. The man who didn't have a face!

'Their mummy made them custard and bananas for their tea,'

Ellie's heart went thumpity in her chest, breaths spiky through her nose as she backed against the far wall of her crate and covered her face with her tied-together hands. Peering out through her fingers.

'And read them lovely stories until they were all sleepy.'

The door opened and The Faceless Man walked into the Scary Room all squinted over sideways cos he was carrying a big plastic carrier thing in one hand – the kind with a grille door that people took kitty-cats to the animal doctor in. He grunted and heaved it onto the workbench in the corner.

'Go up the stairs, you sleepy bears, it's time to brush your teeth,'

Wiggled his fingers and wobbled his hand, cos whatever was in the big carrier had to be *really* heavy.

'Then climb into your cosy beds and snuggle underneath,'

His face was a big flat slab of grey nothing. No nose, no mouth, and no eyes either – all he had were two thin holes with darkness behind them. Much worse than a monster, because monsters were made-believey-up and The Faceless Man was real.

'You elephants must say your prayers and promise to be good,'

He unbolted one of the eight crates and thumped the lid open.

'For Mummy and for Daddy just as every nice child should.'

The Faceless Man went over to the kitten-cat carrier and pulled out a small boy with shiny yellow hair, a red splodgy dirty bit on his face, and sticky tape hiding his mouth. Both hands tied together. The boy's eyes were big as the moon as he tried to wriggle back inside, but The Faceless Man grabbed his arm and ripped the sticky tape off his mouth. Opened a drawer and pulled out a red ball thing like Ellie had on.

'It's time for dreams and sleepy times as you lie in your bunks,
  You teddy bears without a care, you elephants with trunks,'

The boy squirmed. 'Lemmego, lemmego, lemmego!'

But The Faceless Man pushed him down, stuffed the red ball into his mouth and buckled it behind his head. Then scooped him up, carried him over to the open crate and stuck him inside. Thumped the lid shut and clunked the fixy thing closed.

'And Nanny will kiss you goodnight and wish you lovely sleep,
  So close your eyes, my little ones, it's time for counting sheep.'

The Faceless Man picked up the big carrier again.

'Tomorrow is another day, what fun you'll have, and how!'

He turned and looked at them with his empty slits. Waved.

'But today is done and over, so let's go to sleep for now,'

His voice was all kind and warm – like he'd stolen it from Ellie's next-door neighbour, Mr Seafield, who always had sweeties in his pockets and a friendly smile and a doggy you could pat if you promised to wash your hands afterwards. 'You all play nice now.'

'God bless Mummy and Daddy, yes and God bless Nanny too,'

The Faceless Man took the kitten carrier out of the Scary Room, clunking the door shut behind him.

'It's sleepy time, oh loves of mine, and I will—'

The music stopped.

Ellie moved to the front of her crate as the silence got bigger and bigger and bigger.

Then the crying started again.

19

Fiery oranges and pinks glowed on the underside of the coal-coloured clouds, as if the whole sky was made of smouldering embers. Rain hissed against the pool car's windscreen, thickening as they headed across Northfield.

The radio was on again, but at least this time Rennie had the decency to hum along instead of singing. 'You want me to get a lookout request on the go for Freddy Marshall? Maybe try Manchester, Liverpool, and Birmingham? Ooh, and Brighton too.'

'Hmmm...' According to *Cold Blood and Dark Granite* Aiden's photo and description had been circulated by the FBI, Interpol, and most of the world's press.

'Honestly, it's like talking to myself.'

'Hmmm...' All that coverage for about four weeks and then the media moved on to the next terrorist atrocity and celebrity sex scandal. The twenty-four-hour news cycle devouring everything fed to it, then—

Logan's phone dinged. Dinged. Then dinged again. When he pulled it from his pocket, 'Brucie (3)' sat in the middle of the screen. 'Here we go.' He brought up the first message and read it out loud. '"Raymond Hacker, CEO of AberRAD Investigation Services Limited. Used to be a detective sergeant, back when we were still Grampian Police."' Next message... 'Ha! So much for leaving to set up his own business – says here Professional Standards kicked him out for taking bribes.'

172

Rennie nodded. 'I *knew* he was dodgy.'

Message number three: '"Known associates, ex-DC Andy Harris: caught stealing evidence from crime scenes. Drugs mostly. And ex-DC Danielle Smith: done for excessive force. Broke a drink-driver's jaw."'

'I could've taken her though. You know, if you hadn't come along.'

'She'd have had your bumhole for an umbrella stand.' Logan put his phone away and picked up his book again. 'So AberRAD Investigations is full of police officers who've been thrown off the force.'

'You could make an *ace* detective thing on the telly from that.' Rennie put on a big cheesy voice-over voice. 'Once, they were bad cops. Now, they're the last and only hope for those who can't get justice anywhere else...' Then launched into dramatic theme music. 'Dan da-da dan daaaa! Diddly twiddly too dee doo...'

'You're an idiot. You know that, don't you?'

He shrugged and drove on in silence for a bit. Then, 'So why *didn't* you drink your tea?'

'Because I know what ex-police officers are like. And I don't enjoy the taste of other people's spit.'

A look of utter disgust writhed across Rennie's face. 'Urrgh! I *drank* all mine!'

Rennie slowed the pool car as they drove down Queen Street. Pointed across the road. 'Look at these silly sods.'

The protest outside Divisional Headquarters was about three times the size it'd been earlier. Which was quite impressive, given the rain. It hammered down from a burnt-orange sky, yellowed by the street lights, bouncing off umbrellas and placards as they marched round and round and round.

Logan buzzed his window down an inch and rival chants broke through the downpour.

'Find Ellie Morton today! End the uncertainty! Find Ellie Morton today! End the uncertainty!'

A second group stood over by the front doors.

'Bring Ellie Morton back! Catch this sodding maniac! Bring Ellie Morton back! Catch this sodding maniac!'

A third bunch was putting on a show for the TV cameras and journalists, their loudhailer leader whipping them up.

Her voice hissed and crackled out into the rain: 'WHAT DO WE WANT?'

A ragged chorus: 'Ellie found, safe and sound!'

'WHEN DO WE WANT IT?'

'Now!'

Rennie grimaced. 'Yeah, they look friendly...'

Logan tucked his copy of *Cold Blood and Dark Granite* into his fleece pocket. 'I want you to badger Inspector Pearce about that CCTV trawl for Chalmers' car. Make a nuisance of yourself till she does it just to get rid of you.'

'I thought, you know, as I'm SIO, I should pull in a couple of Chalmers' colleagues.' He took the turning around the side of the building, heading up the ramp. 'Give them a bit of a grilling.'

'And get that lookout request going for Fred Marshall.'

'Stick them in a chair with a light in their face.' Putting on a James Cagney voice for, 'You're gonna talk, see? You're gonna talk, or I'm gonna beat the living snot outta ya!' The rear podium car park opened out at the top of the ramp – the usual collection of patrol cars, pool cars, and the small cluster of much fancier vehicles belonging to senior officers glowed in the security spotlights.

'Chalmers was working with DS Steel. So good luck with that.'

'Ah... Yeah. Maybe not then.'

Logan undid his seatbelt. 'You'd be better off having another trawl through DI Bell's old cases. See if you missed anything.'

'Noooooo...' Whining like a teenager asked to tidy their room. 'But I'm SIO!'

'It's not meant to stand for "Sulky, Incompetent, and 'Orrible".'

Logan rolled his eyes. 'You're wrong. You are. Accept it.'

The corridor was all nice and shiny and smelling of pine –

down the far end, the familiar rhythmic whum-whum-whum of a floor polisher echoed off the walls.

Rennie opened the door to their temporary office. 'All I'm saying is: the shark would definitely win.'

Logan followed him in. 'What if they were fighting in a wardrobe? The *bear* would definitely win.'

'Yeah, but why would a shark be *in* a wardrobe in the first—'

The *Addams Family* theme tune belted out of Logan's phone. He pointed at Rennie's computer. 'Go. Do stuff.' Then answered it. 'Sheila?'

A cold, hard voice sounded in his ear. *'Of course not.'* Isobel. Oh joy. *'Have you identified the antidepressants DS Chalmers was on yet?'*

'Isobel. How nice to hear from you again.'

'The antidepressants, Inspector McRae, have you identified them?'

Logan stuck his hand over the phone and grimaced at Rennie. 'Can you remember what antidepressants Lorna Chalmers was on?'

'Ermmm... No?'

'Well, you're a fat lot of help, aren't you?' He turned around and trudged out into the corridor again. 'I'm on my way to do it now.'

'I should think so too.' And then she hung up.

Lovely.

Logan put his phone away and hauled on his best Isobel voice. '"I should think so too." "The antidepressants, *Inspector McRae*."' He dropped the iceberg impersonation. 'God, Logan, you really could pick them...'

At least the rain's stopped...

Sally pulls a handkerchief from her coat sleeve and blows her nose. Huffs out a cloudy breath. Wipes at her stinging eyes.

The play area's busy – scores of kids screaming as they run around the slides and climbing frames and wobbly duck things. Their mums gather at the outside edges, smoking, chatting, or fiddling with their mobile phones, exploiting this break in the weather to tire out their little darlings. Up above, the sky is a solid lump of churned granite, but the setting sun has somehow managed to find a chink between the clouds and the earth, making Westburn Park glow. Turning Aberdeen from a dreich grey lump to a technicolour beauty.

She settles down on the edge of a bench – the only dry bit – and shifts the stroller so it's next to her. The teddy bear strapped into the seat is mostly hidden by the hood and deep walled sides, but it still smiles its dead smile at her, plastic eyes glinting in the sunlight.

Sally takes a deep breath. Bites her lip.

Stares out at the play area.

Look at them all, running and shrieking and laughing, playing tag and pirates and...

She swallows down the knot of wire in her throat. Wipes her eyes again.

The swings were always Aiden's favourites. He would've spent hours on them if she'd let him, squealing for Kenneth to push him higher this time. Higher, Daddy! And Kenneth would smile and push him higher, and they'd all laugh...

The knot of wire is back. Sally bites her bottom lip and tries to keep it all—

'Excuse me, are you OK?'

She looks up and a fat balding man is running on the spot, right in front of her, in Lycra shorts and a fluorescent-orange T-shirt, earphones held in one hand. Face all pink and sweaty. His belly jiggles every time his big white trainers hit the ground.

Heat rushes up her cheeks. 'Sorry.' She dries her eyes again. 'Just being stupid. Sorry.'

'OK, if you're...' He's staring at her. Then his eyes widen. 'You're *her*, aren't you? Yeah, yeah, you are! God. Wow. I read your book!'

'I'm sorry.'

'No, it was really good.' A smile spreads across his chubby face. 'Wow. Sally MacAuley...' He licks his lips. 'Look, I wouldn't normally, but like I said, I read your book...' Then he pulled out a smartphone. 'Can I take a selfie? Yeah?'

'I really don't... I'm not...'

But he does it anyway: pulling a pose and flashing victory

Vs at his phone's camera as it clicks. The two of them captured forever on the screen.

Sally flinches.

He puts his phone back in his pocket. 'You sure you're OK?'

A nod. Holding it in. Please go away. PLEASE GO AWAY!

His smile never slips. 'OK. Great. Well, really nice to meet you. Keep up the good work!' He gives her a thumbs up, then sticks his headphones on again and lumbers off. 'Sally MacAuley... Wow!'

Soon as he's gone, Sally hits herself on the head – thumping her fist into the hair above her ear, making it ring. Then again, harder. And again. 'Stupid! Stupid! Stupid!'

What the hell was she thinking?

She stands, grabs the stroller and wheels the teddy bear towards the exit. Past the play area with its happy children and mothers too tired, or too stupid to realise that *every single* moment with their sons and daughters has to be cherished. Because someone can come along and take it all away in an instant.

She scrubs a hand across her eyes as she gets to the car park. Wheels the stroller over to her rusty old Shogun and opens the boot. It's full of empty feed bags and drifts of orange baler twine, but Sally folds the stroller up and thrusts it inside anyway. Slams the boot shut and stands there, forehead resting against the scratched red bodywork. Scrunches her eyes closed and curls her hands into fists. 'How could you be so *stupid*?'

Quarter to seven on a Saturday night and the streets were virtually deserted. Up above, the sky was still its burnt marmalade colour, the clouds lit from underneath by the city lights. But it had actually stopped raining for a change.

Logan took the slip road at the Lang Stracht junction, onto the dual carriageway, heading for Kingswells. Should be there in about, what, five minutes?

An overexcited DJ burbled out of the Audi's stereo. '...is dinner with local crime writer J.C. Williams and the chance to be a character in her next PC Munro book!'

His phone dinged and buzzed, announcing an incoming text.

Well tough. He was driving.

'And bidding for that stands at two thousand and sixty pounds. Let's see if we can get it to three grand by the end of the show!'

Right at the roundabout, up the hill past the park-and-ride. Trees crowded both sides of the road, leaves shiny and dark. Glistening in the row of street lights.

This time, his phone didn't bother dinging, it launched straight into 'If I Only Had A Brain'. Logan pressed the button on the steering wheel and the radio faded to silence. 'Simon.'

Rennie's voice boomed out. *'First up: Biohazard Bob says thanks for arresting Crowbar Craig. He owes you a pint or two.'*

'That's nice.'

'Oh yeah, it's absolutely lovely. I'm the one got punched in the face! Where's my pints? ... Wait, you sound like you're in a car. Are you in a car?'

'What's second up?'

'Did you abandon me at the ranch and sod off to do something more exciting instead?'

'I need to check those antidepressants at Chalmers' house. You were busy doing things, remember? Now: second up.'

A grunt, a groan, then, *'OK, OK... Had a word with a mate of mine in DI Fraser's MIT. They've got an address for where DI Bell was staying: the Netherley Arms. They're keeping it top secret.'*

The road skirted Kingswells, orange and grey pantile roofs visible over high garden fences.

'Odds on it'll be all over the *Aberdeen Examiner* tomorrow morning.'

'And third up, but not least up: I nagged the team looking through the CCTV footage for DS Chalmers' car, like you asked.'

Left at the junction and into darkest Kingswells. They'd made some effort with the planting, but it was still a sprawling collection of housing estates, bolted together by cutesy-woodsey-named roads.

'And?'

'Not great. Automatic number plate recognition only works if you've got the car on camera and there's only so much of Aberdeen that's covered in cameras.'

'Hmmm…' Logan drummed his fingers on the steering wheel, How the hell were they meant to find out where Chalmers had been with no clues, witnesses, or evidence?

'Does it matter where she went? I mean, if she killed herself…?'

'It matters because she thought she had a lead on the Ellie Morton abduction, but she didn't want to share it. We need to know.'

'Ah, OK. In that case, maybe we'd be better off trying to track her mobile phone instead?'

He'd walked right into that one.

Logan grinned. 'Good idea. Off you go then.'

'Gah…! But it's quarter to seven. On a Saturday! I knew I should've stayed at home…'

'You're SIO now, remember? SIOs get to go home when the work's done.'

Silence.

Logan took a right, then a left, following the satnav.

A long, grudging sigh huffed out of the speakers. Then, 'All right, all right. I'll see what I can do.'

'Let me know.' Logan thumbed the button and hung up.

The DJ on the stereo got louder again. '…twenty pounds from Marion at Chesney's Discount Carpet Warehouse in Milltimber if I'll give a big shout-out to all their staff and customers. Done and done, Marion!'

He pulled onto Chalmers' road, with its collection of boxy wee houses and too-small built-in garages, no two exactly identical, but all cobbled together from the same basic building blocks. As if someone had swallowed a whole bellyful of Lego then vomited it up.

'You're listening to Mair Banging Tunes with me, Kenny Mair, and we're raising money for the Ellie Morton Reward Fund! Next up for auction: dinner for two at Nick Nairn's—'

Logan killed the radio and parked.

Surprisingly enough, the street wasn't as dead as it could have been. Maybe because it was a secluded cul-de-sac, far from the main road? But there were actually kids out riding bicycles, playing in the streetlight, people walking dogs. Lights on in every living room but one.

179

Chalmers' house was in darkness. No car in the driveway.

Logan got out and walked up the path to the front door.

An old lady and her Dobermann pinscher stopped on the other side of the road to stare. Suppose anyone in a uniform would be big news here today. It wasn't every Saturday you got to see the police attending a neighbour's suicide.

Logan rang the doorbell.

No response.

Another go.

Still nothing.

A high-pitched voice sounded behind him. *'Can I help you?'*

He turned.

It was a young man: mid-twenties with a hipster haircut, Skeleton Bob T-shirt, flesh-tunnel earlobes, skinny jeans, and a Kermit the Frog tattoo on his arm – so new it was still swollen and covered in clingfilm. Kermit the Hipster pointed at the house. 'He's not in. Brian, Mr Chalmers, he's not in. Went to stay with friends, I think. Cos of what happened.' Kermit licked his lips, eyes shining. 'My mum's got a key, you know: for watering the plants and things when they're on holiday. I can let you in, if you like?'

Logan gave the weird little man a nod. 'Thanks. But I'd better check first.'

Creepy Kermit stood on the pavement, watching him like a hungry puppy watches a sausage.

Logan shifted his phone from one ear to the other, keeping it between him and Kermit. 'Mr Chalmers? You still there?'

What sounded like singing, somewhere in the background. Not proper professional singing, shower warbling. And was that hissing noise running water?

Brian Chalmers cleared his throat. *'I'm sorry. It's just ... the shock.'*

'Your wife was on antidepressants, Mr Chalmers. I need to know which ones.'

'It... Yes. She... Ever since her father died. It ... the job.'

'Will you be returning home soon?'

The song warbled to an end, the running water fell silent. Still nothing from Brian Chalmers.

'Are you—'

'I'm... I'm not staying there. I'm staying with ... a friend. I can't stand... I can't be in the house. Not after... I'm sorry.'

Logan did another circuit of the driveway. Well, rectangle of tarmac in front of the too-small garage. 'We need access to the property, Mr Chalmers.'

'Fine. Break in. Kick the door down. I don't care. I can't be *there.'*

A voice in the background. Female, warm. *'Brian? Brian, have you seen my hairbrush?'* She paused for a beat. *'Who are you talking to?'*

The response was hard and sharp. *'I'm on the phone!'* Then muffled scrunching came from the earpiece. Probably Chalmers covering the phone to talk to what was her name, Stephanie? The account manager? *'Sorry. I'm sorry, it's... I'll only be a minute. I promise.'* Brian returned at full volume. *'Search the place, burn it down, do what you want. I – don't – care.'* And then he hung up.

Hmph... Hadn't taken Brian Chalmers long to get over his wife's suicide, had it? Body wasn't even post-mortemed yet.

Logan put his phone away. Turned to Creepy Kermit. 'About that key?'

'Yes. Right!' He hurried up the path, produced a pink fuzzy keyring with a single rectangular key dangling from it, and unlocked the front door. Stood aside and made a flourishing gesture. 'After you.'

Logan stepped inside. Stopped. Slipped the key from the lock and pocketed it. Turned to Creepy Kermit and gave him a smile. 'Thanks for your help.' Then closed the door in his surprised and disappointed face.

Weirdo.

And just in case: Logan engaged the snib on the Yale lock. That'd keep the little sod out.

Right: bathroom.

He tramped up the stairs, down the landing and into the small tiled space. Opened the medicine cabinet and called the mortuary. 'Isobel? I've got the antidepressants here.' Logan picked one of the pill packets from Chalmers' collection and peered inside. Almost empty. 'Right first up is … Mo… Moclo…' Oh for goodness' sake, why did they have to make medication *completely* unpronounceable?

Isobel put on her patient voice, as if she was talking to a four-year-old. *'Try sounding it out. Slowly.'*

Yeah, that wasn't emasculating in any way.

He worked his way through them, checking inside each one as he went. 'Mo-clo-bem-ide. Tran-yl-cypro-mine sulphate. Ven-la-faxine hydrochloride. Nor-trip-ty-line. And Aripiprazole. All the boxes are pretty much empty.'

No reply.

Logan put the last packet back in the cabinet. 'Oh come on, my pronunciation wasn't *that* bad.'

'Are these all from the same doctor's surgery?'

'Hold on.' He did a quick comparison on the pharmacists' labels. 'Yes, but different doctors each time. Why?'

'I need to check something.' She raised her voice, as if shouting across the room. *'Sheila? Look up Venlafaxine hydrochloride, please: I need contraindications.'*

Then what might have been the staccato click of fingers on a keyboard, but it was too faint to be sure.

He sat on the edge of the bath.

Look at all those shampoos and conditioners. How did one human being need so many bottles of the stuff? And body lotions! All they did was make you greasy and slithery. What was the point of—

Sheila Dalrymple's voice, barely audible in the background: *'Possible fatal drug interactions with monoamine-oxidase inhibitors.'*

'What about Tranylcypromine?'

Another pause. Then, *'Contraindicated with MAO inhibitors and dibenzazepine-related entities, Professor.'*

'And unless I'm very much mistaken: Moclobemide is an MAO inhibitor and Nortriptyline is a dibenzazepine-related entity. Aripiprazole?'

That was definitely someone typing.

'*Moderate contraindicators with MAO inhibitors and dibenzazepine-related entities.*'

Complete gobbledygook.

He picked up a bottle of shampoo – strawberry and pomegranate. Wouldn't know whether to wash with it or eat it. 'Is all this supposed to make any sort of sense to normal people?'

Isobel put on her talking-to-small-children voice again. '*Mix any of her pills together and you risk a one-way trip to the mortuary. Add alcohol into the mix and you can virtually guarantee it. And as I said, DS Chalmers had consumed a lot of alcohol.*'

Pfff...

Logan put the shampoo down. 'She wasn't taking any chances, then.'

A sigh. '*To be perfectly honest, I'm amazed she managed to make it as far as the garage.*'

20

Logan poked his head into the master bedroom. A couple of cardboard boxes sat on the unmade bed, half-full of clothes. More boxes on the floor, stuffed with CDs and books and DVDs.

Looked as if Brian Chalmers was moving out.

The second bedroom was just the same as it'd been that morning. No packing going on in here.

Might as well have a rummage. After all, you never knew...

He hauled the bottom drawer out of the bedside cabinet and dumped it on the carpet, next to the other two. Reaching into the hollow left behind with one hand, the other holding his phone. 'How are you getting on?'

A groan from Rennie. *'Give me a chance! Do you have any idea how much sodding about you have to do to get phone companies to release tracking data on someone's mobile? On a Saturday? After the office is closed? Because it's loads. Loads and loads and loads!'*

Nothing in the hollow but a pair of black pop socks.

'When they brought Chalmers in, did she have her notebook on her?'

'And look at the time: it's gone seven! *Emma's already been on, giving me grief about not going home when—'*

'Notebook, DS Rennie, notebook.' Logan slotted the bottom drawer back into place. 'Maybe she kept a record of what she was up to.'

'Gah… All right, all right, I'll have a rummage.'

'And see if you can dig out her mobile phone too.'

His voice went all quiet and muttering. 'Ordering me about like I'm an idiot or something. Supposed to be the SIO…'

Logan hung up and finished reassembling the bedside cabinet. Wardrobe next.

Nothing in any of the jackets, trousers, or shirt pockets. Nothing in the pile of boots and shoes either.

Delving under the bed produced a handful of shoe boxes full of old school photographs and some fluff-covered bits-and-bobs.

He lifted up the mattress. A couple of baby magazines sat on the wooden slats beneath it. Would have been better finding sex toys. The magazines, hidden away like that, was just … depressing.

Logan placed them on the bedside cabinet, sighed, then wandered out onto the landing again.

There was a hatch in the ceiling, outside the bathroom.

Right: stepladder.

Probably find one in the garage.

Logan thumped downstairs and into the shelf-lined space. 'Ladder, ladder, ladder, ladder… Ah, there you are.' Hiding behind an artificial Christmas tree in a box.

He wrestled it free and carried it over to the door.

Stopped.

Chalmers' glasses and shoes still sat there, on the shelves. Lined up, all neat and tidy, as if she'd nipped out for a minute and would be back for them soon.

Rennie had been right – it was weird.

Ah well, nothing he could do about that now.

Logan wrestled the stepladder up the stairs and clacked it open outside the bathroom door. Climbed it, shoved the hatch open and peered into the darkness. Like that scene in Aliens… A switch sat right by the opening and when he clicked it on, cold white light flickered into the space.

'Great…'

The place was stuffed full of boxes. They were piled up on every flat surface, jammed in between the joists and rafters, and most of them looked as if they hadn't been opened since Lorna and Brian Chalmers moved in.

Mind you, that cut down the workload a bit, didn't it? Anything covered in dust could be ignored. If Lorna was planking her notebooks up here, hiding evidence, they'd have to be in a box that'd been opened recently.

Logan levered himself up into the cramped space.

And that meant these three nearest the hatch – everything else wore a thick lid of pale-grey fluff. Box one: kitchen gadgets that probably got used once then dumped. Box two: threadbare teddy bears, dolls, action figures, board games – all ancient and yellowed. Stored away, waiting for the child that Chalmers never had. Box three was full of her stuff from police college – photos, textbooks, journals.

He picked a journal and flicked through it: cramped spidery handwriting in blue biro, the occasional diagram that looked as if it'd been copied down at a lecture. Its pages dry and crackling. No sign of any recent additions, scribbled onto the last few pages, saying what had happened to Ellie Morton.

The other two journals were the same.

Logan opened the last one somewhere near the middle.

I graduate tomorrow and I couldn't be prouder. I'm part of something magnificent! Me and Stevie and Shaz and Tommy Three Thumbs are going to make a difference!

I bet Shaz £1,000,000 I'd be the youngest Chief Constable ever and she wouldn't take it! She said only an idiot would bet against me. Look out world, here I come!

He shut the book and placed it in the box again. Folded the lid shut. Sighed.

All that hope and optimism, reduced to this. Some lonely toys, a box full of journals no one would ever read, and a body dangling from the end of an electrical cable in a crappy garage you couldn't even park a car in.

Shaz should've taken that bet.

Anyway, this wasn't achieving any—

186

His phone went *ding*.

That would be Rennie.

Only when he dug his phone out, it wasn't.

HORRIBLE STEEL:

I told you I'd have my REVENGE!

Yes, because today wasn't bad enough already.

He thumbed out a reply.

What revenge? Roberta, what have you
done?

SEND.

Ding.

Oh, you'll find out soon enough...

'All right, all right, I'm coming.' Tara wiped her hands on a tea
towel as she hurried down the hall, following the summoning
chimes of Logan's doorbell. Probably looked a right state with
flour all over the only apron she could find in the kitchen – a
surprisingly un-macho pink number with kittens on it that she
was *definitely* going to make fun of him for when he got home
– and bits of cheese cobbler dough caked all over her fingers.
But tough.

The bell went again – two long, dark, old-fashioned *bong*s.

'Keep your underwear on...' She opened the door. 'Can I
help ... you?'

It was Detective Sergeant Roberta Steel, AKA: The Wrinkly
Horror, standing on the top step with a worrying smile on her
face and a huge bag over her shoulder. God knew what sort of
products she used to get her hair like that. Probably matt varnish
and mains electricity.

The smile got worse. 'Aye, aye: you've got your clothes on,
so I know I'm no' interrupting anything naughty.' She turned,
stuck two fingers in her mouth and whistled.

The call was answered by two little girls. Jasmine, with her dark-brown spiky hair, jeans, trainers, brown leather jacket – a sophisticated look for a ten-year-old, spoiled a bit by the threadbare teddy bear she was clutching. Her little sister, Naomi, waddled up behind, wearing a tatty-looking Halloween pirate costume – not the frilly girly version – holding a cuddly octopus toy above her head like it was a god. Or a sacrificial offering.

Something jagged coiled up in Tara's throat. She swallowed it down. 'Det... It... Detective Sergeant Steel. Logan isn't—'

'In you go, monsters.' Steel gave the girls a push and they scampered inside.

'But...'

'Budge up a bit.'

Steel barged in after them, forcing Tara to flatten herself against the wall.

What was happening? Why was... What?

Outside, in the driveway, Susan waved from the passenger seat of a sensible hatchback – the engine still running. What she was doing with The Wrinkly Horror was anyone's guess. She was a lovely, if slightly frumpy, blonde with a warm smile and dimples, while Steel was a hand grenade in a septic tank.

Tara tried for a smile of her own and waved back, then turned just in time to see Steel dump her bag in the hallway. 'It... But...?'

Any sophistication points Jasmine had left evaporated as she caught sight of Logan's cat and made a noise that wasn't far off a full-on squeal. 'Cthulhu!' She charged off after the poor creature, closely followed by her tiny pirate sister.

'Thooloo! Thooloo!'

Steel had a dig at an underwire. 'Did Laz tell you how come he got the house so cheap? A fancy four-bedroom love nest in Cults must've cost a fortune, right?'

This must be what hostages felt like.

'He... Someone left him money in their will.'

'Oh aye, but this place was going cheap because the old lady who lived here ... *died* here.' She nudged the bag with her boot.

'Everything's in there: pyjamas, toilet bags, sleeping bags, bedtime stories.'

WHAT?

'Sleeping bags?'

'So the old lady has a stroke, or a heart attack or something, drops dead right here.' Steel tilted her head at the big patch of new-looking floorboards at the foot of the stairs. 'Took three months till anyone noticed she was missing. By then most of her had oozed through the floor into the basement. God, the *smell*! Carpet was about two inches thick with dead flies in here.'

A squeaky voice blared out through the living room door. *'Thooloo! Thooloo! Thooloo!'*

Tara swallowed again. 'But—'

'You've looked after them before, you'll be fine.'

No, no, no, no, no...

'But only when Logan was there *too*! I can't—'

'And they like you, which is a bonus.' A wrinkly wink. 'Normally they go through babysitters like vomit through a sock.'

'But I've never—'

'Ooh, look at that.' Steel checked her watch. 'Gotta go, or we'll be late.' She marched towards the front door. 'Naomi's bedtime is eight, Jasmine can stay up till ten, but only if she's behaved herself and done her teeth after dinner. No chocolate.'

'But Logan isn't *here*!'

'We'll see you tomorrow for a nice big slap-up breakfast. Have fun!'

She actually *skipped* out the door, climbed into the driving seat of the sensible family hatchback. Grinned as she fastened her seatbelt.

Susan gave Tara another wave as the car pulled away, while Steel cackled.

This wasn't fair.

'I'm not good with children!'

That tiny voice bellowed out again, like something off *Jurassic Park*: 'Thooloo! Thoolooooooooooooo!'

Tara twisted the tea towel until it was tight as a garrotte. 'Oh God...'

Logan wrestled the ladder in behind the boxed Christmas tree again. Something else that would probably never see daylight again. Never be taken out and covered in decorations...

God, this house was *depressing*.

He turned and made for the door through into the hall. Then stopped.

Chalmers' shoes and glasses. All lined up on their respective shelves.

The glasses weren't anything special – half wire frames with a blueish tint to the legs. He put them back in their place. Then picked up the shoes: grey and black, scuffed around the toe, the laces tucked inside. There was soil caught in the treads. Tiny flecks of green grass.

Now *there* was a thought.

He pulled out his phone with his other hand and scrolled through his contacts. Set it ringing.

A blare of party music got muffled by something. Then, *'Hello?'*

'Dr Frampton? It's Logan. Logan McRae?'

'Ah, Inspector McRae. Let's see it's ... twenty past seven on a Saturday evening, I'm guessing this isn't a social call?'

'I know it's the weekend, but I wondered if you could maybe do me a wee favour?'

'A forensic soil scientist's work is never done. What do you need?'

'I've got a pair of shoes with some dirt on them. I need to know what they trod in and where.'

'Do you now...' A pause. *'Well, I suppose you* did *sort out that thing for me...'* Then a slurping noise came through the phone's speaker. *'It'll have to wait till tomorrow, though: I've been downing Tom Collinses since four and even I wouldn't trust me to run the mass spectrometer.'*

'Thanks. I'll drop them off on my way past. Fifteen minutes?'

'If I'm in the hot tub, you can leave them in the porch.' A smile crept into her voice. *'That or borrow a swimming costume?'*

190

'Can't. Things to see, people to do.'

'Shame. I've got a pair of budgie smugglers you'd look lovely *in.'*

'Actually, I've got to...' He hung up and had a wee shudder. Woman was incorrigible.

Right, all he needed now was newspaper to wrap Chalmers' shoes in and a box to keep them safe from here to Dr Frampton's house.

Logan tucked the Amazon box under his arm and locked the front door.

Kermit the Weirdo was waiting for him, standing on the driveway, the streetlight behind him casting his face and hands into shadow. The creepy effect was somewhat undermined by the fact he was sheltering under a Hello Kitty umbrella. Was that meant to be ironic, or did it belong to some unknown baby sister? Kermit took a step closer, eyes hungry in the gloom. 'You find anything?'

'I didn't get your name earlier.'

Kermit nodded. 'Norman. Clifton. But my mates call me "Tebbit".'

'That's a shame.' Logan held up his hand – the key glinted on the end of its fuzzy fob. 'I'll have to keep hold of this for a couple of days, Norman. Part of the investigation.'

'Oh...' He turned and scuffed away down the drive, shoulders hunched, umbrella canopy glowing like a pink mushroom as he passed beneath the streetlight.

'Thanks for all your help.' Logan smiled and waved him goodbye, keeping his voice nice and low so Kermit the Weirdo couldn't hear him. 'And this way you can't sneak in and lick the floor where she hanged herself, you utter freak.'

More waving and smiling, until Kermit disappeared into his mum's house, then Logan hurried down the driveway – scrambling in behind the Audi's wheel as his phone belted out its generic ringtone.

He dumped the cardboard box on the passenger seat, then answered the call. 'McRae.'

What sounded like a little girl, singing in the background,

came through the speaker. Another, littler girl joined in, getting most of the words wrong.

'*An allosaurus, name of Doris, lived long ago inside a forest,*
She was a stinky dinosaur, everyone told her so...'

Then the whole lot was drowned out by a harsh, hissing whisper. '*You utterly and completely misogynistic bastard!*'

'*It really hurt her feelings to be told she's unappealing,*
So Doris asked a brontosaurus, because she didn't know,
And he said...'

'OK...' He checked the caller ID: 'TS Tara'. Frowned. 'Tara, is that you?'

'*We haven't invented soap, so that's why we're all smelly,*
Or stethoscopes, or skipping ropes, or envelopes, or telly!'

'*Why didn't you tell me? I mean the thing about the old lady rotting her way through the floor was bad enough, but I am not your bloody babysitter!*'

Not another one. He tried not to sigh, he really did.

'Remember when I lent you my key this morning on the condition that you didn't turn out to be a complete nutjob?'

'*Just because I offered to cook dinner doesn't make me your skivvy!*'

'What the hell are you on about?'

A muffled scrunch. Then, '*Don't act like you didn't know: she turned up and dumped Jasmine and Naomi on me then ran away! She. Her. Steel!*'

She dumped...? Oh God.

A cold hard lump ballooned inside his stomach.

How could she *do* that?

'Tara? I'm going to have to call you back. I've got to go shout at Roberta Sodding Steel!' He hung up and stabbed Steel's number in his contact list. Set it ringing as he started the car and pulled away from the kerb.

The Audi's hands-free system picked it up, and a robotic-sounding Steel belted out of the speakers. '*You've reached the voicemail of Roberta Steel. I'm busy, or I don't want to speak to you. Leave a message and you'll find out which.*'

Bleeeeeeep.

He strangled the steering wheel – if only it was her neck! 'You can't abandon Jasmine and Naomi with Tara and sod off! Are you *trying* to ruin everything for me?' He bared his teeth, dragged in a long breath. 'AAAAAAAAAAAAAAAAAAAAAA AAAAAAARGH!' Then mashed the 'END CALL' button with an angry thumb.

Had another scream for good luck. 'AAAAAAAAAAAAAAAA-AAAAAAARGH!'

Called Tara.

She was still doing the angry pantomime whisper. *'Logan?'*

'Steel's not answering her phone.'

The sound of little feet thundered past in stereo. *'Thooloo! Thooloo!'*

'You didn't agree to this in advance?'

'Of course I didn't! I bought bubble bath. I even bought fizzy wine for you to drink while soaking *in* the bubble bath. This is Steel's revenge for me not babysitting last night.'

More thundering feet. Then Jasmine's voice sounded loud and clear. *'Aunty Tara? Aunty Tara, Naomi needs to go to the toilet.'*

'I'm not good with children, Logan. They frighten me.'

'Look, I've got to go to the station and sign out, but then I'll be right home. I promise.'

'You'd better be. Because—'

'Aunty Tara? Naomi really, really needs to go to the toilet!'

'Oh God...' She was obviously trying to put a bit of confidence into her voice. It *almost* worked. *'Come on, Tara, if you can blind a man with your thumbs, you can do this.'* And then she was gone.

Logan grimaced at his reflection in the rear-view mirror. Yeah, that last bit wasn't worrying at all...

21

That's the thing about Aberdeen – as soon as the rain stops, people rush outside, trying to enjoy themselves, as if it's the middle of a summer's day. Only it isn't.

A row of black metal lampposts cast a faint yellow glow into the car park, shimmering back from the puddles. About a dozen assorted hatchbacks and four-by-fours are spread out across the bays, but Sally ignores them, reversing in alongside a dirty grey Luton van in the corner instead. All four tyres are flat, and there's a 'POLICE AWARE' sticker across the windscreen.

Hmph.

Yes, well the police might be 'aware', but, as usual, they're doing sod-all about it.

She leaves enough space between the Shogun and the van to get the passenger door open, backing up till the towbar is a couple of feet from the hedge bordering the car park.

Her head itches, like it's covered in ants. But that's what she gets for listening to Raymond, isn't it? I've bought you a wig, Sally. Put the wig on, Sally. No one will recognise you if you wear the wig, Sally. She tops the long, blonde, curly monstrosity with a baseball cap, flips up the hood on her old brown hoodie, and puts on her sunglasses. She looks like a stroppy teenager, but at least no one will ask for a selfie this time.

Right. Let's try it again.

Sally gets the stroller from the boot, clacks it into shape on the wet tarmac and wheels it away down one of the paths that lead off into Hazlehead Park.

Nearly half past seven and there are lanky kids in AFC tracksuits and head torches, out whacking golfballs where they aren't meant to. A knot of underage couples snogging and smoking and passing around two-litre bottles of extra-strong cider. Hands up sweatshirts and down jeans.

She keeps going, following the path deeper and deeper into the park. Moving from the waxy glow of one lamppost to the next.

Trees and bushes crowd in on the path as she pushes the teddy bear in its stroller. Following the sound.

Shrieks and yells and giggling laughter.

It's not a huge play area: a seesaw, a climbing frame, and a set of swings. Almost a dozen small children have descended on it – some hanging from the bars, two going up and down and up and down, four roaring around and around pretending to be spaceships – while their parents stand on the periphery, looking bored. Chatting to one another or fiddling with their phones. Someone's reading a magazine.

Sally wheels the stroller past them, keeping her head down – along the path as it curls past the far side of the play area and disappears between a clump of thick green bushes.

The kids on the other side screech and roar.

Maybe it would be...

She stops. Frowns.

There's a small girl sitting on the ground beneath one of the bigger bushes where it's dry, playing with a handful of Star Wars action figures. A pretty little thing – can't be more than five years old – in denim dungarees, a wine-red T-shirt, and grubby trainers. Hair a froth of Irn-Bru-coloured curls.

No sign of her mother.

How could anyone just let her wander off like that?

Sally stands on her tiptoes, peering over the top of the bush. The parents barely seem to register the children screeching around in front of them. It's unbelievable, it really is.

She hunkers down in front of the little girl. 'Hello.'

No reply.

'That looks fun.'

Still nothing. So Sally picks up the Darth Vader figure and makes it walk towards her, adopting an over-the-top French accent: 'Ello. I have ze leetle boy who likes space stuff too.'

She doesn't look up. 'That's not how Gunter talks. He's American.'

Right. Of course he is. Sally swaps her Inspector Clouseau for John Wayne instead. 'Well gee, I sure am sorry, partner.'

The little girl attacks a Chewbacca with a Princess Leia, biffing them together. 'It's OK. He's a bit of a tit anyway.'

'A bit of...?'

Chewbacca falls over and Princess Leia jumps on his head.

'That's what Daddy says when someone's not as clever as *he* is.' She puts on a deep growly voice. '"Christ's sake, Becky, but your Uncle Kevin's a bit of a tit!"'

'I see...' Sally forces a smile. 'Well, Becky, would you and Gunter like to come play with my little boy?'

'Is he a bit of a tit?'

Sally bites her lip for a moment, then pulls on the smile again. 'No, he's a lovely, handsome, clever, funny, little boy.' She nods at the teddy bear, strapped into the stroller. 'This is his best friend, Mr Bibble-Bobble. They're playing hide-and-seek.' She brings up a finger and points it at the bushes opposite. 'Can you see him? He's a *very* good hider.'

And at that, the little girl finally looks up from Princess Leia giving Chewbacca a kicking and stares at the bush, eyes narrowing, lips pursed.

Good. You keep facing that way.

Sally slips the homemade gag from her pocket – it's only a tea towel with a knot tied in the middle, but perfectly serviceable. 'Can you see him?'

Becky squints. '... Yes?'

She edges closer. 'Ooh, look: there he goes!' Swinging her finger towards the nearest exit. 'I bet we can sneak up on him if we're all super quiet and *sneaky* like spies.'

Becky scrambles to her feet. 'Gunter is a spy!'

'Quick, jump in the buggy and hide under Mr Bibble-Bobble.' Sally unbuckles the bear. 'He won't expect a thing.'

Becky puts one hand on the stroller ... then stops. Looks back through the bushes at the knot of parents.

Sally tightens her grip on the gag. Come on. Get in the buggy. Get in the buggy.

She scuffs away a step. 'Maybe I better—'

'Unless you're too big a *scaredy*-cat to be a spy?'

'Am *not* a scaredy-cat!' She grabs Darth Vader / Gunter from Sally's hands. 'Come on, Gunter, don't be a tit.' Then clambers into the stroller and pulls the teddy on top of herself. It barely covers half of her, but it'll be good enough from a distance.

She makes little giggling noises as Sally wheels her away along the path.

'Shhh... You have to be very quiet.'

Past the play area, past the snogging underage drinkers. Past the where-they're-not-meant-to-be golfers. Back into the car park. And Becky's *still* giggling...

Sally pushes the stroller into the dark gap between her Shogun and the big manky Luton van. That's when the giggling stops.

Becky sits up and frowns. Stares at her. Then hauls in a huge breath, mouth open and ready to scream.

Sally stuffs the gag into it.

Quick – before anyone sees!

She shoves Becky back into the stroller and grabs her hands – tying them together at the wrists with a double length of baler twine, ignoring the legs kicking against her thighs, the muffled roars as the little girl bucks and writhes.

Soon as she's got the hands secured, Sally ties the gag as well, then hauls the Shogun's rear door open and bundles Becky into the footwell. Pins her against the carpet and ties her ankles together in the dim glow of the interior light.

More muffled roaring.

'Shh...' Sally reaches out to stroke her hair, but Becky thrashes in the footwell like a mackerel in the bottom of a rowboat trying to escape the hook.

'Shh... It'll be OK. I promise, it'll be OK...'

Another length of rope goes around her waist and then around the metal struts supporting the passenger seat. Tied tight so she can't get free.

'It's only for a little bit, I promise. Be a good girl and it'll all be over soon. OK?' And then Sally takes the pillowcase from the back seat and pulls it over Becky's head.

More roaring.

She closes her eyes and lets out a shuddering breath. 'Oh God…' Then backs out of the car, closes the door, shoves the stroller in the boot, and hurries in behind the wheel. Starts the engine and twists on the headlights.

It isn't easy, sticking to the posted fifteen-mile-an-hour limit, but Sally does her best, even though muffled screams and thrashing sounds boom out from the back of the car.

'Please, it'll be OK. Please: shhhh…!' Her voice is shrill in her own ears, panicky, pleading. 'Shhhh…!'

And it makes no difference – Becky keeps going.

So Sally switches on the radio and turns it up to drown her out.

A broad Doric accent joins the cacophony, so thick it's barely comprehensible. '…*an amazin' four thoosand poon! Absolutely crackin'. And dinna forget we've still got a richt load a thingies ye canna buy oanywye else tae auction off fir the Ellie Morton Reward Fund! Noo: fit aboot a bittie music?'*

'Hold still!' Sally tightens her grip on Becky's dungarees, unlocks the shed, then carries her and the teddy bear inside.

It's gloomy in here. The ivy choking the window stops all but the faintest glow from the spotlight above the kitchen door getting through. Rain hisses on the roof, rattles in the ivy, scratches against the walls. It took most of the morning to clear the shed out, and now the only things in here are a couple of yoga mats with a sleeping bag on top, a pillow, a bucket, and the chain – screwed to one of the shed's uprights.

Sally carries Becky over to the sleeping bag and lowers her onto it, which would be a lot easier if she wasn't wriggling and squirming. Growling behind her gag, face still hidden by the pillowcase. Thrashing away on the floor of the shed.

Maybe she'll tire herself out?

Or maybe she'll hurt herself.

Sally grabs her by the shoulders and gives her a shake. 'Stop it! Stop it, please...'

And she does. She *actually* does.

Quick – before she starts up again! Sally wraps the chain's loose end around Becky's chest, just under the armpits, tight enough that she won't be able to get it down over her tummy, and fixes it in place with a padlock.

Good.

Sally stands and puts the sunglasses on again. Makes sure her baseball cap is straight and her hood is up. Then removes the pillowcase from Becky's head, revealing a pair of puffy bloodshot eyes and a bright-pink tear-streaked face.

'Oh my baby...' Sally reaches out to stroke her hair, but she flinches away – growling again. 'Look, I know it's bad. I know. But I'm not going to hurt you, I promise. I...' She lowers herself to the wooden floor, sitting cross-legged in front of Becky. 'I need your help. It's only for a couple of days.'

Becky glowers at her.

'If you promise to be a good girl, I'll untie your legs. Do you promise?'

'Mnnnphgnnnph mmnnn...' She holds up her hands.

'No. Not the hands, the legs. You promise?'

Silence. Then a nod.

'There we go.' Sally undoes the quick-release knot. Tucks the baler twine in her pocket. Sits back again. 'Isn't that a lot more comfortable?'

'Mmmgnnnfff...' Still glowering.

'They took my little boy, Becky. They took him and they sold him to some very bad people.' Sally picks up the teddy bear, squeezing it tight. 'And I know he's still alive, I know it, because people have *seen* him. People have...'

This won't be easy to explain to a five-year-old.

'Becky, they have something called the Livestock Mart: it's like an auction where you can buy and sell people. Children. He's going to be auctioned off again.' She looks down at the teddy bear in her arms. 'I...' Hugs it tighter. 'I'm going to buy my little boy back, but it's not easy. The people who run the auction are ... suspicious of newcomers. If you want to be there you have to prove you're one of them.' Bile stings at the bottom of Sally's throat. She swallows it down. 'You have to have someone to sell.'

Logan pushed into his temporary office.

Rennie was slumped over his computer, nose inches from the screen. Behind him, rain sparked and crackled against the windows – the streetlights turning it into amber fireworks. He looked up and yawned. Stretched. Then a short squeaky trumpet noise sounded from somewhere beneath the desk. His eyes widened. 'Oops.'

Revolting little monster.

'You better not have been saving that up for when I got back.'

Rennie pointed at a collection of evidence bags sitting on one of the other desks. 'Chalmers' stuff. I got everything they took off her at the mortuary. Couldn't find any notebook, though.' He swept an arm out, indicating the cardboard boxes on the other desks. 'DI Bell's stuff. Pick a box, any box.'

'Not tonight, Josephine: time for home. We'll go through his things tomorrow.'

'Cool!' Rennie scrambled to his feet and grabbed his jacket. 'Bright and early though, right? Cos I'm SIO?'

'No. Because one: tomorrow's Sunday. And two: it's a *suicide*. Soon as you sent off your report, that was it. Job's done.'

His bottom lip popped out, trembling. 'But I'm SIO...'

It was like running a nursery some days, it really was.

'Fine. Come in early and draft a press release, if you like. But if you send it *anywhere* before I approve it, I'll have your bollocks for tiny doorstops. Understand?'

Rennie grinned. 'Thanks, Guv.'

'And make sure you remind me to—' Logan's phone burst into the *Addams Family* theme tune and his shoulders slumped. 'Why does God hate me?' But he picked up anyway. 'Sheila. What can I do for you?'

'Inspector McRae, I would request your attendance at the mortuary.

200

It appears we have something that may prove pertinent to the inquiries you make.'

What?

'Why do you sound like something Dickens threw up?' He checked that his computer was switched off. 'You know what, it doesn't matter. I'm heading home, so—'

'Make haste. My mistress has other appointments and a mind to keep them.' And with that, she hung up on him.

Great. Because God forbid Logan McRae should *actually* be able to go home. And no prizes for guessing who Tara would blame for leaving her alone with the kids for however long this was going to take.

Logan groaned. Sagged. Then shooed Rennie away.

'Go. Off with you. Before it's too late to escape.'

Rennie gave him the thumbs up and scarpered.

Lucky sod.

Sheila Dalrymple stood over what was left of Lorna Chalmers. They'd stitched her body closed again, a thick line of puckered flesh and heavy black twine running from beneath both ears, down the neck and out across her collarbones. Another line disappeared under the pale green sheet draped over the remains to cover her modesty. As if that would make up for the post mortem's violation. Skin pale as unsalted butter between the dark red and purple bruises.

But while Dalrymple was still dressed up in her white wellies, blue scrubs, purple nitrile gloves, a green plastic apron, and a hairnet – like Post-Mortem Barbie – Isobel had changed into a dark-grey suit. Very tailored and stylish.

Her hair swept back from her face, high cheekbones, full lips, eyes partially hidden behind narrow steel-framed glasses. The only thing letting the catwalk-model-look down was the pair of mortuary clogs on her feet.

Logan leaned against one of the other cutting tables. 'Well? What was so urgent it—'

'I need you to pay attention.' Isobel clicked her fingers. 'Sheila, if you wouldn't mind?'

Dalrymple gave a weird curtsy / nod thing, then took hold of Chalmers' left arm, raised it straight up and held it there. As if Chalmers was asking to go the bathroom.

'Thank you. Now, Inspector McRae, the crime-scene photographs clearly imply that DS Chalmers committed suicide by hanging herself, do they not?'

'I know. I was there.'

Isobel produced what looked like a pen from her pocket, then pulled it out into a pointer and tapped it against the body's forearm. 'It was your list of antidepressants that made me take another look. Antidepressants, antipsychotics, and alcohol: if you've taken all three of those things, why bother with the rope?'

'Being thorough?' Logan shrugged. 'Or maybe Chalmers hanged herself to punish her husband? It's a bit more dramatic if he has to come in and find her dangling there in the garage.'

'Notice the marks on her wrist and forearm. They're faint, more like the memory of folds pressed into the skin.' The pointer moved. 'The other arm please, Sheila.'

Dalrymple lowered the left with exaggerated care, then walked around the table and raised the right.

'There are matching marks, here ...' indicating Chalmers' wrist, 'and here.' Isobel clacked her pointer in again and turned to Logan. 'If I was a speculating sort of person, which as you know I'm not, I'd be wondering if they were significant.'

OK, no idea.

'And are they?'

'Let's imagine you tie someone's hands behind their back – someone who's struggling to breathe because of the noose around their neck – that leaves very distinct marks. Now imagine you wrap something *else* around them instead.' Isobel mimed doing it. 'Something that doesn't have a single hard line to it. Something large, like a bath sheet, or some foam rubber.'

Logan stared at Chalmers' body. 'Are you saying someone tied her hands behind her back, then *hanged* her?'

'No, I'm saying they *didn't* tie her hands. Because it would have left—'

'Distinctive marks.'

'There are similar marks on her calves and shins too.'

Dalrymple's hand flashed out and grabbed hold of Logan's wrist, squeezing it through his sleeve. Putting some pressure on it.

'Gah!' He flinched, but she held on. Grinning at him like something out of a Hammer House of Horror film.

'See?' She gave it an extra squeeze. 'See how the fabric folds and crumples as I squeeze it? That leaves distinctive marks on the skin.' Dalrymple let go of his wrist and pulled up his sleeve. A network of small white grooves snaked across the red skin, branching and merging – mirroring the wrinkled fabric. Exactly like the ones on Chalmers' arms and legs.

'Oh for Christ's sake... She was *murdered*?'

Isobel pulled the sheet up, covering Chalmers' bruised face. 'The medication and the alcohol would have been enough to make her malleable.'

'Ah-ha!' Dalrymple rubbed her hands. 'But not malleable enough to dangle meekly at the end of a rope, I'll wager. For *that* a means of restraint must be put in place.'

There was silence as Isobel frowned at her. Then, 'What have I told you about speaking like that, Sheila?'

Another strange curtsy / bow thing. 'A thousand apologies, Professor. I shall return to my allotted tasks immediately.' She took hold of a mop and wheely bucket, pushing out of the cutting room on squeaky wheels.

Isobel sighed. 'I suppose it's my own fault for getting her that boxed set of *Ripper Street* as a birthday present. She hasn't even watched the damn thing yet, God knows what she'll be like by tomorrow.'

Logan crossed the ancient brown floor tiles and stood over Chalmers' shrouded body. 'Someone wanted us to think she'd killed herself.'

'That would be a logical conclusion. Unless I'm wrong about the marks on her arms and legs, that is.'

He shook his head. 'When are you *ever* wrong?'

They should be so lucky.

22

Logan knocked on DCI Hardie's door and stood there in the corridor. Waiting.

Actually, you know what? Sod this.

He pushed in without an invite.

Hardie sat behind his desk and a large stack of paperwork. Face flushed and shiny as he wheedled at someone on the phone. '...yes. And all the surrounding streets too. ... Well I don't know, do I?'

He had company – DI Fraser and DS Robertson, the pair of them sitting in the visitors' chairs, Fraser frowning at a clipboard. '...when you've done that: get McHardy and Butler to dig up everything they can on the parents. Facebook, Twitter, the whole social-media circus.' Her shirt-dress thing looked a lot more rumpled than it had that morning. A patch of what might have been dog hair on her lap. 'Maybe someone's threatened them, or maybe *they've* threatened someone? We're looking for motive.'

Robertson nodded. 'Guv.'

Hardie rubbed at his eyes. 'Look, I'm drafting in other patrol cars. ... Yes.'

Robertson picked a pile of papers from Hardie's desk and turned. Jerked to a halt as she clapped eyes on Logan. Forced a smile onto her face and nodded. 'Guv.'

'George.'

She sidled past him and out into the corridor. Footsteps getting quicker as she hurried away.

'Because we're screwed, *that's* why. ... Oh for...' Hardie rubbed at his eyes. 'Just get out there and do what you can.'

DI Fraser gave Logan a grimace. 'It never rains, does it?'

'Something wrong?'

She scowled at her fingernails: long and unpolished, then popped her pinkie-nail in her mouth and gnawed at it, clipping it away. 'Bucketing down. Thunder and lightning.'

Hardie hung up and sagged. Groaned. Rubbed at his eyes again. 'Another little girl's gone missing: Rebecca Oliver, five years old. She was playing in Hazlehead Park, Mum turns her back for two minutes and she's vanished.'

Fraser *thhhpted* the clipped nail out into the palm of her other hand and started in on the next one. 'Monsoon season...'

'No witnesses, no ransom demand. Same as Ellie Morton.'

Logan lowered himself into the chair Robertson had vacated. 'I have some bad news.'

'Noooooo...' Hardie buried his head in his hands. 'Of course you do.'

Tttttpt. Another clipped nail. 'Told you: never rains, but it pours.'

'DS Lorna Chalmers. Professor McAllister thinks she might not have hanged herself after all. She might have been murdered.'

'Murdered?' Hardie peered out from behind his fingers. 'Kim, did he say "murdered"?'

'He said "murdered".' Another nail.

Logan held his hand up. 'Possibly.'

Hardie looked as if he was melting. 'But *murdered*?'

'You might want to put a Major Investigation Team together.'

'Murdered...' He slumped forwards, keeping going till his forehead thumped into the desktop. 'Murdered.' He raised his head an inch, then banged it down again. 'Murdered.' Bang. 'Murdered...'

'Sorry.'

*   *   *

205

Logan parked on his driveway, in front of his skip, in front of his house – at – sodding – last. Then groaned and sagged in his seat for a moment.

According to the dashboard clock, it'd gone ten to nine. And he'd promised Tara he'd be home ASAP what, *two* hours ago? Oh yeah, he was dead. Bloody Roberta Bloody Steel had managed to kill the only good thing that had happened since… No idea. But it was a *long* time ago.

He climbed out, locked the car, and let himself into the house. Clunked the front door shut behind him.

Then froze.

Stared at the hallway walls.

Dinosaurs and pirates and unicorns and zombies snaked across the plasterwork – from about waist-height down – kids' graffiti in lurid shades of crayon and marker pen.

How…? What…?

He draped his Police Scotland fleece over the end of the stairs and stood there, looking up into the gloom of the floor above. 'Hello?'

The only sound oozed out from the living room.

A full-fat American accent with a side-order of cheese: *'Damn it, Poindexter, I'll kick your ass if you touch Clara again!'*

Another professional American, but a bit whinier: *'You don't get it do you, Chuck? I'm not the same nerd you picked on in high school!'*

Logan undid his boots. 'Tara? Sorry I'm late, there's been a murder…'

He scuffed through into the living room.

All the lights were off. The only illumination came from the flickering TV.

An over-muscled blond bloke in a ripped T-shirt grimaced at a classic cliché glasses-and-tank-top nerd with oversized incisors. So that would be vampire schlock horror then. They were obviously meant to be college kids, but the actors playing them had to be in their thirties. The production was a bit ropey too – a dodgy day-for-night shoot outside a doughnut shop where all the colours were wrong.

Tara was slumped on the couch, head back, mouth open,

snoring away. Jasmine had nestled in beside her, doing some snoring of her own.

Only Naomi was still awake, staring at the TV screen with wide eyes and a huge grin on her face. As if this was the best thing in the whole world *ever*.

Nerdy McTanktop gave a terrible fake laugh. *'Bwahahahahahahaaaa! I'm a* vampire *now. A creature of the mother-lovin' night! I'll kick* your *ass!'*

'Get lost, Poindexter! I've got garlic and a crucifix and I'm not afraid to use them!'

Logan crept towards the couch, taking the long way round so he could sneak up behind Naomi. Reached out a hand and put it on her shoulder.

She didn't even flinch. Just sat there, utterly enraptured. 'Vampeeers, Daddy! Vampeers!'

Tanktop did his fake laugh again. *'Garlic and a crucifix? That crap only works in the* movies, *Chuck.'*

'Yeah? Well, lucky I got Betsy here, then, ain't it?' Chuck McMuscles somehow managed to produce a massive chainsaw from thin air. It roared into life.

Logan settled on the arm of the couch. 'Are you sure you should be watching this?'

Naomi squealed with delight, hands covering her mouth, as Chuck turned Poindexter into a collection of very messy body parts.

'Because I think you should be in bed, you bloodthirsty little monster.'

She dragged her eyes away from the screen and blinked up at him, bottom lip trembling. 'Noooo!'

Well … Tara and Jasmine were asleep. And it probably—

Naomi clapped her little hands together, bouncing up and down on the couch.

On screen, Chuck was covered in scarlet and breathing hard. But 'Betsy' was quiet. *'You should've saw that coming, you undead nerd!'*

'Ow...' Poindexter's severed head rolled its eyes and grimaced at him. *'Why didn't I go eat the Chess Club instead?'*

Logan ruffled Naomi's hair. 'You know this'll probably turn you into a serial killer when you grow up, don't you?'

She snuggled into him and grinned at the television.

Becca pushed back against the wall.

It was dark outside, and dark inside too. Dark and full of spiders and stinky smells and stuff that looked like skellingtons hiding in the shadowy bits. And everything tasted like towels.

She struggled her fingers into the gap between her cheek and the gag the Horrid Monster Lady tied around her mouth. Wriggled at it. Pulling left and right. Which was *really* hard with both wrists tied together. But she wasn't giving up, cos it tasted like towels and towels weren't nice to eat, they were horrid.

Something rustle-crunched on the other side of the wall. But it could bugger right off. That's what Daddy always said about Uncle Kevin. *'Christ in a hat, Rebecca, your Uncle Kevin can bugger right off.'* Cos he was a tit.

She strained her chin up, digging and forcing and straining...

The towelly thing came free and she woomphed in a great big breath that tasted of dust and furniture. Coughed a couple of times. Would've spitted too, but the towel had made her mouth all dry.

Another deep breath. 'MUMMY!' Loud as she could. 'MUMMY, I'M IN HERE! HELP!'

The rustly-crunchy thing buggered right off. Scared of *her*.

And so it should be!

'MUMMY! HELP ME!' Becca filled her tummy with air and screeched out a big noisy, 'EEEEEEEEEEEEEEEEEEEEEEEEEEE-EEEEEEEEEEEEEEEEEEEEEEEEEEEEEEEEEEEEEEEEEEEEEEEEEEEEE-EEEEEEEEEEEEEEEEEEEEEEEEEEEEEEEEEEEEEEEEEEEeeee...' until her face was hot and the world went all swimmy.

Outside, something made *'Hoo-hooooooo...'* noises. Like it was laughing.

No one charged in to save her.

So, instead, Becca turned and grabbed the chain the Horrid Monster Lady padlocked under her arms. The other end was screwed into one of the big sticks that held the shed walls together. She dug her trainers into the bit where the stick joined the floor, leaned away from the wall and pulled. And pulled. And pulled...

Then flopped onto the sleeping bag they'd left for her.

Becca sucked in her tummy and tried to get a finger in between the chain and her chest to push it down, but it was too tight and her wrists were tied together and she couldn't get them into the right place and even when she finally managed it she couldn't make the chain move because HER POOPY WRISTS WERE TIED TOGETHER!

'AAAAAAAAAAAAAAAAARGH!'

Stuck. Trapped – in – this – horrible – shed... In the dark. With the spiders.

Becca sniffed. Blinked. Wiped at her eyes with the back of her hand.

No: no crying. No crying allowed.

Big fierce strong girl!

She yanked at the chain again, straining backwards, legs trembling, arms all sore and achy. Pulling and pulling and pulling...

But it was no use. The chain stayed where it was.

Becca sank down onto her sleeping bag.

Stared up at the metal platey thing screwed to the stick.

Sniffed.

No crying...

None.

She wiped her eyes and nose on her sleeve. Glared at the Horrid Monster Lady's stupid teddy bear with its big soppy face. Big floppy ears. Big goofy smile... Maybe he was a prisoner like Becca? Maybe he was scared and frightened, because he was all alone and it was dark and he was only little. He needed someone to look after him and keep him safe and give him a *proper* name, cos 'Mr Bibble-Bobble' was a crap name.

'Don't worry, Orgalorg.' She picked him up in her tied-together hands. Gave him a hug – all fuzzy and squishy. 'I won't let the tits hurt you.'

Becca laid down on her side. The chain around her armpits

209

clinked and rattled as she pulled one half of the sleeping bag over herself, making sure Orgalorg was tucked in too. Breath all jaggy and shaking in her throat.

No crying!

Sally stands at the sink, leaning on the cool stainless steel, staring out of the window. All the lights are off, turning her into nothing but a faint outline in the glass. Tartan nightshirt barely visible. A ghost.

The shed outside is a dark silhouette, one side blurred by the swathe of ivy.

Looking at it makes her chest *ache*.

'I'm so sorry...'

Maybe she should have left Becky with a night light? Or a torch? What if she's afraid of the dark? What if—

'Sally? What are you doing in here with all the lights off?'

She lets her eyes focus on the window again as Raymond's reflection steps up behind her, his naked skin more visible in the glass than she is. Because he's still alive.

'Her name's Rebecca Oliver. Her mother was on the news, Raymond: crying and pleading for her little girl.' Sally huffs out a trembling breath. Wipes her eyes with the palm of her hand. 'Just like I used to do. Standing there with Aiden's photo, *begging* for whoever took him to bring him back safe and sound...'

'You have to stop blaming yourself.' He wraps his arms around her and kisses the skin between her collar and hairline with warm dry lips. 'I know it's horrible, but you didn't have any other choice.'

'But the police—'

'You were careful, remember? No one saw you. And even if they did, they wouldn't recognise you: with the wig and the baseball cap and the hoodie and sunglasses? There aren't any CCTV cameras in the area, no automatic number-plate recognition either. That's why we chose it.' He hugs her. 'No one can connect you with this.'

She looks through his reflection to the shed again. 'She's a little girl.'

'You *had* to do it. They won't let new people into the Livestock Mart without something to sell. It's how they know you're legit.' He takes hold of her shoulders and turns her to face him. Standing there naked in the kitchen, staring at her with those serious grey eyes. The ones that match the two streaks in the swept-back hair at his temples and the stubble on his strong chin. Her knight in shining armour. Only there's nothing shiny about what they're doing. Nothing shiny at all.

Raymond cups her chin and lifts her face to his. Kisses her. 'Listen to me: it'll be OK. We get Aiden back, then we ramp up the reserve price on the girl so high no one will be able to afford to bid for her. We drop her off somewhere safe and call it in anonymously.' A lopsided smile. 'And we come home with Aiden.'

Sally looks away. 'But what if it doesn't work like that? What if someone *can* afford her?'

He sounds so very dependable and reasonable. As if he does this kind of thing every day. 'Then Andy and Danielle follow them home, beat the crap out of the dirty paedo scumbag, and bring the wee girl back. He won't get to lay a finger on her, I swear.' Raymond wraps her up in a hug, his naked skin warm through her nightshirt. 'It'll all be over soon. Trust me.'

— a dish of wasps in aspic —

23

Sunlight barged in through the kitchen window, making the mouldy wallpaper glow, glinting off the toaster and kettle.

Naomi and Jasmine were 'helping'. Which seemed to involve running around the kitchen with plates and tins of ratatouille no one had asked for, while shrieking. Instead of sitting down and eating their breakfast like they'd been told.

Logan poured muesli into a bowl 'You: horrors, put that stuff down and get ready for breakfast.' He slid it across the table where Tara topped it with sliced banana.

The radio played in the background, adding to the general din. '...twenty-one victims in the third mass shooting this week. San Francisco police confirm the gunman was shot dead at the scene...'

He grabbed Naomi as she thundered past. 'Have you washed your hands?'

Jasmine held hers up to be inspected. 'I'm all clean!'

Naomi wriggled. 'All cleeed! All cleeed!'

'Urgh.' Tara poured orange juice into a glass. 'This must be what it's like to work in a lunatic asylum.'

'Looontic! Looontic!'

'...continues for missing five-year-old Rebecca Oliver at Hazlehead Park this morning. We spoke to Detective Chief Inspector Hardie...'

'Sit down, you little monster. Who wants toast?'

The doorbell rang, two long sonorous notes that echoed through from the hallway. Tara put down the juice. 'I'll go.

You ...' she pointed at the disaster, 'deal with this.' Then strode from the room.

DCI Hardie's voice growled out of the radio. '...*want to stress that our number one priority is getting Rebecca home safe and sound.*'

Naomi clambered up onto her chair, singing. 'Toast! Toast! Toast!'

A reporter's voice: '*Is Rebecca's disappearance linked to that of abducted three-year-old Ellie Morton?*'

The Arch Scumbag, Roberta Steel, sauntered into the kitchen, dressed casual in jeans and a jumper. She stopped and frowned at the table. 'What the hell are you feeding my kids? Is that *muesli*? What is this, 1974? Where are the sausages?'

Naomi jumped down from her seat and ran at her, arms wide. 'Mummy!' Grabbing her legs and hugging, staring up at her. 'I seed vampeers! Vampeers!'

Susan appeared in the doorway, perfectly turned out in Laura Ashley's finest. As usual. She thumped Steel on the arm. 'Don't be rude, Robbie. A healthy breakfast never harmed anyone.' Then bent and kissed Naomi's head. 'Hello, teeny horror.'

'Sod healthy – what about bacon. Baked beans. Eggy bread!'

'*...any information, no matter how trivial you think it is – anything at all – call one-oh-one and let us know.*'

'Pfff...' Steel hauled out a chair and slumped into it. Snapped her fingers at Logan. 'Hoy, garçon: coffee. Milk, two sugars. And a decent fry-up! Who do I have to kill to get some black pudding around here?'

Oh joy.

Logan groaned, shook his head, then put the kettle on.

Sunlight breaks through the trees, washing the garden in shades of gold and silver. The wet grass shines, as does the hulking ivy beast slowly eating the smaller of her two remaining sheds. A pair of rabbits sit in the middle of the lawn, nibbling the grass.

Sally stares through the window, mug of tea clutched to her chest, feeling the warmth through her red corduroy shirt. Shame it can't penetrate all the way to her heart.

Red cord shirt, new Markie's jeans, hair brushed, make-up on. Making the effort for Raymond.

He tears another chunk off his croissant and nods at the patio doors. 'Do you want me to go check on her?'

Sally puts her mug down. 'No. No, I'll go. Becky will be hungry.' OK: a bowl from the cupboard and the Coco Pops. She stops on the way past the fridge for the semi-skimmed milk, and heads for the patio doors.

Raymond holds up a hand. 'Aren't you forgetting something?' Then points to the baseball cap, wig, and sunglasses sitting by the toaster. 'Don't want her recognising you.'

Heat blooms in Sally's cheeks. 'No. Sorry. Yes.' She puts on her disguise, slips on her old brown hoodie and pulls up the hood. Slides open the door and steps out into the sunshine.

The rabbits scatter as she picks her way through the wet grass towards the shed, breathing in that heady scent the world has after the rain. Tristan scrabbles at the end of his run, making little yowling noises, wanting out to chase the rabbits. Not that he ever catches any – he's far too big and slow for that, great hairy lug that he is.

Maybe they should take him to Bennachie this afternoon for a walk up Mither Tap? He'll like that. Or out to the beach. Or over to the Bin forest... *Anywhere* but the woods at the back of the house.

A small shudder runs down Sally's spine and she looks away from the greedy trees, tucks the Coco Pops under her arm so she's got a hand free, unlocks the shed door, and steps inside.

Lee adjusted his mask, removed the padlock, slid back the bolt, and stepped into the garage. 'Teddy Bears and Elephants' bounced out of the speakers, jolly and cheery, raising the spirits.

'Go up the stairs, you sleepy bears, it's time to brush your teeth,
Then climb into your cosy beds and snuggle underneath...'

Sobbing came from one of the crates – high pitched and painful. Poor old Lucy Hawkins. She was only three.

Maybe it was time to give the garage another coat of paint? It *was* getting kind of gloomy in here. That might help?

He placed his tray on the workbench and clapped his hands, voice a touch muffled by the mask, but it was safer for everyone this way. What the children didn't *know*, wouldn't get them killed. 'How are we all this morning then, did we sleep well? Did we?'

And right away Lucy stopped sobbing. Good girl.

He took the clingfilm off the sandwiches – well, rolls really – and opened the twelve pack of little water bottles. Humming along with the music as he unbolted Stephen MacGuire's crate.

'Hey, Champ.' Lee undid the gag and handed over one egg mayonnaise with salad. Then one ham, cheese, and coleslaw, and two bottles of water. 'You get those down you.'

He opened the next crate. 'Here you go, Vernon, got to keep your strength up.'

Poor old Vernon. But maybe he'd get lucky this time?

He thumped the crate lid shut again, slid the bolt home, and moved on to the next one. 'Lucy! Who wants lovely sandwiches for breakfast?'

Of course she did, and soon as he had her gag off she was wolfing them down like the tiny trouper she was.

Ellie Morton next.

He opened the crate and Ellie blinked up at him with red-rimmed eyes.

'Good morning, Princess. Egg mayonnaise, your favourite! I even put some cress in there, specially for you.' He smiled at her – not that she could see it, because of the mask, but she'd hear it in his voice and that'd be nice for her. 'You'll be happy to know that *even though* some other kid's gone missing, the police are still looking for you. Yes, they are. Yes, they are!'

Ellie shrank away from him, till her back pressed against the crate's wall. Well, it was all a big change for her. Things would get better when she had a more permanent home. More settled.

He placed the sandwiches and water in her crate.

'Don't worry: I know this Rebecca Oliver's getting a bit of coverage, but you're *still* in all the papers and that makes you worth a lot more money. Isn't that nice?'

He unbuckled Ellie's gag as the song tinkled to an end, then started up again.

'*Teddy bears and elephants went up the stairs to bed,*

They'd had a lovely dinner of tomato soup and bread,'

She snatched up the egg mayonnaise and tore into it, leaving a white smile imprinted on her cheeks as she glowered and chewed.

'That's the spirit. Now you eat them all up. Going to be a big day tomorrow!'

'Good morning, sweetheart, did you sleep well?' Sally squats down in front of her little guest and has a bash at a reassuring smile as she lays the cereal bowl on the wooden floor between them.

Becky's face is grimy with dirt, smeared with dried tears. She sits on top of the sleeping bag, clutching Mr Bibble-Bobble tight. Somehow, she's managed to wriggle out of her gag, but that's OK. She can shout as loud as she likes, the only one who'll hear her is Tristan. And at least her hands are still tied together.

'You like Coco Pops, don't you, Becky? Course you do.' She opens the box and pours a generous portion into the bowl. Then adds milk. 'Everyone likes Coco Pops.' Holding the bowl out as the semi-skimmed darkens. 'Here you go, sweetheart.'

Becky shuffles backwards until she's up against the shed wall, her chain rattling.

'Shhh... It's OK, it's OK. Look,' Sally scoops up a spoonful and swallows it down. 'See? Mmmm, it's *yummy*. Do you want some, Becky? I bet you're really hungry and—'

'RAAAAARGH!' Becky's arms flash forwards, something shiny whipping out at the end of them.

It's the chain, the chain isn't—

The bracket on the end clatters into Sally's temple, sending her sunglasses flying as she crashes sideways against the shed floor. Hot orange noise blares inside her head, followed by an avalanche of gravel and nails. The cereal bowl bounces off the boards beside her, spraying out its brown goop.

'Gnnnn...'

Becky springs to her feet, gathers up the chain, grabs her new teddy, and leaps over Sally – trainers thumping on the shed floor as she lands. 'Only *Daddy* calls me Becky, you stupid tit!' Then the shed door bangs open and she's gone.

Becca slid to a stop on the soggy grass. It was a garden. A big garden, with swings and a slide and things for climbing on. A big hedge with loads of trees on the other side. A big burned thing. A house...

A man inside stared out at her, eyes getting bigger and bigger as his mouth fell open. Surprise, you tit, Super Becca was free!

She tucked Teddy Orgalorg under her arm – not easy with both wrists tied together – and stuck her middle fingers up at the man – like Daddy did every time *Question Time* came on the telly – turned and *ran*.

24

Becca leaped over a big branch, trainers scrunching on the fallen leaves. Running fast as a cat through the gloomy woods. Trees swooshing by on both sides. The chain rattling and clanking in one hand, Orgalorg bouncing along in the other. Ducking under a big spiky bush and out the other side. Arms jiggling in a weird elbows-in way because of the string around her wrists. Legs singing an angry song.

Faster.

Charging through the woods. Grinning. Because she was saving Orgalorg from the Horrid Monster Woman. They were escaping!

Sally staggers out of the shed, clutching her throbbing head, bent almost double. The door frame thumps into her shoulder and she slides down it, sitting with her legs on the wet grass as the world spins.

Tristan goes from little yowling noises to full-throated diaphragm-rattling barks as Raymond slithers to a halt in front of her.

His mouth moves, but nothing comes out.

Blood drips between her fingers, disappearing into the red of her shirt.

Raymond stares. 'What—'

'I'm fine. Go. Go!'

A blink. Then he turns and sprints across the lawn to the

gap in the hedge and stops. Looks left, then right, head cocked to one side as if he's listening for something. Then he darts forward, disappearing into Skemmel Woods.

Sally clutches the door frame and does her best not to be sick.

Becca scrambled around a clump of jaggy green bushes. Jumped over stones. Ducked under a fallen tree. Running and running and running.

She darted around a tree and her trainers skidded in the slippy leaves, but she didn't fall over! She thumped a shoulder into a branch, stayed upright, and kept going. Through the woods.

Looked back over her shoulder, but there was no sign of the Chasing Man.

Maybe he'd given up?

She slowed to a walk. Trees everywhere. All around her.

An old house sat off to the left – tumbled down and broken, its windows just big black holes in the stones. Roof a rusty saggy lump like wet cardboard. Could hide in there... But what if they set the Big Dog on her? What if the Big Dog sniffed her out and then bit her and she'd have to go in the Horrid Monster Lady's shed again and they would chain her up and she'd be all sore from being bitten.

No. No hiding. *Running.*

Becca clutched Orgalorg tighter and ran away again.

A big green splodge of bushes blocked her way, covered in long brown beans that rattled as she fought her way through it – hissing like angry snakes as she wobbled out into a space where there wasn't many trees at all.

They gathered around the outside, like kids waiting for a fight to start in the playground. But inside it was all sunny and bright and warm. The leaves beneath her trainers were orangey and yellow, like jelly and custard. Scrunching and crunching as she walked over to a gurgly stream.

Someone had tied flowers and an old grey teddy bear to a tree on the other side of a little wooden bridge. Its eyes were all scuffed and dull, most of its fur either missing or covered in greeny-black mould. Who would *do* that to a dead teddy bear?

She hugged Orgalorg, pressing his big soppy face against her chest so he couldn't see.

All she had to do was cross the stream, march through the woods on the other side and she'd be free. They were going to make it. They were going to—

Behind her, the bush made its angry-snakes noise again, joined by crashing and snapping.

Becca barely had time to turn before the Chasing Man burst from inside the bush and leaped at her, arms out like the rugby people on the telly.

He thumped into her and Orgalorg went flying as they bashed down into the leaves. Rolling over and over. Only when they stopped, the Chasing Man was on top, pinning her down, face all red and sweaty, teeth bared, breathing hard.

'HELP! MUMMY! HELP ME!' She kicked and she squirmed and she bit, but he held on tight. 'HELP! HELP—'

The Chasing Man slapped his hand across her mouth, but she kept on screaming – even though all that came out were muffled grunts.

'Hold still, you little monster!'

No. Never.

Big fierce strong girl!

She writhed and wriggled and fought as he stood, dragging her with him.

He looked around. Smiled a nasty smile at Orgalorg – lying there in the churned-up leaves and twigs.

'If you don't hold still, I'm going to hurt your teddy bear. You want that? Want me to rip his arms off and poke out his eyes? That what you want?'

No!

Becca went limp.

'Good girl.' He scooped up Orgalorg. 'No more bad behaviour, *or else.*'

The Chasing Man marched her back through the hedge into the garden again, one hand holding onto her dungarees and the other holding the chain. Being all rough and shovey, like a big bully. But she didn't cry.

Becca squeezed Orgalorg to her chest. Cos he was scared. Cos he was only a teddy bear.

The Horrid Monster Woman was sitting in the shed doorway, holding onto her head like it was a broken egg – the side of her face covered in slithery red.

Good.

'Keep moving.' The Chasing Man shoved Becca across the garden till they were right in front of her. 'Are you OK?'

The Horrid Monster Woman looked at them, eyes all puffy and pink, tears and blood on her face. A really good lump growing on the side of her head with an oozy red slash across it.

Becca grinned at her.

Big fierce strong girl!

The Horrid Monster Woman looked away. 'I'm sorry.'

The Chasing Man pushed Becca closer. 'You got something you want to say to the nice lady?'

'My mummy's going to kill *both* of you tits.'

'Gah...' He shoved her into the shed. 'Don't know how you got free, but you're *not* doing it again.'

Ice melts through the tea towel, sending cold dribbles down Sally's face to drip off her chin and onto the kitchen table. Even after two ibuprofen, two aspirin, and a couple of paracetamol, the world thuds and lurches. Like her head is a bass drum and God is stomping on the pedal.

Raymond slides the patio door open and steps in from the garden. Thumps it closed behind him. 'Here.' He flicks a small silver disk onto the table, it bounces and skitters to a halt by the tiny puddle in front of her. 'Five-pence piece. She used it to unscrew the hasp from the wall. I've sunk four bolts through the upright and tightened the living hell out of them. She's going *nowhere.*'

He walks over and peels the ice-filled tea towel from her forehead. Makes a pained face. 'You might need a couple of stitches.'

'I'm fine.'

'No, I really think you need stitches.'

Why does no one ever listen to her?

She tries to hold it in, but it claws out anyway: 'I'm – fine!'

And Raymond flinches, like he's been slapped. Because it always has to be about him, doesn't it? *Men.*

Sally stares at the coin, shiny and glittering as the puddle of meltwater envelopes it. She sighs. 'I'm sorry. Just … don't make a fuss.'

He rubs her back, between the shoulder blades, as if that makes up for everything. 'She's seen our faces.'

'I know.'

Then Raymond presses the towel into her hand and marches out of the room, leaving her alone with the shiny five-pence piece.

It's amazing – Becky's only five years old, according to the morning news bulletins, and she managed to unscrew her chains with *that*. Concrete fills the bottom half of Sally's lungs, dragging her chest down towards the tabletop. A five-year-old, alone and scared. How does this make them any different from the people who took Aiden?

Raymond reappears, carrying a leather satchel. He opens it and pulls out a plastic Ziploc bag. Tips the bag's contents out in a small pile: blue pills, green pills, white pills, some tiny sheets of paper divided up into squares by perforated lines – like miniature postage stamps. Takes one of the mugs from the draining board and fills it with water. Drops two of the green pills into it.

Because no one *ever* listens to her. They always have to know best.

Sally stiffens. 'I told you I'm *fine.*'

'It's not for you.' He sticks a spoon in the mug and stirs. 'It's a little something to help our guest relax and not attack people.' Stirring and stirring and stirring, till the water turns a pale-blue colour.

'Ray, don't hurt her! Please.'

He picks up one of the sheets of mini stamps. 'I'm not hurting

225

her, I'm ... protecting her. She'll wake up and she won't be able to remember any of this. You *want* her to remember this? You want her to have nightmares for the rest of her life?'

'But she's—'

'We're doing this for Aiden, remember? And it's better for *her* this way. Some Rohypnol to forget, a tab of acid so she doesn't get PTSD.'

How are they any better?

Sally's breath thickens in her throat, warmth spreading through her eyes as the kitchen blurs and a tear splashes into the meltwater puddle.

Raymond walks over and strokes Sally's arm. 'Shh... It's OK. We'll bring Aiden home tomorrow, you'll see.' He leans in and kisses her lightly on the non-bloody side of her forehead. 'I promise.'

25

Logan stood in front of the medicine cabinet and popped a couple of Aripiprazole out of their blister pack. The orange tablets snuggled into his cupped palm, like a small child watching a vampire movie. He filled his tumbler from the tap, right up to the brim, and—

Banging on the door, accompanied by Naomi's high-pitched I-want-something squeal: *'Daddy! Daddy! Daddy!'*

'Give Daddy a minute, Little Monster.' He palmed the pills into his mouth, washing them down with every drop of water in the tumbler.

'Help! I needs to make wee-wee!'

He closed the medicine cabinet – his reflection grimaced back at him. 'Oh joy.'

Susan, Steel, and Tara stood at the open patio doors, nursing mugs of coffee while Naomi and Jasmine played catch-the-leaf with Cthulhu in the garden. Jumping and pouncing between the puddles.

Logan tucked his Police Scotland black T-shirt into his Police Scotland itchy black trousers and joined the coffee drinkers. 'At least it's stopped raining.'

Susan wrapped an arm around Steel. 'You know what we should do today? We should go to the park. Big family picnic. That'll be nice, won't it?'

'Oh aye?' Steel looked at her. 'With all those kids being snatched?'

'Well, how about the beach then?'

Logan straightened his epaulettes. 'Actually, I can't. Got to go hand over the Chalmers investigation. Now it's a murder.'

'Ooh...' Steel turned. '*Murder*?'

'Someone's going to have to run an MIT and we all know it won't be me.' Epaulettes straightened, he tapped Tara on the shoulder. 'Do you want a lift, because you've got that thing, don't you?'

She frowned at him. 'Thing?'

He nodded at Naomi and Jasmine, shrieking their way around the garden.

'Oh, *that* thing! Yes. Definitely. I'll grab my coat.'

And they were off – hurrying through the living room and out into the hallway. Struggling into their jackets as Steel finally realised what was going on.

'Hey! Wait a minute!'

Logan zipped up his fleece, voice an urgent whisper. 'Quick, quick!'

Steel burst into the hall as they made for the door. 'Wait, who's—'

'Bye!' He bustled Tara outside, making for the car. 'Lock the door behind you, and that litter tray needs cleaning!'

'But...'

Logan thumped the front door shut. 'Run!'

They scrambled into the Audi, he cranked the key in the ignition and pulled out of the driveway while Tara was still fastening her seatbelt.

And: escape!

Logan pulled up outside an imposing block of modern flats on Riverside Drive. The kind of place that looked as if it'd been modelled on GCHQ. Still, the top-floor flats must have had a great view of Craiginches prison, till they closed it. Bulldozed it. And turned it into yet more flats.

Tara opened the passenger door and climbed out. Walked around to the driver's side.

He buzzed down his window. 'Sorry about that. I really didn't … you know.'

'Pfff…' A shake of the head. 'Yeah, well, maybe it wasn't *exactly* the fifth circle of hell.' Though she didn't look convinced.

'The kids aren't that bad when you get to know them.'

Still didn't look convinced.

'OK, maybe they are, but it's like drinking really cheap wine. The first couple of glasses kill your taste buds and after that you're too numb to care.'

She sighed, then leaned in through the open window and kissed him. Smiled. 'You're a terrible boyfriend.'

'I know, I know.'

Tara turned and strutted towards the flats, putting a bit of hip into it. 'You can spend the rest of the day trying to think how to make it up to me!'

Logan grinned and drove off.

Logan tucked the case folder under his arm and raised a fist to knock on DCI Hardie's office door. Stopped, knuckles inches from the wood, as a voice bellowed out:

'FOR GOD'S SAKE, GEORGE, JUST DO WHAT YOU'RE BLOODY TOLD FOR ONCE!'

The door jerked open and Logan jumped clear as DS Robertson burst into the corridor.

Hardie was visible in the gap between her and the door frame – sitting at his desk with his head in his hands while DS Scott tried to hand him a form.

DS Scott stuck it on the desk instead. 'I'm going to need you to sign—'

'AAAAAAAAAAAAAAAAAAAAAARGH!'

Robertson closed the door behind her, shutting him off. Then leaned back against it, grimacing at Logan. 'I gave up my Sunday for this.'

'Now not a good time?'

'A good time?' She pulled her chin in, lip curled, as if Logan had suggested battering puppies to death with a hammer. 'It's

229

like being trapped on the waltzers with an angry badger. I'd leave it at least an hour, if I was you.'

Fair enough.

What most people don't realise is that it's not the grief or even the shock that gets you when you lose someone. Maybe, if it's natural causes, but not when it's murder.

Yes, those things are there, but what really gets you, what really consumes your soul is *anger*. Rage. Hatred for the person who did that, not just to your husband or your loved one (the one they killed), but to you and everyone in your family. To everyone who ever knew the happy, funny, sweet, lovely man you married before some animal murdered—

The office door thumped open and Logan looked up from *Cold Blood and Dark Granite*.

It was Rennie, returned with the spoils of his important mission: two mugs of coffee. He had something tucked under one arm, making him all lopsided as he pushed the door shut again. 'You're not *still* reading that, are you?'

'Hmmm...'

you married before some animal murdered them.

Because murder isn't something that happens to one person in isolation, it happens to everyone they've ever met. Kenneth didn't just *die*, he was *taken* from us. From me, his wife, from his mother and father, from his brother and his nephews, from his friends at work. From his son.

Rennie thunked a mug down on Logan's desk. 'Nightshift CID think they're clever, but you've got to stay up pretty late to get one over on Detective Sergeant Simon Rennie. Ta-da!' He dug into his armpit and produced a packet of custard creams. 'Hidden inside a half-empty box of past-its-sell-by-date bran flakes. As if I wasn't going to look in there.'

'Hmmmm...'

Like a bomb going off in a crowded supermarket, a murder might 'only' kill one person, but it injures everyone around it. And some of them will never recover.

Logan turned the page and there were the photographs again. The happy family snaps before the bomb went off.

Rennie sighed. 'Don't know why I bother.' He thumped into his seat and ripped open the biscuits. 'Have you approved my press release yet?'

Kenneth MacAuley, standing at the family barbecue – in the back garden at Skemmelsbrae Croft, going by the playset and the sheds behind him – cooking sausages and chicken. Shorts and a Pink Floyd T-shirt. Sunglasses perched on top of his head. Eyes squinted against the smoke. A smile on his face as he toasts the photographer with his free hand and a bottle of Beck's, big fancy watch dangling from his wrist. Massive Newfoundland Monster Dog in the background...

'Hello? Press release?'

Logan *stared*.

It'd been right there, all along.

'Earth to Inspector McRae, are you receiving me? Over.'

He grabbed his desk phone and dialled the custody suite.

'Downie.'

'Jeff? It's Logan. Crowbar Craig Simpson – have you still got his property?'

'For my sins. He's been a complete pain in the ring all morning. "My tea's too cold." "My porridge's too hot." "My—"'

'I'll be right down.'

Sergeant Downie tipped the contents of a brown paper bag into a blue plastic tray. Spread it out, then held up the chunky silver watch Crowbar was wearing when they arrested him. 'One rip-off Rolex.'

Logan took it – holding it next to the photo of Kenneth MacAuley at the barbecue. That arm raised in salute. The big fancy watch hanging off of it.

The two watches were identical. Which was either a *massive* coincidence or...

He turned the watch over. The words, 'To K From S With LOADS Of Love' were engraved on the back. Bingo. 'Stick Crowbar in an interview room.'

Downie puffed out a breath. 'You got any idea how long it'll take to get a duty solicitor down here on a *Sunday*?'

'Then you'd better get cracking, hadn't you?'

Logan stopped outside Hardie's office. Again. This time the door was open and no one was shouting. Which was nice.

The place was a bit crowded though: Hardie behind his desk, DS Scott on the phone, DS Robertson changing things on a whiteboard, DI Fraser on one of the visitors' chairs – in a green shirt-dress today – frowning at printouts of something as DS Becky McKenzie handed them to her. DI Porter had the other chair, playing with the mole on her cheek while she scrolled through something on an iPad. Everyone talking over everyone else.

DS Scott pinned the phone between his ear and shoulder, then checked some paperwork. 'Yes. ... OK, no. ... No, put the POLSA on, OK? ... Look, put her on, please.'

DS McKenzie handed Fraser another sheet. 'And that's the third death threat since Friday...'

Fraser shook her head and sighed. 'What is wrong with people?'

Porter looked up from her screen and grimaced at Hardie. 'I honestly don't see how we can do more without at least another dozen uniform.'

He grunted. 'Where am I supposed to get twelve officers from? We're stretched razor-thin as it is.'

'Well go find her then!' DS Scott thumped his paperwork down on Hardie's desk. 'God's sake, Constable Guthrie, it's not University Bloody Challenge!'

Logan knocked on the door frame.

Hardie gave another grunt. 'Where the hell have you been?'

'I came by earlier, you were busy. Who do you want me to

232

hand the Chalmers investigation over to? Oh, and I *might* have a lead on the Kenneth MacAuley murder, if you've got someone free?'

McKenzie handed Fraser another sheet of paper. 'This one's a threat to rape. There's six of those.'

Hardie sagged. 'Do you know how much crap I've got on my plate right now?'

Fraser handed it back. 'What about the usernames?'

'No one's using their real names. It's all MummyLover1962 and SlipsterDavie stuff.'

'Tell you what,' Hardie held up his hand, 'let's count them, shall we?' Ticking the fingers off one by one: 'Search for Ellie Morton. Search for Rebecca Oliver. Murder inquiry into DI Bell's stabbing. Murder inquiry into whoever it was Bell killed two years ago. *Chalmers'* murder.'

DI Fraser nodded. 'OK: get onto Twitter and find out who they really are. They must have IP addresses, *something*.'

'Not to mention a huge drugs bust I can't postpone, because it's been set up for weeks.'

DS Scott settled his bum on the edge of Hardie's desk, still working the phone. 'Stringer? ... Stringer, it's Charles Scott. ... Yeah. ... Yeah, look: I need you to widen your search. ... Yeah, it—'

Hardie slammed his hand down on the desk, making the pen holder rattle. 'Can everyone just *shut up* for thirty sodding seconds?' Silence. Everyone stared at him, sitting there, looking as if his head was about to go *boom*. 'Can't hear myself *think*.'

Someone appeared at Logan's shoulder, peering in from the corridor, dressed in full Police Scotland black with combat trousers and matching riot accessories. Sergeant Rob Mitchell, so big he had to stoop to look through the door, arms thick with muscle and corded with sinew. A wee smile as he waved at Hardie. 'Sorry to interrupt, Boss, but we're going to have to get the briefing underway or we'll lose the dog team.'

Hardie covered his face with his hands and screamed.

26

Hardie hauled open the door, revealing a tiny galley kitchen off the MIT office and a uniformed officer in the middle of doing a little dance. Short, with a Lego-style black bob. Bopping and shimmying away with her back to them, earbuds in as the kettle boiled.

PC Dunn did a Michael-Jackson-style spin and froze, one hand clutching the crotch of her trousers. She yanked out her earbuds. 'Chief Inspector. I was... It's not what—'

'Give us a minute, will you, Stacey?' Hardie hooked a thumb over his shoulder.

'Yes. Sorry.' She glanced at the six mugs lined up in front of the kettle. 'I can... Yup.'

Hardie had to shuffle out of the way to let her squeeze past. Then stepped inside. 'Inspector?'

Logan joined him and closed the door. 'Are you OK?'

The two of them pretty much filled the place.

'It's like trying to juggle jelly, broken bottles, and hand grenades all at the same time.' He slumped against the sink, pointing towards his office. 'How am I supposed to organise everything if they won't leave me alone for five minutes?'

The kettle clicked and Hardie started filling PC Dunn's mugs. 'Officially, Superintendent Young is SIO on the Chalmers murder. Dead police officer, so it had to be someone senior. Which means *I* have to run the actual investigation. Which

234

means DI Jackson should have been in charge of operational matters. Which means…?' Letting it hang there.

'Wait: "should have been"?'

Hardie put the kettle down. 'Jackson's son was hit by a car this morning. He's only five.'

Oh no… 'Is he…?'

'Touch and go. And I can't get anyone to fill in for Jackson till Monday morning at the earliest. Maybe Tuesday.' Hardie gave Logan a pained smile, then raised his eyebrows. 'So…?'

Logan pulled in his chin. 'Why are you looking at me like… No.'

'There's no one else.'

'I'm *Professional Standards*, we don't do murder investigations. That's not what we do!'

'It's only for *one* day. One. Two tops. Set things up, get them running.'

'We investigate dodgy police officers. Nothing else.'

Hardie shrugged. 'You were investigating Chalmers anyway.'

'It's not the same thing!'

'And I've spoken to Superintendent Doig: he's happy for you to take the reins. Chalmers was a *police officer*, Logan. We can't stick her murder in a drawer and forget about it.'

Argh… He was right. Chalmers deserved more than that.

'Fine. What about my lead on the Kenneth MacAuley case?'

'I can repeat everything I've just said, if you like?'

'Gah…' Logan scrubbed his face with his hands. 'But I get minions! And *real* ones this time, not like the fake ones I was promised for looking into DI Bell's not-suicide.'

'Done.' Hardie stuck his hand out for shaking. 'You can have … how about DS Steel and PC Quirrel? They worked with Chalmers on the Ellie Morton case, so they should be *some* help. I'll get George to call the pair of them in.'

Terrific. Wonderful. Absolutely great.

Logan grimaced. 'Oh yeah, Steel's going to *love* that.'

The phone rang and rang and rang. Logan shifted it to his other ear and went back to marking Lorna Chalmers' last known movements on the whiteboard. And still the phone—

A thin, wobbly voice replaced the ringing. *'Hello?'*

'Dr Frampton? Hi, it's Logan. Any joy with the soil analysis on those shoes yet?'

'Shoes…? Urgh… Give me a chance – I was up drinking cocktails till one this morning. Head feels like it's packed full of fragmented schist with calcareous inclusions.'

'I'm sorry to be a nag, but it's a murder investigation now and the victim was a police officer. So…?'

The sound of rushing water burst out for a couple of seconds, followed by a couple of *plink*s and a hissing fizz.

'Dr Frampton? You still there?'

'Can't a woman enjoy her Alka-Seltzer in peace?'

'Only we're—'

'I know, I know. Pfff… Give me half an hour and I'll drag myself to the lab.'

'Thanks. I appreciate it.'

A thunk. Then, *'I really do feel like schist…'*

Logan left her to her hangover.

Rennie dunted the office door open and lurched inside, only his legs visible – the rest of him hidden by the stack of file boxes. 'Little help!'

Logan put Lorna Chalmers' service history down, hurried over and plucked the top two boxes off the pile, revealing a shiny-pink face with sticky-up blond hair.

'Argh… These weigh a ton!' Rennie staggered to the nearest desk and dumped the rest of the boxes, bent double and grabbed his knees. Puffed and panted for a bit. 'And … and Downie says … says that Crowbar … has seen … his solicitor. Urgh…' He straightened up and rubbed the small of his back. 'Think I pulled something.'

Logan lowered the other two boxes onto the desk. 'They ready?'

Rennie nodded at the pile. 'Every case Chalmers worked on in the last two and a half years. Records are still trying to dig out the six months before that.'

'Rennie, *focus*. Are they ready?'

'Waiting for you in Interview Two, but Downie says you're not to get it all messy this time.'

'And Crowbar doesn't know what we're after?'

'Thinks we want more dirt on Fred Marshall.' Rennie grinned. 'Thought we'd leave the victim's watch as a nice surprise.'

Crowbar slouched on the other side of the interview room table, arms folded, a sneer twisting his handlebar moustache. A tiny old man sat next to him in a shiny grey suit and grubby glasses. One hand trembling as he fiddled with a biro. Rennie had his pen out too, poised over his notepad, ready to strike.

Logan sat forward. 'Well?'

Crowbar shrugged. 'Nah. Like I was saying to Winston here, it's a total witch-hunt, yeah?'

'Actually,' the little man raised a shaky finger, 'it's Albert. Not Winston.'

'Whatever.' Crowbar lounged back in his seat. 'They *fishing*, Winston. They got nothing.'

Rennie put down his pen and picked up an evidence bag. 'We've got this?' He dipped inside and came out with the fancy watch. 'Recognise it, Craig?'

'I...' Blinking at it. The tip of his tongue snaked across his top lip. 'It's a watch.'

'You told Sergeant Downie it was a "knock-off", remember that?'

'Never seen it before in my life.'

'Really?' Logan pulled out his copy of *Cold Blood and Dark Granite* and laid it on the table. Opened it at the Post-it note acting as a bookmark, revealing the photo of Kenneth MacAuley burning sausages and chicken on the barbecue. 'Because *I* have.'

Crowbar jerked his chin up. 'Yeah, so?'

'Your statement to DS Savage claims Fred Marshall told you he'd murdered Kenneth MacAuley and abducted Aiden. And yet, here you are wearing Kenneth MacAuley's watch.'

The only sound was the wind, growling against the window.

Crowbar licked his lip again.

His solicitor tutted. 'Ah. Now, I'm sure there's a perfectly good reason for that. Isn't there, *Craig*?'

'Yeah, there's … gotta be lots of watches, you know, *exactly* like it. Isn't there? Heaps of them.'

Logan took the watch from Rennie, turning it over to show the back. 'Only *this* one is engraved, "To K from S, with *loads* of love".'

'Winston, you going to say something here, or what?'

Albert didn't.

'Fred Marshall didn't kill Kenneth MacAuley, did he, Craig?'

'I wanna…' Crowbar cleared his throat. 'No comment.'

'All that talk about how Kenneth's brains looked when they were pounded out with a rock. All those little details you told us. It wasn't Fred, it was you. *You* killed him.'

'No comment!'

'It wasn't Fred who was offered two thousand pounds for Aiden MacAuley, it was you. Wasn't it?'

He grabbed his solicitor's arm. 'Come on, Mr Wolfe, say something!'

A slow smile spread across Albert's lips. 'I've been practising law in Aberdeen since before you were born, Craig, and I always find "no comment" the best option.'

'Here's how this is going to work. You're going up before the Sheriff on Monday for the two outstanding warrants, breaching your parole conditions, resisting arrest, and assaulting a police officer, so—'

'You promised! You said if I told you about Fred, you'd drop the charges.'

'Yes, but you *lied* to me, Craig. You sat there and lied to my face. Fred didn't kill Kenneth MacAuley, you did. And then you fitted him up so you could move in on his wife.'

'It wasn't… I…' Big pleading eyes.

Albert took off his glasses and polished them on a hanky. Taking his time. 'I think it might be wise to pause at this point so I can confer with my client for a wee bittie. If that's all right with you?'

There was a shock.

* * *

'Course, in the good old days, you could've beaten a confession out of him.' Rennie rocked on the balls of his feet, staring at the closed interview room door.

Logan leaned against the corridor wall. 'I'm going to pretend you didn't say that.'

Crowbar was having some sort of argument with his solicitor in Interview Two, their voices too muffled to make anything out. The tone was clear enough, though.

Rennie raised his eyebrows. 'You sure we can't lug-in at the door?'

'You do remember we're Professional Standards, don't you? Professional Standards? The people who make sure everyone follows the rules?'

'Was only asking.'

'And if you think you're getting to join us full time, you're going to have to start acting the part.'

Rennie pulled on a lopsided smile and a Yoda voice. 'Come over to the Dark Side, you must. Penguin biscuits, we have.'

Inside, the argument murmured to an end. There was a thump, then the interview room door swung open and Albert poked his head out. 'Sorry to keep you waiting. Shall we have another shottie?'

Crowbar Craig shifted in his seat. Looked at his solicitor. 'I...?'

An indulgent fatherly smile. 'It's all right, Craig, do it like we practised.'

Deep breath. 'The watch in question was a gift from Fred Marshall.' He sounded about as natural as a pornstar's breasts. 'Fred said it was a knock-off Rolex he'd found at a flea market in Amsterdam. I had...' Crowbar's face puckered as the words dried up, as if he'd just sat on an unlubricated lemon. 'I had...'

Albert nudged him. 'No idea.'

'Yeah, I had *no idea* that Freddy was lying about the watch's ... providence.'

'He means "provenance", but you get the idea. The watch was a gift. He didn't kill anyone.' Albert polished his glasses again. 'Now, unless you can prove *otherwise*, I think we're done here. Don't you?'

Logan poked the tabletop. 'Someone paid you two thousand pounds to kill a man and abduct a child, Craig, and I want to know who!'

'My client isn't prepared to answer any further questions unless you have evidence of wrongdoing, Inspector.' A smile and a shrug. 'Without it, this is all supposition.'

Of course it was. But that didn't mean Crowbar Craig Simpson couldn't do the decent thing, save them all a heap of work, and admit he'd done it.

Logan stared at him.

And stared.

And stared.

Crowbar sat there, like an Easter Island head with ridiculous facial hair.

Fine.

At least they'd tried.

But this wasn't the end of it. Somewhere, out there, was evidence linking Crowbar Craig Simpson to Kenneth MacAuley's murder. And when that evidence surfaced, the vicious little sod was going to spend the rest of his life in a small grey cell.

Logan thumped Rennie on the arm. 'Call it.'

'Interview terminated at eleven fifty-two.' Rennie clicked off the recording equipment.

And as soon as he did, Crowbar scooted forward in his seat. 'They'll kill me! I tell you anything and they'll – *kill* – me.'

Albert shook his head. 'I advised against this, Craig.'

Now this was more like it. Logan put on his sympathetic voice. Tried not to smile. 'Who'll kill you, Craig?'

'You gotta get us protection, right? Me and Irene and Jaime and Tyrion?'

'Protect you from who?'

'Cos I'm saying *nothing* till I get a new identity somewhere … somewhere warm, like, I dunno, Sydney or something.'

Aye, right.

Logan sat back again. 'We're not allowed to export our

240

criminals to Australia any more, Craig. They're a lot more picky these days.'

'Well … *Spain* then, or Italy. Somewhere they'll never find us.'

'*Who*? Where *who* will never find you?'

Had to hand it to him – if this was an act, he was teetering into Tom Hanks territory.

Crowbar shook his head. 'Nah. Not till the four of us is protected. Till then I'm saying sod-all.'

27

Logan knocked on Hardie's door and slipped inside.

He was behind his desk again, forehead resting on a stack of reports, hands wrapped over the top. As if he was trying to physically shove his whole head through the thing and out the other side.

DI Fraser looked up from her iPad and grimaced at Logan. 'Please tell me you've got some good news?'

'I think we *might* be able to prove that Crowbar Craig Simpson killed Kenneth MacAuley and abducted Aiden MacAuley.'

Hardie raised his head, face breaking out into a smile. 'That's great!'

'Only trouble is, he's claiming it was on the orders of a third party, and he won't talk unless we guarantee safety and new identities for him, Fred Marshall's wife, their kid, and an exceptionally ugly miniature sausage dog called "Tyrion".'

Hardie banged his head back down. 'Arrrgh... How the hell am I supposed to swing that?'

Fraser shrugged. 'Well, I suppose it's worth a try?'

'Arrrrrgh...'

'Yeah.' Logan sucked a breath in through his teeth. 'Assuming Simpson isn't lying about the whole thing to get away with murder.'

Hardie raised his forehead four inches off the desk ... then thumped it into the reports again. 'Arrrrrgh!' *Thump*. 'Arrrrrgh!' *Thump*. 'Arrrrrgh!' *Thump*.

Fraser puffed out her cheeks. Put her iPad down, raised her eyebrows at Logan, then nodded at the door.

Fair enough.

The pair of them stepped out into the corridor, Fraser easing the door shut behind her. Keeping her voice down. 'Look, leave it with me, OK? I'll see what I can do with DCI NRC.'

'NRC?'

'Not Really Coping.' She shook her head. 'It's Sunday. All I wanted was a lie in, a nice spag bol for lunch, bucketful of gin and slimline, and *Armageddon* on the telly. Instead of which I'm stuck here trying to stop our beloved leader from having an aneurysm.' Fraser ran a hand through her hair – the nails she'd bitten down were all filed to perfect crescents again, painted the same green as her dress. 'He's like an unexploded zit. One good squeeze and his head will go *pop*! Gunk and yuck everywhere.'

'Kim?'

'Yes, Logan?'

'Never take up poetry.'

She smiled. 'We'll do our best to organise some sort of protection for Simpson and his hangers-on, but don't get your hopes up. It's incredibly difficult to get new identities authorised. If it's not major drugs, organised crime, or terrorism-related, they're not usually interested.'

'Assuming—'

'Assuming Crowbar's not just a lying scumbag.' Fraser sighed. 'Which we both know he is.'

Wullie sounded as if he were calling from Mongolia on a tin can at the end of a bit of string, rather than sitting in Bucksburn station. *'Aye, that's it set up for you now: one HOLMES instance. I'll email you the login details.'*

'That's great, thanks, Wullie.' Logan hung up and ticked the word 'HOLMES' off on the whiteboard.

The office door thumped open and Rennie lurched in, carrying another pair of large boxes. 'They found the missing six months of case files. And look who *I* found!'

Steel appeared in the doorway, face like someone had suggested a threeway with Donald Trump and Kim Jong-un. She hurled her coat at an empty desk. 'Let's get one thing crystal clear, OK? I was on a day off. We were going to buy a new sofa. After which I was planning on watching last night's *Strictly*, getting fruity on prosecco, and rolling around naked with my wife on it.'

Urgh...

Logan shuddered. 'There's an image.'

Rennie added his boxes to the pile. 'So that's us now got every case DS Chalmers worked on in the last three years.'

'Two:' Steel held up both fingers, 'I am no' your sodding sidekick. Understand?'

'You want me to start going through the files, Guv?'

Logan opened the nearest box, pulled out about half a dozen folders and dumped them into Rennie's arms. 'Pass them round: most recent files first. Maybe someone in here decided to get revenge and kill her.'

'Three:' two fingers on one hand, one on the other, 'I'm not driving you about like a bloody chauffeur.'

The office door bumped open again and in swanned Tufty – dressed in jeans and an original-series *Star Trek* T-shirt. 'Morning fellow travellers on the highway to justice!'

Steel gave him the benefit of her three fingers. 'Oh, shut your twit-hole.'

Logan clapped his hands. 'Right, listen up, people. We are *nowhere* near enough bodies for a Major Investigation Team, but for the next two days we're all we've got.'

Tufty settled into an office chair and pulled out his notebook and pen. Keen.

Steel sniffed. 'We'd better be getting overtime for this.'

'Detective Sergeant Lorna Chalmers was found hanged in her garage, yesterday morning.' Logan picked up a sheaf of paper. 'She'd been seriously assaulted at least twice on Friday. Preliminary forensic report says she was stuffed full of alcohol and probably antidepressants too. Marks on her arms and legs look like they were caused by someone restraining her while she died.'

Tufty put his hand up. 'What about the husband?'

'Brian Chalmers has no previous, but he was planning on leaving his wife the day after her birthday. Claims he didn't see her suicide-note text till the next morning, then went downstairs and found her. I want him brought in and questioned.'

A grin. 'I'll grill him like sausages!'

'No you won't. Rennie will.'

Rennie nodded. 'I went on a course.'

'Tufty: you're going over to Chalmers' house and looking for her mobile phone.'

'No sausages?'

'No sausages. She texted her alleged "suicide" note at ten thirty on Friday night, so where's her phone?'

Rennie perched on the edge of his desk. 'Maybe she sent the message from somewhere else first, *then* went home and killed herself?'

Steel threw a whiteboard marker at him. 'Well it's no' like she could've sent it *afterwards*, is it?'

Honestly, it was like being in charge of a kindergarten, full of delinquent drunken monkeys.

Logan pointed at Tufty. 'Go through her bins, search the garage, kitchen, bathrooms, car. It has to be somewhere.' Then pointed at Steel. 'You worked with her on the Ellie Morton case.'

'Oh aye?'

'Chalmers was very cagey about who assaulted her, but she said she'd recently interviewed the stepfather. I want to talk to him.'

Steel crossed her arms. 'Russell Morton? Can't drag him in: press would have a field day.'

'Then we go to him.'

Steel gripped the steering wheel, as if she was trying to murder it. 'You're a rotten, scum-filled, pus-faced—'

'Privilege of rank.' Logan stretched out in the passenger seat. 'That's what you used to tell me when I had to ferry *you* all over the place.'

245

Outside the pool car's windows, playing fields drifted by on the left. And on the right: Aberdeen University's contribution to brutalist architecture, AKA: the Zoology Building. A narrow-windowed block of crenellated concrete stuck on top of what looked like a double-storey car park.

Steel gave the steering wheel an extra murder. 'That's no' the point!'

'Yes it is. Tell me about Russell Morton.'

'I won't be a detective sergeant forever. I'll get promoted to DCI again, and see when I do? *Revenge!*'

Logan smiled at her. 'And until then, you're my sidekick.'

The playing fields gave way to communist-style tenements, arranged in squares.

'I'm no' your sodding sidekick!'

'And I shall call you "Binky" and if you're a good little side-kick you shall have a sweetie.'

The muscles bunched and pulsed in her jaw.

Trees reached up on either side of the road now, naked branches dancing in the wind, a cluster of tiny wee houses jammed in behind them.

She jerked the car into a left turn, opposite a development of pink-and-white flats. 'You're enjoying this *far* too much, you know that don't you? Gloating turdmagnet.'

'Now: Russell Morton.'

She rolled her eyes, driving deeper into Tillydrone. More terraced housing – painted in slightly different shades, as if that would disguise how ugly they were. Terraces. Small blocks. More terraces. 'Russell Morton is the kind of guy who's never earned an honest bob in his life. Benefits, gambling, and a bit of B-and-E. Closest he's come to a proper job was growing cannabis in a polytunnel up Mintlaw way.'

'Violent?'

'Officially? Couple of drunken assaults, other side dropped the charges both times.'

A squat tower block loomed in the distance in shades of grey and brown. Windows glinting in the sunlight. Glowing like a burning brick.

246

'And unofficially?'

Steel shrugged. 'Him and Ellie's mum have been knocking lumps off each other for years. Serious lumps as well: I'm talking the odd week in hospital for both of them.'

'What about Ellie?'

'Battering *her*, you mean? If they are, no one's noticed it.'

The pool car turned into a parking area between two rows of tenement flats. Six flats to a communal door. Bland and a bit shabby. Someone had tried the different-coloured-paint trick here as well. It hadn't worked.

A handful of fancy four-by-fours sat outside one of the communal front doors, all occupied. Conspicuous amongst the hatchbacks and rusty white vans.

'Aye, aye.' She parked a few doors down. 'Our mates from the press are still hanging about, then.'

Logan undid his seatbelt. 'And if we're *really* lucky, we won't have to talk to any of them...'

The living room was crowded with furniture – more than it could really cope with – two floral sofas and a pair of matching armchairs almost filled the space between a pair of sideboards, a Welsh dresser, and a TV unit topped by a massive set. Every single flat surface covered in floral tributes, cards, and teddy bears.

Not bad going for a two-bedroom flat. Even if there was barely enough space to squeeze sideways through the gaps.

Russell Morton had the armchair with its back to the window, the light framing him as if the chair was a throne and he was King of Laura Ashley Land. Tall and thin. Long fingers. Shoulder-length brown hair and mid-cheek sideburns. A polo shirt and paint-spattered jeans.

He curled his lip at them. 'So how come you've not found our Ellie yet?'

The sound of someone singing along to a boiling kettle rattled through the open door to the kitchen.

Steel slouched on one of the couches, knees akimbo. She smiled at Logan. 'I think you should answer that one. Seeing as I'm just the sidekick.'

Logan eased himself into the space in front of the TV. 'You spoke to one of our colleagues a few days ago: Detective Sergeant Chalmers.'

The lip curled some more. 'She that frizzy-haired bint? Bit rough around the edges, but still kinda doable if you've had a couple of pints?'

Steel nodded. 'That's the one.'

'Yeah, I spoke to her.' Russell Morton shook his head. 'Bitch wanted to know where I was when Ellie got snatched, didn't she?' Pause. 'Cos I was with me *mates*.'

Of course he was.

'You were flashing cash about that night, weren't you Russell? Bought pizza for everyone and gave the delivery man a big tip.'

A shrug. 'I'm a nice guy.'

'Oh aye.' Steel nodded. 'A veritable *prince* among men.'

'I got a bit of cash in my pocket, why not splash it about? Spread the happy, yeah?'

Logan checked his notebook. OK, so there was nothing actually written there, but Morton didn't know that. As far as he was concerned Logan *knew* things. 'Where were you this Friday, Russell?'

'Pfff... About. You know, helping search for Ellie and that. Cos she's missing.'

'What about Friday night?'

He spread his hands, indicating his floral-print domain. 'Back here, with Katie. Poor cow's broken up about Ellie, isn't she? Cos you lot can't get your finger out long enough to *find* her.'

'Where did you get the money from, Russell?'

'But you're doing sod-all aren't you? Too busy harassing me.'

The singing someone emerged from the kitchen with a mug in each hand. Angela Parks, from yesterday's media scrum outside Mrs Bell's house – the thin androgynous one. She had the same suit on, her shirt looking worn and unwashed. She shuffled her way through the upholstered obstacle course and offered one of the mugs to Russell Morton. 'Milk and three.'

He took it without a word of thanks. As if it was his due.

Sipped at it, staring at Logan. 'You want to know where I got the cash?'

'Cash?' Angela Parks turned. 'What cash?'

'Got it on a scratcher, didn't I? *Three* grand. Sweet as hell, like.'

She stuck her free hand towards Logan for shaking. 'Angela Parks, *Scottish Daily Post*. Why are you asking him about cash?'

Morton jerked his chin up. 'None of anyone's business, though, is it?' He jabbed a finger at Angela. 'And you don't print a word about it, right? Katie doesn't know and it's *staying* that way or you can kiss your exclusive ta-ta.'

Steel clamped her legs together. 'You won three grand on a scratch card and didn't tell your wife?'

'Course I didn't. *She* didn't win the cash, did she?' Another sip of tea. 'Anyway, better not to. Money changes people, yeah? And Katie's got enough on her plate as it is.'

'Unbelievable...'

Logan pulled out his notebook. 'Where did you buy the scratch card? I'll need the address.'

'See, you lot swan in like something off *Downton Abbey* and you think we're gonna be all bowing and "Yes, m'Lord", don't ya? Your frizzy-haired bitch was the same.'

'Supermarket, newsagent's, garage?'

'But we got the power, don't we? Us. The little people. The working class ain't taking your crap no more.'

Steel laughed, slapping her thigh as if it was the funniest thing she'd ever heard. Laying it on thick. 'Working class? You have to do some actual *work* to be working class, Russ.'

He bared his teeth and stood, chest out. 'You calling us a scrounger?'

'A scrounger?' Angela Parks looked as if she was about to wet herself with glee. 'Oh, I am *so* going to quote you on that.'

'Not my fault there's no jobs, is it?' Morton's voice got louder. Sharper. 'Austerity. Banking crisis. Downturn in the oil price and that.'

'Mr Morton is coping bravely with the disappearance of his little girl and you're here calling him a *scrounger*? That's going right across the front page tomorrow!' She painted the headline with her hand. 'Callous Cops Brand Ellie's Dad A "Scrounger"!'

And at that, Morton turned on her. 'You think this is funny?' He put his mug down, curled a pair of fists. Stepped towards her. 'Ain't no one's business but mine if I got a job or not, you skinny munter *cow*. You try to make me look like a fanny in print and I'll have you. We shiny?'

She shrank away from him. 'It... We... I was only trying to *defend* you.'

Louder. Closer. 'Well you're doing a piss-poor job of it, aren't you?' And then, as if someone had thrown a switch, he was back to normal – smiling at Logan. Nothing to see here, Officer. 'I can't remember where I bought the scratcher. Got wankered with my mates, right? Found it in my pocket the next day – head like a broken hoover, mouth like a septic tank. Then it comes up three grand.' The smile turned into a grin. 'Best hangover ever.'

Logan tried to keep the disgust out of his voice. 'Where did you cash it?'

The smile brittled. 'Nah. Think I'm done being nice to you tossers.' Morton jerked his head towards the door. 'Don't let it hit your arse on the way out.'

Angela Parks followed them down the shabby hallway with its collection of shabby coats and shabby shoes gathered by the shabby door. Keeping her voice down. 'Course, he's going to change his mind about me printing the story, you know that, right?'

Steel glowered at her.

She shrugged. 'Not my fault you called him a scrounger, is it?'

A sniff. A look of disgust. 'Here, Laz, Can you smell something rank? Cos I can smell something *rank*.'

'Don't be like that. I could make it all ... go away if you like? Pretend I never heard you insulting the stepdad of a missing child?' Parks inched closer, eyes shining. Eager. 'What do you know about something called the "Livestock Mart"? Where they sell kids to paedos? It's a real thing, isn't it?'

'Nope.' Logan held up a hand. 'Don't know what you're talking about. Never heard of it.'

'Ellie Morton and Rebecca Oliver: abducted here, Stephen MacGuire in East Kilbride, Lucy Hawkins in St Andrews. Three kids in eight days, all of them under five.' Parks grabbed at his sleeve. 'They've been abducted to order, haven't they?'

'I think we can show ourselves out.' He removed her hand.

'I won't stop digging, whether you help me or not! This is your chance to avoid a PR *disaster*.'

He opened the door and Steel followed him into the rain.

Parks stayed in the hall, glaring at them. 'I mean it: I'll splash "Scroungergate" right across the front page!'

And that's when Steel paused, turned in a graceful pirouette, stuck up two fingers and blew her a long wet raspberry. 'And you can quote me on *that*!'

28

Steel puckered her lips, whistling something cheery as she drove them away from Ellie Morton's house.

Sitting in the passenger seat, Logan stared at her. Doing his best. Really, really doing his best to stay calm. 'What the goat-shagging hell was that supposed to be?'

She stopped whistling and turned onto the main road. 'That song off *Timmy and the Timeonauts*. The one about the stinky dinosaur who—'

'Not the bloody whistling: goading Russell Morton!' OK: now he wasn't doing quite so well at the staying-calm thing. Starting to get a bit shouty, to be honest. Which was perfectly justifiable in the circumstances.

'He's a scroungy—'

'His step-daughter's missing!'

A shrug. 'Yeah, but he's the one probably—'

'And you did it in front of a journalist!' Getting even louder. 'Because *God forbid* you go to all that trouble acting like an arsehole without an actual audience!'

She took one hand off the steering wheel and gave him the same Vs she'd given Angela Parks. Long and slow. 'For your *information*, sunshine, Russell Morton is an abusive, sexist, misogynistic *wankspasm*.'

'I don't care if he's Jack the Ripper – you want to rattle him to see what falls out? That's fine. But you *don't* do it in front of a reporter!'

'Aye, well, doesn't matter, does it?' Steel took them out onto Tillydrone Avenue again. 'You heard him: if she prints a word of it, he'll "have her". And where does that lanky strip of puke get off calling her a "skinny munter cow"? *He* looks like the bastard lovechild of Frankenstein's monster and a bicycle-seat sniffing smackhead.'

Unbelievable.

'You think that makes it *OK*?'

'Course it does.'

The woman was completely unbelievable.

'What would've happened if I'd done something that stupid when I was working for *you*? You'd have blown your rag.'

'Blah, blah, blah.'

Why did he bother? Why? What was the point?

He thumped back in his seat. 'I should've stuck with Rennie. You're a crap sidekick.'

'Oh aye. And if you *ever* shout at me like that again I'm going to rip your nadgers off and feed them to your cat.'

North Anderson Drive slid by, taking its tower blocks, rounda-bouts, and soggy housing estates with it.

Steel overtook a rusty Land Rover with a yellow 'Bearded SexGod On Board' sign stuck to the rear window. 'See, if you ask me—'

'Which I didn't.' Logan poked at his phone again. No new text messages.

'We're wasting our time searching for Ellie Morton.'

'She's a little girl!'

'She's a *dead* little girl.' A right at the roundabout, onto King's Gate – with its squat granite bungalows and cycle lanes. 'Russell Morton comes home drunk and stoned, tries it on with her – cos he's that sort of guy, you can tell just by looking at him – she screams, he kills her.'

'And where's Ellie's mum when all this is happening?'

'Probably passed out on the couch, surrounded by empty lager cans and copies of *Dysfunctional Family Monthly*.'

Trees lined the road, opening up into parkland, the grass so waterlogged after the last few days it had grown its own lochan.

'He was with his mates, remember?' That was the trouble with Steel – never paid any attention to anything. Or anyone.

'Aye, if you believe Ellie went missing when they *say* she did.'

Ah... Logan nodded. Good point. 'So when Chalmers checked his alibi...?'

'Exactly.' She smiled across the car at him. 'See? We'll make an inspector of you yet.'

'Cheeky sod.'

Righty-diddle-doodie, let's do this.

Tufty grabbed the folder from the back seat of his pool car and a-rummaging he did go. 'For whosoever pulls the sword from the stone...' Found it. He held the key aloft, his other hand curled into a claw beneath it, teeth bared, belting the word out: 'EXCALIBUR!'

And so began the glorious reign of Tufty Drizzleborn; first of his name; Lord of Flat 24, Martin House, Hazlehead; Protector of the Great Biscuit Tin, Breaker of Teapots; Father of Rubber Ducks.

Who was about to get wet.

He climbed out into the rain and hurried up the driveway to the front door – sheltering under the teeny porch while he unlocked DS Chalmers' house and let himself in.

Not a bad place. A lot bigger than his, that was for certain. And they had stairs! How cool was that? Your very own stairs that went all the way up and all the way down again.

Now, where best to start searching? Up those lovely stairs, or down here?

How about a compromise: kitchen.

Kitchen it was.

Tufty wandered down the hall, pausing to frisk his way through the pockets of the six assorted jackets hanging there:

lint, some change, a roll of dog-poo bags – which was a bit weird as Chalmers didn't own a dog – a couple of takeaway menus, and a packet of peppermint Rennies. No phone.

Onwards ever...

Tufty stopped. Frowned.

There was a weird noise coming from behind a white-painted panel door on the left. A sort of grunty, *panting* noise. Maybe Chalmers did have a dog after all? And if she was dead, and her scumbagular ex-husband was off playing naughty games with an account manager called Stephanie, who was feeding and walking the poor wee thing?

'Tufty to the rescue!'

He yanked open the door.

A small garage lay on the other side, lined with shelves full of boxes and tins and bottles and sports stuff and things. Exposed joists, for the room above, ran from side to side, but one near the middle had a chunk of white electrical flex wrapped around it. The end snipped clean where they must have cut down Lorna Chalmers' body.

And right underneath that was a naked man. Well, not *entirely* naked, he did have a set of super-huge over-ear headphones on – connected to the laptop sitting on the concrete floor in front of him. Next to a squirty container of hand cream. Which he was massaging into his erection with quite a lot of vigour.

Smiling and grunting. One tattooed arm pumping up and down.

Yeah... No way Tufty was feeding *him* and taking him walkies.

There was some sort of candid camera footage on the laptop's screen: Lorna Chalmers, in her back garden and a bikini, on a sun lounger. Working on her tan.

Dirty wee monkey.

There was a packet of non-stick scrubby pads for doing the dishes on the shelf next to the door. Tufty grabbed it and lobbed it at the onanistic halfwit. It bounced off the back of his head.

Woot!

'Ten points!'

The guy turned, a scowl on his face, then his eyes locked onto Tufty's. They widened. A look of horror spread like custard.

Then he *screamed*. Covering his willy with one hand, the other slamming the laptop shut, heels scrabbling at the hand-cream-spattered concrete.

Tufty grinned. 'Get your clothes on, you filthy sod. You're *utterly* nicked!'

Tufty propelled No-Longer-Naked Norman the Naughty Knob Noodler down the hallway – both hands securely cuffed behind his back in 'pat the dog' position.

The filthy sod snivelled and sniffed. 'Please, this is all a misunderstanding, yeah?'

Tufty picked 'Sergeant McRae' from the contacts list on his phone and set it ringing as he gave Norman another push towards the front door.

'You don't have to arrest me: I'm not hurting anyone! How am I hurting anyone?'

The Sarge's voice whumped out of the phone, a bit tinny and boomy like he was in a car. *'Tufty?'*

'Guv? I've just arrested someone.' He followed Norman into the rain, grabbing a handful of checked shirt to stop him getting away while the house door got locked.

'Who?'

A couple of teeny kids danced about on next-door's lawn in wellies and waterproofs.

Norman lunged at them. 'Leo, get Mum, yeah? *Please* get Mum! Get Mum!'

Tufty tightened his grip. 'Shut up you.' Then pinned the phone between his ear and shoulder so he could dig out the pool car's keys and plip the locks. 'Caught him in Chalmers' house. He'd broken in and was giving himself a wee treat on the garage floor right under where she was hanged.'

'Help! Mr Ghent! Police brutality!'

On the other side of the road, an old bloke with grey hair and a Metallica T-shirt looked up from putting out his wheelie bin. Sniffed. Then shuffled off to get the recycling.

'Let me guess, hipster hairdo and a brand-new Kermit the Frog tattoo?'

'AKA: Norman Clifton. Stark naked on the floor, hammering away like he was playing Whack-a-Mole.' He steered the aforementioned pervert towards the parked pool car.

'Bet he's got another spare key: confiscate it. And did you find that phone yet?'

Tufty plipped the locks and 'assisted' Norman into the back, holding his head down so he wouldn't bash it on the roof. 'Not even looked yet, Guv. I've been too busy getting No-Longer-Naked Norman here dressed again.' Tufty thumped the door shut and leaned on the roof. 'Think he might have something to do with it? Maybe he's the type who lets himself into other people's houses in the dead of night and Whack-a-Moles away while they're lying there sleeping? Maybe he finds Lorna Chalmers all unconscious with booze and antidepressants and decides, "Way-hey, my luck's in tonight!"'

'Could be. Get him processed and stuck in a cell. And not a nice one either, one of the scabby ones next to someone with a smack habit and Tourette's. Soon as his solicitor's had access, I want the hipstery wee pervert in an interview room.'

'Hurrah: finally someone to grill like sausages!'

'No. No sausages for you until you find that phone.'

Oh poo...

Tufty sagged. 'Guv.' He hung up and opened the car door. Loomed inside with his scary police-officer face on. 'Right, Norman, one chance and one chance only: how did you get into Mrs Chalmers' home? Did you break in, or have you got a key? You've got a key, haven't you?' Tufty stuck his hand out. 'Give.'

Norman Clifton blinked at him, bottom lip wobbling like strawberry jelly on a washing machine, and burst into tears.

A big grey slab sat on the other side of the junction, with 'THE JAMES HUTTON INSTITUTE' on it, complete with strange wavy logo and a bunch of arrows pointing the way to various access routes and bits of the campus.

Steel followed the one marked 'Reception', driving through a set of wrought-iron gates and onto a winding, narrow road through the trees. '...the upshot of which is: you and Ginger McHotpants take the kids that week and *I* take Susan to Reykjavik for pickled fish and naked fireside-wriggling on a bearskin rug.'

Logan put his phone away. 'OK, one: no. Two: don't be disgusting. That's a horrific image to plant in anyone's mind. And three: stop calling Tara "Ginger McHotpants"!'

Steel reached across the car and thumped him on the arm. 'Who are you calling a horrific image? Think your naked body is anyone's idea of a Monet oil painting? Because I've seen it, and *believe me*, it isn't.'

He stared at her. 'We swore never to talk about that ever again!'

'I still have nightmares.'

'Oh yeah? Well I got Post Traumatic Stress Disorder from seeing your—'

'Don't!' Her finger hovered centimetres from his nose. 'Just don't.'

Fair enough.

The Hutton Institute campus emerged from the trees – an old two-storey granite building tacked onto a massive white shopping-mall-style extension that completely dwarfed it.

The car park was empty, except for a red Porsche four-by-four parked near the reception.

Steel slid the pool car in next to it. Then sat there, hands still on the wheel, frowning out at the institute. 'Might wait here. Dr Famptonstein always gives me the willies with her,' Steel put on her best B-movie vampire voice, '"the soil is the life, ah ... hah ... haaaaah..." shtick.'

Logan climbed out. 'Don't be such a big boy's pants. And don't look at me like that: apparently we're not allowed to say "big girl's blouse" any more. It's sexist.'

'Pfff...' She locked the car and scuffed her way towards reception. Shaking her head. 'And they made *you* an inspector...'

Dr Frampton fiddled about with what looked like a huge espresso machine, but probably cost about half a million. Pressing buttons with her purple-nitrile-gloved fingers. Peering at the display through a pair of little round glasses.

The units and workbenches were littered with expensive-looking bits of equipment, sample containers, more equipment, computers, cupboards marked 'HAZARD!'...

Steel slouched in the corner, eyes down, poking away at her phone.

Logan leaned against a worktop – not touching anything. 'Sorry to drag you in on your day off.'

Dr Frampton looked up from her ... whatever it was. 'Well, I suppose. I've got a conference in South Korea next week so it doesn't hurt to clear the decks a bit. I can knock off a couple of outstanding analyses before Edward's got the joint out resting and the roasties in the oven.' A smile. 'I'll be heading off to Seoul with a clear conscience for a change.' Then over to the screen hooked up to the thing. 'Come on, little mass spectrometer, work for Mummy...' A bleep and data filled the screen. 'There we go.'

'Where?'

'It's a mixture of noncalcareous gleys with peaty gleys, and going by the mineral distribution ... that gives us...' She shuffled across to a desktop computer and punched things into the keyboard. Waved Logan over.

A map of Aberdeenshire appeared, covered in bruise-pattern swirls of blue and red and yellow and brown and purple.

'The blue bits are all the areas in the northeast with mineral gleys, but ours are from this bit, west of Newtonhill.' A click and the map zoomed in. 'Our samples also contain coprostanol and 24-ethyl coprostanol, plus an unusually high ratio of plant sterols to fatty alcohol levels—'

'Doctor?' Logan gave her a pained smile. 'Bearing in mind that we don't all have PhDs in organic chemistry...'

'Sorry. OK, in layperson's terms: we've got good biomarkers for faeces here. Most *likely* porcine. So you'd be looking for a pig farm...' Her fingers danced across the keyboard again. 'Which gives us eight possible locations, but when we factor in the organic aggregates...' Clickity click. '*Et voila.*'

She made a flourishing hand gesture and turned the screen to face Logan.

He peered in closer. A blue amoeba sat in the middle of a yellow splodge, overlaid on an Ordnance Survey map. West of Portlethen, not far from where the Aberdeen Western Peripheral Route carved its way through the countryside. 'And you're sure?'

'The soil never lies, Logan. It speaks to us from beyond the grave, whispering its secrets to those prepared to listen.'

Steel didn't bother looking up from her phone. Just took a deep breath and went, 'Ah ... hah ... haaaaa...'

'And in this case, I mean that literally. There are traces of cadaverine in the sample. And where there's cadaverine...?'

Great.

Logan covered his face with his hands. 'Oh God, not *another* dead body...'

29

Steel kicked a stone across the weed-flecked concrete, phone clamped to her ear. 'Nah, I'm fannying about on a disused pig farm in the middle of sodding nowhere.'

It must have been quite impressive in its day, but that day was *long* gone. Someone had panned in all the farmhouse windows – possibly the same someone that had daubed 'MALKY WAZ HERE!!!' across the front of it in drippy red paint. The house was surrounded by a collection of crumbling outbuildings, their corrugated-metal roofs sagging in rusty grandeur.

A huge metal barn stood off to one side, the far corner collapsed – trapping big round bales of rotting hay beneath.

Logan turned.

Downhill, the fields were a mess. Thigh-high swathes of docken and reeds. Uphill, it wasn't much better. Whin and broom hunched in jagged green herds, reaching along the fence line as if they planned on devouring the place.

Steel sent another stone on its clattering way. 'Oh come on, Susan! Don't blame me, it's no' *my* fault.'

Between the farmyard and the devouring gorse lay the decomposing hulks of about two hundred pig arks, their dull brown semi-circular roofs making a regular grid pattern across the hillside. And right at the top, diggers and bulldozers growled, prowling the ridge.

Posts and ropes and survey poles marked out a strip of land from there, straight down the hill, through the farmyard, the outbuildings, the farmhouse, and out the other side. Wide enough to fit two lanes, a central reservation, and the road verges either side.

Goodbye, Nairhillock Farm.

Logan wandered over to the farmhouse.

'What?' Steel raised her voice, no doubt making sure he could hear her. 'Because, *Buggerlugs* McRae thinks it's OK to drag me in on my day off to ferry him about the place. ... Aye, I told him that too.'

The door was wasp-stripped and swollen. The grey wood flecked with speckles of red paint. He gave it a couple of kicks. It juddered in an inch – so not locked – then wedged to a halt.

'What? No! Did she?' A throaty laugh. 'Bet she did...'

Logan waded into the weeds and around the side. More weeds. And no sign that anyone else had tried to force their way through them.

He pushed between rattling spears of rosebay willowherb, sending puffs of white drifting off into the dank air. Peered in the windows.

A bedroom rotted on the other side of the broken glass, its lath and plaster swollen and distended, freckled with mould and mildew. What was left of a wooden bedframe and a sagging mattress.

The back door was swollen and jammed too.

Living room – peeling wallpaper, manky furniture, a swathe of bird droppings beneath a couple of house martin nests up in the corner.

Kitchen – crumbling units with the doors hanging off, a hole in the wall the size of a bulldog, an ancient range cooker puffed up with rust. The remains of a table and skeletal chairs. All the charm of a biopsy.

He stepped out in front of the building again.

Steel was still mooching about. 'I don't know, do I? Depends when Herr Oberleutnant Von Arseface decides to stop wasting everyone's time with this jiggery piggery pokery.'

Logan crossed the yard, making for the metal farm gate – wide open on sagging hinges.

'You liked that did you? … Yeah, thought you would.'

He leaned on it, frowning.

All those rusty pig arks, stretching up the hill. Regular as the squares on a chessboard.

The grass was tussocked and dark green, littered with thick-stalked docken – the colour of dried blood. Animal trails snaked away through the undergrowth.

'So, come on then: what are you wearing?'

Logan climbed onto the gate.

'Well, that's no' very erotic, is it? Joggy bottoms? Least you could do is make something sexy up!'

More dark grass. More docken…

There – a rectangle of lime-green grass, about a hundred feet into the field. From the ground, it'd been hidden behind one of the pig arks, but from up here on the gate it stood out like a neon sign. And now he'd seen it, it was obvious what else was wrong with the scene. The pig ark in front of that lime-green rectangle wasn't in line with the others. Two-hundred-odd rusty metal semicircles and *this* was the only one out of place.

'Ooh, that's better!'

He clambered down from the gate and waded into the grass, keeping clear of the animal trails. No point disturbing potential evidence.

Steel gave a dirty chuckle. 'You saucy minx…'

A perfect rectangle of pale green, peppered with the twisted, stunted stalks of docken. Like they'd been covered with something for a long time, sheltered from the light. The grass between it and the misplaced pig ark was flattened and torn, gouged with scrape marks that ended at the mini Anderson-shelter shape.

Logan peered inside.

The grass *inside* the pig ark was dark green, but rutted and mismatched, filthy with clods of soil. A brown seam marked the joint between the clumps and the rest of the field. Spade marks?

He squatted down, grabbed a handful of grass and pulled. A chunk, about the size of a placemat, lifted away like a grimy toupee revealing churned earth underneath.

Logan curled his top lip. Sniffed.

There was something lurking beneath the rich dark-brown scent of newly turned earth. Something... He leaned in and sniffed again.

Gah!

Rancid meat. Like a stack of suppurating roadkill, or those floorboards at the foot of his stairs.

He stood, wiped his hands on his trousers. Backed away from the ark.

Steel's voice battered out behind him. *'Hoy! You finished twatting about yet?'*

Logan turned and pulled his phone out.

She tapped her watch. 'Lunchtime!'

It took three rings for someone to pick up. *'Control.'*

'Yes. This is Inspector McRae: I'm going to need an SE team.' He peered into the sty again. 'And tell them to bring their shovels.'

The sky darkened like a bruise.

The Scenes Examination Transit sat next to Logan's pool car, its back doors open – exposing the cages of equipment and rows of seating inside. A scruffy blue Fiat Panda four-by-four was parked on the other side, with an immaculate Range Rover nearest the farmhouse.

Isobel checked her watch. 'Is this going to take long? I have DNA results pending.'

Logan shrugged. 'Don't look at me: I told Control to let you know what was going on, not get you out here.'

A blue plastic marquee hid the pig ark from view. The lightning-flash of photography made the walls glow, casting the silhouettes inside as larger-than-life distorted monsters.

Someone in full SOC regalia exited the tent, carrying a blue plastic evidence crate, lugging it towards the farmyard.

The Procurator Fiscal clasped his hands behind his back, feet shoulder-width apart, as if he was at parade rest. Not the tallest of men, in a blue pinstripe suit and long red tie. Glasses, grey hair, and a military moustache. A voice about three times larger than he was: 'There might not even be a *body* in there. Cadaverine does not a human cadaver make, it could be a dead dog, or chicken...' He looked around him, one eyebrow raised. 'Or pig.'

Oh for God's sake.

Logan sighed. 'Look, I called Control and asked for an SE team, OK? It's not my fault they mobilised everyone and their Uncle Jim.'

'So you say.' Isobel folded her arms. 'I managed to pull what looks like saliva from DS Chalmers' cheek, two centimetres below her left eye.'

'What, someone *spat* on her?'

'Not spat, no. The saliva acted as an adhesive, fixing the hairs on that part of her cheek *upwards*: opposite to their direction of growth. So I'd say whoever it was *licked* her.'

The Procurator Fiscal's moustache twitched. 'I suppose it's too much to hope for that the saliva belongs to our killer and he's in the database?'

She shook her head. 'We won't know until the results come in.'

A filthy Vauxhall lurched its way up the rutted farm track towards them. Because it wasn't as if Logan didn't have enough people to deal with.

The SE tech with the evidence crate stopped in front of Logan and pulled down their facemask – revealing scarlet lipstick, stubble and a deep manly voice. 'That's us finished with the fingerprints and photographs.'

Behind him, two of his fellow SOC-suited techs backed out of the marquee, hauling the pig ark with them, one foot at a time. A lone voice wafted down the hill, *'One, two, three: heave!'* The ark moved another foot.

Logan peered into the crate – brown paper evidence envelopes, the forms printed on them all filled in with red biro. 'Anything?'

'Nah.' He shook his head. 'A bunch of smudges and that's it. I'm not going to bet the farm on it, but I'd say they looked like leather gloves. You can tell by the grain patterns.' He stomped off towards the van. 'Gotta go get the shovels.'

'One, two, three: heave!'

The Procurator Fiscal rocked on his parade-ground shiny shoes. 'I don't like it when murderers lick the people they kill. Next thing you know, you've got three more victims and the media are screaming "Serial Killer Stalks Aberdeenshire!"'

'One, two, three: heave!'

The filthy Vauxhall lumped to a halt beside the SE Transit and DS Robertson climbed out. She stared up at the hill with its blue marquee, then stomped over. Nodded at the PF and Isobel. 'Professor. Fiscal.' Grimaced at Logan. 'Could you not give over discovering dead bodies, Guv? The boss is doing his nut. I swear he's going to pop something.'

The Procurator Fiscal held up a finger. 'Now let's not jump to any conclusions. It's not necessarily a dead *human* body, DS Robertson. Cadaverine is produced by—'

'It's all right, Richard.' Isobel put a hand on his arm. 'I don't think the poor Detective Sergeant needs a discourse on decomposition products.'

'One, two, three: heave!'

The SE tech lumbered back from the Transit, struggling under the weight of a half-dozen shovels. He stopped and smiled at DS Robertson. 'Hey, George.'

Robertson just grunted.

'Oh come on, I *said* I was sorry.'

Isobel snapped her fingers at him. 'I want every bit of soil retained for analysis. And not all in one big lump either! A separate bag for every cubic foot. And *number* them.'

The tech's shoulders slumped, his red-lipsticked mouth sagging at the edges. 'Aww…'

Robertson pointed at the blue plastic sheaths on his feet. 'And you'd better not be planning on returning to the locus with those booties on! Didn't you do cross-contamination training?'

A groan, then the tech dumped his shovels in a clattering pile, turned on his heel and stomped off to the Transit again.

Robertson shouted after him, a great big grin on her face. 'Suit and gloves too!' The smile faded as she realised they were all staring at her. 'What?'

Logan swapped the umbrella from one shoulder to the other and stuck his spare hand in the pocket of his padded fluorescent jacket. From here – at the top of the field, looking down towards the crumbling farm buildings – there was a perfect view of where the road was going to go. Right through the middle of Nairhillock Farm and up the hill on the other side, disappearing into a stand of trees. And that put the Scene Examination marquee smack bang in the middle of the northbound carriageway.

A grimy SOC suited figure emerged from inside, wrestling a wheelbarrow full of bagged dirt across the field, making for their Transit van.

Now the only vehicles left were the SE van, Logan's pool car, and Robertson's mud-spattered Vauxhall. Everyone else had sodded off.

That was the trouble with procurators fiscal and pathologists – no patience.

Mind you, at least they were bright enough to get in out of the rain. It made pale grey sheets that drifted across the landscape, drummed on the skin of his Crimestoppers brolly, dripped off the edge.

Logan's phone launched into David Bowie's 'Space Oddity'.

He dug it out. 'Tufty?'

'Guess what I has, go on: guess.' Sounding like an overexcited spaniel.

'Genital warts?'

'Ew... Shudder.' There was a crinkling noise. *'No, I has a mobile phone. DS Lorna Chalmers' mobile phone, to be precise. Screen's all cracked like someone's stamped on it.'*

Yes.

Logan turned his back to the wind. 'Where was it?'

'*In her garage.* Technically. *Because Naughty Naked Norman Clifton had it in the pocket of the trousers he wasn't wearing.*'

Finally something was going their way.

'Has his solicitor turned up yet?'

'*Nope, but his mum has. She's screaming the place down as we speak. Listen:*'

The sound went all echoey, a woman's voice clearly audible in the background, roaring like a wounded wildebeest. '*HOW DARE YOU! I DEMAND TO SEE MY SON! DID YOU HEAR ME? I DEMAND TO SEE HIM RIGHT NOW!*'

A clunk and Tufty was back again. '*What do you want me to do with the phone?*'

'Get it fingerprinted, then down to the forensic IT team. See if they can access the thing – I need to know who she's called, all her text messages... Everything they can get.'

'Guv.'

Logan hung up. Frowned down at the tent and the pig arks again. At the blue plastic marquee covering the patch of earth that stank of death. 'What were you doing here, Lorna?'

A voice sounded over Logan's shoulder. Indignant and official. 'Can I help you? Only you're not supposed to be here.'

Logan turned and there was a large man in a high-viz jacket of his own, but instead of natty blue-and-silver reflective bands, his had a Transport Scotland logo on it. Big puffy cheeks, thick sausagey fingers, as if he'd never said nay tae a pie in his life.

Captain Pies tapped the plastic safety gear perched on top of his marshmallow head. 'And this is a *hard-hat* area!'

Logan unzipped his waterproof and pulled out his warrant card. Held it out. 'Police. Are you in charge here, sir?'

His eyes widened. 'Yes? No. Kind of.' He cleared his throat. 'Sorry, Officer. I... The umbrella was covering your ... the bit where it says "Police" ... and I...' Captain Pies tried for a smile. 'Erm ... would you like a cup of tea?'

Steam fogged the windows, dribbling down in rivulets by the small canteen area crowbarred into the corner of the Portakabin.

Little more than a mini fridge stuffed under a small table with a kettle and some tins of tea, coffee, and sugar.

Captain Pies handed Logan a mug of tea that smelled of Styrofoam and burned toast. 'Sorry about that, but you wouldn't *believe* the amount of people we get sightseeing up here. I mean, we're building a bypass, it's hardly the Grand Canyon, is it?'

The office was clean enough, but this obviously wasn't its first construction site. Dents rippled the walls between the maps of the bypass taped up there, the lino floor scuffed and permanently scarred by thousands of muddy work boots. Desks lined the walls, with a row of filing cabinets at the far end. Back-to-back file cupboards made a waist-high island down the centre, covered in more detailed plans.

The ghost of something huge and yellow growled its way past the steamed-up windows, making the walls vibrate.

Logan sipped his tea – tasted every bit as nasty as it smelled – and stood in front of the section of map covering Stonehaven to Cove. 'Thought the bypass went through east of here?'

Captain Pies nodded. 'Yup.' He picked up a pen and tapped it against the thick line that curved across the map, tracing the route north as he called out the points with obvious pride in his voice. 'Our stretch starts at Stonehaven,' *tap*, 'B979 to Bridge of Muchalls,' *tap*, 'Netherley,' *tap*, 'B979 to Portlethen,' *tap*, 'Crynoch Burn,' *tap*, 'and joining the bypass at Cleanhill.' He made a circle over the countryside to the left of the road. 'But they want to open this area up for development, so now we're putting a slip road in. Roundabout too.'

He turned and shuffled through the plans on the central island, hauling one out and laying it on top. 'See?'

It was an OS map of the surrounding area, with the slip road and roundabout marked up, annotated, and all measured out.

The marker pen tapped a crosshatched area. 'That's us there. There's planning permission in for two thousand houses, a retail park, and a swimming pool.'

Logan put his finger on the bit of map to the right of it, where the new road cut straight across the fields and through a handful of small grey rectangles. 'What about this place?'

'Nairhillock Farm? Got the bulldozers going in, Wednesday.' He put his hand up. 'But don't worry, nobody's lived there for *years*. Didn't even have to compulsory purchase it – farmer left it to the city in his will before he committed suicide. Shame not everyone's so public-spirited. You wouldn't believe the abuse we get bulldozing people's—'

'This slip road: when did you decide to put it in?'

Captain Pies puffed out his cheeks. 'Oooh... Now you're asking.' He frowned for a while, then bit his bottom lip. 'I can find out if you like?'

30

Rain drummed on the barn roof, like tiny hammers, twenty-five feet above their heads. The metalwork buckled and twisted its way down to the collapsed corner and rotting bales of hay.

Shirley unzipped her manky SOC suit, flapping the sides to get some air circulating. 'Urgh...' Steam rose from her green polo shirt, along with a funky onion smell.

Logan moved away a bit. 'How much longer?'

'At *least* another hour. Maybe two?'

DS Robertson stared up at the warped metal roof. 'Oh for God's sake.'

A steamy shrug. 'We don't even know how deep it is.'

'*Two* hours?'

'It's doing it one square foot at a time that's the killer! Everything has to be logged and numbered and witnessed. Bloody pathologist is a nightmare.'

Logan stared out into the rain, where a lone figure in a muddy SOC suit was fighting the wheelbarrow down towards the SE Transit van again. Slipping and sliding in the damp grass. Poor sod.

Shirley sighed. 'The only thing we *do* know is that someone's dug it out recently. The soil in there isn't all compressed and hard – it's been moved.'

'How recently?'

'Week? Two weeks?'

271

'Well, at least that—' Logan's phone launched into 'The Monster Mash' and he pulled it out. 'Sorry, give us a second.' He pressed the button. 'Dr Frampton?'

Something chugged and beeped in the background, then her voice boomed out of the speaker – as if she were shouting at the phone from the other side of the room. *'Logan? It's Jessica. I've got a bit of a problem.'*

Great. Because things weren't going slowly enough.

'What kind of problem?'

'I think we've got some sort of cross-contamination going on in the equipment. It's giving us screwy results.'

'We've found what looks like a grave, so your soil analysis this morning was spot on.'

'No, you see, that's the thing: I tested a sample from a different case and it produced identical readings. Twice. So I asked Tony to come in and double-check my methodology.'

A laidback voice called out from the same kind of distance. *'Inspector McRae, wassup, dude?'*

Ah, OK – so he was on speakerphone. That explained the shouting.

'Hi, Tony.'

'I can only think that something's got stuck in the mass spectrometer, but we're getting the same problem with the gas chromatograph, so maybe it's me?'

'We've totally run it, like, a dozen times now. Cleaned all the stuff and everything.'

'Well, at least we got...' Hold on a minute. 'Wait, what? You've got another case that's coming up with soil from Nairhillock Farm?'

'And pig faeces.' Her voice went all distracted. *'Maybe I got the samples mixed up when I processed them? I should never have come to work with a hangover.'*

Robertson and Shirley were staring at him.

He turned away. 'Which case?'

'Oh. I managed to extract it from a shovel and a pick that came in. Someone'd had a damn good go at cleaning them, but soil isn't so easy to get rid of. It sticks in screw heads and between joints.'

'Yes, but which *case*?'

'There's two different layers on the tools: the one on top is peaty podzols, but the one underneath is mineral gleys and we keep getting a false positive for Nairhillock Farm from them.'

Logan licked his lips. Paced across the cracked concrete to the barn's edge. 'Pickaxe and a shovel? That's the DI Duncan Bell stabbing, isn't it?'

Robertson and Shirley were still staring at him.

He pinched the bridge of his nose, eyes closed. 'Of course it is. Where's the second soil from? The peaty postles.'

'Podzols. It's a kind of soil you get in areas associated with coniferous forest and—'

'Fine, OK: *podzols*. Where?'

'Ben Rinnes, about four and a half miles southwest of Dufftown.'

'And they were the top layer, so the Nairhillock soil got stuck to the shovel first, *then* the stuff from Dufftown?'

A sigh. *'I'm sorry. I don't know what's wrong with the equipment, but we'll get it fixed – I promise.'*

'I don't think there's anything wrong with your equipment, Jessica. You're a star!'

'I am?' Sounding a bit flustered. *'Are you sure?'*

'Text me coordinates for the peaty podzols, OK? And thanks. I owe *you* this time!' He hung up.

Robertson pulled her chin in. 'Why do you keep saying "peaty podzols"?'

Logan pointed at Shirley. 'Leave a couple of people to keep digging. I need the rest of you to follow me: we're going to Dufftown.' He marched out into the rain, towards the pool car, Shirley and Robertson hurrying after him.

Robertson grabbed his arm. 'Wait! What the hell is going on?'

'There's nothing in the hole: the body's gone. DI Bell dug it up and reburied it out on Ben Rinnes.'

'Argh...' Shirley stopped where she was and sagged. 'Not *more* digging!'

He pulled open the pool car door.

Steel was slumped in the passenger seat – reclined all the

way back – eyes closed, mouth open, belting out wind-screen-wiper-rattling snores.

Logan banged his palms on the roof.

She snorted and spluttered, sat bolt upright. 'It wasn't me! I never touched her boobs, it was...' Then blinked, wiping drool from the corner of her mouth. 'What? Where? Eh...?'

'Start the car: we're going hill walking.'

Fields swished past the windows in shades of grey and brown and yellowing green as they hammered up the dual carriageway. Water pooled along the drystane dykes, miserable sheep lumbering through the mud.

Logan tried not to flinch as Steel overtook an oil tanker on the inside. Focused on his phone call instead. '...I'd been looking at it all wrong – Chalmers *wasn't* trying to crack the Ellie Morton case on her own. She was after DI Bell.'

Hardie groaned. *'Oh in the name of... Because that was more important than a missing three-year-old girl?'*

'You know what she was like.'

'Not really, but I'm beginning to get the idea.'

'I need a dog unit: something cadaver trained.'

'I'll see what I can do, but they're all tied up looking for Ellie Morton and Rebecca Oliver.'

'And a POLSA.'

'Same answer.'

'Well ... can we draft some bodies in from N or D Division?'

'What exactly *do you think I've been trying to do all weekend, painting my toenails?'*

Bennachie appeared through the rain, its sides dark and brooding beneath that heavy lid of low grey cloud.

'All I've got is two thirds of a Scene Examination team and a DS who drives like a drunken rally driver on acid.'

Steel grinned across the car at him. 'Vroom, vroom! Beep, beep!'

'Logan, every spare officer in the country's been requisitioned for that stupid anti-capitalist thing in Edinburgh. We're on our own till Tuesday.'

'I'm trying to investigate a murder here!'

'And there's literally *nothing I can do about that: you're going to*

have to manage till I can get something sorted, OK? I'm sorry, but this is what it is right now.'

Of course it was.

'Guv.' He hung up. Sighed. 'It never gets any better, does it?'

Steel put on what was probably supposed to be a sympathetic face, but it made her look more like a lecherous uncle. 'You know what might help? Lunch.'

'No. No lunch. We don't have time.'

'Aye, good luck with that. It's gone half three and if we don't stop for lunch soon I'm going to pull over in a layby, murder, and eat *you*.'

They'd grabbed a table by the big wall of glass that ran along the front of the café, overlooking a rain-drenched patio area and the rain-drenched car park, across the rain-drenched A96 and off to the rain-drenched trees and hills opposite.

Not exactly picturesque.

A fork clattered against the flagstone floor and Shirley bent down to retrieve it. It was ... weird seeing her out of the usual SOC get-up. Like catching your granny in a gimp suit. She'd pulled her hair back with an Alice band, her green polo shirt and its funky oniony smell constrained by a pink cardigan.

The rest of the Scene Examination team were equally unfamiliar in civvies: Bouncer, in cords and a replica Peterhead FC shirt, with his long nose buried in the menu again – even though they'd already ordered – one hand smoothing down the thinning hair combed across his bald patch. Charlie had a compact mirror out, fixing his make-up, the top three buttons on his lumberjack shirt open to expose a gold chain nestling amongst thick wiry black hair. Polly's chair was empty, because the silly sod was outside, wrapped up in a high-viz jacket, sheltering in the lee of the Transit van so she could smoke a cigarette and shout at someone on her mobile phone.

Logan checked his watch. Again. Ten to four. If they didn't get a shift on it'd be dark before they'd found anything. So they'd have wasted the whole—

'Will you stop fidgeting?' Steel didn't look up from her

phone, thumbs poking away at the screen. 'People got to eat.'

A voice sounded behind Logan's head: 'OK, so I've got a fish pie, a stroganoff, and a cauliflower cheese?' Their waitress couldn't have been much more than thirteen, her teeth all constrained behind the train-track wires of a set of braces.

'Cauliflower cheese?' Logan stuck his hand up. 'That's—'

'Mine!' Steel put her phone down. 'With extra chips?'

A railroad smile. 'With extra chips.'

'Gimme, gimme, gimme...'

The plate clunked down. Shirley took the fish pie, and Bouncer got the stroganoff.

'Ooh, ta.'

The waitress wandered off and everyone tucked in.

Steel grinned at him, mouth full. 'You snoozed so you loozed.'

Child.

Logan pulled out his phone, scrolling through his text messages to the one from Dr Frampton:

> If you follow this link it will give you the
> rough area to search!

He tapped the link and waited for the screenshot to download. It was another swirly bruised pattern of blue, yellow, red, purple, and grey overlaid on an OS map of Glen Rinnes.

Frampton had added a couple of big white circles with arrows pointing at them and, 'TRY LOOKING HERE!' Both circles sat over red bits on the slopes of Ben Rinnes, what looked like a track running through each.

Shirley leaned over and had a squint at the phone's screen, a prawn skewered on the end of her fork. 'Those our search areas? What are they, about two, maybe three hundred feet across? Lot of ground to cover.'

Bouncer grimaced. 'Tenner says it's all gorse and heather. Be an absolute nightmare to find anything in that.'

'Aye, in the rain too.' Steel shovelled in another mouthful of cheesy cauliflower. 'I'll stay in the car. Make sure no one steals it.'

Oh no she sodding wouldn't.

Logan put his phone in the middle of the table, where everyone could see. 'DI Bell won't have buried it under a gorse bush. He'd want somewhere secluded but easy to dig.'

The waitress appeared again, with three more plates. 'Got a meatloaf, chicken Provençal, and another cauliflower cheese?'

Charlie pointed at Polly's empty chair. 'Meatloaf.' Then at himself. 'Chicken.'

Logan put his hand up again. 'I'm the cauliflower cheese.'

She winked at him. 'I got you extra chips too, so you wouldn't feel left out.'

'Thanks.' It was about time something went right. He stabbed a chip with his fork, using it as a pointer. 'No one carries a body more than fifty metres from their car, so that'll cut it down a bit. We start with whichever area's more difficult to see from the road, then we—'

His phone buzzed, then launched into 'Space Oddity' as the word 'Tufty' replaced the map.

So much for that.

'Why me?' Logan lowered his chip, picked up his phone and answered it. 'Tufty? Can it wait? I'm in the middle of something important.'

'Do you want the bad news, or the worse news?'

'Let me guess: Norman Clifton's solicitor hasn't turned up?'

'Forensic IT say they can't even look *at Chalmers' phone for about a fortnight.'*

He sagged back in his chair. 'Oh for God's sake!'

'Said they've got about two dozen laptops from that hacking farm in Ellon to do first. You know, the ones who leaked all the SNP's emails, when—'

'And the worse news?'

'Oh. OK. So I had a go at unlocking it myself.'

Oh no. No. No. No. No. No...

Steel stared at him. 'Did something just crawl up your bum? Cos it looks like something just crawled up your bum.'

'Guv?'

'Tufty.' Logan tightened his grip on the phone, forcing out

each individual word as if it was made of uranium: 'What – did
– you – do?'

*'Only unlocked it on the third try! I has a genius. See, when I was
in her house I noticed all these—'*

'How is this "worse news"? What was on it?'

'Don't you want to hear my tale of genius and derring-do?'

Why did everyone have to be a pain in his backside? Was
there some sort of competition going on? Because right now,
Tufty was winning.

'What – was – on – the – phone?'

'Pff... I bet Inspector Morse never gets—'

'Tufty: I swear on my father's grave...'

*'All right, all right. There was nothing there. Someone had deleted
everything: call history, texts, photos, the lot.'*

Logan slumped again. 'Urgh. That is "worse news".'

*'But they did leave one entry in the phone's history: a fifteen-minute
outgoing call at ten twenty-two.'*

'Any idea who she was calling?'

'The Samaritans.'

So either Isobel was wrong about the marks on Chalmers'
arms and ankles, and she *did* kill herself after all, or someone
was covering their tracks.

'But then I has another genius.' There was a scrunching papery
sound. *'Someone might have deleted everything, but that doesn't mean
it has to stay deleted. You can get all manner of things off an SD card
if you know what you're doing. And fortunately for us, Constable
Stewart Quirrel is like a sexier Stephen Hawking.'*

'You recovered it? *All* of it?'

'Oh yes.' More scrunching. *'And my clever doesn't stop there. Her
phone's got GPS built in. Which is trickier to hack, but if I can pull a
Mitnick we'll know everywhere it's been in the last six days.'* There
was a small pause, followed by a swanky proud tone. *'Are we
impressed now?'*

Damn right we were. Even if we didn't have a clue what a
'Mitnick' was.

'You, my little friend, have earned yourself a whole packet
of sweeties!'

'Woot!'

'Now get back to work.' Logan hung up and dug the chip on the end of his fork into the cauliflower cheese. Grinned. Today was going to turn out *just* fine after all.

31

The Huntly Asda glowed beneath the low, heavy clouds as Steel took them across the roundabout. And the rain fell. Sheets of grey and darker grey set the landscape out of focus, robbing it of colour as the windscreen wipers squeaked.

Steel nudged him. 'Anything juicy?'

Logan looked up from Tufty's email. 'Not so far. Most of Chalmers' texts are her fighting with her husband. "Why didn't you empty the dishwasher?", "Don't you ever dare speak to me like that again.", "You're disgusting Brian." Only she's spelled "disgusting" wrong.'

'How about naked pics? She must have some of those on her mobile. *Everyone* has those!'

He stared at her. 'Remind me *never* to borrow your phone!'

'Hmph.' Her nose went up. 'Done. Don't want to send you into an onanistic frenzy.'

Logan shuddered and went back to the email as they drove off into the wilds of Aberdeenshire.

'Well, *this* is romantic.' Steel pulled up on the little rectangle of tarmac acting as a car park at the side of the road. 'Wish I'd brought some lubricant, now.'

Ben Rinnes loomed in front of them – a lopsided lump of a hill, dark purple with heather. A track cut across it, pale tan in the never-ending rain. Another hill loomed behind them – more

280

tussocky heather with the odd pine tree to break up the monotony.

Headlights swept over the pool car as the Scene Examination Transit crept past and turned onto a chunk of hardstanding in front of a padlocked metal gate with 'NO PARKING ~ KEEP ENTRANCE CLEAR' on it.

A small river had formed, coming down the track, out under the gate, and across the road. And still the rain fell.

Yeah, searching in that was going to be *loads* of fun.

Logan reached into the back of the car and grabbed his peaked cap and high-viz jacket. 'We're going to get soaked, aren't we?'

'You are. I'm staying put.'

He handed her the other high-viz. 'Not a chance in hell.'

'Gah...'

They wrestled their way into their jackets and climbed out into the downpour. Then Logan hurried around to the boot and got the Crimestoppers umbrella. Popped it open.

It twitched and thrummed in the wind.

Steel grabbed it off him and glowered at the rainswept hill. 'For future reference, this was the moment I decided to kill you.'

Lovely.

Logan pulled on his hat and jogged over to the Transit van. Knocked on the driver's window.

As it buzzed down, what sounded like Queen's *Greatest Hits* belted out for a couple of beats, then clicked into silence, leaving only the engine's diesel grumble, the thunk-squeak of the windscreen wipers, and the hiss of falling rain.

Polly put both hands back on the wheel and bared her top teeth. Staring straight ahead.

On the other side of the gate, the track reached away around and up the hill. Little rapids marked the bigger stones and potholes as the water coursed down it.

She sucked in a breath. 'I'm not sure this is a good idea. I mean, if we had a big four-by-four, maybe...?'

Steel banged on the side of the door. 'Just get the bloody gate open. We're drowning out here!'

Polly turned in her seat. 'Bouncer?'

Bouncer zipped up his jacket, pulled up his hood, and hopped down from the passenger side, armed with a large pair of bolt cutters. He strode over to the padlock and snipped right through the shackle – the hinges squealing as he hauled the gate open.

Logan hurried around to the passenger side and climbed in. Scooted across to the middle seat as Steel clambered in after him and thunked the door shut.

The Transit growled and juddered its way onto the track, then stopped so Bouncer could close the gate, open the side door and scramble inside.

Grit and gravel crunched beneath their wheels as the Transit crawled uphill. Lurching through the riverbed potholes and rapids, heather thick on either side.

Polly bared her teeth again, knuckles white where she gripped the steering wheel. 'Still say this is a bad idea...'

She was probably right, but what choice did they have?

No one said a word as the van grumbled its way up the narrow track. Thumping and groaning. Windscreen wipers squealing and moaning. It listed left for a moment, then thudded down again – everyone bouncing in their seats.

Polly's knuckles went even whiter. 'Eeeek!'

Steel grabbed the handle above the passenger door.

The little red dot on Logan's phone crawled along Dr Frampton's map.

Another lurch to the left, the hillside falling away like a heather-covered cliff face as the van swayed and bounced.

Someone in the back laughed – high-pitched and nervous.

And on they went, climbing the river / track. On and on and on and—

Logan thumped his free hand on the dashboard. 'That's us.'

Polly's face was fixed in a pained rictus grin. 'Oh thank God for that!' She hauled on the handbrake and sagged in her seat, arms dangling by her sides, head drooping, eyes shut.

He didn't have the heart to tell her they'd probably have to reverse most of the way down again. Well, it wasn't as if they'd be able to do a three-point turn up here.

Directly in front of the van, the track narrowed even further. To the right, Ben Rinnes stretched away uphill, to the left, it fell towards a line of trees, four, maybe five hundred feet distant.

Charlie poked his head between the front seats and frowned at the drenched landscape. 'Good a place as any, I suppose.'

Logan undid his seatbelt. 'What about trace evidence?'

'In this?'

Bouncer snorted. 'You'll be lucky. If it'd been dry: yes.'

Polly nodded. 'Anything viable would've washed away *days* ago.'

'Right, people,' Shirley clapped her hands together, 'get your waterproofs on. We've got a deposition site to find.'

It didn't matter that the rain had downgraded itself from a full-on torrential downpour to the standard Scottish drizzle, Logan was still soaked. Bulbous clumps of heather grabbed at his legs, hiding roots, rocks, puddles, holes, and other assorted fun ways to break an ankle.

Every step came with the sibilant squish of waterlogged socks.

He picked his way through yet another clump – no dead body – then turned, looking uphill.

The Transit marked the middle of the search area, lurking on the path about eighty feet away. Which meant there was still another eighty-odd to go. God, this was going to take *forever*.

Five fluorescent-yellow figures inched their way through the treacherous undergrowth. All spread out across the downhill side of the search area. Maybe he should have split the team and got one half searching the uphill side at the same time? The sun was already sinking towards the hills. They only had, what, an hour and a half before it set?

But then, three people would take twice as long to search the same area, so in the end it would've made sod-all difference.

Thank you very much, Detective Chief Inspector Stephen 'I can't spare anyone' Hardie. How was Logan supposed to—

'The Imperial March' blared from his phone, partially muffled by the thick high-viz jacket. He hauled it out. The words 'HORRIBLE STEEL' filled the screen. He answered it anyway. 'Have you found something?'

'*I just stood in a dirty great puddle!*'

'So watch where you're putting your feet.'

'*I'm cold and I'm wet and how are we supposed to find anything in this godforsaken hellhole?*'

'Keep looking.' He hung up.

About seventy feet away one of the high-viz figures made very rude hand gestures in his direction.

Heather grasped hold of his right ankle and Logan toppled forward, arms outstretched, a bush rushing up to punch him in the face.

And BANG! Right into it, branches and leaves scratching at his cheeks and hands. An eruption of water as the rain-soaked undergrowth gave up a fair portion of its moisture.

'Arrrrrrrgh!' He struggled on to his soggy knees. Wiped the water and bits of vegetation from his face. Spat out some peaty-tasting soil. 'Sodding heathery bastards!'

He forced himself upright, bellowed in frustration, then gave the traitorous bush a *serious* kicking. 'AAAAAAAAAAAARGH!' Kick, bash, boot, batter, thump.

Logan stopped and bent double. Hands on his knees. Face and shoulders prickly with heat, panting out great billows of steam. 'Argh...'

This was impossible. Completely and utterly—

His phone rang again and he yanked it from his pocket. Stabbed the button. 'No, you can't go back to the van for a kip! You can search like the rest of us!'

Silence from the phone.

Water dripped from the hem of his high-viz jacket.

'What, no sarky comeback?'

'*Erm... Guv?*'

Oh. It wasn't Steel, it was Shirley.

'Sorry. Thought you were someone else.'

'*By my reckoning, we've gone a hundred and eighty feet from the van.*'

Logan turned. The Transit was a lot smaller than last time he'd checked, the rest of his team were all spread out, the ones in the middle distance like tiny Lego figures. 'OK. We head back and try the other side of—'

'HEY!' A voice bellowed out across the hillside. 'HEY!' The Lego figure furthest away jumped up and down, waving her arms in the air. 'OVER HERE!'

Logan waded into the heather, fought his way past a clump of broom, more heather. Yet more heather...

Everyone fought their way through the undergrowth, all converging on where Polly stood, still waving. As if they wouldn't be able to find her by the glow of her massive fluorescent-yellow coat.

Logan clambered over a ridge and stopped.

Polly stood in the middle of a natural hollow, surrounded by heather that looked a lot browner and droopier than the stuff around it.

He took one step down into the hollow and stopped. What was that *horrible* smell? Rotting sausages and... He retreated a couple of steps, breathing through his mouth. Urgh, you could *taste* it – rancid and greasy. 'Dear Lord...'

Charlie lurched up beside him. 'What's...' Then his eyes bugged and he slapped a hand over his nose and mouth, hiding the scarlet lipstick. 'Aw, *Jesus*, that stinks!'

Polly pointed to a bush, three feet from her foot. 'He's had to grub up the heather to get at the soil for digging. That's why it's all brown. Dying.'

Shirley stumbled to the brow of the hollow. Narrowed her eyes and wafted a hand in front of her. 'Can't be a very deep grave if it smells this bad out here.'

Bouncer sagged. 'Not *again*.'

And last, but not least, Steel appeared. Hands in her pockets. She stopped at the edge, flared her nostrils, and took a good sniff. Then nodded. 'I ate a kebab that smelled like that once. Tell you, my arse was like a Niagara Falls of oxtail soup for a whole week.'

Everyone stared at her.

'Oh, like *you've* never done it.'

* * *

285

'…absolutely stinks. And I mean *spectacularly*.' Logan shifted in the driver's seat, looking through the window and down the hill. Phone pressed to his ear.

A newly erected blue plastic marquee squatted over the deposition site, the walls glowing – Shirley and her team turned into monstrous shadow puppets by the crime-scene lights. It was one of the bigger ones, too. Could probably have parked a couple of minibuses in there.

Rain drummed on the van roof, its grey blanket hiding the fields and hills opposite. As if the setting sun wasn't doing a gloomy enough job.

Hardie's voice took on a hopeful edge. *'Don't suppose there's any ID on the body, is there?'*

'Difficult to tell. According to the SE team, everything's been swallowed by the adipocere. Victim looks like he's been carved out of solid lard.'

'Pfff… I don't like it, Logan. I don't.'

'Only bright side is the ground around here isn't as diggable as the stuff at Nairhillock Farm.'

'Ding-Dong was one of us. It was bad enough he'd killed one person, but two?'

'Body was barely three feet down. And they must've been three *hard* feet to dig.'

'How many more did he kill? How long was he at it?'

'Managed a good six feet down at the pig farm. It's—'

The van's sliding door rattled open, letting in a gust of wind that set jackets and paperwork and takeaway menus rustling.

'Shut the door!'

Steel clambered in. 'What did you think I was going to do? Sit here with it open?' She hauled it closed with a thunk and collapsed into a seat. Sat there with her arms held out to her sides. 'Freezing, sogging-wet, buggering horrorfest…'

Hardie made a little groaning noise. *'Let me guess: Detective Sergeant Steel?'*

She cupped her hands and blew into them. 'Should've brought a thermos of coffee with us.' Then she leaned forward and thumped Logan on the arm. 'Why didn't *you* think of that, you're *supposed* to be in charge!'

Logan hit her back. 'Get off me! And there's a kettle in the equipment rack – plug it into the cigarette lighter and make yourself useful for a change. I'll have a tea.'

She rolled her eyes, flipped him the Vs, then stood and slouched away down the van. 'What did your last slave die of?'

Logan shifted the phone to his other ear. 'Sorry about that. Look: we haven't got *definitive* proof DI Bell killed anyone yet.'

'Do you really think that matters? I know he did it, you know he did it, everyone and their bookie's dog knows he did it.'

'Yes. But...' Logan sighed. 'I worked with him for ten years and till we found his body in that car... A killer? I wouldn't have believed you.'

'Me neither.'

Steel made a show of hauling the kettle out of its rack, banging and clanging her way up the van clutching it and a two-litre bottle of mineral water.

'Any ideas for motive?'

'Maybe this is why he had to fake his own death? Something gets out of hand and next thing he's got a dead body to get rid of.'

'Buried six feet down where no one would ever find it.'

Steel filled the kettle with mineral water, then stuck it on the floor, jamming the adapter into the cigarette lighter slot like she was performing a vigorous sex act.

'Until Bell discovers the Western Peripheral Route is going to stick a slip road right through the middle of his secret grave-yard.'

She set it on to boil. 'Where's the teabags?'

'I'm on the *phone*!'

'Gah...' Steel stomped off down the van again.

'Post mortem?'

'Knowing Isobel? Tomorrow morning? Maybe? If we're lucky? Won't find out for sure till she gets here.' Logan tried for a smile. 'At least we've got a body for her this time.'

That had to count for something.

* * *

287

Four spotlights lit up the marquee's insides like a bright summer's day. The effect was slightly spoiled by the big diesel generator roaring away in the corner, the stench of rotten flesh, the five figures in white SOC outfits, the dug-up heather, the water-logged shallow grave, and the muddy peat floor, but other than that it was indistinguishable from a fortnight in Torremolinos.

Actually, scratch that. The one and only time Logan had been to Torremolinos, there had been shallow graves and dead bodies too. No one ever put that kind of thing in the brochures, though, did they?

Polly and Charlie were stuffing the dying heather plants into bags, while Shirley squatted at the side of the grave, looking up at Isobel. All of them glowing like aliens in the spotlights.

Logan stepped closer. Stared down into the grave.

A man-shaped mass of yellowy-white fat glistened at the bottom of the hole, liberally smeared with earth, peat, and mud. A lard golem.

'Well?' He pointed at the remains.

Isobel put her hands on her hips. 'At least you've actually got a body for me this time.'

'Yeah, I said that.'

She frowned at him.

'Never mind.'

'You're extremely lucky I got here as quickly as I did. If it wasn't for a fatal stabbing in Insch, you'd still be waiting.'

'We need an ID soon as possible.' Logan pointed. 'Any chance…?'

'You want me to do a post mortem today? On a Sunday evening?'

'That would certainly *help*.'

Isobel stared into the grave for a bit. Then sighed. 'All right, but I shall expect time off in lieu.' She snapped her fingers at Shirley. 'Get the remains bagged and back to the mortuary ASAP.' Then she turned and swept from the marquee, leaving the tent flaps billowing behind her.

Shirley waited till Isobel was *definitely* out of earshot. 'I hope your arse falls off, you rancid lump of yuck.' She patted the adipose-encrusted remains with a purple-gloved hand. 'No offence.'

288

32

Sally grips the steering wheel tighter, like that's going to stop her hands shaking. Eases off the accelerator as the village limits glow in her headlights: 'LYNE OF SKENE ~ PLEASE DRIVE SLOWLY'.

'The Happy Pirate Jamboree' bounces out of the CD player. Aiden's favourite. His little face beamed every time she put it on and they'd sing along to the adventures of Captain Wonkybeard and his silly crew.

'*There was panic on the poop deck, as the Kraken he awoke,*
Wrapped his tentacles around the ship, and the captain: he got soaked.'
Sally tries to join in ... but it's not the same without Aiden. Nothing is.

She takes a left at the junction, past a row of small cottages and some new-build homes, lights shining from their windows as their occupants settled in for a nice Sunday evening in front of the television.

Out through the limits, into the countryside and darkness again.

A breath shudders out of her: sharp and painful.

She's doing the right thing. For Aiden. It doesn't matter how bad she feels about it, or how *guilty* – this is what she has to do to get her baby boy back.

She glances in the rear-view mirror, past the red-eyed woman in there with the big square of sticking plaster on her bruised forehead and the long curly blonde wig, to the Shogun's boot. Separated from the rear seats by a heavy-duty dog grille, the boot cover pulled all the way across so no one can see what she's got in there. 'Not long now, I promise.'

Not long...

A track leads away into the woods – the junction marked by a teddy bear cable-tied to a tree...

Sally slows at the junction and stares at it. It's different to the one in Skemmel Woods, but it *means* the same thing. Only this time she's complicit.

And it's too late to turn back now.

So she pulls onto the track, the engine growling as the Shogun rolls and bounces through the potholes, water rearing up over the wheel arches even though she's keeping the speed down so Becky won't get thrown around in the boot.

Deeper into the woods, headlights dragging trees from the darkness, before letting them fade away. Past the looming hulk of a collapsed metal structure. Past piles of logs and a thicket of brambles. Eyes glittering in the woods to either side, their owners lurking beyond the headlights' reach.

Deeper.

A ruined cottage emerges from the gloom up ahead, sagging at the side of the road. No roof left, the windows nothing more than ragged sockets in the building's skull. Walls smeared with moss and streaked with rain. A garden in front of it choked with weeds: brambles, bracken, docken, and the grey-brown spears of rosebay willowherb. Like something out of a Brothers Grimm tale.

She stops in front of it, gripping the steering wheel even tighter as she glances in the rear-view mirror again. Swallows down the thing growing in her throat.

'I'm sorry. I'm really, *really* sorry, but I haven't got any choice. I need my little boy. I need him so very, very much...'

Becky doesn't reply, but then she can't.

Sally wipes her eyes. Huffs out a breath. Then another. And another.

'Come on, Sally, you can do this. Do it for Aiden.'

Yes.

She puts on her baseball cap and sunglasses, adjusts the wig, then pulls up the hood on her hoodie. Checks her reflection again.

Even without the disguise, would she recognise the woman looking back at her? After everything she's done?

Probably not. But what choice does she have?

She climbs out into the gloom as the rain starts again – like the pitter-patter of tiny feet on the car and trees and earth.

The Shogun's headlights pick out the pale skeletal forms of branches and trunks up ahead, casting a thin grey glow along the front of the cottage, leaving everything else in darkness. Its engine grumbles, exhaust trailing scarlet in the tail-lights' glare.

Sally stands there, breath fogging around her head.

No sign of anyone.

Come on, you can *do* this.

She pulls a torch from her pocket, clicks it on, and follows its glow to the four-by-four's boot. Pops open the tailgate. Forces a smile as she slides the cover away. 'Hey, you...'

Becky lies on her side, cosseted in a nest of sleeping bags and blankets and towels. Hands tied with baler twine, ankles too. Sally tucks Mr Bibble-Bobble in between Becky's arms and chest – she moans behind her tea-towel gag, eyes barely flickering.

Two more green pills and another mini stamp.

'I know. I know. I'm *sorry*.' Sally reaches in and lifts them both from the boot, cradling them against her chest as she crosses the weed-strangled verge to the cottage's rusted gate.

She takes a deep breath. 'HELLO?'

The only sounds are the car's engine and the falling rain.

'HELLO? IS THERE ANYONE THERE?'

She shifts her grip on Becky and runs the torch across the cottage. Something scurries into the brambles. A rusting jumble of metal casts a twisted shadow along the wall.

'I CAN'T JUST LEAVE HER OUT HERE IN THE RAIN!'

She turns on the spot, playing the torch across the garden, the trees, the track, the Shogun. 'HELLO? IS ANYONE—'

A muffled voice growls out behind her. *'What part of "clandestine" did you not understand?'*

Sally moves to face him, but something hard presses against her hoodie at the back of her neck. There's a metallic *click* and she freezes. It's the unmistakable soundtrack to a million action films – a gun's hammer being cocked.

'No, no, no.' He sounds patient, like he's talking to a small, but favoured, child. *'I get to see you. You don't get to see me. That's how this works.'*

She holds Becky tighter. 'But—'

'Genuinely, it makes no difference to me if you survive this handover or not. I leave with the girl either way.' The gun presses harder into Sally's neck. 'Put her down on the ground. Nice and gentle – don't want to damage the goods.'

Sally tenses. 'How do I know you won't hurt her? How do I know you won't … *touch* her?'

'Well, one: no one wants to buy damaged goods. And two: I'm not the kind of guy who's into little kids. I leave that to perverts like you.' This time, he doesn't push with the gun, he shoves. *'Now, put – the kid – down.'*

She lowers Becky onto the wet ground, steps away, and stands there with her hands up.

'There we go.'

There's a rustling noise, then Becky moans.

'What's wrong with her?'

'We…' No. Probably best to make him think she's working on her own. 'I gave her something to keep her calm.'

There's a pause that grows and grows and grows.

Then, *'Fair enough.'* More rustling and a grunt.

Becky moans again – has he picked her up?

'Go stand over there, both hands on the bonnet.'

Sally picks her way through the weeds and does what she's told.

'Now, you know the rules for tomorrow, right? Cash sales only. I so much as suspect that you're dodgy: you go home in bitesize chunks.

Well, you know, dodgy for a paedophile. Bar's set a bit differently for you people.'

'I understand.'

'You come alone. You don't tell anyone. You don't bring anyone. You pay in cash. And you never ever tell anyone about this. Not even on pain of death.'

Sally grits her teeth. 'I *said* I understand.' No one ever listens.

His voice is getting fainter, as if he's backing away. *'You get to keep eighty percent of anything your "contribution" makes on the night, collectible at the end of the evening.'*

'But you haven't told me where to—'

'You'll get a text with the time and place. Don't be late...'

She stands there, hands on the warm bonnet, the engine's grumble drowning out everything but the rain thumping against the brim of her baseball cap. Breathing hard. Every exhale a glowing grey ghost in front of her face.

Is it safe to turn around yet?

Count to a hundred, that would be long enough, wouldn't it?

One... Two... Three...

By the time she finally turns, there's no sign of Becky or the man with the gun.

Sally wraps her arms around herself for a moment, squeezing till the trembling subsides. Then closes the Shogun's boot and climbs in behind the wheel.

The track is a bit tight for a three-point turn, but she manages it – heading back the way she came, one hand wiping the tears from her cheeks.

At least it's done. She's one step closer to saving Aiden.

It doesn't matter how much it burns inside, it's for Aiden.

She thumbs the hands-free button on her steering wheel and calls Raymond's mobile.

He picks up on the first ring. *'Sally? Sally, is everything—'*

'It's on for tomorrow night.'

The Shogun rides the potholes harder this time as she puts her foot down, not having to worry about damaging her precious cargo any more. Past the thicket of brambles and the pile of logs – their shapes looming in the headlights, then sinking into darkness again.

'*Sally, are you OK?*'

Past the crumpled metal hulk. Hands tight on the steering wheel, the muscles in her jaw clenching.

'*Sally?*'

Scowling out through the windscreen. 'Of *course* I'm not OK! I handed a little girl over to a bastard with a gun, so he can auction her off to a bunch of paedophiles!'

Filthy liquid crashes over the bonnet as she thunders through a waterlogged rut.

'*We'll get her back, remember? Andy and Danners won't let her out of their sight. I promise.*'

Sally shakes her head, scrubs a hand across her eyes again. 'I don't know if I can go through with—'

'*Yes you can! You can do this, Sally. You just have to be strong for Aiden.*'

But that's easy for him to say, isn't it? He isn't the one who has to bloody do it.

On the one hand, drugging children really did seem wrong, but on the other, they really were a lot less … *wriggly* afterward.

Lee shifted his grip, making sure Rebecca wasn't going to slip off his shoulder, tucking her teddy bear under his arm as he picked his way through the rattling spikes of rosebay willow-herb. Gloomy out here and getting darker. But no point hurrying and having an accident.

Around the back of a clump of spiky holly.

Rebecca groaned.

Poor wee thing. 'Shhh… Almost there.'

And over to the Volvo. Hidden from the road by a huge swathe of brambles and rhododendron.

He opened the tailgate and reached in – careful to hold her in place with his other hand, didn't want to drop her, after all – and pulled the pet carrier over. Eased her inside. Patted her on the cheek.

Looked like a sweet kid.

He placed the teddy in beside her, closed the carrier door, draped the tartan rug over the whole thing, then shut the boot. Walked around to the driver's door and climbed in out of the rain. Smiled. Nothing quite like the satisfaction of a job well done.

Lee plucked the cheap burner phone from his pocket and dialled from memory. Listened to it ring as he started the car and pulled out onto the track, driving in the opposite direction to the woman and her mud-spattered four-by-four. No point taking any risks. And yes, *technically* it was against the law to use a mobile phone while driving, but this was a private road, so there you go.

Jerry, sounding cheerful, but noncommittal: *'Hello?'*

'Our final item is now in stock.'

'Excellent. No issues?'

Trees and bushes slid past the car, dark and brooding. Have to turn the headlights on in a minute, once he was a safe distance from the cottage.

'Some people need the rules explaining to them, that's all.'

'Good. Excellent. Well, in that case, I think you're all in for a lovely evening tomorrow.'

'Looking forward to it.' He hung up, slowed for the junction, flicked on his headlights and turned right onto the narrow road. Threw back his hoodie's hood, removed the grey mask, and placed it in its box on the passenger seat.

Lee turned in his seat. 'Hope you're ready to make some nice new friends, Rebecca! Well, maybe not *nice*, nice, but at least they'll give me a lot of money, and in the end isn't that what matters?'

Of course it was.

— in the dark woods, screaming —

33

The stairwell rang with the sound of feet and voices, coming from the floors below as Logan plodded his way up. One hand on the bannister, one on his phone. 'I'd love to, but I've no idea when I'll get finished tonight.'

Tara sighed. *'You sure?'*

'I know I'm only in charge for forty-eight hours, but it's still a murder inquiry.'

A tiny PC thundered down the stairs, carrying a stack of case files. He nodded at Logan on the way past. 'Guv.'

'Damien.' Logan kept on climbing.

'And have you decided how you're going to make things up to me yet, or do I need to impose sanctions?'

'Sanctions?'

'Oh, I'll go all United Nations on your arse. You'll think North Korea's *getting off lightly.'*

'OK, now you're being cruel.' He walked past the lifts and pushed through the double doors, into the corridor beyond.

'I got dumped with your kids last night, Logan. I'm allowed to be cruel.'

'Yeah, you've got a point.'

A couple of doors down, Rennie poked his head out of the temporary office and waved. 'Thought it was you. DCI Hardie's throwing a wobbly!'

Wonderful.

'Sorry: got to go.'

I know, I know. "It's a murder."' She hung up.

Logan sighed and put his phone away. 'Has Norman Clifton seen his solicitor yet?'

'I'm not kidding about Hardie: this isn't just any old wobbly, it's a full-on, five-star, man-the-lifeboats, *wibbly* wobbly. He's about thirty seconds off exploding and taking everyone with him. Wants you in his office A.S.A.F.P.'

Wonderful.

'What's gone wrong *now*?'

34

Hardie's office door was open, letting the sound of muttered voices ooze out into the corridor, overlaid by the harsh electronic ringing of his desk phone.

Logan stopped, hand up – ready to knock.

DS Robertson and DS Scott had Hardie hemmed in behind his desk and he did *not* look happy.

Scott dumped a huge stack of paperwork into the in-tray. 'Five hundred door-to-doors and not a single lead.'

'What a shock.' Robertson grabbed the ringing phone. 'DCI Hardie's office. ... Uh-huh. ... Uh-huh...'

DI Fraser fumed in one of the visitors' chairs, arms folded, eyebrows down, as if someone had spat in her ear. 'Completely unbelievable that anyone could be *that* stupid. It's a PR disaster! How are we supposed to get the public to trust us after this?'

Hardie shook his head. 'As if I haven't got enough to deal with already...'

DS Scott tapped the pile of paper. 'We've done another appeal for witnesses, but you know what it's like: soon as they find out there's a reward we're swamped with crazies, loonies, time-wasters, chancers, and conmen.'

Fraser shook a finger at the ceiling. 'It's unforgivable!'

Logan knocked on the door frame.

No one paid any attention.

'Hold on, I'll check.' Robertson put a hand over the phone's mouthpiece. 'Boss, they can get you on the six o'clock news for another appeal. Interested?'

Hardie sagged. 'Urgh... OK, OK. Six o'clock.'

Robertson went back to the phone. 'Yup, six is fine. ... OK.'

'You're busy.' Logan hooked a thumb over his shoulder. 'I can pop by later if you like?'

Hardie looked up, face darkening. 'Oh no you don't!' He reached for his in-tray, stopped, then scowled at Scott's big stack of forms. 'Oh for *God's* sake!' He snatched them up and dumped the paperwork into Scott's hands. Then hauled out a sheet of paper and thrust it in Logan's direction. 'The *Aberdeen Examiner* faxed over Monday's front page, wanting a comment.'

Why did that sound like a threat?

'OK...' Logan stepped into Hardie's office and took the sheet of paper. The headline blared, 'HEARTLESS POLICE SLANDER ELLIE'S DAD' above a photo of Russell Morton looking stern and disappointed. And for some bizarre reason an inset photo of Logan sat on the right with the subheading 'POLICE HERO TURNS CRUEL COP'.

Oh for...

He poked the page with a finger. 'How did they get hold of this?'

Hardie folded his arms, chin up, teeth bared. 'Go on then: read it.'

'Because this isn't—'

'Out loud for all the boys and girls!'

Great.

Logan took a breath and did what he was told. '"In a shocking move, police officers visiting Ellie Morton's worried parents branded her stepfather a 'workshy scrounger'..." That's not *strictly* true.'

Hardie's fist banged off the desk. 'It shouldn't even be *vaguely* true! What the bloody hell were you thinking?'

'Me? Oh, no, I'm not...' He clamped his mouth shut. Paused. Then, 'How did the *Aberdeen Examiner* get hold of this?'

'How could you be so *stupid*?' Getting louder and louder. 'I

302

thought the key to being in Professional Standards was acting like a bloody professional!'

'It wasn't—'

'YOU DON'T CALL VICTIMS' PARENTS "WORKSHY SCROUNGERS"!'

Logan turned.

A couple of PCs stood outside in the corridor, gawping. And as soon as he made eye contact, they were off, bustling away towards the stairwell as if the host of hell was right behind them.

Logan closed the office door then turned back to Hardie. Kept his voice nice and calm. 'Number one: I didn't. Number two: I get that you're stressed, but that doesn't make it OK to scream at people. Number three: this is nothing more than Russell Morton playing power games.'

Hardie glowered back, lips shining with spittle. 'I am *trying* to run a department here!'

'Who wrote this...?' Logan checked the byline. 'Colin Bloody Miller.' He pulled out his phone, stuck it on speakerphone and dialled. The tinny ringing noise sounded from his palm. 'Morton promised to sell his story to the *Scottish Daily Post*. Probably got paid handsomely too. This is him showing them who's boss.'

Fraser jabbed a finger at Logan. 'Do you have any idea how damaging this is to NE Division?'

'Yes, Kim, I'm *aware*. That's why—'

Colin Miller's Weegie accent belted out of the phone. *'Well, well, well, if it's no' my old pal Laz. Who's been a naughty—'*

'You sent a story over to DCI Hardie for comment.'

'Oh aye, well, it's only fair, right? I'm thinking of calling it, "Scroung-ergate".'

'Very original.' Logan scowled at the screen. 'How did you get hold of it?'

'Poor guy's lost his stepdaughter and you're there callin' him workshy?'

'Thought Morton had an exclusive deal with the *Scottish Daily Post*?'

Silence from the other end.

Then, *'Did he now? That's no' what he told me...'*

'Oh, I'll bet he didn't. He's playing you off against them, Colin. You're *leverage.'*

'Ah well. Still a good story.'

Hardie's glower hadn't shifted any.

Logan paced the carpet tiles between the filing cabinets and the whiteboards. 'Russell Morton said I called him a "workshy scrounger" and you believed him?'

'You saying you didn't, but?'

'Damn right I am. All I did was question him about the meeting he'd had with DS Chalmers and where he got the money he's been flashing about.'

'Yeah, but heat of the moment—'

'And I've got a witness: DS Steel was there the whole time. So unless the *Aberdeen Examiner* can produce evidence I said it – which you can't, because I didn't – you'd better get your lawyers warmed up, because you're going to *need* them.'

'All right, all right, keep your pants on, man. I'm no' wantin' to measure dicks here.' A sly tone crept into Miller's voice. *'Suppose I do you a favour and kill the story, gonnae have a* big *hole on the front page to fill...?'*

'Hold on.' Logan pressed the 'MUTE' button and jerked his chin at Hardie. 'See?'

Hardie picked at his desk diary, not meeting Logan's eyes. 'Yes, well...' He cleared his throat. 'As you say, this is a very *stressful* time for everybody.'

'Do you want to give him something to print? Something that helps us?'

'Hmmm...' Hardie pursed his lips. Put his head on one side. Then held out his hand. 'Give me the phone.'

Logan was on his way up the stairs again when Rennie came clattering down, a blue folder tucked under one arm.

He screeched to a halt. 'Guv, that's Norman Clifton all lawyered up and ready to go in Interview Two.'

Pfff...

Logan checked his watch – seven fifty-two. Only nine and a

half hours since he'd come on shift, so why did it feel like a week? This was what he got for coming into work on a Sunday.

He let out a long, weary breath, then turned and headed down the stairs again.

Today was *never* going to end.

Norman Clifton didn't look much like a criminal mastermind. He sat, all hunched up, on the other side of the interview room table in a white SOC suit, arms wrapped around himself, eyes all red and puffy. Sniffing and wiping away tears, before going back to hugging himself.

Sitting next to him was a plump middle-aged woman in a brown cardigan and mumsy haircut. And as soon as they made scowling an Olympic sport, she was going to win gold for Scotland.

Rennie was perched and ready to go in chair number three with all his interview notes spread out on the table in front of him. Pen in hand.

Logan leaned back in chair number four. Watching Clifton in silence.

Watching him sniff and wipe and fidget and tremble.

Clifton's solicitor pulled at her cardigan sleeve and checked a little gold watch. 'Are you actually going to say something at some point, or can I get my knitting out?'

Logan smiled at her. 'Making anything nice?'

'An extremely itchy jumper for a nephew I hate.' She straightened her cardigan. 'Now, you've heard my client's statement: he understands that his actions may seem inappropriate, but this is his first offence and he's committed to getting psychological help. It's time for you to release him.'

'"May seem inappropriate"?' Logan raised an eyebrow. '"*Seem*"?' He leaned forwards. 'Norman, you were masturbating, naked, in your dead neighbour's garage, so really—'

'And he's apologised for that.'

'—I think "seem" is kind of redundant, don't you?'

Norman sniffed. 'I didn't mean to...'

His solicitor put a hand on his arm, voice warm and reassuring. 'It's all right, Norman, I'll deal with this.' The warmth leached away as she turned to Logan. 'I've known Norman his whole life. He's a good boy who's maybe got a bit … *confused* about his feelings.'

Rennie held up his pen. 'Is there anything else you'd like to tell us before we go any further, Norman?'

That got him a worried look.

Rennie tried again. 'Anything we need to know?'

Mrs Scowly Cardigan gathered up her papers. 'All right, I think we're quite done here.'

'Because, do you remember when you were arrested and processed? They took a DNA sample, didn't they?'

She dumped a massive handbag on the interview room table and stuffed her papers inside. 'If you're trying to put my client at the *scene of the crime*, you can save your breath. He's already admitted being there.'

Rennie raised his eyebrows. 'You wouldn't believe how quick the computers can process those DNA samples these days. Used to take ages and ages, *now* we can get a result in an hour.'

She clicked her handbag shut. 'Is there a point to this?'

Logan picked a sheet of paper from Rennie's folder and placed it on the table. 'We got a match from your DNA, Norman.'

The hipstery wee sod flinched. Stared at his solicitor, bottom lip trembling.

She put her kind voice on again. 'It's all right, Norman, you haven't done anything wrong.'

'Actually…' Rennie sucked in a theatrical breath. 'Are you *sure* there's nothing you want to tell us?'

'My client has already told—'

Logan tapped the tabletop. 'You licked her face, didn't you, Norman?'

'I…' His eyes widened. 'It…'

'We found your saliva on Laura Chalmers' cheek.'

'Wow.' Rennie tried a sympathetic voice. 'Was that before, or after you killed her, Norman?'

Mrs Scowly Cardigan stared at Norman, open-mouthed. 'What did you…' Then blinked and shook her head. Fussed with the buttons on her cardigan. 'I think I need to consult with my client again. In *private*.'

The vending machines droned away to each other: one wholesome – full of crisps and chocolate and bags of sweeties – while the other was pure EVIL. They sat like Cain and Abel, next to the empty chiller cabinet. Nearly all of the canteen chairs were stacked on the tables, legs in the air, giving the place a cold and hostile look. Ready to repel invaders.

That hadn't stopped Logan and Rennie, though. They sat at the table nearest the scrubbed-down counter, nursing evil-tasting coffee in an evil plastic cup from the evil vending machine.

Rennie pulled out his phone and poked at the screen. 'Nearly twenty past. Taking their time, aren't they?'

'Be fair, she's just found out her client was up to a bit more than an inappropriate wank.'

'True.' A nod and a frown. 'Do you think he did it? I think he did it. You can't trust people with those flesh-tunnel ear things. It's not right.'

'What happened with the missing person reports?'

'Even the word's perverted, isn't it? "Flesh tunnel". Who goes into a shop and asks for a "flesh tunnel"?'

'Stop saying "flesh tunnel".' Logan reached across the table and thumped him. 'Now focus: missing persons?'

'Which ones?'

'For the love of … I *told* you to go through every missing person report for the month DI Bell faked his own death!'

'Oh, *that*. Did that ages ago.'

The evil vending machine buzzed.

Someone walked past the canteen door, whistling the theme tune to *Danger Mouse*.

Logan reached across the table and thumped Rennie again. '*And*?'

'Oh, right. Won't be a tick.' He scrambled out of his chair and hurried from the room.

'I'm surrounded by idiots.' Logan took another sip of hot

brown yuck. 'Urgh...' Then called up the contact list on his phone, found 'HORRIBLE STEEL', and set it ringing.

Her voice crackled in his ear, all echoey and distorted, as if she'd answered from inside a filing cabinet. *'What?'*

'"Workshy scrounger". Remember that?'

A papery rustling noise. *'I'm kinda busy.'*

'I had to defuse an unexploded DCI Hardie, because you couldn't keep your mouth from running away with itself in front of Russell Morton!'

More rustling. *'Says here there's a guy in Dundee who's grown a six-foot marrow. It's in the* Sunday Post, *so it must be true.'*

'So much for "if she prints a word of it he'll have her".'

'Who wants to eat a six-foot marrow? Be like chewing a roll of linoleum stuffed with mouldy peas.'

Typical. She couldn't even be arsed paying attention to a bollocking.

'You really don't give a toss, do you? We're trying to find missing kids and track down cop killers and you simply don't care!'

'Course I care. Waste of good courgettes, letting them grow that big.'

'Hardie thought it was my fault!'

'Well, you were *the senior officer, so he's got a point. If you can't control the people working for you...'*

'You dirty, rotten, two-faced, backstabbing—'

'Temper, temper.' A hollow knocking sound echoed out in the background. Steel raised her voice. *'Occupied.'*

Oh no!

Logan recoiled from the phone. Holding it away from his ear. 'Please tell me you're not on the *toilet!*'

More knocking. *'Are you smoking in there? Because you're not allowed to smoke in there!'*

'Occu-sodding-pied!'

'Oh God, you're on the toilet, aren't you?'

How could *anyone* be that manky?

The canteen door thumped open and Rennie staggered in, all red in the face and breathing hard. Holding a folder above his head like a revolutionary flag. 'Got it!'

'Now, if you don't mind, I'm in the middle of making wee Russell Mortons here and you're putting me off my stroke.' And with that, she hung up.

'Gahhhh...' Logan put his phone down and wiped his hands on a napkin. Probably have to scrub his ears with bleach now. 'The woman's a horror show.'

Rennie collapsed into his seat and sagged there – one arm dangling, the other hand clutching his ribs. 'Arrgh... Stitch.'

A shudder rippled its way across Logan's shoulders. 'On the *toilet.*'

'Anyway,' Rennie opened the new folder, 'just to be safe, I did an extra month before Bell didn't kill himself as well. Eliminated anyone too tall, too short, too womany, the wrong number of limbs, or who's been found since – and that leaves us with...' He produced three printouts and laid them on the table in front of Logan – mugshots with personal details underneath. 'Number one: Joseph Horman. Librarian from Buckie. Been suffering from depression for three years, then one day he walked out of the family home and never came back.' Rennie tapped the next mugshot. 'Number two: Barry Linwood. Self-employed accountant from Mintlaw. Wife reported him missing after a four-day bender. And number three: Evan Forshaw. He was a Church of Scotland minister who vanished off the face of Peterhead in the middle of the night. Turned out he'd been embezzling cash from a fundraising thing. Sick kids in Syria, I think.'

'Yeah...' Logan examined each one in turn. Horman's flat forehead, Linwood's jowly face, Forshaw's sticky-out ears. 'None of them look much like DI Bell.'

'Which is why I present, for your viewing pleasure, Bachelor Number Four.' Rennie delved into the folder again and pulled out one more printout, laying it on top of the others with a flourish. 'No one reported him missing, but Rod Lawson here disappeared at some point during the week Bell's meant to have died.'

'At some point?'

A shrug. 'Was supposed to see his parole officer on the Wednesday. Never turned up. No one's heard from him since.'

Just like Fred Marshall.

Logan picked up Rod Lawson's mugshot.

A sullen, hairy man scowled out of the picture, a police measurement chart clearly visible on the wall behind him, his name in magnetic letters on the small board he was holding. Bags under his eyes, a smattering of cold sores around his mouth. Blotchy skin.

'Let me guess: drugs?'

'To a band playing. DI Bell did him a couple of times for possession with intent. Same height as Bell, same basic build, same hairiness. About ten years younger, and the nose, ears, and eyes are all wrong, but if you're blowing his head off and setting fire to the remains...?'

'Close enough.' Logan puffed out his cheeks. 'Of course, if we could find his *teeth* we might actually have some DNA to do a match with.'

'Yeah... Well, maybe?'

'Get a warrant sorted – I want his medical records. And don't let them fob you off this time!' Logan grabbed his phone and called Control. 'I need you to put me through to Sergeant Rose Savage.'

The sound of muffled fingers on a keyboard rattled out for a bit, then: *'I'm sorry, Sergeant Savage isn't on duty today. Do you want to leave a—'*

'Then put me through to her mobile.'

Rennie stuck bachelors one-through-three in the folder again. 'They're not going to give me a warrant without corroboration or probable cause. How am I supposed to—'

Logan held up a finger, silencing him as Sergeant Savage answered.

Her voice dripped with suspicion. *'Who's this?'*

'When you worked with DI Bell, do you remember him mentioning Rod Lawson at all?'

No reply.

'Hello? You still there?'

'Sorry, you broke up a bit. Did Ding-Dong mention...?'

'Rod Lawson.'

'*Rod...? No, that doesn't ring a...*' Another small silence. '*Oh, wait, you mean* Hairy Roddy Lawson*? The Sandilands Sasquatch? Oh, I know him fine. Did him for possession and shoplifting more times than I can count. Haven't seen him for ages, though. Why, has something happened to him?*'

'That's what I'm trying to find out.' Logan tried another sip of evil coffee. Nope, still horrible. He pushed the cup away. 'Did Bell mention him?'

'*Not that I can remember. But it was a long time ago.*' Something clunked in the background. '*Sorry. Is it important?*'

'And when you ID'd Bell's body, there wasn't anything *suspicious* about it?'

'*What, other than the fact he'd blown his own head off and then burnt to a crisp? Other than that, you mean?*'

'Fair point. But—'

The canteen door thumped open. 'Inspector McRae?' A lanky PC with a centre parting waved at him.

'Hold on a second.' Logan put a hand over his phone's mouthpiece and raised his eyebrows at the constable. 'Yes?'

'Your guy's solicitor says they're ready to make a statement.'

'Thanks.' He went back to the phone. 'Sorry, got to go. If you remember anything, give me a shout, OK?'

'*Will do.*'

Logan hung up and stood. Curled a finger in Rennie's direction. 'Come on then, let's see what kind of lies Norman Clifton's got for us this time.'

35

Norman Clifton had swapped the sniffing and eye wiping for tiny silent sobs, bottom lip wobbling. Which might have been due to the amount of trouble he was in, or it might have been down to the bright pink handprint swelling up on his left cheek.

His solicitor sat all prim and proper next to him, cardigan buttoned all the way up to her neck.

Logan nodded at Norman. 'In your own time.'

Norman sat there, not making eye contact. Digging away at a mole on his right wrist with his fingernails. Worrying at it till tiny drops of scarlet stained the pale surrounding skin.

Mrs Cardigan sniffed. 'My *client* wishes to make the following statement.' She picked a sheet of handwritten paper from the table in front of her, reading out loud. '"I want to apologise for not being completely honest with you earlier. I was worried that you would jump to the wrong conclusion if I told you that I had seen Mrs Chalmers' body after she had died."'

Rennie snorted. 'Wrong conclusions? Us? Whatever gave you that idea?'

'"I let myself into the Chalmers' household using one of the spare keys my mother holds for them, as has been my habit over the last eight months."' She paused and directed a foul look at Norman. '"I like to be in the house when they are both asleep. I find it peaceful and … *stimulating*."'

'Ooh, I see.' Rennie leaned forward, voice all conspiratorial. 'Is that a polite way of saying you have a bit of a wank?'

Tears welled up in Norman's eyes, making them glisten. A tiny bubble of snot popped from one nostril.

'"I realise now that this was misguided and that I need professional help."'

'Oh it's too late for—'

'Look,' she lowered the statement and glared at him, 'do you think we could do without the snarky running commentary?'

'Sorry.'

'"When I entered the premises at two in the morning I could not see Mrs Chalmers in her bedroom. Searching the house I discovered her body in the garage. I was traumatised by this and left immediately, returning home."' Mrs Cardigan cleared her throat. '"Where, reflecting on what I had seen, I became … stimulated. Afterwards, I revisited the garage and was again … stimulated."' A warm pink flush spread up her neck and into her cheeks. '"It was then that I *inadvertently* licked Mrs Chalmers' face while trying to comfort her remains with a kiss."'

Norman's shoulders jerked as a massive sob burst free.

His solicitor dug a hanky out from the sleeve of her cardigan and thrust it at him. '"I realise that this was a severe error of judgement on my part and would like to offer my sincere condolences and apologies to Mr Chalmers."' She placed the statement down in front of him and folded her arms.

Logan raised an eyebrow. 'Finished?'

'Finished. I have advised my client to respond to any further questions with "no comment" until we can have him assessed by a mental-health professional.'

Rennie curled his top lip. 'Well … he certainly needs one.'

Another snot bubble burst, but Norman didn't wipe it away, he sat there sobbing, tears shining on his cheeks, eyes as pink and swollen as the handprint on his cheek. 'I'm sorry... I'm sorry I … I didn't … didn't mean to...' He looked at Logan for the first time since they'd sat down. 'I just … just wanted to taste her dying tears...'

* * *

Rennie leaned in close, his voice barely a whisper. 'You think he did it? Killed her, I mean.' He made a big show of pantomime glancing at the custody desk, where Mrs Angry Cardigan was in conversation with Aberdeen's answer to inbreeding – Sergeant Downie.

A fiver said he had gills and a vestigial tail.

And speaking of weirdos: Norman Clifton's sobs echoed out from behind a closed cell door. Huge and deep and wracking. Which served the wee sod right.

Logan shrugged. 'Pfff... Maybe he sneaks into the house and he finds Chalmers doped up on antidepressants and booze? Thinks this is going to be his one opportunity to watch someone die, carries her into the garage, and hangs her. Or maybe he finds her trying to kill herself and decides to lend a hand? Or maybe he's telling the truth and all he did was get turned on by a dead woman?'

A shiver. 'Creepy little pervert.'

'Better organise a search warrant for his mum's house. You don't get to be that weird without leaving traces.'

'Guv.' Rennie hurried off as Mrs Cardigan stepped away from the custody desk, glowered, stuck her nose in the air, and stomped over.

She stopped right in front of Logan, hands on her hips. 'You're not *really* charging him with murder, are you?'

'Give me one good reason why I shouldn't.'

'I've known Norman since he was a baby; I was at school with his mother.' The nose went up another inch. 'He's always been a bit ... odd. But this? *Killing* someone?'

Logan took out his notebook. 'Didn't torture any family pets as a kid, did he?'

She cleared her throat. Looked away. 'I don't think it's appropriate for me to discuss this case any further until Norman has received the help that he needs.' And she was off, thundering out through the custody suite doors like a bowling ball in a brown cardigan.

Yeah, Norman Chalmers was definitely a pet torturer.

Logan put his notebook back in his pocket on the way to the

stairwell. Grinding to a halt as the *Addams Family* theme tune belted out of his phone. He pushed through the doors and answered it. 'Sheila.'

'Professor McAllister requests the pleasure of your company at our humble mortuary. And if you wouldn't mind getting a shift on, that would be grand. It's late and some of us have love lives to struggle through.' She hung up.

Great. Summoned like a small child or an errant dog.

He stared at the screen for a moment. Then turned and thumped through the doors again. Muttering to himself. 'Thought the whole point of being an inspector was people ran about after you, not the other way around.'

The extractor fans roared. Not that it achieved very much, the mortuary still *stank*. The source of the smell lurked on the cutting table, caught in the glare of half a dozen working lights. All glistening and greasy, like it'd been carved from rancid butter.

That thick layer of adipocere had smoothed away most of the detail, leaving a sort of revolting jelly-baby shape behind.

Isobel stood beside it, an SOC suit on over her usual mortuary scrubs, complete with booties, full-facemask, gloves, wellies, and a green plastic apron over the top. What every well-dressed pathologist was wearing this season. She'd arranged all the cutting tools on a stainless-steel trolley, everything looking clean and unused.

Sheila Dalrymple was dressed exactly the same, her face creased with concentration as she wrestled a digital X-ray machine into place over the body's jelly-baby head, aligning the machinery for a sideways view.

Logan stayed where he was – in the doorway. SOC suit or not, that was the kind of smell that oozed into your hair and clothes and skin. And no amount of scrubbing would get rid of it.

'Right.' Dalrymple pulled a remote control from the equipment and fiddled with it. 'Anyone *not* wanting a dose of X-rays should retire to the other room.'

Oh thank God for that.

He backed into the prep room: all work surfaces and cupboards, a couple of plastic chairs standing guard over a stack of boxes at the far end.

Isobel followed him, carrying a laptop. She stuck it down on the worktop and turned it to face him. 'You need to see this.'

The X-ray of a knee filled the screen in shades of white and grey. Not a good knee, though. There was something wrong with the way it fitted together.

Dalrymple appeared, holding the remote control. She pointed it into the cutting room and the X-ray machine bleeped. A nod, then she marched back inside again.

Isobel traced a purple finger along the screen. 'The light areas are bone, the dark areas tissue.'

Lovely.

'I have seen an X-ray before, I'm not *completely* stupid.'

'Good. Then I won't need to tell you what *these* are.' Her finger traced along one of the twisted grey lines that clustered around the kneecap.

He leaned in and squinted at them. They looked a bit like worms, but that probably wasn't the right answer. 'Nope. No idea.'

'They're distorted now, but if you can imagine the knee bent at ninety degrees, as if the victim was sitting, they would be perfectly straight. And approximately sixty millimetres long.'

'OK. Still no.'

A long-suffering sigh. 'Imagine taking a drill to someone's kneecaps.'

He winced. 'Please tell me it was accidental.'

'The first time? Perhaps. But not the eighteen other ones. Both knees, both elbows, both ankles, shoulders... Four in the bottom jaw alone.'

Something heavy congealed in Logan's stomach. 'He was tortured.'

It was bad enough finding out DI Bell was a murderer, but *this*?

Dalrymple appeared from the cutting room again. Stood with her legs apart and her hands hanging by her side, Wild West gunslinger-style. Then she snatched the remote control up. Fast. *Beep.*

She blew across the end of the remote, mimed slipping it into a holster, then sashayed through the cutting room door as if it was the entrance to a saloon.

Isobel ignored her, fiddling with the laptop instead so a fractured clavicle appeared on the screen. 'Then there are the percussive injuries. Possibly a hammer.'

'God.' Logan huffed out a breath. 'DI Bell tortured him...'

'And last, but not least, there are nicks in the ribs.' A section of ribcage appeared, small dark Vs marring the white curves. 'See how they line up in pairs? That's consistent with multiple stab wounds to the chest from a double-edged blade. Going by the pattern and number, most likely a frenzied attack.'

Wonderful.

Just. Sodding. Great.

Logan sank down into one of the plastic seats. 'Any idea who our victim is?'

She stared at him, face as dead as her patient's.

He shrugged. 'Because if you *don't*, then I've got a suggestion you could look into?'

Dalrymple moseyed out into the prep room and stood there, facing away from the door ... then snapped around holding the remote in one hand and mashing the button with the palm of her other in one swift seamless motion. *Beep.*

Another blow across the 'barrel', then she spun the remote and holstered it. 'Aaaaand, we're done, pardners.'

Isobel didn't move. 'We don't do *nominative* investigations here, Inspector McRae. We follow the evidence.'

'Which is great, but you *might* find it leads you to Fred Albert Marshall. DI Bell was convinced Marshall killed Sally MacAuley's husband and abducted her son. He was obsessed with it.'

Still nothing.

Logan stood and backed towards the exit, both hands up. 'OK, I can take a hint.'

She strode into the cutting room. 'We'll be in touch.'

'Y'all come back, now.' Dalrymple tipped an imaginary Stetson at him, then cowboyed off after Isobel, leaving him on his own.

'Only trying to help.' Logan stripped off his SOC get-up, chucked it in the bin, and got the hell out of there. Along the corridor, through the doors, up the stairs, and onto the rear podium car park.

OK, so it was raining, but at least he wasn't *enveloped* in that horrible stench any more.

You could add that to the list of 'Reasons Why It Is Not A Good Idea To Sleep With Pathologists'. Very difficult to get amorous when the object of your affections smelled like rotting cadavers.

He hurried across the car park and in through the rear doors. Shook the rain from his shoulders and trouser legs. Pulled out his phone and called Rennie on the way to the stairwell.

Rennie picked up with a sigh. *'Guv.'*

'Have you got that warrant sorted for Rod Lawson's medical records?'

Through the double doors.

'The Sheriff won't give us one till he's read the post mortem report. I emailed it over, but he says it's nearly nine on a Sunday night and we should know better.'

Typical.

'What about the search warrant for Norman Clifton's mother's house?'

'Same. Only he used fewer words. Three of which were quite rude.'

Logan headed up the stairs. 'You told him this is a murdered police officer we're talking about?'

'No, I left that bit out, because clearly I'm some sort of bum-sniffing moron!' A groan. Then another sigh. *'Sorry, Guv. Been a long day.'*

'Yeah.' Logan stopped on the landing. 'Look, pack up, sign out, and go home. Spend some time with your family.'

'Donna will be in bed by—'

'And tell Tufty and Steel they can sod off too. But I want everyone back here tomorrow – seven sharp.'

'Half seven for cash?'

'Don't push it.' Logan hung up. Sagged for a moment. 'Right. One more stop to make and we're done for the night.'

*   *   *

Hardie stared at him, mouth hanging open.

Logan shifted in his seat.

It was a bit like facing down a goldfish. A goldfish in an ugly suit. That needed a shave.

Then finally, Hardie's mouth clicked shut. A blink. 'He was *tortured*?'

'That was pretty much my reaction.'

DI Fraser stretched in her seat, stifled a yawn. 'The media's going to love this.'

'How could Ding-Dong torture someone? I was at his twenty-first wedding anniversary...'

'I've sent the team home for the night. Can't do much else till the warrants come in.'

Fraser nodded. 'Good idea. My lot are stumbling about like half-shut knives too. Maybe it *is* time to pack up for the night?'

Hardie rubbed at his face. 'We've got two missing girls; an ex-police-officer who was stabbed to death; an exhumed murder victim no one can identify; a *serving* police officer who's been hanged; and *now* you say the body you dug up in the middle of nowhere wasn't just murdered, it was tortured first!' He pressed his palms into his eye sockets and made a muffled screaming noise.

Logan and Fraser grimaced at each other.

Then she stood and put a hand on Hardie's shoulder. 'Come on, Boss, you're tired. We all are.' She gave the shoulder a squeeze. 'Inspector McRae's right. Time to pack up and go home for the night. Get some rest. Things will look a lot better in the morning.'

Hardie's shoulders slumped even further. 'You're right, Kim. Of course you're right. I didn't mean to...' His head fell back and he stared at the ceiling tiles. 'God, I hate being a police officer.'

'Then do what I do – go home, make yourself a nice big vodka-and-Diet-Coke, and soak in the bath till you look like an elephant's knee.'

*   *   *

319

'How come you don't do kebabs?' The wee loon in the Man United tracksuit and expensive trainers stuck his bottom lip out.

Idiot.

Logan settled onto the windowsill, next to an avalanche of yesterday's red-top tabloids. 'JUNGLE LIZZY IN UNDERWEAR HORROR', 'POLICE SCANDAL SUICIDE SHOCKER', 'Mum's Tearful Plea: "LET MY BOY DIE!"', 'Scottish Yobbos' W.T.O. Rampage', 'CANDLELIT VIGIL FOR MISSING MILLIE'.

The takeaway wasn't that busy. Just Logan; a woman waiting for salt-and-pepper squid, chicken chow mein, beef in black bean sauce, and a prawn-fried rice; the grim-faced auld wifie behind the counter; and Little Lord Kebab.

Who turned and flounced out of the Chinese takeaway, ramming a baseball hat on his head. 'You're getting a one-star on TripAdvisor!'

Logan pulled out his phone and sent Tara a text:

> If it helps, I'm getting those spare ribs in Peking sauce you like?
> This is me trying to make it up to you, by the way.

SEND.

Ding.

TS TARA:

> Can't. I'm going round unlicensed sex shops with Dildo the Boy Wonder, tomorrow morning. A Trading Standards Officer's work is never done.

Hmm...

> Prawn toast, crispy chilli beef, Szechuan char sui pork, Mongolian king prawns, special fried rice, and Singapore noodles.
> I've ordered enough for six!

Send.

Mrs Salt-and-Pepper-Squid kept sneaking glances at him. Sitting there in his Police Scotland fleece, itchy trousers and muddy boots. And every time he caught her looking, she developed a sudden overwhelming interest in the menu mounted on the wall.

He thumbed out another message:

> I'm never going to eat all this on my own.
> And Singapore noodles give Cthulhu the
> squits.

Send.
Ding.

Well, she was replying straight away, so that was a good sign. Wasn't it?

> It's really late Logan & I've got work in
> the morning. So do you. See how things
> go tomorrow.

Ah. Maybe not so good.

Mrs Salt-and-Pepper-Squid was at it again.

Logan smiled at her. 'Can I help you?'

Her cheeks flushed and her nose went up. 'Why aren't you out there trying to find that wee girl?'

Great.

'I can assure you we're doing all we can.'

'You're not! You're sitting there, ordering Chinese takeaway and playing on your phone!'

The miserable old lady behind the counter dinged a small bell. 'Order for McRae.'

Logan stood. Bit back the reply.

What was the bloody point?

Pfff...

Logan hauled on the handbrake, switched off the headlights, then the windscreen wipers, killed the engine, and climbed out of the car. Sagged for a second in the darkness and drizzle. Reached into the passenger footwell for his takeaway. Plipped the locks and made for the house.

God, what a day.

He let himself in, thumped the door shut and deadbolted it. 'Cthulhu? Daddy's got Chinese for tea!'

Heavy-pawed thuds walloped down the stairs, then Cthulhu sashayed over – her huge plumed tail sticking straight up in the air as she purred and coiled around his ankles.

At least *someone* wanted to spend the evening with him.

'Wrrrnnnggh!' Logan sat bolt upright, the duvet crumping down around his waist, and blinked in the gloom. Heart lump-thumping like Long John Silver staggering down a staircase.

Cthulhu gave an irritated *prrrrrrp* and jumped down from the bed with all the delicacy of a breeze block.

Faint orange light oozed in around the curtains' edges, the only other illumination coming from the alarm-clock-radio: 23:45

'Urgh...' A whole thirty-two minutes' sleep. That's what he got for eating all those spicy—

He froze.

A pale-yellow glow outlined the bedroom door.

Either the aliens had come to abduct him, or something a whole lot worse.

He eased over in the bed, dropped his right hand to the floor and felt about underneath. Cat fluff. Toy mouse. Discarded sock. Ah. Now *that* was more like it. His fingers curled around the pickaxe handle.

Right.

Let's see how clever whoever-it-was felt when he caved their skull in.

And that's when the door thumped open and there was Tara, looking a little dishevelled about the hair, wearing a padded jacket over a set of tartan jammies. Slippers on her feet.

She clicked off the hall light and scuffed into the room. Closed the door behind her.

Logan let go of the pickaxe handle. 'Thought you had an early start.'

Tara hauled off her jacket, dumped it on the floor and slipped into the bed. 'Don't get your hopes up: this is *not* a bootie call.' She helped herself to two thirds of the duvet. 'Idiots in the flat upstairs are having a party and they – won't – shut – up.'

'It's lovely to see you too.'

She turned her back to him, searching for his legs beneath the duvet with her feet. 'No funny business.'

'Aaargh!' Her horrible feet were like bags of frozen peas. 'If this is your idea of foreplay, you've been watching the wrong porn films!'

'You gave me a key; this is what you get.' Tara snuggled down. 'Now stop wriggling and go to sleep. Some of us have work in the morning.'

36

Logan paused on the landing – health and safety first – and took a sip from his wax paper cup. Decent coffee. Proper coffee. Made by Wee Hairy Davie, instead of the Evil Vending Machine. Ahhhh…

He shifted the folder, pinning it beneath his armpit as he started up the stairs again.

The sound of stomping feet clattered down from the floor above, and Jane McGrath, Media Liaison Officer to the stars, thundered around the corner. Her hair and make-up might have been perfect, but she had a face like a wet weekend in Rhynie. She had a folder of her own too, only she was holding it in a strangling death grip.

She thumped past him. 'Unbelievable!'

'I think the word you were looking for was "excuse me".'

McGrath stopped. Turned. Threw her hands in the air – waving the folder like a club. 'Excuse me, oh great and all-*powerful* Professional Standards Person.' She hurled the folder onto the stairs at her feet. 'Did you see what they splashed all over the front page of the *Aberdeen Examiner* this morning?'

Oh no.

Colin *Bloody* Miller.

He promised!

Logan stuck his chest out. 'I never called Russell Morton a workshy scrounger!'

Her face froze for a moment, eyebrows lowering into a frown. 'What? No.' She snatched up her folder and yanked out a sheet of newsprint. Unfolded it. Jabbed it towards him.

The whole front page was given over to a photo of an attractive young woman in a frock, lots of brown hair, looking flirty at the camera. An inset picture sat on the right, by her buttocks: a shed with a collapsed roof. All beneath the banner headline: 'POLICE PERVS INJURED PEEPING ON PRETTY PAULINE'.

McGrath thrust it towards him again, making the edges crinkle. 'Look at it. LOOK AT IT! They weren't injured chasing a *burglar*: they fell through that shed roof because they were up there ogling an eighteen-year-old divinity student jigging about in her bra and pants!'

'Ah...' So not Colin Miller after all.

'I told the world they were *heroes*! Listen to this.' She straightened out the front page and glowered at it. '"At the end of a long day's studying I like to relax by dancing about to my mum's old Showaddywaddy records, while I get changed. I can't believe they were out there, night after night. I feel so violated,' sobbed Pauline, brackets, eighteen." *Eighteen*!' McGrath crushed the front page into a ball. 'Some neighbour filmed it all on their mobile phone: crash, right through the shed roof! How am I supposed to put a positive spin on that? Police pervs!' She hurled the front page down and stamped on it, grinding the article into the concrete as her face got darker and darker. 'Aaaaaaaargh! Why do I bother? Why do I *sodding* bother?'

Wow.

Logan licked his lips. 'Erm...'

She stood there, glaring at everything, shoulders heaving, eyes bugging, teeth bared.

PC Guthrie appeared on the landing behind her, smiling up at Logan like a happy potato in a police uniform. 'Inspector McRae? Have you got a minute? There's an auld mannie in reception, wants to see you.'

'Yes. Right.' He gave McGrath a sympathetic smile and picked his way past her on the stairs. Pausing to pat her on the shoulder. 'I'm sure it'll all blow over eventually.'

She took a deep breath and screwed her eyes shut. 'AAAAAAAAAAAAAAAARGH!'

Dear Lord, what was that *smell*? Sharp, filthy, and dirty all at the same time. Like someone had piddled in a bucket of mud then left it on a hot radiator all day.

Logan blinked. Breathed through his mouth. And lowered himself into the seat opposite, keeping as far back as he could. 'So, Mr ...' he checked Guthrie's Post-it note, 'Seafield. The Desk Sergeant tells me you've got some information?'

Mr Seafield was hunched in the other seat, shoulders curled forwards as if he were afraid someone was going to steal the tank-top-and-tie combination he had on under his suit jacket. A pointy nose stretched out from his jowly face; no hair on top of his head, lots of it growing out of his ears; big round glasses; teeth so white and straight they *had* to be falsies.

He nodded at the ancient border terrier snuffling away at his feet. 'It's not me, it's Gomez.'

OK. So he was one of *those*. Great.

Logan's smile got a bit more difficult to maintain. 'Your *dog* has information for me?'

'No: the smell. Dirty wee sod likes to run under bigger dogs while they're having a pee.' He reached into his jacket pocket and pulled out a folded sheet of paper. Slapped it down on the tabletop. 'I wouldn't speak to any of those other fannies because they don't know, do they?'

'Know what, Mr Seafield?'

Mr Seafield slid the paper across.

Logan unfolded it. Stared.

It was a printout from the *Aberdeen Examiner* website: 'HEART-LESS POLICE SLANDER ELLIE'S DAD' complete with the wee photo of Logan and its subheading, 'POLICE HERO TURNS CRUEL COP'.

He promised. The dirty, two-faced, lying—

'That's right.' Mr Seafield thumped a hand down on the table. 'Workshy scroungers, the lot of them!'

'I never *said* this!'

'Course you did, and you know why?' He leaned forward, bringing with him the sweet woody scent of pipe smoke. 'Cos it's true. Russell Morton *is* a workshy bastard – pardon my French – wouldn't know an honest day's graft if it bit his arse for him! Him and that whore of his, living there, right next to decent God-fearing folks. With their *parties* and their *drugs*, and their loud *bloody* music at all *bloody* hours!' He bared his false teeth. 'Scroungers! And it's about time someone had the guts to say it.'

Logan folded the printout in half, then half again. 'Where did you get this?'

'I've been complaining about the Mortons for *years*, but would anyone listen?' He pointed at the folded paper. 'Soon as I saw that on the internet I said to my Avril, I said, "Finally! Here's someone who says it like it is! I'm going down there right now to shake that man's hand."' To prove it, he stuck his hand out, an expectant look on his face.

Urgh...

Logan shook it, the skin dry and sandpapery. 'It wasn't—'

'You want to know what happened to little Ellie? That poor wee girl, growing up with those ... animals? He sold her. Russell Morton *sold* her to buy drugs.'

Of course he did. And thirteen bacon butties were flittering their way over Divisional Headquarters at that very moment. Logan had been right the first time: Mr Seafield was a nutter.

'He sold her.' Logan kept his voice nice and neutral. 'Russell Morton sold his stepdaughter.'

'To buy *drugs*.' Mr Seafield's eyes were bright as buttons.

Gomez made whimpering yowling noises beneath the table.

A mad man and his stinky dog.

'Right. Yes. I see. Well, we'll definitely look into that.'

'I know you will, because you're not one of these PC idiots running about mollycoddling scroungers and layabouts.'

Logan stood. 'Thank you for bringing it to my attention. We better not take up any more of your valuable time.' AKA: bugger off.

*   *   *

Logan smiled through the safety glass panel as Mr Seafield and his arthritic stinkhound turned and hobbled across the reception area and away through the main doors.

Soon as the doors closed, Logan hauled out his phone and stabbed at the screen. Listened to it ring.

'Colin Miller.'

'What the bloody hell are you playing at? I thought we had a deal!'

There was a thump and a faint buzzing noise. *'Can't a man have a wee prowl through his colleagues' packed lunches without police harassment?'*

'You promised me you'd spike the story! You bloody promised me!'

'And I did. Did you see it on the front page? No, you didn't. Because I got my hands on a juicy wee exposé about a couple of pervert coppers who—'

'Then why, *Colin*,' getting louder as he unfolded the sheet of paper, 'why am I holding a printout of the thing from your piece-of-crap website?'

'Moi? Nah, that wasn't me, that was the system. *Automatically flags articles to publish online. Me? I deleted it, but you know what newspapers are like these days: Wee Shuggy Public is desperate for content! Blogs, tweets, feeds, podcasts—'*

Logan forced the words out through gritted teeth. 'I will *personally…*' Ram a photocopier up his backside? Slam his head in the fridge he was raiding? Rip the rest of his fingers off? Deep breath. Calm. *Calm.* 'Get it off the internet, Colin. Get it off NOW!'

'What's this I spy in lovely Tupperware? Is that leftover pie?' The *crunk* of a plastic lid being removed. *'Ooh, payday.'*

'Colin, I'm serious!'

'Aye, aye, keep yer frilly lace panties on.' What sounded like a microwave door opening was followed by it slamming shut and some beeping. *'I'll get it deleted off the website. But favours begat favours, right?'*

'Gah!' Logan hung up. Stood there, trembling. Gripping his phone like a stone ripe for the hurling. Then turned on his heel and stormed off down the corridor. 'They don't have to put up with this in North Korea! They'd just execute the bloody lot of them...'

He thumped through the office door. Bloody Colin Miller. Bloody Colin Scumbag Lying Tosspot Miller!

Tufty was bent over a laptop, fiddling away at the keyboard. He'd put his uniform on today, so looking a lot less scruffy. Rennie waded through a box of manila folders, shirt sleeves rolled up to his elbows, tie tucked in between two buttons, the jacket of his used-car-salesman suit draped over the back of his chair.

And then there was Detective Sergeant Roberta Steel, scuffed boots in need of a clean and up on her desk. A silk shirt with what looked like egg stains on the front. Holding the phone to her ear with one hand and rummaging about in her cleavage with the other. 'No, Barry, I'm no' being unreasonable. ... No.'

Because why set a good example when you could set a bad one instead?

Logan thumped the door shut and scowled at her.

She gave him a cheery wave in return. 'You think *this* is unreasonable, you wait till I get started.'

He raised his voice to the room in general. 'Anything?'

Rennie looked up from his box. 'Sheriff's working on our search warrant for Norman Clifton's mum's house. Says to give it an hour. So I'm going through Ding-Dong's old cases again: see if we missed anything.'

'You think?' A nasty chuckle from Steel. 'Oh I'll do you one better, Barry: I'll come down there myself, and see when I do?'

'I need you to try getting hold of Fred Marshall's dental and medical records again. If he's what we dug up yesterday, I want to know for sure.'

'*Again.*' Rennie sagged. 'Oh joy of joys.'

'Oh aye? Think I won't? You just try me, Barry.'

Logan crossed his arms. 'And while we're at it: what's happening about dragging Chalmers' husband in for questioning?'

'He's having a dirty weekend in Glencoe with an account controller called Stephanie from Kennethmont. I've asked Northern to send a car round. See if we can't spoil the lovebirds' mood a bit.'

'Good. Now: dental records. Go.'

'Guv.' Rennie grabbed his jacket and hurried out the door.

Tufty looked up from his laptop. 'Sarge? Do you want those—'

'You: dig up whatever you can on one Mr Graeme Seafield. Says he's been complaining about Russell Morton for years.'

The lazy wee sod pulled on a spanked puppy-dog face. 'But I made—'

'*Now*, Constable.'

'Eek...' He turned and battered away at his keyboard.

Logan paced the room – pausing only to glare at Steel on the way past.

She gave him a wink in return. 'Oh, you better believe it. Like a ton of the proverbial, Barry. With hobnail boots on.'

'Okeydokey.' Tufty scrolled through the search results he'd got back from the Police National Computer. 'Graeme Seafield... Ooh, he's been busy.' Then silence.

'Well?'

'There's a *massive* catalogue of complaints he's made against the Mortons. Everything from putting out their wheelie bin on the wrong day to... Wow: "Undertaking satanic child-sex rituals in the back garden." Uniform investigated – apparently it was a kids' Halloween party.'

And that was why you always went on your first impression.

'So he's a nutter.'

'Like a squirrel's underpants.' Tufty spun around in his seat. 'Now, do you want to see these maps I made?'

'Maps?'

'From the GPS on DS Chalmers' phone? I did has a genius, remember?'

Steel raised her heels an inch, then thumped them down on her desk. 'Oh aye. ... That's right. With *both* boots.'

'Go on then.' Logan held out his hand and Tufty dug a folder from his desk, produced half a dozen sheets of paper and passed them over. Each one had a screenshot from Google Maps on it, printed in colour, with little red, green, and blue lines criss-crossing Aberdeen city and shire – peppered with tiny arrows.

'See, most people don't know their phones store GPS data, but if you access—'

'Are these in any sort of order?'

'I dated them in the top corner and put arrows on the lines so you can see which direction she was going in and when. See?'

Logan spread the maps out on the desk.

'No, thank *you*, Barry. Been a pleasure doing business with you. … Aye, and the same to you with knobs on.'

Tufty scooted his chair over and sorted the maps into date order. 'So this is yesterday – her phone basically stays at home in Kingswells till I arrest Naughty Naked Norman Clifton.' He poked the sheet of paper next to it. 'Saturday: all day at King-swells.' The next sheet. '*This* is the day she died.'

It was a larger scale map than the others, the lines tracing back and forth across Aberdeen, out to Kingswells...

'You've got the arrows going both ways here.'

'Ah, yes.' Tufty traced the route with his finger. 'That's because she went out to this industrial estate, then came all the way across town to here and stopped at this pub, then went home, then went off to the industrial estate again.'

Steel stretched out in her seat, hands behind her head, eggy shirt riding up to expose a yoghurt-pale slash of belly. 'You may all now bask in the glory of my magnificence.'

Logan picked up the map and peered at it.

The scale was so large it was hard to make out *exact* details, but the bit Tufty called 'this pub' looked familiar. 'That's Huge Gay Bill's Bar and Grill, isn't it? Chalmers was in the pub toilets when I tracked her down.'

Tufty glanced at Steel, his face all shifty and puckered. Trying to keep his voice innocent. 'And I didn't help you with that at all. You found her all on your own.'

Steel frowned at the pair of them. 'Well, don't all rush at once!'

Logan followed the line to Northfield. That shonky green duck shape underneath it looked like Allan Douglas Park. Which meant Chalmers had been...

Sod.

He grabbed his fleece from the coatstand. 'Tufty – get the car!'

'Guv.' Tufty snatched up the printouts, his stabproof vest, and equipment belt, jamming his peaked cap on his head as he bolted from the room. Logan hurried after him.

'Oh for...' Steel's voice rang out into the corridor. 'Does *no* one want to bask in my sodding magnificence?'

37

Tufty stopped at the junction with Broad Street. Morning rush-hour traffic crawled past: buses, cars, taxis, vans, and lorries full of miserable-looking people trying to get to work for nine. And probably failing. The new development loomed on the other side of the street – a massive block of grey and glass – Satan's Rubik's cube, all streaked and gloomy in the rain. Marischal College squared up opposite it, façade like a cathedral in granite with spikes and turrety bits.

Tufty sat forward, pulling his seatbelt tight. 'Where to, Sarge?'

'"*Inspector*", you muppet.' Logan took out his wallet and selected Raymond Hacker's business card from the dog-eared collection of social workers, lawyers, senior officers, and other assorted layabouts.

A small off-white rectangle with the ram's-head logo on it, 'AberRAD Investigation Services Ltd.', and the company address, website, and Twitter handle underneath. Complete with Hacker's mobile and office number.

According to the info printed on the back they were open Wednesday to Sunday, ten till half six. Which was sod-all use at twenty to nine on a Monday morning.

Logan called Hacker's mobile.

It picked up on the fourth ring. '*Yup?*'

'Mr Hacker, it's Inspector McRae. We met on Saturday.'

'*McRae? Oh right. Yes. You wanted to know about Ding-Dong.*'

'I need to ask you a couple of follow-up questions. Tell you what, give me your address and we'll come to you.'

'*Ah…*' There was a faint whirr, click, whirr, click noise in the background and was that someone whistling? '*Sorry, the office is shut till Wednesday and I'm out of town. Working.*'

Aye, right.

'Oops, sorry, can you hold on for a second, my DS wants something…' Logan pressed 'MUTE' and stuck out his hand at Tufty. 'I need your phone.'

Tufty unlocked his mobile and handed it over.

Logan pressed 'MUTE' again. 'Sorry about that, Mr Hacker. You know what the Job's like. Monday mornings, eh?' Logan thumbed the AberRAD office number into Tufty's phone.

'*Right, well, I'll get in touch with you next time I'm in Aberdeen.*'

The office number rang on Tufty's mobile. And, in a *weird* unforeseeable coincidence, a phone rang in the background of Logan's call to Hacker. Strange that. It was almost as if he'd *lied* about being away on business.

Logan smiled. 'If you would, that would be very much appreciated, Mr Hacker. Enjoy your trip.' He hung up both phones. Returned Tufty's. 'Northfield. And step on it. I want to get there before Hacker realises we're on our way.'

'Oooh, lights, camera, action!' Tufty hit the button on the dashboard and the blue-and-whites hidden behind the pool car's front grille flickered into the rain, accompanied by the siren's mournful wail.

The rush-hour traffic parted … and they were off.

Anderson Drive ruined their winning streak. Even with the lights and sirens on, the traffic was thick as day-old porridge. Why did no one get out of the bloody way any more?

So Logan killed the lights-and-music, then moved on to the next GPS map from Chalmers' phone.

The windscreen wipers protested their way across the glass, clearing greasy arcs in the rain.

Tufty reached a hand for the car radio, fingers hovering over the controls. 'Can I…?'

'Why not?'

'Groovy.' He clicked it on and something upbeat and jangly bounced out of the speakers. 'Ooh, I like this one.'

Logan pointed at a high-level map that extended all the way south to Stonehaven. 'She was at Nairhillock Farm five days ago.' He pulled out another one that extended north to Dufftown. 'Four days ago she visited Ben Rinnes.'

'And never said a word about it, either. Sodding sloped off when she was *meant* to be helping me and DS Steel interview people about Ellie Morton.' He shook his head. 'Not exactly a team player.'

Tufty took the first left at the roundabout, onto Provost Fraser Drive. Strange little houses drifted by on the left, the red-brick penitentiary of Northfield Academy on the right.

'OK.' Logan shuffled the maps into an orderly stack. 'What else did you get off the phone? You said texts ... and?'

'Photos. And there's printouts of her call history in the folder.'

Logan reached behind him and plucked the folder off the back seat. Flicked through the contents. 'Where's the photographs?'

That got him a smirk. 'You're kidding, right? Had to upload the photos to my phone, there's loads and loads and *loads* of them.'

'Hmmm...' He pulled the call history from the folder. Tufty had married up all known numbers with their contact name in Chalmers' phone, printing everything out in a table with number called, time, duration of the call, and whether it was outgoing or incoming.

Logan's own number appeared a fair few times, each instance tied to the contact, 'McRae: AVOID!!!' Charming. 'What about fingerprints?'

'On the phone? Mix of Chalmers and Norman Clifton.'

They passed more strange little houses. A fenced-off area. Then a row of bungalows. All brown and bleak in the rain.

The Granite Hill Transmitter loomed in the middle distance, huge and ominous, warning lights shining red against the heavy dark clouds. Like a massive angry Dalek.

Logan frowned at the list. 'Why would she delete everything *except* the Samaritans call? Doesn't make any sense, does it?

Even if there's something incriminating in here, what do you care? You're killing yourself anyway.'

A cheery mishmash of guitars and drums and saxophones brought the song to an end and the DJ blared out instead. *'Kitten-Heel Pirates there, with their latest single: "Onion Boy"!'*

Tufty turned right onto Kettlehills Crescent. 'Maybe she was covering for someone?'

'Maybe...' Didn't feel right, though.

'Don't forget we're helping raise money for Ellie Morton's family all week here on Silver City FM.'

They drove past a wall of bushes.

'And I'm delighted to announce that in addition to putting up a reward for any information, local company Whytedug Facilitation Services Limited have pledged a thousand pounds to the fund!'

Past the swimming pool.

'Aha!' Tufty held up a finger. 'Maybe it wasn't her! Maybe Naughty Norman deleted it?'

'No. He'd want to keep every last thing he could. That way he can sit in his bedroom reading Chalmers' texts and "stimulating" himself.'

'—delighted to say that Jerry Whyte, CEO of Whytedug, is on the line with us now. Hello, Jerry!'

There were a lot of numbers with no contacts next to them. 'Did you reverse look-up any of these?'

Jerry Whyte's voice smugged out of the radio. *'Hi, Tina, great to talk to you.'*

'Ah...' Tufty pulled his chin in and his eyebrows up. 'Sorry?'

'What matters is making sure we get little Ellie Morton back. It's—'

'Then we'll have to do it the old-fashioned way.'

'—and I know, if we all pull together, we can—'

Logan clicked the radio off, pulled out his phone and dialled the last number on the list:

'10:22 → 15 MINS → OUTGOING.' The one to the Samaritans. It rang and rang and rang.

Then, *'Hello, Samaritans, how can I help you?'* A friendly voice, like someone's grandad.

'Hi, this is the police. I need to talk to whoever answered a call at ten twenty-two on Friday night, from mobile number: zero seven eight—'

'I'm sorry, but we can't do that.'

Oh really?

'I can get a warrant.'

Clumps of terraced housing sulked in the rain on the left, reaching away into deepest darkest Northfield. On the right: a wide expanse of featureless grass, shut away behind a high chain-link fence, trapped beneath the thick grey clouds. And still the angry Dalek loomed.

'I know, but that probably won't help. The volunteers who answer the phones don't see the caller's phone number. We don't record calls. And unless the caller chooses to give us their details, it's a hundred percent anonymous.'

'The woman who called is dead.'

A disappointed sigh. *'I'm sorry for her family's loss. But we still can't give you any details without a warrant, assuming we have any. Even after death.'*

'Oh.' So much for that.

The car rocked its way through a set of speed humps.

'Now, is there something I can help you with? I'm not trying to tout for business or anything, but it can't be easy being a police officer these days. Must be very stressful.'

Logan blinked. 'Me? No. Er... No, thank you.'

'OK. If you're sure...?'

He hung up and scribbled the words 'SAMARITANS: WARRANT?!?' next to the number he'd just rung.

Tufty frowned at him across the car. 'No joy?'

'No joy.'

Second last entry on the list was 'BLOODY BRIAN', so Logan skipped that one and moved on to the third last. Poked in the number.

It rang. On and on and on.

Maybe there was nobody—

'Hello?' A woman's voice: thin and nervous. Familiar, but not familiar enough to put a name to. The sound of a small dog, yapping in the background. A whining baby.

'Hello? Who am I speaking to?'

'Craig isn't here.'

'My name's Inspector Logan McRae, I'm looking for...' Oh. He put the phone down. 'She hung up.'

He tried the number again. Only this time it went straight through to an automated voice. *'THE NUMBER YOU ARE CALLING IS NOT AVAILABLE, PLEASE TRY LATER.'*

Oh, don't worry: he would.

Tufty pointed through the windscreen. 'Nearly there.'

A small industrial estate appeared through a break in the hedges – little more than a row of big metal sheds in matching shades of grey.

The next number on the list was: 'McRae: AVOID!!!'

Tufty took a right at the junction.

The number after that looked like... He pulled out Raymond Hacker's business card again. Yup. It was the office number.

The pool car stopped at the junction with Quarry Road, waiting as a dirty big removals van rumbled by.

Logan dialled, listened to it ring.

'AberRAD Investigation Services Limited?' That sounded like the woman who was going to kick Rennie's backside for him. Danielle? Something like that anyway. *'Can I help you?'*

The pool car nipped across the road once the van had passed, and into the industrial estate.

'Hi. Is Raymond Hacker about?'

Tufty parked outside the AberRAD Investigations Portakabin.

'Hold on, I'll get him. Who's talking?'

Logan leaned across the car and thumped his palm down on the horn. A harsh *'Brrrrrrrrreeeeeeeeeeeeeeeeeeeeeeeeeeeeeeep!'* blared out.

Danielle's face appeared at the window, one perfectly shaped eyebrow raised.

He waved. 'I am.'

Logan smiled across the desk. 'How nice of you to cut your trip short for us.'

Hacker took another sip of coffee, face blank. 'We like to be civic-minded.'

The fish tank gurgled and hissed. Tufty hovered in front of it, bent over, staring in at the multicoloured inhabitants with a big smile on his face. 'Oooh...'

Other than that, the only noise was the rain, thumping down on the Portakabin roof.

Danielle appeared in the open doorway and knocked on the frame. Shoulders back, chin up. Like a particularly unhappy bouncer. She nodded at Hacker. 'That thing? Just got a text: it's tonight.'

'Thanks, Danners. Do us a favour and tell Andy he can head off home soon as he's finished that report on Mrs Floyd, OK? Want to make sure he's nice and fresh.'

'Guv.' But she didn't move. She stayed where she was. On guard.

Hacker turned a thin smile on Logan. 'Not that it isn't nice to see you again, Inspector ... Mackay, wasn't it?'

'McRae.'

'Sorry. Inspector *McRae*.' The smile warmed a bit. 'But we don't usually work on a Monday. Had a long weekend photographing cheating spouses and insurance fraudsters. You know how it is: guy claims he's got crippling whiplash from a rear-end shunt and next thing you know we're snapping him having a threesome with a dinner lady and someone dressed as a kangaroo.' A shrug. 'And it all needs written up.'

The tank gurgled.

The rain thumped.

Logan opened the folder from the car and pulled out one of the phone logs. 'When we spoke on Saturday, you didn't tell me you'd already met with a colleague of mine.'

'Didn't I?'

'Detective Sergeant Lorna Chalmers. She was here on Friday. Twice.'

Hacker raised his eyebrows. 'Was she?' Look at me, I'm so innocent, I never done nuffink wrong, Officer.'

'*And* she phoned your business number,' he held up the printout, 'at nine fifteen that evening.'

'We close at six.'

'The call lasted five minutes.'

No reply.

Logan had another go: 'Why was she here?'

'Danners, you remember a DS called Chalmers?'

Danielle made a big show of thinking about it. Then. 'About yay tall with spaniel-perm hair? Yeah, she came past a couple of times looking for the boss.' Shrug. 'He was out. Told her to come back later.'

No one said anything.

No one moved.

'I love tropical fish.' Tufty shuffled closer to the tank. 'Did you know the scientific name for Angelfish is Pterophyllum? It's from the Greek for "winged leaf".'

Logan returned the phone log to the folder. 'And when Chalmers turned up again?'

The pair of them shared a look. Then Hacker gave Danielle a small nod. As if he was granting permission.

'She wanted to ask about DI Ding-Dong Bell. Same as you did.'

The tank went on gurgling.

Outside, a van did a six-point turn, bleeping every time it reversed.

For goodness' sake. Logan gritted his teeth. 'This would go much quicker if I wasn't having to play dentist, here.'

Hacker sighed. Made an 'after you' gesture with one hand. 'It's OK, Danners.'

'She was flapping her top lip about how Ding-Dong was running round the countryside, acting all Batman and Robin. Course we tried to tell her she was off her head – Ding-Dong died ages ago. I was at his funeral, so were Andy and Ray. But she wasn't having any of it. Got a bit rowdy, so Andy and I had to … calm her down a bit.' Danielle shook her head. 'Of course, the next day it's all over the news that DI Bell's turned up stabbed to death in a crashed car, but we weren't to know that, were we? Lorna…' A small smile, then Danielle cleared her throat. 'Chalmers *sounded* insane at the time.'

Tufty pointed at the tank. 'Angelfish breed for life. They're

340

like albatrosses, or my Great Aunt Effie. Once their mate dies, that's it – might as well not even have genitals.'

She glowered at him. 'Will you shut up about fish?'

'Sorry. I was wondering about fidelity: what with you guys specialising in cheating-spouse cases and DS Chalmers' husband being at it with someone from work?'

'You want to know if she was a *client*? Pff... We can't confirm or deny that without a warrant. Data protection. Isn't that right, Guv?'

Hacker nodded.

Funny how people like that were so keen on the law when it suited them.

The seat creaked beneath Logan as he turned to Hacker. 'What else did Chalmers want?'

'She thought Ding-Dong was caught up with these so-called "Livestock Marts".'

'And was he?'

'If they even exist. Bunch of sketchy paedophiles getting together to sell-on abducted kids? Been hearing rumours ever since I joined the Job, but...' Hacker shrugged. 'Don't know if I believe it. I mean, if you're that kinda guy, why take the risk?'

Interesting.

Sometimes, what *wasn't* said was more telling than what was.

'You didn't answer the question.'

'Didn't I?'

'You work for Sally MacAuley. Her husband was killed trying to stop their son being abducted.' Logan sat forward, setting the chair creaking again. 'You know what *I* think? I think someone was paid a lot of money to snatch Aiden MacAuley. I think killing Kenneth MacAuley made Aiden even more saleable. All that controversy?'

'No one's ever proved the Livestock Mart even exists.'

'Are you saying you've been working this case for *three* years and you never looked into it? Sounds to me as if Sally MacAuley needs to get better private detectives, because you and your useless bunch of idiots are taking her money and doing sod-all.'

Pink flushed up Hacker's neck, darkening his cheeks. 'We are doing everything possible!'

'You're ripping her off!'

He shoved himself upright, looming over the desk. 'We *will* get Aiden back!'

'Oh, I'm sure the three of you are great at taking bribes, nicking stuff, and beating up motorists, but *actual* detecting?' Laying it on thick.

'What do you bloody know? Three years and you haven't got anywhere near these people, while...' A light must have flickered on somewhere inside Hacker's brain because he clamped his mouth shut. Took a deep breath. Lowered himself into his seat again. All calm and collected. 'I see what you're doing. Very good.'

'"Not got anywhere near these people, while" what, Mr Hacker?'

'When I was a DS, Force Headquarters was awash with stories about the *great* Detective Sergeant Logan "Lazarus" McRae. How you were the brains behind that wrinkly disaster area Steel. That you solved all those cases, not her...' Hacker stuck his feet up on his desk, coffee mug held against his chest. 'After all that, you'd think they'd at least have made you Assistant Chief Constable. But here you are, nothing more than a lowly inspector.'

'Keeps me humble.'

He toasted Logan with his mug. 'AberRAD Investigation Services are committed to bringing Aiden MacAuley home to his mother. We haven't billed her a penny in two years. We – will – bring – him – home.' A broad smile. 'Now, if you'll excuse me: Danielle will see you out. I've got work to do.'

Rain spattered up from the drenched tarmac as Danielle held the Portakabin door open for them.

Tufty smiled at her. 'Thanks.'

'Keep walking, Skinny Malinky Short Legs.'

Logan dug out one of his Police Scotland business cards. 'In case you remember anything else.'

'Oh right. Yes.' She fluttered her eyelashes at him. Then tore the card up and sprinkled it into the nearest wastepaper basket like seasoning. 'Now, if you don't mind – it's meant to be my day off and I'd like to go home.' She shooed them out of the door and into the pounding rain. 'Go on. Away. Sod off.'

As soon as they stepped outside she slammed the door shut and flipped the sign to 'Sorry, We're Closed'.

Logan hurried over to the car, jumping in as soon as Tufty plipped the locks. 'Urgh.' Absolutely drenched. *Again*.

Tufty clambered in behind the wheel. Shuddered. Turned and frowned out of the passenger window. 'They were … nice.'

Danielle rattled down the blinds, one by one, until there was nothing to see.

'You know what, Guv? I get the feeling that they didn't has a truthful.'

Logan clicked on his seatbelt. 'They discovered something about the Livestock Mart and Chalmers found out about it. Possibly DI Bell too.'

'Maybe *that's* why they were killed?'

'And if Chalmers can find out, so can we.'

Tufty started the car, driving away from the Portakabins – headlights on, windscreen wipers at max. He drifted to a halt at the junction. 'Back to the station?'

Maybe there was another way to go about this?

'If you were Raymond Hacker, and you were getting close, would you tell your client?'

'Sally MacAuley? Don't see why not, after all…' He puckered his lips, eyes narrowed. 'Actually: no. No, I wouldn't. You'd be getting her hopes up, wouldn't you? What happens if it doesn't pan out? She thinks her son's coming home, but he isn't.'

'True.' Still: might be worth a try.

Difficult to see how to do it without tipping them off, though.

A white Clio pulled up alongside the pool car, Danielle Smith behind the wheel. She revved the engine a couple of times, giving Logan the cold hard stare. Bared her teeth at him. Then drove off.

Logan watched the Clio disappear into the rain. 'Is it just me, or would you not trust Hacker and his merry band further than you could spit them?'

'Nope.'

'Me neither.'

38

'Thanks for your help.' Logan hung up and wrote 'Argos' next to the number he'd just dialled.

The office was quiet – nobody but him and his phone.

He called the next one on the list.

An over-the-top cheery voice belted out of the earpiece. *'Sparkles! Your hair is our flair! How may I assist you on the road to your fabulous best today?'*

You could dial it down about three notches.

'I need to speak to someone about Lorna Chalmers.'

'One moment.' Some flappy, clacky typing sounded in the background. *'Yes indeed. Lorna's coming in to see us on Tuesday at six for a cut and colour. Does she need to change her appointment?'*

'Well, she died on Friday night, so I don't *think* she'll be able to make it.'

'But we confirmed it with her on Thursday?' As if that was going to make any difference to the situation.

'I can check, but I'm pretty sure she'll still be dead.'

'Oh, OK.' Every bit as cheerful. *'Well never mind, that's that cancelled now.'* A bleep. *'Please hold, I have a caller on line two.'*

No chance.

Logan hung up. Wrote 'Hairdresser' next to the number.

Well, that settled things, didn't it? People planning on killing themselves didn't make appointments to get their roots done.

Right: next number.

'Yeah, about a week ago?' There was a muffled voice in the background. *'Ooh, hang on a second, I think our man's come out of the... No. Sorry, it's not him.'*

Logan swivelled in his chair. 'What did she want?'

A knock on the door and DI Fraser stuck her head into the room. 'You about ready?'

He pointed at the phone in his other hand, then mouthed 'Two minutes.' at her.

'It was weird. Chalmers calls us up, completely out of the blue, like, wanting intel on Fred Marshall. Last known whereabouts, associates, home address, outstanding warrants etc.'

'She say why she wanted it?'

'Nah, but you know what Chalmers is ... was like. Never wanted to share anything with anyone. She... Ooh! That's definitely *him this time. Got to go.'* The clunk of a car door opening. *'HOY! YOU! STAND—'* Silence. He'd hung up.

Logan wrote 'DC OWEN' next to his number. Stuck the list in the 'pending' tray, grabbed the case report and an A4 notepad. Stood. 'Right. Shall we?'

'Yes, because nothing lifts the spirits like sitting in a three-hour ongoing-cases meeting when we could be out, oh, I don't know ...' she rolled her eyes, 'actually solving crimes?'

'So if you turn to page seventeen in your briefing you'll see the numbers.' DI Vine wheeched his laser pointer across the screen, circling the pie chart. 'Car crime is a particular concern, especially in zones E through H...'

Logan turned the page and nodded. Then went back to doodling in the margins of his pad.

It wasn't that Vine was boring – though he really, *really* was – it was just very difficult to get excited about car crime when there were murder investigations to get on with.

'You'll note that vandalism is on the up in zone B as well...'

The meeting room was packed – a dozen officers sitting there with their piles of briefing notes, printouts of PowerPoint slides, notebooks, glasses of water, cups of terrible tea and nastier coffee, waiting for their turn with the laser pointer, all doing their best to look interested. Most of them failing.

And still Vine droned on. And on. Standing there, like a heavyweight boxer with his broken nose, squinty eyes. A massive forehead that ended in a pointy black widow's peak.

'Page eighteen.' The slide on the screen changed to a bar graph. 'Antisocial Behaviour Orders.'

Pff....

Of course, the *real* question was: how did Chalmers find out about DI Bell in the first place? She'd been to the pig farm where he'd buried the body, she'd been to the mountainside where he'd reburied it last week, she'd even been to the crash site where they'd found Bell's body in the car.

But how did she know?

Maybe she'd seen him somewhere? Recognised him, realised he wasn't dead, and started digging.

'...that right, Inspector McRae?'

Or was she looking into something else and somehow managed to stumble across him that way?

There had to be a connection. All Logan had to do was figure out what it—

'Inspector McRae?'

Someone nudged him.

He blinked.

The whole room was staring at him.

Sod.

No idea what the question was. So Logan nodded, pulling his face into a thinking frown as if he were actually considering it. 'In what way?'

DI Fraser nudged him again, hooking her thumb at the screen where his name was projected in big block capitals above the words, 'Investigation Into Ex-DI Duncan Bell's Falsified Suicide. Investigation Into Lorna Chalmers' Alleged Suicide.'

Ah. Right. It was his turn with the laser pointer.

*　　*　　*

DI Fraser stuffed her stack of briefings, printouts, and other assorted nonsense into her massive handbag as the rest of the room filed out. Keeping her voice down. 'Three and a half hours. Three and a *half*.' She smiled and waved at Hardie as he lumbered away, already on his phone. 'Did you see the colour Hardie went when McCulloch kept talking over the top of him?'

Logan gathered up his papers. 'Would've gone a lot quicker if that idiot McPherson hadn't broken the projector.'

'What do you expect: it's McPherson.'

He followed her out into the corridor. 'True.'

'Think we're too late to get something from the canteen?'

'Mushroom stroganoff today. That or breaded haddock.'

'Blearg. Mushrooms are the devil's bumfungus. And so are fish.' She did a quick turn, the hem of her black skirt-dress flaring out, and stared towards the stairs. 'Come on then: how much of your briefing was a load of old testicles?'

He smiled. 'Don't know what you mean, Kim. Why, how about yours?'

'Twenty, maybe twenty-five percent.' A sigh. 'In real life we've no idea *who* stabbed Ding-Dong or why. Would help if we had an ID on the body you dug up.'

'You think it was a revenge attack? DI Bell killed their friend, so they killed him?'

She pushed into the stairwell. 'Makes sense. He comes back from Spain, digs up the guy he tortured to death, and reburies him. Then a couple of days later someone parks their knife in Ding-Dong's side.' She gave Logan a sideways glance as they started down the stairs. 'You *sure* you don't know who it is?'

'A hundred percent? No. And the last time I suggested who it *might* be, I got my head bitten off by our delightful pathologist.'

'Go on then.'

'Ever heard of a thug-for-hire called Fred Marshall? We're trying to get hold of his dental and medical records for comparison.'

'Fred Marshall... Fred Marshall...' Fraser stopped on the landing and frowned. 'Wait, wasn't he one of Crowbar Craig Simpson's cronies?'

'Yes, but a knife's not really Crowbar's style, is it?'

'People change.' A smile spread across her face. 'I might go pay Mr Simpson a social call. See if I can't rattle something out of him.'

'You're in luck – we arrested him on Saturday morning. He's not up before the Sheriff till half four, so if you hurry…?'

'Now you see me.' And she was off again, clattering away downstairs on her three-inch heels.

Logan watched her go. Oh to be young and enthusiastic again.

He used his elbow to turn the handle and pushed through into the temporary office, both hands tied up with a fish-finger buttie on a paper plate and a wax-paper cup of proper coffee.

Tufty looked up from his computer and stretched, mouth wide open in a huge yawn. He raised his eyebrows at the sight of Logan's plate and smiled. 'Why yes, I'd *love* a little smackerel of something.'

'Get your own. This is my lunch.' He plonked the plate and the cup on his desk, then dipped into his fleece pocket for the half dozen plastic sachets of tomato sauce and mayonnaise. 'Where's Stinky and Wrinkles?'

'DS Rennie's away picking up medical and dental records for Fred Marshall and Rod Lawson, while the esteemed DS Steel has an appointment with a search team and Naughty Norman Clifton's mum's house. And I …' he did a small drumroll on the desk with his fingers, 'have gone through and reverse look-up'd all the numbers in Chalmers' call history. It's in your in-tray, and are you sure none of that buttie's for me?'

'Positive.' Logan opened it and slathered the fish fingers inside with red and white blobs. Took a big crunchy bite. Hot and fishy and delicious. Talking with his mouth full. 'You'll be pleased to hear that Hardie's putting DI Vine in charge of you bunch of miscreants. As of tomorrow morning, you're his problem.'

'Not DI Vine!' Tufty's face sagged. 'He's the police equivalent of having your verrucas and eating them.'

Another bite of buttie, washed down with coffee. Logan held his hand out. 'Give me your phone.'

'My phone?'

'You said you'd copied all of Chalmers' photos onto it.'

'Oh, my *phone*!' Tufty dug it out. Looked at Logan's sauce-smeared fingers. 'Yeah. Maybe after you're a bit less … sticky?'

Such a baby.

Logan polished off his buttie and scrubbed his hands clean on a wee individual moist towelette pilfered from last night's takeaway. 'Happy now?'

'Cool.' Tufty scooted his chair over, cradling his phone as if it were a tiny baby and he the proud father. 'I fitted an extra-large SD card: two hundred and fifty-six gig. Utterly *massive* storage capacity.' He laid it on the desk with careful reverence. 'There's rumours they're working on a one *terabyte* micro SD card, how mind-blowing's that? I know, right? A thousand gigabytes in something smaller than your—'

'I'm waiting for the passcode, you idiot.'

'Ah. Six, six, two, six. If you need an easy reminder it's the first four digits of Planck's Constant.'

Weirdos and freaks…

Logan punched the four digits into the smartphone's screen, then poked the icon for its photo gallery. A folder right at the top was marked, 'CHALMERS' PHONE PICS!!!'

He selected it and the screen filled with thumbnails.

'These in any sort of order?'

'By date, oldest to newest.'

He scrolled through them with his finger. Flicking faster and faster. There were hundreds and hundreds of the bloody things. Who took that many photos on their mobile phone?

Finally, the screen wouldn't scroll any more. He'd reached the end of the list.

'Let's see what we've got.' He tapped the last thumbnail and a pig ark filled the screen. It was the one from Nairhillock Farm – the rectangle of stunted lime-green grass was clearly visible next to it.

Scrolling backwards produced another eight or nine photos of the same sty, and another dozen of various bits of the farm. The picture after that – or before it, chronologically – was a selfie of Chalmers, staring out across Aberdeen Beach towards the North Sea. Brooding and moody. Auburn hair tangled by the wind.

Next up: three pics of a chicken Caesar salad.

And after that... 'Oh for God's sake.'

It was DI Bell, sitting behind the wheel of his Trans-Buchan Automotive Rentals car, parked somewhere in the Bridge of Don, by the look of. The next one was the same. And the one after that.

Logan turned the screen to face Tufty. 'She found DI Bell days ago! If she'd bothered her backside to *tell* someone, we could've brought him in and he'd still be alive!'

A sage nod. 'Maybe *she'd* still be alive too?'

'Gah...'

Some more photos of Bell coming out of the Netherley Arms, carrying his pickaxe and shovel.

'This is what happens when you're not a team player, Tufty.'

Two shots of a big bowl of mushroom tagliatelle.

Then another selfie.

'You end up ostracised, fired, or...'

Hold on.

Logan zoomed in a bit. The selfie was Chalmers posing in a shiny black bomber jacket with 'SECURITY' embroidered on the left breast. Danielle Smith from AberRAD was mugging over her shoulder, sticking her chin out and one eyebrow up. She was wearing an identical jacket.

Tufty sat forward in his chair. 'Or – dot, dot, dot – what?'

The next photo showed the pair of them again, at some sort of concert, both throwing air-guitar poses – the band an out-of-focus blur in the background. There were another five pictures at the same venue, each one showing Chalmers and Danielle. Chums. Besties. Muckers. Mates. BFFs.

Logan grabbed the desk phone and dialled.

'Control?'

'I need a home address for one ex-Detective-Constable Danielle Smith.'

* * *

Traffic crawled along the South Deeside Road, winding its way along the course of the River Dee, past the sprawling mass of new-build houses at Blairs. On through the trees, twisting and turning till the view opened out on the right, exposing the gargantuan earthworks where the new bridge reached across the dark and swollen river like a vast grey slab.

Ahead, tail-lights stretched into the distance, brought to a halt by temporary traffic lights and a coned-off section.

Tufty hauled on the handbrake, then slumped in dramatic-fainting-Victorian-lady mode. '*Please* can I stick the siren on?'

'No. Anyway, it's not going to make much difference, is it? You overtake something on a bend down here and we'll end up in the mortuary. And I'm not keen on Isobel ever seeing me naked again.'

'Ooooh. Is that gossip I sense?'

'No. And shut up.'

'Fair enough.' He puffed out a couple of breaths, lips pursed like a duck's bum. 'Course, you know the trouble with this bypass, don't you? Going to be a green light for development. Aberdeen's going to spread and spread, till it gets stopped by the road. Like a moat of tarmac around a city state. Or a wall around a megacity from *2000 AD*. Or the belt on a really, really fat man.'

Logan stared at him. 'Honestly, feel free to shut up any time you like.'

'We could talk about physics instead? Where do you stand on Bohmian mechanics? Cause if it's right, it's a *totally* valid mechanism for explaining wave-particle duality!'

He covered his face with his hands and muffled out a scream.

So this was what it felt like to be DCI Hardie…

A line of temporary metal fencing ran along the side of the road and down both sides of the building plot – the kind made of panels, held upright by concrete blocks, and peppered with 'WARNING: BUILDING SITE', 'AUTHORISED ENTRY ONLY', and 'THESE PREMISES PATROLLED BY GUARD DOGS'. It sat on the edge of an older housing estate, the beginnings of a

351

house slowly rising from the ground about thirty yards in at the end of a rough driveway. Nothing but the foundations and a few courses of breeze blocks to mark out the shape.

Stacks of more blocks sat off to one side, along with two pallets of bricks and a big pile of something covered by tarpaulins. Probably timber.

A small caravan was parked halfway down the site, partially surrounded by a wicker fence, its lights shining in the gloomy afternoon. A shadow moved across the drawn curtains. So *someone* was in.

Logan pointed through the windscreen. 'Block the entrance.'

Tufty did, parking right in front of the driveway. 'Good cop, bad cop?'

'Good cop, silent cop. And in case you're wondering which one you are...' He climbed out into the rain, pulled his peaked cap on and hurried over to the line of fencing.

A padlock and chain secured one side to the other, but it was slack enough to squeeze through, so Logan did.

Tufty locked the car and scurried after him, up the driveway, past Danielle Smith's white Clio and over to the caravan in its wickerwork enclosure.

The sound of Blink 182's 'Miss You' pounded through the caravan walls, the whole thing rocking slightly as whoever was inside danced and sang along. Logan strode over to the door and did his police-officer knock: three thumps, loud and hard.

Barking bellowed out from the other side of the door as something massive slammed against it. The song clicked off. More barking, loud enough to rattle Logan's fillings.

That dog had to be absolutely sodding *huge*.

He backed away from the door a couple of steps, till his legs bumped into a sodden garden table and chairs. He cleared his throat and turned to Tufty, Hissing it through clenched teeth – nice and quiet. 'Did you bring any Bite Back?'

'I didn't know we'd be arresting Cujo!'

The barking faded, and Danielle's voice boomed out instead. *'Go away, Jason. I'm not interested!'*

Logan inched forward and knocked again.

'*Don't be a shitebag, Jason. Take the hint or I'll set Baskerville on...*' She wrenched the caravan door open. Stood there wearing combat trousers, a Led Zeppelin T-shirt, and a frown. She directed it at Logan. 'What do *you* want?'

Behind her, the barking exploded into life again as a huge German Shepherd lunged forward, mouth big and red and full of teeth and oh God why didn't they bring any Bite Back with them and they were all going to die and—

Danielle grabbed the dog's collar, holding it back. 'Baskerville: enough!'

Instant silence.

Logan licked his lips, not taking his eyes off the dog for a second. 'Can we come in?'

'You got a warrant?'

'Do I need one?'

She stood there, staring at him, eyes narrowed. Then nodded. 'I'm getting ready to go out. You can have five minutes.'

39

Unlike the TARDIS, Danielle Smith's caravan was smaller on the inside. Every wall had at least one architectural drawing Sellotaped to it, the built-in shelves groaning with books on building and crime novels.

She pointed at the front of the caravan, where bench seating bracketed a foldaway table. Baskerville jumped up onto the cushions, padded to the far end, and sat with his mouth hanging open. One paw on the tabletop – as if waiting for his dinner.

Danielle stared at Logan and Tufty. 'You two as well. Sit.'

Logan took the empty bench seat, so Tufty had to squeeze in next to the massive dog. Sitting there, staring at it. Looking about as comfortable as a mouse in a blender.

'So...' Logan nodded at the plans and elevations. 'You're building your own house? That's got to be stressful. Builders never show up when they say they will.'

'Dear God, it's like I'm sharing a caravan with *Sherlock Holmes*!' Sarcasm dripping from every word. 'How ever did you deduce that?' She opened the tiny fridge and pulled out a couple of takeaway containers. 'Yes, I'm building my own house. What else am I going to do with a degree in mechanical engineering and a tanked oil industry?'

Now that was impressive.

'You're actually doing the construction *yourself*? Wow, that's—'

'Look, can we skip the fake rapport-building and get on with it? I've got places to be.' She opened the containers' lids a crack, then stuffed them both into the microwave and set it buzzing.

'OK.' He stretched his arms along the seat cushions. 'When we spoke at your office, you said you didn't know DS Lorna Chalmers.'

'No I didn't.'

'Didn't you?'

'Who says I knew her?'

Logan pulled out Tufty's phone and tapped at the screen. ... Nothing happened. Oh for God's sake – the thing was locked again. He looked at Tufty. 'What's the code?'

'Planck's Constant?'

Nope.

Tufty rolled his eyes and sighed. 'Give it here.' A quick flurry of fingers and he handed it over again, unlocked this time.

Logan brought up the photos and pointed the screen at Danielle. 'That's you and Chalmers doing security at a concert.'

She turned her back. Took a bowl from a cupboard. 'And?'

'There's more pictures, if you like? The pair of you look very cosy.'

'We worked a couple of security gigs together,' Danielle kept her face to the wall, 'so what?'

'Then why pretend you didn't know her?'

The microwave buzzed.

Nobody moved.

'Looks as if you were friends to me.'

Her voice went all bitter. 'Yeah, well it did to me too.' The microwave bleeped and she opened the door, turned the containers. *Slammed* the door shut. Set it buzzing again.

'So you weren't that bothered when she "hanged herself"?'

A shrug. 'What's for you won't go by you, will it?'

And the microwave kept buzzing.

Tufty fidgeted.

The dog turned to look at him.

Tufty sat perfectly still.

Then the microwave bleeped again.

Danielle's shoulders curled forwards. 'I met Lorna at a Fleet-wood Mac tribute act. It was her first security gig. A bit green behind the lugs, but she was OK. She was Job, I was ex-Job, so we hated some of the same people. We got on.' The containers were retrieved from the microwave and their contents tipped into the bowl. Rice first, followed by something wet and lumpy.

The warm, spiky scent of Thai green curry filled the caravan.

'We did the Rolling Stones gig at Glasgow SECC together.' She turned, a smile on her perfectly rouged lips. 'Man, that was some concert. I'd have worked that one for free...' Danielle thumped the bowl down on the table, following it up with chopsticks.

She shooed Logan over, sat, and got stuck into her food. 'So yeah, I knew her.'

Pretty proficient with those chopsticks. Ferrying chunks of vegetables in soft green sauce from the bowl to her mouth. Scooping up chunks of rice.

She stopped and looked up. 'What?'

'What did she do?'

'Let's see... There was me, thinking she was my *friend*, thinking she was a decent human being, *sympathising* with her because her husband Brian's a complete dickhat, but we weren't really friends at all. It was all an act.'

Tufty waggled his eyebrows. 'You weren't...?'

She stared at him. 'I will genuinely take you outside and break every single one of your bloody limbs.'

A low growling noise rumbled out of Baskerville and Tufty edged away from him.

'Eep...'

Danielle dug into her curry again. 'Lorna started asking all these questions about Sally MacAuley and loads of other cases we were working on at AberRAD. Next thing you know she's wanting me to do little *favours*.' Her voice changed to a pretty decent imitation of Chalmers' Highland drawl. '"Introduce me to this guy.", "Introduce me to that guy.", "What have you found out about so-and-so?"'

'She was using you.' Logan sat forward. 'Is that why you had to, how did you put it, "calm her down a bit"?'

'Lorna kicked off when I called her out on it. I kicked back.'

'And did you? Introduce her to all those people?'

'Till I realised what she was doing.'

Interesting.

'You think she joined the security team *specifically* to target you?'

Danielle frowned, chopsticks frozen halfway between the bowl and her mouth. 'No. No, that came later. Wasn't till…' She cleared her throat. 'Look, I'm going to have to change in a minute, so if it's all the same with you I'd rather finish my dinner in peace.'

Logan stayed right where he was.

A big, long-suffering sigh. 'All right, all right: she overheard me asking the other security guys about Fred Marshall.'

'And why would *they* know about Fred Marshall?'

'Because they worked for the same agency Marshall did. Why do you think I joined it in the first place: the sexy uniforms?' She pointed at the window with her chopsticks. 'Marshall's out there somewhere and he knows what happened to Kenneth MacAuley. He knows where Aiden is.'

Tufty sucked air in through his teeth. 'Yeah… You see: Fred Marshall's—'

Logan kicked him under the table.

'Ow!'

'And did these security guys tell you anything?'

She plucked a chunk of baby sweetcorn from her bowl, crunching on it. 'Marshall's too thick to keep his gob shut. Sooner or later he's going to make contact with someone. And when he does, we'll get him.'

Tufty rubbed at his leg. 'That hurt!'

'Good.' Logan watched Danielle polish off the last of her curry. 'So, this gig you've got tonight – anything interesting?'

The chopsticks froze again. Then, 'Nah: local-celebrity wedding anniversary party. Got to keep the riff-raff out.'

'Don't mean to be personal,' Tufty pointed towards the work surface, 'but your handbag's vibrating.'

'Bloody...' She got up and rummaged through it, producing an iPhone just in time for it to fall silent. 'Arrrgh.' She poked at the screen and turned away from them. Put the phone to her ear. 'Andy? ... No. I know. ... I said I *know*! I'm getting ready now. ... Yes, I know I'm always late, but— ... I'm getting ready! ... Yes, when they *tell* us, I'll be there. ... Because you won't get off the bloody phone!' A nod. 'OK, bye.'

She stuck the phone in her bag.

Logan smiled. 'Andy from work?'

'OK, I'm getting changed now. You've got thirty seconds to get out or I set Baskerville on you.'

Logan scooted down a bit in the passenger seat, watching Danielle's building plot vanish in the wing mirror.

Tufty sniffed. 'Why don't dogs *like* me?'

'Can't shake the feeling that she's up to something. You hear that pause before she said what she was doing tonight?'

'Maybe she really *is* working security at a local-celebrity wedding anniversary?'

He treated Tufty to a wee scowl. 'Don't make me kick you again.'

'That really hurt, by the way.' Tufty pulled onto the main road, joining the crawling traffic. 'Not much point going straight home to headquarters, is there? Unless you fancy getting stuck in rush hour again. What do you think: try the *North* Deeside Road this time?'

'Might as well. It's not as if—' His phone dinged at him. A new text message.

IDIOT RENNIE:

> Productn stors jst bean on th phn – sgt
> Moor fnd th teeth U wz looking 4! 3 uv
> thm filed in th wrng bx!!! Gtng DNA dn
> nw!

What?

He squinted at the screen. 'It's like a foreign language.'

What the hell did... Aha!

He grinned at Tufty. 'They've found some teeth from DI Bell's fake-funeral pyre.'

'Coolio.'

Logan thumbed out a reply:

> Make sure you stand over them and get
> those results to me ASAP!
> And what have I told you about texting
> like a 1990s schoolgirl?!?

SEND.

His phone was barely halfway to his pocket before it launched into 'The Imperial March', the words 'HORRIBLE STEEL' glowing in the middle of its screen.

Yes, well no thank you.

He pressed 'IGNORE'. Stared out of the window at the tiny semidetached houses and oversized bungalows. 'This whole thing makes me itchy, Tufty.' He counted them off on his fingers: 'DI Bell, Sally MacAuley, AberRAD Investigations, Fred Marshall, Lorna Chalmers, Rod Lawson – if that's who we exhumed... Itchy.'

A bus stop drifted by on the left, populated by a gang of OAPs with their headscarves, bunnets, shopping trolleys, and wee dogs.

'Erm,' Tufty glanced across the car, 'Sarge?'

'*Inspector*.'

'Yeah, but see if you ever go back to proper police work—'

'Professional Standards *is* proper police work!' Cheeky sod.

'Yeah, but see if you do: can I be your sidekick again?'

They accelerated out through the limits, following a mud-brown baker's van.

'Thought you were DS Steel's sidekick now.'

'Yeah, but she's *mean* to me. Well, she's mean to everyone, but if you're stuck in the car with her, you can't escape like normal people.'

'True.'

Fields of barley lined the road – bent, battered, and half drowned by the rain.

'And if I *was* your sidekick, would it be OK if I requisitioned DI Bell's laptop? The one they found in his hotel room? Cos we *know* the forensic IT Smurfs won't get near it for weeks. Would that be OK?'

'Don't see why not.'

Tufty nodded. 'Good. Good. Erm... Because I *might* have said you'd already OKed it. A teeny weeny bit.'

Logan stared at him. 'You've been hanging round DS Steel too long, she's starting to—'

'The Imperial March' started up again.

'Oh sod off...' He hit 'Ignore'.

'Maybe it's something important?'

Aye, right. 'She'll be wanting a moan. It's all she ever does.'

'But what if—'

Tufty's pocket launched into 'Ding Dong! The Witch is Dead'. He dug a hand in and produced his phone. Grimaced across the car at Logan. 'Can you get it? I'm driving.' He poked his thumb at the screen, unlocking it, then held it out. 'Please?'

'Like I'm his secretary...' But Logan took it anyway. Held it up to his ear. 'PC Quirrel's phone?'

Steel's voice growled out at him. *'Oh I see. That's how it is, is it?'*

'Urgh... It's *you*.' Well, at least that explained the ringtone.

'Ducking my calls. Very mature. Thought you were supposed to be SIO on this one?'

He glared at Tufty. The little sod knew it was her and tricked him into answering it.

Tufty kept his face forwards, not making eye contact.

'If you've phoned up to whinge, you can—'

'You bunch of spunghammers were given the opportunity to bask in the glory of my magnificence, and did you?'

'Moan, whinge, gripe, whine...'

'You want to know what I dug up or no'?'

'We'll be there in twenty minutes. Plenty of time for you to dig out some biscuits and get the kettle—'

'It's happening tonight.'

Logan pulled his chin in. 'What is?'

'*Ah, see:* now *you're interested.*'

More fields of ruined barley, a huge puddle of water spreading out from beneath a five-bar gate onto the road.

The baker's van slowed, sending up big curls of dirty water.

Tufty hummed a wee song to himself as they surfed through after it.

Logan puffed out a breath. 'And are you actually going to tell me?'

'*You were banging on about missing kids, so I spoke to a pervert of my acquaintance: Barry the Nonce. Took a bit of leaning, but he's been away speaking to his slimy wee pals and guess what he's just told me. Go on, you'll no' guess, but have a go for your Auntie Roberta.*'

'OK, I'm going to hang up now.'

'*You're even less fun than you used to be, you know that, don't you?*' There was another pause as she milked whatever it was. '*It's no' Santa Claus that's coming to town tonight, it's the Livestock Mart. And I mean* the *Livestock Mart.*'

Logan sat upright, eyes wide. Turned to Tufty. 'Stop the car!'

'Aaaaaaargh!' He slammed on the brakes and the car slithered to a halt in the middle of the huge puddle. 'What? What's happened?' Looking around, frantic. 'Did I hit something?'

Behind them, someone leaned on their horn.

Logan shifted his phone to the other ear. 'Where and when?'

'*Nah, we're no' that lucky. Whole thing runs on an invitation-only basis. From what Barry hears: if you make the cut, you get a text with the* when *so you're ready to go and, a couple of hours later, another one with the* where.'

Tufty stuck a hand against his chest and slumped in his seat. 'Nearly gave me a heart attack!'

A Ford Escort drove around them, the driver sticking up one finger and mouthing obscenities as he passed.

'And Barry the Nonce...?'

'*He's no' on the list. But it's still happening tonight. What we gotta do is figure out where.*'

So *that* was why Chalmers wanted him to keep DI Fraser out

of her hair for seventy-two hours. She knew when the Livestock Mart was scheduled.

He turned in his seat and stared out through the rear window. The line of traffic behind them was getting shorter as each one gestured and swore their way past. They couldn't be more than a couple of miles from Danielle Smith's caravan. There was still time.

Logan faced front again and thumped Tufty on the arm. 'Do a U-turn and get back to that building site ASAP. Wherever Danielle Smith's off to: that's where we're going too.'

Tufty hauled the wheel around.

40

Danielle tapped her nails against the tabletop, staring at her iPhone. Hurry up and *ring*.

Baskerville had picked up on the tension, pacing the length of the caravan, making semi-growling noises.

Come on and ring!

She'd done her make-up twice, her hair once, changed into three different all-black outfits – before settling on cargo pants, black trainers, a black sweatshirt and a silky bomber jacket. Maybe the bomber jacket was a mistake? What if she got someone's blood on it? How was she going to get that out of silk? Gah... No: leather jacket. And not the good biker one either, the Sixties one from the vintage shop. In case she had to burn the thing.

She stood and stripped off the bomber jacket.

Frowned.

What about the canvas night-camouflage one from—

Her phone buzzed on the tabletop and she snatched it up, unlocked it.

Number Withheld:

> 19:15 Location 6F – Doors open 20:30 for
> 21:00

Yes!

She stuck the bomber in the wardrobe again and put on the

night-camouflage jacket instead. Checked herself in the mirror – definitely the right choice – loaded up the pockets with the essentials, pulled on a pair of black leather gloves, and climbed out of the caravan. 'Baskerville: stay. Guard.'

He gawped at her, mouth hanging open, tongue dangling out like he hadn't a brain cell in the world.

'No, I'm not falling for the idiot look, and you're not coming with me.'

Baskerville gave a miserable whine, then lay down with his big triangular head on his paws. Staring up at her.

'And that's not going to work either.' She clunked the caravan door shut and locked it, ignoring his yowls as she jumped into her Clio and drove down to the makeshift fence / gate at the end of the drive. Did the whole unlocking-the-padlock-driving-through-and-locking-it-again routine, before punching the coordinates for '6F' into the satnav and pulling out onto the road.

The car drifted past rain-drenched streets. People hurrying home from work.

The satnav was estimating forty-five minutes, but on a rainy Monday evening with rush hour in full crawl? Quarter past seven was *maybe* doable. As long as she considered the speed limit more of a suggestion than a rule.

She poked the icon on her dashboard screen and set the hands-free kit ringing.

The suburban streets gave way to darkened countryside.

Hacker's voice banged out of the car's speakers. *'Danners? Is it in?'*

'They've texted through my watchpoint. It's the far side of Bennachie. On my way now.'

'Great! Good. You all set?'

Danielle reached into her jacket pocket and pulled out the semiautomatic: Smith & Wesson, M&P 40 2.0. A thing of utter beauty. She ran a gloved thumb along the safety catch. 'Better believe it.'

'We're going to get Aiden back tonight, Danners. We're finally going to do it.'

*   *   *

Sally digs her fingernails into the placemat, one leg twitching under the table, staring out through the patio doors.

Raymond paces along the edge of the patio, shoulders hunched against the rain, phone clamped against his head.

Please. Please. Please. Please...

He stuffs his phone in his pocket and hurries to the doors, hauls them open and slips inside, a huge grin nearly splitting his face in half.

She swallows. 'It's happening?'

'It's happening!'

Sally grabs hold of the table and lets a huge breath rattle free. 'It's happening. After all these years, it's actually happening.'

Raymond fetches the red rucksack from the cupboard under the stairs. Dumps it in front of her. 'You need to be ready: they'll be in touch soon.' He marches off again.

After everything she's gone through, it's finally happening...

He returns with an armful of carrier bags, tipping the contents out onto the table: bundles of twenty-pound notes. A thousand pounds per bundle. Raymond counts them into the rucksack. '...fifteen, sixteen, seventeen...'

Fifty thousand pounds from selling her father's house.

'...thirty-two, thirty-three, thirty-four...'

The five thousand she got from the publishers for her book.

'...fifty, fifty-one, fifty-two...'

The four thousand she's saved over the years.

'..sixty-three, sixty-four, sixty-five.'

Sixty-five? Sally frowns. 'That's not right, it's meant to be—'

'I cashed in my ISA: got us another six grand.' He zips up the rucksack. 'Better safe than sorry.'

She stands and holds out her arms, trembling, tears making the kitchen wobble as he wraps her in a big hug, burying his face in her neck.

She stares over his shoulder at their reflections in the patio doors. Standing there like ghosts, hovering in front of the darkened garden, the ivy-covered shed barely visible on the other side.

He kisses her forehead. 'We're going to get Aiden back.'

Something curdles in her lungs, making it hard to breathe. 'What if—'

'Hey, it's OK.' He kisses her again: frowning, serious. 'You do whatever they tell you, follow *all* their rules ... and leave everything else to me and the gang.' Then that grin spreads again. 'This is it!'

After all this time.

She hugs him. 'I can't believe it's finally happening...'

A sliver of sky glowed a pale shimmering blue, the clouds above it painted in violent shades of pink and orange. Everything else was a dark heavy grey.

'Don't lose her!'

Danielle Smith's tail-lights burned red, disappearing as the road twisted along the flank of Bennachie. Trees loomed over them, turned into scratchy inkblots by the pool car's headlights. Dark fields. The shining windows of a farmhouse in the distance.

Tufty shifted his hands on the wheel. 'I'm not *going* to lose her. I didn't lose her on the dual carriageway, did I? Or all the way out here? No, brave Sir Tufty stuck to her like a secret sneaky sticky ... stain?'

'Be careful, OK? Can't afford to screw this one up.'

'How am I screwing it up? I'm doing everything it says in the manual! Regulation distance for following a vehicle on quiet roads at night is—'

'Oh shut up.' Logan pulled out his phone and called Steel. 'We've pulled off the A96 at Port Elphinstone. Heading west on the B993. I repeat—'

'Heard you the first time. I'm irascibly sexy, no' deaf.'

'Where's Rennie?'

The sound grew echoes, the clatter of Cuban heels on stairs reverberating underneath. *'Getting himself a pool car and hopefully some Tic Tacs. Boy's got breath you could strip paint off the Forth Bridge with.'*

'What about my firearms team?'

'I've got two words for you: "awa" and "shite".' More clattering.

'Oh you're kidding me!'

The clattering quietened down a bit, followed by the thump of a door and louder echoes. *'Well, what did you expect? We've got no actual intel, we've got no corroboration, we've got no proof. We haven't even got a sodding location. All we've got is your scar-puckered gut to go on.'*

'But—'

'Course they're no' giving us a firearms team.' Another thump, and the sound opened up – no more echoes. *'So we follow this private investigator woman of yours till she leads us to the Livestock Mart, we call it in, and then we get a firearms team.'* A shrill whistle ripped out of the earpiece.

'Aaargh!' Logan yanked the phone away from his ear.

'RENNIE, YOU USELESS LUMP OF BADGER SPUTUM, WHERE THE MOTHERFUNKING...' A car horn blared in the background. *'Oh. About time too!'*

'You nearly deafened me!'

'Oh, boo-hoo.' Some rustling and clunking was followed by a loud thunk and the sound of an engine starting. *'Don't just sit there:* drive!'

Logan hung up. Stuck a finger in his ear and wiggled it as he frowned out through the windscreen.

Dark. No rear lights.

'Tufty?' His eyes widened. 'Where's Danielle Smith's car?'

'Ah... Funny you should mention that...'

Logan crumpled forward in his seat, until the seatbelt stopped him, and covered his head with his arms. 'Aaaaaaargh!'

'Sorry?'

'For God's sake, Constable. Why didn't you—'

'I'm *sorry!* You were shouting and there was all this...' He grabbed Logan's arm. 'There! Look, thar she blows! Woot! Jodrell Bank, we does has a liftoff!'

Danielle's tail-lights snaked through the darkness up ahead, headlights casting the trees into sharp relief as she passed them.

Logan slumped back. 'Don't *do* that.'

Tufty pulled on a sickly smile. 'Anyone can make a mistake...'

*   *   *

Raymond paces up and down the kitchen, hands clenching and spreading and clenching and spreading.

Sally's mobile sits on the table in front of her, the dark screen reflecting her face: thin, bags under her eyes, the bruise on her forehead spreading out from beneath its skin-coloured sticking plaster – already starting to go green and yellow at the edges.

She clears her throat. 'Maybe they—'

Her phone buzzes and she snatches it up, unlocking it with shaking fingers.

A text message.

NUMBER WITHHELD:

> 57°18'43.1"N 2°29'34.7"W – No later than
> 19:45
> Watchword: "Foxglove"

Raymond hurries over. 'Is it them?'

'Map coordinates.'

She copies and pastes them into the phone's map app which churns and churns and finally fills with an unnamed road northwest of Inverurie. Pressing 'GET DIRECTIONS' sets it churning again. Then brings up a blue line from the croft to the designated spot with an estimated journey time of twenty-two minutes.

Sally stares at the microwave clock – '19:10' – then scrambles to her feet, grabbing the rucksack and her jacket. 'I have to go!' Rushing into the hall.

Raymond blocks the front door. 'Wig!'

The bloody wig! She snatches it off the coatrack and jams it on her head as she rushes out through the front door, wrenches open the Shogun's door and throws herself in behind the wheel. Slamming the door shut as Raymond runs down the track towards the gate.

Sally dumps the rucksack in the passenger footwell, jams the key in the ignition and twists it: the engine roars into life.

She can do this. For Aiden.

Her hands shake on the steering wheel as she accelerates down the drive.

Raymond's waiting for her, right in the middle of the track, the gate lying wide open behind him.

Get out of the bloody way!

She slams on the brakes and buzzes her window down. 'Raymond, I—'

'It's going to be OK. Deep breaths. You can do this.'

'I have to *go*.'

He steps up onto the running board and leans in through the window. 'You know I'd come with you if I could.'

She nods. Blah, blah, blah.

'We're going to bring Aiden home tonight, Sally. That's all that matters.'

She stares at him. 'That's all that's *ever* mattered.'

He wraps a hand around the back of her neck, pulling her into a kiss. His lips taste of bitter coffee and Extra Strong Mints. Then he lets her go and hops back to the ground again. 'You can do this!'

For Aiden.

She puts her foot down.

Raymond jumped away from the puddle as Sally's four-by-four hammered out through the open gate, sending up twin walls of dirty brown spray. This was it. Succeed or fail, it was all down to her.

He pulled out his phone, dialling as he picked his way over to the side of the track, steering clear of the puddles. 'Andy?'

Andy's voice crackled from the earpiece, distorted and broken. *'Guv? I can barely hear you.'*

'Are you on?'

'Guv? Hello? ... Hello? ... Can you— me? Gu—'

Oh in the name of Christ. Not now. Not tonight!

'Andy? Andy!'

Damn it. He hung up and tried again.

Straight to voicemail. *'Hi, this is Andrew Harris. Leave a message after the bleep.'*

No point. Either they were ready, or they weren't. He'd just have to trust them.

He put his phone away. Stood there, at the gate, watching Sally's tail-lights get smaller and smaller, then disappear.

She was a strong woman – a lot stronger than she thought. She could do this. And Danners and Andy would look after her.

Ray grabbed the gate and hauled it shut again. Clipped the hooky thing onto the chain. 'Please, God, let it be this time. Let us *finally* bring Aiden home.'

What really hurt was that he couldn't be there to help.

He sighed, shook his head, and walked back to the croft.

Danielle slowed the Clio and turned off the stereo – right in the middle of Jimmy Page's big 'Heartbreaker' solo. The road stretched away into the darkness ahead, not a house in sight, not even the distant lights from a lonely farm. Nothing but trees and bushes crowding in on all sides.

The satnav's voice broke the silence. 'YOU HAVE REACHED YOUR DESTINATION.'

The only feature in sight was an unmarked track on the left, cutting deeper into the woods, wide at first, then narrowing. A black Range Rover gleamed at the edge of her headlights. It'd reversed up the track about twenty / twenty-five feet and sat there. Like a funnel-web spider. Waiting.

She pulled off the road and onto the track, parking in front of it – nose to nose. Killed the engine. Stuck the gun in her pocket again. Put on a plain baseball cap. And climbed out into the rain.

It drummed on the hat's bill, pattering against her shoulders as she walked across to the big car. The lights were off, but the engine was running – the exhaust clouding in the cold air, drifting away into the trees.

Danielle stopped by the driver's window and raised her hand to knock. Her knuckles hadn't even made it that far before the window buzzed down.

Probably a man, going by the build, in a light-grey hoodie

370

and a black leather jacket. Black leather gloves, like her own, and a featureless grey mask. No mouth hole, no nose, or decoration of any kind. A grey slab with two narrow horizontal slits for eyes.

Anonymous as hell.

She gave him a nod. "Sup, Jason Voorhees?'

His voice was deep, authoritative. The kind of guy who expected people to follow orders. 'You're new, so you get one chance at this and one chance only. Give me your phone.' He held out a gloved hand. Ah, why not. She passed it over and he tucked it away. 'You'll get it back at the end of the night.'

She better.

He produced a big brown envelope with the letter 'A' printed on it. 'You stay here until you've passed all three clients on to the location. You don't chat to them, you don't remember them, you don't let them see your face.' He reached across to a card-board box on the passenger seat and came out with another mask. Only this one was a dull-blue colour, with a big white '6' on it. Heavier than it looked, with a thick strap to hold it in place.

OK.

Danielle took off her baseball cap and put the mask on. The world shrank to the view through the two narrow slits. She wedged her cap over the top – tight, but it fit.

'Better. Park where I'm parked and remove your number plates. Anyone who gives you the watchword gets a card from envelope "A". Anyone who *doesn't* give you the watchword gets sent here instead for a special surprise.' He passed her another envelope marked 'B', same size, same shape. 'Fingerprints on *nothing*. Understand?'

She held up her gloved hands, showing them off. 'Way ahead of you.'

'No one gets to bring a friend. No one gets to take their mobile phone with them. No one gets to record or photograph anything. If in doubt: confiscate it. Search *everyone*.' One more envelope, this one with a big 'C' on it. 'When your last client is on their way, give them five minutes, then get your arse to the venue. Details in there.' He stared at her, head tilted slightly to one side. 'Any questions?'

It was … weird. There was something about that blank face and the calm voice that set alarm bells ringing all the way up and down her spine. Like he was a cat and she was a juicy little mouse.

She cleared her throat. 'What do I do if someone kicks off?'

'What do you *want* to do?'

That was more like it. She wasn't the mouse, she was the attack dog. A grin spread across her face – making her cheeks brush the inside of her mask. 'I'm going to enjoy this.'

He clicked the Range Rover's headlights on and stuck it in drive.

She waved. 'Wait: what do I call you?'

'You don't.'

OK.

Danielle stepped aside as the Range Rover backed up, pulled around her Clio, bumped onto the main road and drove away. She stood there till its rear lights disappeared into the rainy night. Then nodded. Took a deep breath. 'Right. Turn the car round, then number plates…'

41

Fat yellow sycamore leaves drifted across the road, caught by the pool car's headlights as they danced and weaved their way to the rain-rivered tarmac. Danielle's tail-lights went in and out of focus as the windscreen wipers thunked back and forth across the glass.

Getting nearer...

Logan grabbed Tufty's arm. 'Kill the lights. Kill the lights!'

Tufty killed them and the car drifted to a halt in the darkness. 'What?'

'She's stopped.'

'Oooh.' He grimaced. 'Maybe she's on to us?'

They sat there, in the dark, engine running.

Tufty leaned forward, peering out through the windscreen wiper's temporary arcs. 'Or maybe she's trying to make sure nobody's following her? Hiding up and waiting for us to drive by, then POW!'

Logan looked over his shoulder. The road behind them was barely visible. 'Or maybe she's meeting someone.' Why else would she be out here, in the middle of nowhere, in the middle of the night? Well, not *night*, but definitely early evening. 'Get the car off the road, find a wee track or something... Up there, where the trees get thicker.'

Tufty eased the car forward, nose inches from the windscreen, bottom teeth bared. 'Talk about your all-inclusive Stygian gloom.'

Twenty feet on, a track disappeared off into the woods on the right. Rutted and bumpy, with a thick line of grass down the middle. Tufty turned onto it, the car lurching and bumping along in slow motion. Shapes loomed in the darkness, swallowed by the rain. 'Argh, this is horrible…'

A huge lump of whin scraped its way down one side of the car.

Logan tapped the dashboard. 'OK. You can stop here.'

'Oh, thank the Great Green Arkleseizure.' He pulled on the handbrake and killed the engine.

Now the only sound was the rain, pattering against the car roof.

Tufty undid his seatbelt. 'And now we…?'

'One of us has to go out there and see what she's up to.'

'Urgh.' He slumped in his seat. 'Oh noes… Poor Tufty…'

'Don't be such a drama queen.'

'It's always the lowly police constable, isn't it? Squelching about in the rain. Dying of pneumonia. Getting all chafed.'

Oh for goodness' sake.

'Fine! *You* stay with the car.' Logan took out his phone and set it on vibrate. Then did the same with his Airwave. 'If she drives off, you follow her. *Discreetly.*' He grabbed his peaked cap and pulled it on. Then climbed out into the rain. 'And don't lose her this time!'

Something squished beneath his feet as he picked his way around the bonnet of the car, breath misting out around his head. He'd got as far as the driver's side when Tufty cracked the door open and put on a big theatrical whisper:

'Guv! You forgot your waterproof!'

'Yes, because creeping through the woods, in the middle of the night, is so much easier in a fluorescent-yellow jacket!'

Idiot.

Logan turned and stepped off the track, and onto a slippery patch of fallen leaves. Yeah, this was going to be a barrel of laughs.

He pushed through a clump of dying nettles, ducking under the branches of a huge Scots pine and into the woods proper.

Lichen-crusted beech snatched at his black fleece, their fingers brittle and rattling.

They gave way to Forestry Commission pines, standing guard like sentries in the dark. Their trunks pale against the suffocating gloom.

He scrambled up a small ridge of needle-matted ground, then down the other side. Stepping over the drainage channel at the bottom. It was a lot darker in here, but at least the canopy kept most of the rain off. And he had to be virtually invisible in his black Police Scotland fleece, trousers, and boots.

Logan crept on, crouched over to avoid the lower branches, feet scuffing through the rolling sea of fallen needles. Every step smelled of old houses, stale bread, and pine disinfectant.

The sound of a car engine idled up ahead. Getting louder.

He stopped.

There – through the trees. Danielle Smith's white Renault Clio. Parked down a rutted track of its own. Only she'd reversed up hers, the car sitting nose out. For a quick getaway?

Logan sneaked closer.

She was squatting down by the boot of her car, fiddling with something.

Urgh. She wasn't having a—

No. She stood, holding the rear number plate in one hand, screwdriver in the other.

OK, so she was definitely up to *something*. Innocent people didn't anonymise their motor vehicles.

He could probably get a bit nearer if he—

Logan froze as his phone buzzed in his pocket.

He dug it out – the screen was like a searchlight in the gloom. He slapped it against his chest, smothering the glow, and ducked behind a tree trunk. The word 'Tufty' filled the screen.

Logan answered it, keeping his voice so low it was barely there. 'This better be important!'

Tufty crackled on the other end. *'Guv? There's a ... comin— Guv? ... –ello?'*

'I can't hear you.'

'...car com— ... see it? I—'

He hung up and thumbed out a text instead:

> Reception is terrible. Have located Smith.
> She's parked up a small track, taking off
> her number plates.

SEND.

Headlights glowed in the middle distance, coming this way.

Logan turned down the brightness on his phone and crept around to the front of the tree again. Slipped in behind a clump of jagged broom, keeping low and out of sight, then peered through its branches.

A rusty old Jaguar rolled to a halt at the junction where the track met the road and sat there, windscreen wipers *click-thump*ing. Then eased onto the track. Stopping a couple of feet in.

Danielle Smith stood.

At least, it was *probably* Danielle Smith. Her face was hidden behind a smooth dull-blue mask with a big white number six on it. A baseball cap hiding her hair. She popped open the Clio's boot and chucked the number plate inside. Thunked it shut again. Checked something in her pocket. Stood there. Still and silent.

The Jag's driver wound down his window. Overweight with a mop of greying hair and an open-necked shirt. Sweaty and jowly, like a proper child molester. He waved at her, voice booming out, 'HELLO?'

She didn't reply. Instead she stood there, with her head on one side, as if trying to decide which of his bones to break first.

Logan started up the camera app on his phone and clicked off a few shots. The results were all grainy in the low light, but they were good enough to make out the Jag's number plate. He took a few more, trying to get the driver's face.

Sweaty McChildMolester checked his watch. 'CAN WE GET ON WITH THIS PLEASE? I DON'T WANT TO BE LATE!'

She ran at him, from zero to a full-on sprint, covering the ground to his car in seconds, arms out, growling.

Sweaty ducked inside again, but she was too quick – before he could wind up his window her hand snapped forward, grabbed him by the collar, and hauled his head out into the rain. The other hand dipped into her jacket and when it reappeared... Great. A semiautomatic pistol. Because this whole thing wasn't screwed-up enough.

She ground the barrel into Sweaty's forehead.

He scrunched his eyes shut. 'Oh God, oh God, oh God, oh God...'

Logan tensed. OK, so running out there and getting between Sweaty and a bullet was a stupid thing to do, but he couldn't sit here and watch her *murder* the guy.

Danielle growled it out: 'You didn't say the magic word.'

'Wormwood! Wormwood! The magic word is Wormwood...'

Come on, Logan. Charge in there and save the day.

Maybe she won't even shoot you?

Or at least, not *fatally*.

Maybe.

Here we go.

Deep breath.

In three. Two...

She yanked the Jag's door open and dragged Sweaty out onto the road. Stuck the gun in her pocket.

Oh thank God for that.

Sweaty tumbled onto his back, squealing and whimpering, both hands covering his face as she searched him.

'Where's your phone? WHERE'S YOUR PHONE?'

She yanked it from one of his inside pockets, then shoved him over onto his front so she could check the rest of him.

Then stood.

Nodded.

And gave the car a quick search as well. Fast and efficient.

Logan tried a few more photos.

She stood over Sweaty, holding his mobile phone between two gloved fingers like a soiled nappy. 'You can pick this up at the end of the night.'

He whimpered and curled into a ball.

'In the car. NOW!'

Sweaty scrambled into the Jag and sat there, trembling and muddy.

'Better.' Danielle thumped the door shut and stepped away from the car. Then reached into her pocket and produced an envelope. Pulled a card from it and held the thing out just a *tiny* bit too far from the open window.

Sweaty ran a shaky hand over his dirty face. Licked his lips. Then nodded and reached for the card. Stretching for it. Podgy fingertips searching the air … almost … almost…

She let him take it. 'Pleasure doing business with you.'

He snatched his arm in again and wound the window up. Eyes darting left and right as he reversed off the track, the *scrunch* of grit giving way to the squeal of tyres as he stuck his foot down and the old Jaguar roared off into the night.

Danielle waved after him, the grin obvious in her voice: 'YOU'RE WELCOME!'

Logan cupped his hands in front of his mouth and blew a warm breath into them. Fog escaped through the gaps between his fingers as he huddled there, sitting on the forest floor, hidden from the track by a lump of broom. He clamped his knees together and leaned against a tree trunk. Wrapped his arms around himself and shivered. At least the pine needles gave a bit of insulation to his bum, everything else was half frozen.

Danielle had returned to her car, sitting in the passenger seat, still wearing her Number Six mask. Nodding away to a song belting out of the stereo: something loud with pounding drums and a bloke banging on about 'loving this feeling'.

All right for some.

Logan's phone buzzed and he dug it out.

TUFTY:

You OK?

He poked out a reply with shivering thumbs:

378

> No I'm not. Bloody freezing out here!!!

SEND.
Another buzz.

> Want to play I-spy?

Did he...?

> How about we play "hide my boot in your
> arse"? You

But before he could tell Tufty what he was, the phone buzzed again.
TUFTY:

> Car heading your way!

Logan peered through the bushes as a dark green Audi pulled off the road and onto the track. It wasn't easy, holding the phone steady, but Logan took a handful of photos. Zoomed in on the car's nose...

Sod: the Audi didn't have any number plates.

The driver got out and stood there with her hands empty and visible. Calm, in a high-necked jumper, jeans, and trendy trainers. Dark hair tied up in a bun. All perfectly normal, except for the green snake mask that covered her whole face. And not a cheap plastic one either, it looked custom-made and expensive.

Logan took some grainy pixelated photos of it. Probably completely useless, but you never knew.

Danielle climbed out of her Clio and stalked across to Snake. Slow and menacing.

Snake didn't move. Her accent was crisp and well spoken – one of those privately educated voices. 'Hello, my name's *Nightshade*. I'm looking for my friend, have you seen him?'

'Arms.' Danielle gestured with her gloves.

'But of course.' Snake adopted the search position, arms out, legs shoulder-width apart. 'My phone's in my jacket pocket – left side.' She stood, still and quiet as Danielle searched her, didn't complain when her phone was confiscated, didn't so much as fidget as her car was searched.

Danielle handed her a card.

Snake nodded. 'Thank you kindly.' Then got in her car and drove away as if this was all perfectly normal and happened every day.

The world was full of weirdos.

Logan jammed his elbows in a little tighter, trying to hold his hands still enough to text. All ten angry-pink fingers burned and itched. Ears like someone was sandpapering them. The only plus was that his toes didn't ache any more.

He clamped his jaws together to stop his teeth rattling.

> Can't feel my feet. No idea how many
> people she's going to stop and search.
> Could be here for hours!

SEND.

On the other side of the broom, Danielle was rummaging about inside a mud-spattered Toyota Hilux. No number plate on the vehicle.

Its driver stood off to the side, arms crossed, quiet and patient. About six / six-two, wearing red corduroy trousers, Cabotswood boots, a checked shirt, a green Barbour jacket, and a tiger mask. None of which photographed particularly well on Logan's phone.

Should've got one with a better camera.

Might as well submit a drawing in crayon to the procurator fiscal.

His treasonous phone buzzed again.

TUFTY:

> Maybe we should arrest her, before you do
> a hypothermia?

Logan's thumbs kept hitting the wrong keys. Every shivering word had to be corrected as the Hilux's big diesel engine rumbled into life then faded away into the distance.

> Don't be an idiot: she's got a gun! We're
> just going to have to keep tabs and see
> where she

Sod.

He went perfectly still, not shivering, not even breathing as the barrel of Danielle's gun pressed against his cheek.

She tutted. 'Well, well, well...'

OK. He had one chance at this. If he—

She pressed the gun in harder. 'I *really* wouldn't do that if I was you.'

Yeah, maybe not.

'Danielle. You were a *police officer*, you don't have to—'

'Oh, but I *do*, Inspector McRae. I *do*.' She backed away out of reach, face hidden by her Number Six mask, the semiautomatic pointing right at the middle of his chest. 'Now toss the phone over here. *Gently*.'

'They're paedophiles, Danielle, they—'

'Tell you what, I'll swap you the phone for a bullet. How's that sound?'

He tossed the phone onto the ground at her feet.

'Good boy.' She eased down, keeping the gun on him the whole way, and picked up his mobile. Swiped a thumb across the screen. Stared. Then obviously realised the screen wouldn't react to leather-gloved fingers, because she stuck her left hand in up under her mask and pulled the glove off. Tried again. Nodded. 'How nice, it's still unlocked. Let's make that permanent, shall we?' She fiddled with the settings then nodded. 'On your feet: you and I are going walkies.'

It took a lot of effort to get his aching legs and stiff back into position, but Logan struggled upright.

She jerked her gun towards the track and her car.

He limped around the clump of broom, arms up as far as

they'd go – given the branches overhead. Ducked under the last of them and onto the track. Dirt and gravel crunched beneath his boots, the rain pattering against his peaked cap, stealing what little heat remained in his skin.

Logan stopped. 'You know I'm not here on my own, don't you, Danielle? They'll come looking for—'

Bright white light blared out, robbing detail from the world, followed by a rushing, crashing noise. Then burning daggers slashed across the back of his head as the light faded and everything went...

Down like a bag of tatties.

Danielle stood over him for a moment. Never coldcocked someone with a gun before. Certainly seemed to work, though. As long as it hadn't damaged the gun, of course.

She pulled on her other glove, then hunkered down next to him and went through his pockets: keys; some change; a hanky; a wallet containing a photo of a big fluffy cat, a photo of a pretty woman with bright-red hair and tattoos, twenty quid in cash, a debit card, a bunch of receipts, and some business cards; a hanky; a police-issue notebook – he could whistle for that; and an Airwave handset. He could whistle for that too. Everything else got stuffed into one of his fleece's pockets.

Probably better get a shift on now, in case he woke up. She popped open the Clio's boot and levered the bass board out of the way – thing weighed a ton. Then pulled out her abduction kit: a packet of thick black cable ties, a roll of bin bags, and one of duct tape. A lot of people would be surprised how often something like that came in handy.

Now: first things first.

She shoved McRae over, so he was lying face down, pulled his wrists behind his back and zipped a cable tie around them. Then did the same with his ankles. Rolled him onto his side, balled up his hanky and stuffed it into his mouth. Stuck a big strip of duct tape across his face to keep it in there. It took a couple of minutes, lining the boot with the bin bags, but it was worth it. Who wanted DNA and bloodstains all over their nice new car?

Danielle dug two hands in under McRae's armpits and dragged him around to the Clio's boot. Heavier than he looked. She wrestled him inside, made sure all his limbs were secured, then sealed him in with the hefty pine bass board. Lovingly hand-crafted for maximum solidity.

'Sweet dreams.' She scooped his peaked cap up off the ground and chucked it in with him, clunked the tailgate shut, and climbed in behind the wheel. Dumped the Airwave on the passenger seat, removed her gloves, took out his phone and checked the recent text messages.

Hmm... About a dozen outbound texts and the same number of replies from that idiot sidekick of his, all about hiding in the bushes like a pervert watching her. No point deleting them – they'd be on the sidekick's phone anyway, and more people got caught trying to cover something up than actually doing what they'd done – but that didn't mean she couldn't make this work *for* her. She killed the Clio's engine, made sure all the lights were off. Well, except for the smartphone's screen.

Let's see...

She deleted the 'Don't be an idiot: she's got a gun!' text and thumbed out a reply of her own:

She's driven off – heading east!

SEND.

And five, four, three, two...

The phone buzzed in her hand.

TUFTY:

Get to the road & I'll pick you up!

Oh no you don't.

No time you idiot! Follow her! I'll catch up later!

SEND.

Shouldn't be long now.

Danielle fastened her seatbelt.

Come on 'TUFTY' – which was a stupid nickname, by the way – soon as you like…

Ha! A manky old Vauxhall raced past the end of the track, heading east.

'One elephant. Two elephant. Three elephant.' She turned the engine on and crept back onto the road – look left, look right. Not a single police officer to be seen, so she turned west, clicked her headlights on, set Jimmy Page's solo belting out of the stereo again.

After a mile, she picked the Airwave handset off the passenger seat. The Airwave with its built-in GPS and panic buttons and here-comes-the-cavalry. No thanks.

Danielle pulled into the next passing place. The ground dropped away on the left: trees and bushes clinging to the side of the hill. Good enough. She buzzed down her window, stuck her arm out, and lobbed the Airwave over the roof of the car. It sailed off into the darkness and vanished.

Even if they activated the thing's GPS and sent out a search team it'd take them forever to find it. And by the time they did, she would be *long* gone.

She buzzed her window up again and drove off into the night.

Now, the big question was: what to do with Inspector McRae?

42

A single standing stone flares in her headlights – pink and notched, its surface covered in intricate swirls and knotwork – and Sally's phone dings at her, the red circle at the end of the line flashing. This must be it.

Please still be here. Please still be here. *Please...*

There's a small parking area not far from the stone, at the side of the road, with spaces for about eight vehicles, separated by fading white lines. But there's only one car there: a single black hatchback, no number plate, engine idling. The glowing red tip of a cigarette flares to a hot orange, then fades to red again.

Sally parks two spaces away. Pulls her sunglasses on and her hoodie up, the curly ends of her wig sticking out. She takes a deep breath and climbs into the rain. Hurries over. Stands there, cold water seeping into her hoodie as the wind whips away her fogging breath. Shifts from one foot to the other.

The cigarette flares orange again.

She knocks on the passenger window. 'Hello?'

It buzzes down, a curl of smoke escaping into the night. 'What?'

Please...

Sally bends forward, resting her arms on the sill. 'Excuse me, I'm sorry, but I was sent a text...'

The man in the driver's seat is big as a nightclub bouncer,

dressed all in black. For a moment it looks as if he hasn't got a face, but he's wearing a mask. It's barely visible in the dull glow of the hatchback's instrument panel: a dull-blue feature-less slab, marked with a large number four. Eyes nothing but two thin slits. His huge hands covered in red leather gloves.

They match the accents on the car's upholstery.

He places his cigarette in the ashtray and gets out of the hatchback.

Sally's bladder clenches: he's even bigger than he looked, cricking his neck from side to side, rolling his shoulders as he limps over and looms above her.

She shrinks against the Shogun. Everything about him radi-ates violence.

She clenches her hands into fists. Not to *fight* him – he'd kill her – but to keep them from shaking. 'I was sent a text? They said to come here and...'

Four clenches a huge red fist of his own, snapping it up, ready to—

'Foxglove! The password's Foxglove!'

He nods, then beckons her forward with a finger. And when she steps towards him he slams her back against her car, hard enough to make her teeth rattle against each other. Bellowing in her face. 'YOU'RE LATE!'

'It was flooded outside Meikle Wartle! I had to—'

'And where's your mask?'

'I didn't—'

He grabs her hoodie, pulls her forward, and shoves her against the Shogun again.

'Please, I didn't—'

'Bloody amateurs.' Four slams a red glove down on her shoulder and spins her around, so she's facing the car, then thumps her into it again.

Pain cracks across her ribs. 'Aaargh!'

'Shut it!' He forces her legs apart with his foot, then goes through her pockets, hard and fast. Hauls her phone out of her jacket and spins her around again. 'What's this? You going to film us? That it? You going to call the cops? You got GPS on it?'

The tears roll down Sally's cheeks, cold as the rain. 'I don't... I didn't... *Please*, I don't know what to do!'

He pockets her phone then points at the far edge of the car park, where a tarmac path leads up to the stone. 'You stand there and you keep your pervert mouth *shut*.'

So she does, standing huddled into herself, arms wrapped around her aching chest, shivering in the rain as he searches her car with the kind of efficiency you'd expect of a policeman or someone from the armed forces. Even checking under the floor mats and seats.

Four pulls out the red rucksack and rummages through it.

Sally's breath catches in her throat, but he doesn't take anything. He nods and dumps it in the passenger footwell again. Then turns and beckons her over.

He reaches into his pocket and produces an envelope. Throws it at her with a flick of the wrist, like he doesn't want to risk touching her again. In case he catches something. 'Address is in there. And you'd better get your skates on – the Auctioneer isn't as forgiving as I am when paedos are late.'

She nods. Scoops down and picks up the envelope – already starting to grey as the rain soaks into it.

Four lunges forward a step. 'Well don't just stand there, you snivelly bitch, MOVE!'

And Sally does, scrambling into her Shogun, jamming it into reverse, roaring out of the parking space then off into the rainy night.

The air catches in her throat, short, panting, rasping.

Sally pulls in to the side of the road and sits there with her head on the steering wheel, throat dry, everything shaking, heart like an angry man hammering on a locked door.

Breathe.

Come on: for Aiden.

She sits up and takes the damp envelope from her pocket. Sticks on the interior light. Opens the thing with trembling fingers and slips the card inside free. The words 'BOODIEHILL FARM' stretch across the top in big inkjet-printed letters – the

387

text beginning to spider where the damp has got to it. And underneath that: a map and directions.

Sally nods, takes a deep shuddery breath, props the card up behind the steering wheel and pulls out onto the road again.

A sign looms out of the darkness as Sally slows for the junction: 'BOODIEHILL FARM ~ AGRICULTURAL PROPERTY FOR SALE'. The wood it's painted on is bloated and swollen, streaks of green and black staining the white surface like it's been there for a long, long time.

The track beside it stretches away into the darkness, towards a cluster of large agricultural buildings, a faint glimmer of lights twinkling between them.

This is it...

She turns onto the track, accelerating. Can't afford to be any later than she already is. But she's barely gone a hundred yards before someone flashes their headlights at her.

Sally slows.

A hatchback sits in the entrance to a field – dark blue, with no number plates, windscreen wipers sweeping from side-to-side in the rain.

She stops in front of it, palms damp against the steering wheel, trying to calm her breathing as a large man, dressed all in black, climbs out of the hatchback and marches over. Not quite as big as Four was, but every bit as menacing in his dull-blue mask. Only this one has the number three on it.

Sally pulls on her sunglasses again, flips up her hood, and buzzes her window down.

He stoops and stares inside. 'You looking for someone?'

'I... Foxglove. Foxglove.'

He holds out his hand. 'You want to make a deposit.' Not a question, a statement.

Which makes no sense at all – she's already *given* Becky to the man with the gun. 'A deposit?'

Three shakes his head. 'You don't bid cash, you make a deposit and bid on account. You get back anything you don't spend at the end, less a handling fee. Now: *do* you want to make a deposit?'

'Yes! Yes, I want to make a deposit.' She leans over, grabs the rucksack from the passenger footwell and holds it out to him. It doesn't weigh as much as it should, given what's in it. 'Sixty-five thousand pounds in twenties. They're nonconsecutive. I took them out over the course of about...'

But he's not listening, he's carrying the rucksack around to the hatchback's boot. A clunk, and the tailgate swings up, bringing on the internal light. He's got some sort of machine on the parcel shelf and one-by-one he feeds the blocks of cash into it, making notes as he goes. Then he takes something from the boot, thumps the tailgate shut, and marches over to the Shogun again. Tosses whatever it is in through the window. 'Put that on.'

It's a mask – green and scaly, with sharp teeth and red eyes, a snout that has flames coming out of the nostrils, all rendered in thin plastic. Slightly better quality than the sort of thing you can buy from a petrol station at Halloween, but not much. She slips it on and tightens the elastic, so it's secure against her wig, adjusting the mask until she can see out properly.

'Your name is "Dragon". You do not tell anyone your real name. You do not ask them *their* real names. You share no personal details at all. If you do, you will be disciplined. Do you understand?'

Her voice sounds strange in her ears, deeper, more echoey. 'I understand.'

'You have sixty-three thousand, three hundred and seventy-five pounds to spend on the item, or items of your choice.'

'But I gave you—'

'Two and a half percent *handling fee*.' He turns and thumps away through the rain, shaking his head. 'Bloody newbies.' Climbs into his car and clunks the door shut.

She looks at Dragon's face in the rear-view mirror. Then pulls up her hoodie again, leaving fake blonde curls hanging down over her chest. Nods at her reflection.

Dragon looks back at her. 'You can do this.'

Because what other choice does she have?

Sally puts the Shogun into drive again, headlights picking

out fields of stubble and dirt on either side of the track as she goes past – all the way to the end, where it opens out into a courtyard flanked by two large metal barns with a dark farmhouse lurking at the far end. The only light comes from a handful of dim yellow fittings, fixed to the barns' corrugated walls.

About a dozen cars are parked between the two agricultural buildings, four-by-fours, hatchbacks, estates, a new-ish Audi... All of them stripped of their number plates, except for a tatty old Jaguar.

Sally parks next to the Audi. Takes a deep breath. And steps out onto the rain-slicked concrete. The smell of sour straw and animal waste taints the air.

Muffled voices ooze through the walls of the building on the right, where a sub-door lies open – inset into a much larger sliding one.

Another big figure, dressed all in black and a dull-blue mask, stands in front of it. Tall and broad with the number two slashed across her face. Her voice is every bit as hard and aggressive as the other Numbers. 'You're late.'

'Sorry. It took longer than I thought because—'

'You're late again, you get disciplined.' Two sticks out her hand as Sally hurries over. 'Car keys.'

'What?'

'Give me your car keys!' Jabbing her hand forward again. 'No one leaves till *everyone* leaves.'

'Oh. I see. Yes.' Sally digs her keys out and drops them into Two's gloved palm.

'Now: inside.'

'Yes. Sorry.' She swallows, straightens her shoulders, and ducks through the door.

Warm air wafts over her, bringing with it the soft vanilla scent of cattle and the pungent brown stink of dung. Inside, the cattle court is one big open-plan space with a raised walkway down the middle, each side divided into three large pens by chest-height metal barriers. All lit from above by twin rows of buzzing strip lights.

Chunks of agricultural machinery crowd the pens on the right, but the ones on the left have been cleared down to the straw-covered floor – a stack of pallets and a dozen large round bales of haylage, wrapped in pale green plastic, lined up along one wall.

The only animals in here are people.

Eleven of them, standing in a group, none of them talking to any of the others. Mostly men, going by the clothes, all wearing masks: a rat, pig, goat, tiger, horse, chicken, monkey, rabbit, dog, some sort of lizard, and a bull. The only one of them that looks as nervous as she feels is Chicken – fat and fidgety in mud-scuffed jeans and a tatty tweed jacket. He plays with the buttons on it, twisting them in his pudgy fingers.

Two Numbers stand off to the side, talking in voices too faint to make out... Sally freezes. The bigger one is Four: the thug from the standing stone. He's talking to someone a good foot-and-a-bit shorter than him, with a number five on his mask, Shorter, maybe, but there's something about Five that makes the pit of Sally's stomach *crawl*.

She sticks to the side of the pen furthest away from them, making her way through the gap in the barriers toward the gathering of animal masks. No one says anything, or even nods a greeting, but they turn to stare at her with their immobile plastic faces and hollow eyes. Most of their masks look a lot more expensive than hers did in the mirror, all except for muddy fidgeting Chicken.

Sally joins them, making the gathering an even dozen.

Twelve little animals, all in a row...

She wraps her arms around herself, steam rising from her damp hoodie.

A warm, confident voice booms out across the cattle court. *'Ladies and gentlemen!'*

Almost as one, they turn their gaze from her to the walkway. Standing up straight. Eager. Like dogs awaiting titbits from their master.

There's a man on the walkway, dressed in a black leather jacket, black leather gloves, a grey hoodie and a featureless grey mask. No number. He's got a roll of clear plastic sheeting tucked under one arm and when he gets halfway down the walkway he props it up against the guardrail. 'Now that Dragon is here, we can begin.'

Everyone shuffles forward.

That voice – it's the man from the derelict cottage. The one who took Becky. The one with the gun. The Auctioneer.

He throws his arms wide, mask tilted towards the ceiling as he bellows it out: 'WELCOME TO THE LIVESTOCK MART!'

— secondhand children —

43

The Auctioneer lowers his arms. 'Before we begin tonight's sale, we have a bit of housekeeping to do. If you hear a fire alarm, please make your way calmly from the building using either of the exits being pointed out to you now.'

Five swings an arm up at the door Sally came through, Four points at a metal one at the opposite end of the cattle court.

'Today, we welcome two new members to our congregation: Dragon and Rooster. Big round of applause for Dragon and Rooster!'

The clapping lasts all of three seconds, then peters out. Chicken / Rooster shrugs and shuffles his feet like he's been nominated for an award.

'We have one more item of business to attend to before we can begin our auction this evening.' The Auctioneer turns and waves. 'Number One?' Then he picks up the roll of clear plastic sheeting, unfurls it with one smooth movement – about the size of two double duvets joined side to side – and lays it out on the concrete walkway.

A huge man with the number one painted on his dull-blue mask pushes through the door at the far end, propelling someone in front of him. A man, dressed all in black, with his hands secured behind his back and a black bag covering his head and shoulders.

Pig rubs his fingers against his jeans. 'Ooh, a floorshow...'

Number One shoves the man and he stumbles, tripping over his own feet and tumbling to the straw-covered floor with a muffled cry. Like he's been gagged.

Number One grabs him by the arm. 'Get up.' He hauls the man to his feet and drags him onto the walkway.

Pig rubs at his jeans again. 'I do *love* a good floorshow.'

Tufty parked the pool car at the junction and hopped out. Scrambled back inside for his peaked cap, and hopped out again.

The headlights blazed in the darkness, turning the rain into shiny things, making the wet tree trunks glow. He stepped in front of the bonnet and his high-viz fluoresced radioactive yellow. Looked out into the Deep Shadowy Woods of DOOM.

He checked his phone again. Nothing since,

SERGEANT MCRAE:

> There isn't time you idiot! Follow her! I'll
> catch up later!

Tufty shifted from one foot to the other and dialled the Sarge. It rang straight through to voicemail.

'Hello, this is Inspector McRae. I can't come to the phone right now, so please leave a message after the beep.'

Try to sound calm. 'Sarge, it's me … again. Where are you? Just wondering.'

He hung up. Fidgeted in the headlight's glow – his shadow long and dark before him as he cupped his hands to his mouth in a makeshift loudhailer, breath billowing out. 'SARGE?'

The engine grumbled. The windscreen wipers *whonk*ed. The rain pattered.

Tufty turned and tried again. 'HELLO?'

OK, this was bad. This was really, really bad.

He hiked as far up the track as the headlights reached. 'INSPECTOR MCRAE!

COME ON, THIS ISN'T FUNNY!'

Nothing. Not even an echo.

Tufty bounced on the balls of his feet, eyes raking the dark tangle of branches and trunks. Where the hell had the Sarge gone?

Like it or not, it was time to own up and ask for help.

He scrambled down the track and jumped into the pool car, unzipping his jacket as the windows began to fog. Pulled out his phone and selected 'THE PRINCESS OF DARKNESS!' from his contacts.

It rang. And rang.

'Come on, come on, come on...'

Steel's voice crackled in his ear, breaking up. *'Where the bl—
...ell have— ...ello?'*

'I can't find him!'

'Hello? Tuf— ...odding useless—'

'He said I had to go after Danielle Smith's car and I did but I couldn't find it and I circled round to pick him up and now I can't find *him*. He's not answering his phone or anything!'

Tufty rocked back and forward in his seat.

What if the Sarge died of pneumonia? Or hypothermia? Or fell down a hole and broke his neck?

'...uck's sake! This... pointless— ...ear a word.'

And then silence. She'd hung up.

He fidgeted with the steering wheel for a bit. Then climbed out into the rain again. Grabbed the big Maglite torch from the boot and clicked it on – sweeping the beam across the trees either side of the road. Left or right?

Right?

OK.

He took a deep breath and followed the torch's glow into the dark woods.

He could do this. He could and he would.

Because if he *didn't*, Steel was going to kill him.

Roberta scowled at her phone. 'NO SIGNAL', as if she couldn't tell that by the complete and utter lack of being able to talk to Tufty, let alone give him the biblical bollocking he so *desperately* deserved. 'Useless lanky wee fudgemonkey.'

Rennie looked over from the driver's seat. 'No joy?'

'Pfff…' She stuffed her phone in her pocket and scowled out the car window at the dark fields whooshing past in the rain. 'The idiot's lost Laz. How do you lose a stupid great big-eared lump of Professional Standards like that?'

Roberta snapped her right hand out, catching Rennie a stinger, right across the arm.

'Ow!'

'I should drag the lot of you down the vets and have you all tagged. And neutered as well.'

You could hear the wee sulker sticking his bottom lip out. 'You decided where we're going yet?'

Gah…

No point returning to the station – they'd nearly made it as far as Inverurie. And it was no' as if they could stop at the next petrol station and ask for directions to the nearest auction house specialising in buying and selling abducted wee kids.

She slumped in her seat and gave her armpit a good rummage. Chasing the itch. 'Given we've sod-all idea where the Livestock Mart is and Tufty the Idiot's let our only lead drive off into the sunset, suppose we'd better go help him find Laz.'

And after all this Logan had better be in real motherfunking trouble. Because if she had to go sodding about in the rain looking for him and he *wasn't* in trouble? He bloody well soon would be.

The figure in black tries to pull away as he's dragged down the walkway towards the Auctioneer. He's shouting something, but all that makes it out through the gag in his mouth and the bag over his head are muffled grunts.

The Auctioneer leans forwards, forearms resting on the hand-rail, looking down at them. 'That's right, ladies and gentlemen, we have an uninvited guest! And you know what we do to uninvited guests, don't you?'

Everyone but Sally and Rooster belts it out in unison: 'Discipline them!'

Rooster tries to join in, but he's two seconds too late. 'Discipline them…' He shuffles his feet. Looks away.

A nod from the Auctioneer. 'Number One?'

There's a small pause, then Number One shoves the man onto the plastic sheeting and slams a fist into his kidneys. A muffled cry as knees bend, spine arching, head thrown back in its black fabric bag.

Number One batters an elbow down on the man's face and he collapses onto the plastic sheet, moaning and writhing, hands fixed behind him as the blows hammer down. Fists first, then feet.

Sally gasps, retreats a couple of steps, but Rabbit grabs her arm.

Rabbit doesn't look at her, keeps his face turned towards the walkway and his voice at a whisper. 'Don't. You show weakness and they'll turn on you.'

So she stands there and watches as boots slam into the man's ribs and stomach. On and on and on. Hard and furious and unrelenting. The sound of muted crunching and dull thumps coils out across the cattle court, punctuated by muffled screams and grunts of exertion.

Number One keeps on going, even when the muffled screams fade away – stamping on his victim's chest and head. Then more kicking and punching: on and on and on and on, long after the poor man is nothing more than a ragdoll made of meat and bone and Number One's mask is peppered with tiny red dots.

Then, finally, the crunching, thumping noises stop and Number One sags against the railings, puffing and panting. 'Fin … finished… Pfff…'

And through it all, the Auctioneer doesn't even bother turning to watch. 'We *discipline* them.'

Sally forces herself to breathe.

They killed him. Beat him to death. Right there, in front of everyone. Like it doesn't even matter.

Number Five climbs up onto the walkway and folds the bloodstained plastic sheeting over the body. Wrapping it up. By the time he's finished, Number One is upright again and together they drag the package out through the door.

'There we go.' The Auctioneer claps his hands, voice cheerful and warm, like a man hasn't just been murdered right behind him. 'Now, let's begin. Our first item in tonight's catalogue is lot number one: Stephen MacGuire all the way from East Kilbride!'

Number Three appears through the same door, pulling a small fair-haired boy by the arm across the pen. He shoves Stephen and the boy stumbles forwards, then stands there, blinking up at the Animals with his tearstained face full of freckles and an angry claret birthmark.

They move in, making a semicircle with Stephen at the centre, staring at him.

'Stephen is four, a natural blond, and he likes kittens and chocolate-chip ice cream. He's never been touched.'

Monkey put his hand up. 'Can he sing? I like it when they sing.'

'He has the voice of an angel. Now, who wants to start the bidding? Do I hear "five thousand"?'

Monkey blurts it out. 'Five thousand!'

Pig shakes his head. 'Six thousand.'

'*Eight* thousand.'

Becca pressed her face against the wall of her crate, peering out through the gaps. A lightbulb hung in the middle of the big metal room, making loads of thick dark shadows. They lurked behind the rusty old tractor and the chunks of metal stuff piled up next to it. Made a stripy pattern on the wall underneath the racks of shovels and rakes and things. Made a jungle of dark bits and light bits between the six crates from the Grey Man's garage.

Six crates, one open and empty, the rest of them full of little children – looking out through the gaps, like her. Someone was crying – louder now that the Grey Man had taken off their gags and untied their hands so they'd look 'pretty for the nice people'.

Well, the 'nice people' could go poo themselves, because Becca was getting out of here.

She shuffled into the middle of her crate, bunched her legs

under her and shoved her back against the lid. The crate rocked, but she was still stuck.

Another go... *Thump.*

A little boy's voice came from one of the other crates. *'Shhh! You'll get us into trouble!'*

Come on Becca: big fierce strong girl!

She squatted down as far as she could and banged her whole self up into the lid, pushing at it with her shoulders till they were all achy and her legs trembled and shook.

No use. The bolty thing was too hard.

She sagged against the crate wall and hugged her teddy. 'Don't worry, Orgalorg, we'll get out of here. We will. I *promise.*' Becca kissed him on the head. 'Don't cry.'

Orgalorg was probably just tired. And cold – all the crates were near a big slidy door that was open a bit, letting the rain in, making the straw on the floor all damp and soggy.

On the other side of the room, a littler door banged against the metal wall and two of the tits backed in, dragging a big plastic parcel between them. Shuffling backwards with their bums sticking out until they'd pulled the parcel onto another sheet of plastic.

It looked like a *dead* person. You could see it through the stuff! All red and black and icky.

Becca stared. A real dead person. Right there. In the same room!

The tit with a number five on his face wiped his gloves on his trousers. 'You got this, yeah?'

'Yeah.' The number one tit wrapped the other plastic sheet around the dead person and fixed it all together with a big roll of scritchy sticky tape. Like a really nasty Christmas present.

Then he stood and flexed his fist. Nudged the parcel with his foot. 'Serves you right.'

He turned and looked at the crates – the light reflecting off his nasty blue mask with a big number one on it – *looking* at them with those horrid black slits for eyes. The tit marched over to Becca's crate, undid the bolty thing, and threw the lid open.

She bared her teeth at him and growled like an angry cat.

He reached in with a big gloved hand and grabbed her by the throat. 'Any more of that and I break your arm, understand?' He lifted her out of the crate and took a handful of her dungarees, dragging her and Orgalorg towards the door he'd come in through. 'Come on: *smile*, Princess. You want to look pretty for the nice people, don't you?'

No. No she didn't.

She wanted them all to die.

Andy kept his voice down, face hidden by his Number Seven mask. 'I don't like it, Danners. I really, *really* don't.'

The space between the cattle court and the machine shed was home to three dirty hatchbacks, an estate car, a couple of big four-by-fours, the Auctioneer's black Range Rover, and Danielle's pristine-white Renault Clio, all lurking in the gloom of a low-wattage bulkhead light. And not a single one of them was wearing a number plate.

Suppose it was quite telling – the difference between the workers' cars, parked back here, out of the way, and the customers' ones round the front. But then, if you were the kind of person who could afford to splurge tens of thousands on buying a child to molest, why *wouldn't* you drive something a bit more fancy?

But round here, everything smelled of engine oil and cow dung.

She popped open the Clio's boot, lifted the bass board, and gestured Andy closer.

He edged over and peered inside. Hissed some air in through his teeth. 'Is he dead?'

McRae lay on his side: bound and gagged, still as a headstone.

She shrugged. 'I barely touched him.'

'Yeah, Danners, but … he's *police*.'

'He's Professional Standards.'

'Oh…' Andy nodded. 'True. What we going to do with him?'

'Could hand him over?'

'Nah, they'd kill him. Better keep him here and hope no one finds out. Cos if they do…'

The bass board clunked into place again, hiding McRae's top half. 'Yeah.'

'You saw what they did to that journalist: battered him to death.'

As if she hadn't been standing right there, watching it happen. Stomach full of wasps. Bile churning at the base of her throat. 'I *know*, Andy.'

Andy shook his head. 'Right in front of everyone.'

'Oh shut up.' She closed the boot again, hiding the rest of Inspector McRae. 'We'll just have to hope no one finds him, then, won't we?'

'Well, I think we can all agree that's an excellent start to the evening!' The Auctioneer rubs his hands as Number Five drags Stephen MacGuire off. The little boy's whining cries fade away into the other room as Number One marches in with Becky.

She's still got Mr Bibble-Bobble with her, hugging him to her chest. The sight of it makes something inside Sally burst, stinging, causing the cattle court to swim as tears run down her cheeks. Hidden by the mask.

'Lot number two: Rebecca Oliver! Rebecca's five and, if you're local, you'll know there's been a good furore whipped up in the media about her disappearance. Ooh, exciting!'

Number One shoves her into the semicircle, where she glares at all the animal masks. A defiant set to her chin and shoulders.

'Rebecca plays the recorder and wants to be a famous footballer when she grows up. Assuming her new owner lets her live that long.'

That draws a couple of chuckles from Tiger and Dog.

Sally stands there, staring at the girl she abducted. Blinking through the tears.

'Given the media interest, ladies and gentlemen, I'm going to start the bidding at fifteen thousand. Who'll give me—'

'I will!' Rabbit's first: 'Fifteen thousand.'

Bull steps forward, circling Becky. 'Seventeen.'

'Thank you, Ox. I have seventeen, any advance on seventeen?'

'Eighteen.'

Becky bares her teeth, snarling it out. 'My mummy will kill *all* of you tits!'

'Well, aren't you *feisty*?' Horse's voice drips with hunger. 'I bid twenty!'

44

'Mmmmmnnnnghph!' Logan's eyes snapped open on darkness.

Still alive. Still alive...

Something cottony filled his mouth and a hard rectangle pulled at the skin of his cheeks and lips – holding the cottony thing in. A gag. He wriggled and cramp twisted its way up his arms and across his shoulders.

Gah... Sodding... Oh that hurt.

Then it did the same with his legs.

'Mmmmmmmnnngnggphhh!' With bells on.

He screwed his eyes shut again. Deep breaths through his nose. Deep breaths. Relax. Let it pass. Let the cramp—

It surged back for another go.

'Mmmmgn fggggnnn mmmgggsssttmmmmmnd!'

Deep breaths. Deep breaths.

And at last it passed.

He rested his head against something crinkly that smelled of fresh bin-bags. Reached up with his right elbow and clunked into something solid and hollow sounding. Wood? He gave it another thump, but it wouldn't move. Legs next: but he couldn't straighten them more than halfway without his feet bashing into ... metal? Sounded like metal anyway.

Rocking back and forth and back and forth set the whole

thing bouncing. Not a lot, but enough to know there were springs involved. Big ones, because as soon as he stopped rocking the world settled down again.

Well, there you were then: he was in a car boot. A car boot lined with bin-bags.

Yeah, not a good sign.

And as if that wasn't bad enough: his ankles were fastened together, wrists too – something thin and hard. Not handcuffs. Not rope. Cable ties?

Today just got better and better.

OK. He could do this.

He took another deep breath and curled up into as small a ball as he could, reaching with both arms at full stretch ... down his back, thighs, knees, calves ... feet!

And now his hands were at the *front* of his body instead of behind him.

He sagged against the bin-bags and panted for a bit. Then scrabbled his fingers at whatever it was holding the gag in. Duct tape. Definitely duct tape. Logan found the edge and ripped it off his mouth then dug out the cotton wad and spat. Coughed. Gasped for air.

The world rotated around him once, twice, three times...

He screwed his eyes shut again, slowing his breathing until everything stopped spinning.

OK. Two things down. Three to go. Four, if you counted getting out of the boot.

Next up: whatever it was holding his wrists together.

He raised them to his stinging lips, feeling his way along them. Definitely cable ties. Question was, were they the industrial heavy-duty max-strength ones, or your common-or-garden domestic variety?

Only one way to find out.

He twisted his wrists to the side and gnawed on the ties like a hungry rat. Teeth clicking and clacking as they slipped over the tough plastic.

God, this was going to take *forever*.

*   *   *

'Lot number four is an old Livestock Mart favourite: Vernon Booker!' The Auctioneer sweeps an arm out as Number Five shoves a skinny boy into the circle.

He's older than the first three children, dressed in nothing but pyjama bottoms, with heavy bags under his sunken eyes. Shoulders hunched, head low, not looking at anyone. Shivering. His bare arms and chest are peppered with tiny circular scars – the skin puckered, pink, and shiny against his pale skin. Like someone's stubbed a million cigarettes out on him.

'Back for his fifth auction, eight-year-old Vernon has been *fully* housebroken. Who'll start the bidding at three thousand pounds?'

Silence.

'Three thousand pounds for this compliant, well-trained young man.'

No one moves.

'Two thousand?'

No one speaks.

'Well, *one* thousand then.'

Vernon's bare feet scuff on the straw-covered floor as he shrinks a bit more with every drop in price.

'Come on, people, this is a perfectly serviceable boy here! A bit worn, but there's life in him yet.'

He's so thin, so terrified...

Sally licks her lips. Maybe she should buy him? It's only a thousand pounds. She'll *still* have more than sixty-two thousand to spend on Aiden, plus the money Horse bid for Becky.

And Vernon's so small and cowed. So broken.

She can *save* him. Hand him over to the police, or social services. Anonymously, of course. Raymond will know how to do it so they don't get into trouble.

'OK, do I hear five hundred?'

But what if she doesn't have enough left afterwards? What if she needs every penny to get Aiden back and she can't because she's spent this money on Vernon?

'Two fifty? Come on, I'm practically *giving* him away!'

The breath catches in her throat.

What if Aiden gets sold to one of these horrible perverts and she – can't – stop – it?

Why, because she feels *sorry* for this boy? This stranger? What makes *him* more deserving than her own flesh and blood?

'Going once, going twice...' The Auctioneer sighs. Shrugs. 'Bad luck, Vernon. Never mind, I'm sure you did your best.' He turns his grey mask to the Animals. 'This lot is officially withdrawn.' Then snaps his fingers and points. 'Number Five? Ex-stock.'

Number Five grabs the boy by the arm and hauls him away.

'No!' Vernon looks at them for the first time since he was brought in. Eyes darting from one bestial mask to the next as he's dragged out. 'I'll be good, I promise! I swear I'll be a good boy!'

He breaks free of Number Five and runs towards the Animals. Throws himself at Rat's feet, hands clasped together in prayer. 'Please! I'm a good boy, I'll do whatever you—'

'Urgh!' Rat backs away. 'Get *off* me!'

'Please, I can—'

Number Five backhands him, sending him sprawling across the straw. Then grabs a handful of Vernon's hair and starts towards the door again.

'PLEASE! I'M A GOOD BOY! I AM! DON'T LET THEM KILL ME! DON'T—'

Blood sprays from his nose as Number Five smashes a fist into it.

The Animals look away, shuffling their feet as he's dragged away.

Come on, come on, come on...

The coppery tang of blood overlaid the dark waxy taste of plastic.

Probably be lucky if he had any teeth left at the end of this.

Assuming Danielle didn't come back halfway through and shoot him.

Logan gnawed and gnawed and—

The cable tie gave with an audible *snap*.

Ha, ha!

Pins and needles coursed through his fingers as he sagged onto the bin-bags again.

Two more things to do.

He reached down and yanked at the cable tie around his ankles. Hauled. Pulled. Wrenched...

Nope.

OK. So even if he managed to get out of the boot, what was he going to do with his ankles fastened together: make a hop for it?

Maybe there was something in the boot he could use, like an emergency toolkit?

He scrabbled through the black-plastic bags down to the boot's rough carpet lining, fingers searching... That was probably a roll of duct tape. That was a plastic bag of what felt like more cable ties. That was a roll of bin bags. And that was his peaked cap.

No toolkit.

Sod.

He ran his fingers around the boot again. There was a ridge in the carpet, running from side to side, right through the middle. As if it folded... Of course – the spare wheel and all the bits and bobs needed to change it! And if the carpet folded in the middle, there had to be a handle or something at the edge closest to the bumper.

He found a small gap to put his fingers in and pulled.

The whole front half of the boot's floor tried to lift up in one solid flap. Only he was lying on top of the thing, so it couldn't.

Aaaargh!

Kinda weird, the way life turns out – the stuff you end up doing for a living.

The kid was waking up, so Ian dumped him on the floor. No point carrying him if he could walk.

Now, you know, the guys at the golf club would've been appalled to see this. Wee boys and girls? Oh heaven forfend you do anything *nasty* to the tiny ickle angels! Yeah, well, if you wanna go down that road then you might as well go vegetarian. Or worse: vegan, like bloody Sarah with her sulky teenage sighs and passive aggressive bullshit.

Nah, when you strip it all back: human beings? Just animals, weren't they. No different from cows, or pigs, or chickens, and nobody cried when *they* got put out their misery, did they?

'Cept the vegetarians.

And Sarah.

Swear to God she only did it to wind him up.

Ian grabbed a handful of Lot Four's hair – better to think of them as numbers: once you started giving them names, it was a slippery slope – and dragged him through the equipment store. Past the crates with all the other kids in them. And out the door into the rain.

Dirty – bastarding – bloody – wanking – boot!

'Move, you piece of shit!'

How? How was he supposed to do this? How?

How was this even supposed to be possible?

Thumping back and forward didn't make any difference. It was impossible to lift the flap when he was lying on top of the bloody thing.

AAAAAAAAAAAAARRRRRRGH!

OK: forget the toolkit. Get out of here first and *then* find a sharp edge to cut the cable tie round his ankles. Scissors, hacksaw, a knife...

Logan shuffled over onto as much of his back as he could and slammed both palms upward into whatever was over the boot.

Thunk.

It barely budged. Had to be thick chipboard? Something like that. Something solid and wedged in tight.

Thunk.

Still nothing. Who the hell had a wooden boot cover?

His hands scrabbled across it ... wires and what felt suspiciously like the underside of two speakers. Which explained the wood – it was a heavy-duty DIY speaker board.

He struggled his way over onto his front, tensed his arms, shoved, and slammed his back into it.

Thunk.

Thunk.

Harder!

THUNK.

And it wasn't like he hadn't tried, was it?

Ian hunched his shoulders as the rain battered down. Should get some decent lighting installed out here. Something better than a couple of manky wall-mounted jobs with low-wattage bulbs in them. A faint orangey glow wasn't gonna deter thieves, was it?

All them foreign holidays. Travel's supposed to broaden the mind, but you try broadening a sulky bloody fourteen-year-old's mind when she won't eat bloody *pain perdu* cos it's got honey in it and honey's 'cruel to bees'.

Cruel to bloody bees!

Ian dragged Lot Four across the concrete, not bothering to go around the puddles.

Got to hand it to him – the kid kept his mouth shut. Not a lot of them could manage that. They'd be whingeing about the cold, or the rain. Or what was gonna happen next.

I mean, they're only bloody *bees*.

And you didn't need a degree in psychology to know what it was really all about. Well, you know what? Wasn't easy raising a daughter on your own. Wasn't his fault Kirstie got breast cancer. Wasn't his fault the chemo didn't work. Think that was fun for him? Watching her wither and die?

Soon as they were within three yards of the truck, Enfield did his car alarm bit – lunging at the canopy window, barking his great big head off. Teeth flashing in the dim orange glow of them half-arsed wall lights. Good boy.

Why couldn't Sarah be more like...

Ian stopped. Turned.

There was something up with the white Clio parked three cars down. Rocking on its springs like someone was going at it

411

in the back seat. And this really wasn't the time, or the place, for vigorous lovemaking.

He let go of Lot Four's hair. Pointed a finger at the concrete beneath the kid's bare feet. 'Stay. You move: I don't put you out of your misery before I feed you to Enfield.'

Lot Four nodded, scarred arms wrapped around himself for warmth, blood dripping off his chin from the broken nose.

See? *Some* kids could do what they were told.

Ian walked over to the Clio. Had a good squint inside – no one in the front, no one in the rear, but the boot? Now that was a different matter. The internal cover thing was bumping up and down, shifting as something moved underneath it.

Might be a dog?

Or it might be something else.

He reached into his pocket and pulled out the butterfly knife: nice, titanium, really good balance. He flipped it open with a basic horizontal, then a quick fan, into a backhand twirl. The blade shone as it spun in and out.

Oh yeah.

Whatever was in the boot, was about to get a new hole in it.

Ian grabbed the boot release with his other hand.

Clunked it open...

Seriously: who gave a toss about bees?

He yanked the tailgate up.

Logan exploded from the boot, arms outstretched and curled into fists. Both ankles still cable-tied together. Snarling. Barrelling into a someone wearing a mask like Danielle Smith's, only with a big number five on it instead.

'Aaargh!' Number Five staggered, falling backwards, crashing into the wet concrete with Logan on top of him. 'Get off me you—'

Logan smashed a fist into the guy's mask.

His head bounced off the concrete.

Then again. And again.

His left hand wrapped around Logan's throat, squeezing, the thumb digging into his Adam's apple.

412

'Gggnnnphnnnng...' Logan grabbed Number Five's head and battered it into the concrete with a dull grating thunk. Pulled it up and battered it down a second time, putting his weight behind it.

Thunk.

The hand around his throat loosened.

Once more for luck.

THUNK.

The mask flipped off, skittering away under the hatchback.

Number Five's eyelids flickered, as if the wiring inside was faulty. Then they closed and he sagged, strangling arm flopping out across the ground. Mouth open, breath steaming in the rain. An unconscious wee nyaff with forgettable features and a bloody nose.

Logan sat up, pushed himself to his knees, and collapsed sideways against Danielle's Clio.

Why did...? What...?

He looked down – not at Number Five, but at...

Oh God.

No.

His black police-issue fleece glistened in the dim orange glow of a bulkhead light. The handle of butterfly knife stuck out of the fabric, at a jaunty angle, halfway between his bottom right rib and his hip.

Ox 'oohs' and 'ahs' as a tiny girl, dressed like an angel, is led into the cattle court by Number One.

Number One doesn't drag her, he holds her hand and lets her walk through the straw at her own pace, with her blonde curly hair, flowing white robes, cardboard wings, and a tinfoil halo.

'I'm sure our next auction lot needs no introduction, but just in case: it's Ellie Morton!'

The Animals stare as she's guided into the middle of the semicircle and Rooster bursts into a one-man round of applause that peters out into embarrassed silence when nobody joins in.

'Ellie's been the subject of a massive search by police, with

413

articles and news reports published and broadcast all over the world.' The Auctioneer points at her with a pantomime flourish. 'Whoever goes home with *this* little girl will be the envy of everyone here!'

Goat and Dog move in for a closer look, but Ellie backs away from them, scuffing through the straw till she bumps into Sally's legs.

Ellie lets out a little squeak.

Sally flinches like she's been burnt and Rabbit catches her arm.

His voice is still too low for anyone else to hear. 'Steady...'

'Ellie's only three and, I think you'll agree, *magnificent*. Who'll start the bidding at twenty thousand pounds?'

Goat nods. 'Twenty.'

Dog: 'Twenty-one.'

Snake raised a finger. 'My client bids twenty-five.'

Logan gritted his teeth and took hold of the knife's handle. Huffed out three short panting breaths.

Come on.

You can do this.

He pulled and the blade slid free with a wet *sucking* noise.

Logan clamped his other hand over the wound. Blood oozed out between his fingers.

Didn't hurt though. That was something. Probably in shock.

He tightened his grip on the knife and sawed through the cable tie around his ankles.

Stood. Staggered against the Clio.

Looked down at Number Five and his stupid unconscious face.

Logan slammed his boot into the guy's ribs. Hard. 'A knife!'

Kicked him again.

This isn't helping.

You need to stop the bleeding, you idiot.

Yes. Right.

He reached into the Clio's boot, searching the corners with his free hand. It had to be here somewhere... Ha! Duct tape.

Logan ripped off a palm-sized chunk, then unzipped his fleece and eased up the hem of his T-shirt. The dim orange glow turned the blood dark and glistening, like used engine oil. He wiped his sleeve across his side, taking the worst of it off, revealing a tiny black hole in the pale smeared skin. It oozed more oil.

Somehow, seeing it made all the difference. It went from being a numb, slippery thing, to a burning oil-well – the flames ripping through his insides, burning up into his chest and down to his knees.

'Arrrrgh...'

He gritted his teeth, wiped the blood away again and slapped the strip of duct tape over the top.

Yeah, that wasn't going to stay there, was it.

He took the roll and wrapped a length of tape all the way around, behind his back, across his front, pulling it tight, then added another layer, keeping the pressure on. A sort of sticky silver tourniquet. But the bloody thing still oozed.

It would have to do.

He tucked his T-shirt in again. Zipped up his fleece. Turned.

A skinny boy stood beside a massive muddy four-by-four, arms wrapped around himself. Shivering. Wearing nothing but a pair of pyjama bottoms. So thin that his ribs stuck out like knuckles on a clenched fist. Hair plastered to his head. Blood running from his squint nose. Shuffling his bare feet in the rain.

So it was true: the Livestock Mart was real.

They were actually selling *children*.

Logan staggered over and a huge dog went off in the four-by-four, spraying the rear window with saliva as it lunged and barked. What was it with these people and massive weaponised dogs?

He hunkered down in front of the wee boy, trying not to wince. Failing. 'Are you OK?'

No reply, just a trembling stare.

Up close, his pale skin was covered in small circular scars. Someone had put cigarettes out on him. So many cigarettes that it looked as if he had measles. Poor sod.

'I'm a police officer. You're all right. But I need you to…'

What?

Logan swallowed, looked across the rain-puddled concrete at Number Five lying sparked-out in front of the parked cars, between a pair of large agricultural buildings. The gable end of a cottage was visible at one end of the gap. A five-bar metal gate at the other. Eight parked cars – all with their number plates removed. No sign of Sweaty's ancient Jag, Snake's Audi, or Tiger's Hilux.

He put a hand on the boy's shoulder. Did his best to sound confident and in charge. To sound as if he wasn't *bleeding to death* because someone had stuck a knife in him. 'Are there any other children here?'

The boy stared at him with big dark eyes.

'Are there other children like you here?'

A tiny nod, eyes flicking towards the agricultural building on the left. The one with an open door and lights on inside.

Great.

So much for stealing a car and speeding off to the nearest hospital. Now he had to stay here and figure out a way to rescue them. Without getting himself killed.

Well, it wasn't as if he actually knew how to hotwire an engine anyway.

Gah… Why did everything always have to be so hard?

Come on, Logan. Focus.

First – get the boy to safety. Or as near to it as possible.

He pointed. 'You see those lights in the distance? I need you to go that way. I need you to keep low, and I need you to run. OK?'

No response.

OK. So it wasn't *ideal*, but at least it was a plan.

Logan unzipped his fleece and winced his way out of it. Draped it around the boy's shoulders. 'I need you to run till you find another farmhouse, far away from here, and you call the police. Can you do that for me?'

Those big dark eyes stared up at him.

For God's sake!

416

Logan patted him on the shoulder, trying really hard not to shout at the silent wee sod. 'Can you be a good boy and *do that* for me?'

His bottom lip wobbled. 'I'm a good boy.'

'Good. Great.' He cupped Chatterbox's face with his hands. 'Off you go then.'

The boy backed away a couple of steps, Logan's bloody handprints on his cheeks, gathered the fleece around himself, turned, and *ran*. Past the end of the house, into the darkness.

Logan gritted his teeth and levered himself upright again, left hand clutching his side as the oil-well burned.

A tiny flash of white in the gloom as the wee boy took one last look ... then he was gone.

'And *please* don't get caught.'

45

Number One leads Ellie Morton from the cattle court, holding her hand again, like a perfect gentleman.

'Wasn't she adorable?' The Auctioneer sighs, then performs a booming drumroll on the walkway's handrail with his gloved hands. 'And now, ladies and gentlemen, we come to our most anticipated item of the evening ...' Letting the silence hang. Building the tension. 'LOT NUMBER SIX!'

He throws his arms in the air and everyone turns to towards the door.

Only nothing happens.

Sally's throat tightens, like someone's strangling her. Aiden. Lovely, beautiful, wonderful Aiden. She's going to see her baby again.

The Auctioneer's still got his arms up. 'Lot number six!'

Still nothing.

She places a hand against her chest, blood thumping in her ears, mouth dry, skin tingling. And still Aiden doesn't appear.

The Auctioneer turns to one of his men, voice tight and clipped. 'Number Four, will you *please* go see what's taking Number Five so long?'

'Nae probs.' Number Four limps out through the door, flexing his shoulders as if he's about to do someone an injury.

'Sorry about this.' The Auctioneer runs his fingers along the rail. Clears his throat. 'Well, while we're waiting, why don't we go over the catalogue listing for lot number six?'

Everyone turns to face him, their masked faces expressionless, but their bodies trembling with expectation.

Sally tries very hard not to tremble. Where *is* he? He's meant to be here. She went through all that horror just for this moment. She abducted a child for Christ sake. HE HAS TO BE HERE!

'Our final lot of the evening is the one, the *only*, Aiden MacAuley!' The Auctioneer leans closer. 'Abducted at the age of three, Aiden's father was *brutally* murdered, leading to an international manhunt, *extensive* worldwide press coverage, a bestselling book, and now there's even talk of a *film* being made.' The pause that follows is like a razorblade, slicing its way through Sally's throat as the Auctioneer raises his arms again. 'Imagine *owning* that child.'

Logan limped over to the Clio's boot, retrieved his peaked cap and jammed it onto his head. At least that would keep *some* of the rain off. He dug out the packet of cable ties and wipped one around the guy's wrists, then did the same with his ankles. Slapped a big strip of duct tape across his mouth. Then grabbed him by the armpits and dragged him away across to the agricultural building on the other side. The one the wee boy hadn't looked at when Logan asked him where the other kids were. The one with no lights on inside.

Every step was like being kicked in the stomach.

Which is what Number Five was going to get as soon as they were out of the rain. Possibly more than one. Heavy, ugly, stabby scumbag that he was.

The door wasn't locked.

Logan shifted his grip and hauled him over the threshold and into a big metal space – every panting breath echoing around him.

It was some sort of machine shed: two tractors, a JCB digger, and a huge yellow combine harvester loomed in the darkness. The air scented with diesel and rust.

419

He dumped Number Five behind the combine and gave him another free boot in the ribs. Then hissed his way down and rummaged through the stabby sod's pockets.

'Come on, you have to have a phone here somewhere.'

But he didn't. Nothing but lint, change, and a bunch of used tissues. Not even a wallet with ID.

'Arrrgh! Bloody, bastarding...'

Deep breaths.

Logan slumped there, *breathing*, then forced himself to his feet. Wobbled a bit. Put a hand on the combine harvester to steady himself.

The cottage – they'd have a phone. All he had to do was sneak in, call 999 and hope they could trace his location, because he didn't have a sodding clue where in the hell he was right now. Get the cavalry to descend on the place like a million angry bricks.

He lurched away, leaving a bloody handprint behind.

All the breath rushes out of her body as the door opens and Number Four leads Aiden into the room.

Her Aiden.

Oh God, he's beautiful. Her beautiful baby boy.

The world blurs. She blinks and blinks, but more tears come.

Aiden.

Six and a half now, but still small, with blond ringlets hanging around his beautiful face in delicate curls.

Oh Aiden.

They've dressed him up in shorts, white socks, sandals, and a Paddington Bear T-shirt. He doesn't smile. Or cry. In fact, there's no expression on his face at all – like he's been unplugged.

Oh, Aiden, what have they *done* to you?

Pig groans, both hands clenching and unclenching in front of his groin. Tiger stands up a bit straighter. Rat makes a nervous giggling sound. But *everyone* stares.

The Auctioneer turns his palms upward and stares at Number Four, who shrugs in reply.

Aiden's so close now. It doesn't matter what they've done:

she can fix it. It doesn't matter what *she's* done: it was worth it. Everything was worth it, to be here and see him again. To save him. To bring him home.

She would've killed a thousand Beckys, to hold him in her arms.

'Ladies and gentlemen, before we begin, please remember that Aiden MacAuley has only had one careful *loving* owner since he was abducted three and a half years ago. And that this is a very reluctant sale, due to ill health.' The Auctioneer claps his hands together. 'Now, shall we start the bidding at twenty-five thousand pounds?'

Logan hurpled around the side of the cottage, keeping to the shadows. Not that there was a lot of light about anyway. Rain thrummed against his peaked cap, thumped into his shoulders, dripped off his hands, stole warmth from his bare arms.

What idiot decided it was a good idea to make police uniform a T-shirt? What happened to nice thick sleeves?

He staggered to a halt at the gable end, where a big grey BT box was mounted beneath the guttering. A cable dangled from it, the end cut clean across.

Great.

He turned. A telegraph pole sat a hundred or so yards away, the other end of the cable drooping to the ground.

Because it couldn't be *that* easy, could it? No, of course it couldn't. Nothing ever was.

He lurched around the corner again.

Well, if the cavalry wasn't coming, he'd have to do it himself, wouldn't he?

Assuming he didn't bleed to death first.

Logan limped his way across the grass to the concrete slab between the two buildings. Then snuck over to the open door and peered inside.

It was a space about the size of a really large double garage, walled off from the rest of the shed. An ancient tractor rusted in the corner with a couple of chunks of agricultural equipment stacked up beside it. Racks of tools around the walls, most of which looked as if they'd last seen service digging for victory. But the really interesting things sat in the middle of the straw-strewn floor: six wooden crates, each one with 'LOT' and a number spray-painted on the top.

LOT 4 and LOT 6 lay open, but the other four were still bolted shut. Little eyes peered out at him from between the slats.

And they weren't the only ones in here, either. What looked very much like a body was bundled up in bloodstained plastic sheeting, beneath a rack of antique shovels.

There, but for the grace of battering Number Five's head off the concrete...

Logan lumbered over and unbolted LOT 1.

A little boy flinched away from him, cowering in the corner of his crate. Blond hair, a dark port-coloured birthmark reaching across his cheek and down one side of his nose. Stephen MacGuire. The wee boy abducted from East Kilbride.

Logan put a finger to his lips. 'Shh...' Keeping his voice soft and quiet. 'It's OK. I'm a policeman.' He reached in, took hold of Stephen under the arms and lifted him out. Ow! Ow! Flames raced around Logan's torso. Put him down. PUT HIM DOWN!

He lowered Stephen to the ground and promptly doubled over, both hands clutching at the hole in his side, eyes screwed shut, teeth gritted so hard his cheeks ached.

Deep breaths. Deep breaths.

OK. Not doing that again.

Dragging was bad enough, but lifting was *horrific*.

He straightened up and limped over to LOT 2. Undid the bolt. A little girl topped with an explosion of Irn-Bru-coloured curls glowered up at him, teeth bared. She lunged towards his fingers, mouth open.

He snatched his hand away before she could sink her teeth into it. 'Yeah, you can definitely get yourself out of there.'

LOT 3 opened to reveal a small girl in pink dungarees with embroidered sunflowers on them. She clambered from her cage and stood there staring at him with her thumb in her mouth.

Logan unbolted LOT 5. Smiled down at the wee girl with the

blonde curls and big green eyes. Kept his voice down. 'Ellie Morton, I presume?'

For some strange reason, she was dressed up in a white smock with wings and a coat-hanger-and-tinsel halo. Ellie climbed out to join her fellow auction lots and the whole bunch of them stood and stared at him as if he was some sort of weird and amazing animal. Well, all except for Bitey McIrn-Bru, glowering away on the edge of the group, clutching a lumpy-looking teddy bear.

He nodded at the open crate with 'LOT 6' painted on it. 'Where's number six?'

Bitey bared her teeth again. 'One of the *tits* took him!'

'Shhh!' Logan put a finger to his lips and hissed it out. 'You have to whisper.'

The little girl in the pink dungarees pointed towards the door at the other end of the equipment shed.

'Thank you.' Logan limped over, opened the door a crack, and peered through the gap.

A cattle court, divided in two by a central walkway. Farm machinery on one side, people on the other. One, two, three … about a dozen of them in assorted animal masks, six in numbered masks, and a guy up on the central walkway in a grey one. The Animals were gathered around something, blocking Logan's view – so probably LOT 6.

A woman's voice cut through the air. Hard and precise. *'Thirty-seven thousand.'*

Then a different woman. Softer. *'Thirty-eight thousand.'*

Nineteen of them.

And he'd nearly died taking on just one.

Logan wiped his mouth with the back of his hand, leaving a harsh metallic taste behind.

What the hell was he supposed to do?

Couldn't leave LOT 6 behind. Could he?

No, of course he couldn't.

So what: charge in and get himself killed? Then all the kids he'd set free would be rounded up and handed over to whichever paedophile had bid the most for them? Yeah, that sounded like an *excellent* plan.

Logan eased the door shut again, then winced down in front of Bitey. 'You're the bravest one here, aren't you?'

She nodded.

'OK. Good. What's your name? And *quietly* this time.'

'Rebecca.' She held up the bear. 'This is Orgalorg.'

'Rebecca. Right: I need you to look after the others, Rebecca, can you do that?'

A frown put wrinkles between her orange eyebrows.

He took off his peaked cap and plonked it on her head. 'I'm making you and Organthingumy official deputy police officers.'

It was far too big for her, but she frowned up at him from beneath the brim and nodded. 'Does that mean we can arrest people for being tits?'

Wow. Not so much as a smile. She was serious.

'Er… Not *today*, but maybe tomorrow? Today you're going to help me get these kids to safety.' He winced his way upright again. 'Everyone hold hands and follow me.'

Logan stuck his hand out and Rebecca took it, gave him the bear, then jabbed her other hand towards Stephen MacGuire.

He didn't take it. He leaned over to one side and frowned at the courtyard instead. 'But it's *raining*.'

'Don't be a tit or I'll arrest you.'

He did as he was told. Then Ellie took *his* other hand and Pink Dungarees took hers. All in one short-ish crocodile.

'We have to be quick and super quiet, OK?'

They nodded and he led the way out the door and into the rain. Across the concrete, past the parked cars and the big barky dog. Through the gap between the cottage and the machine shed, where the concrete gave way to a small grass verge bordered by a barbed-wire fence.

Logan had a good long look at the farm buildings – no sign that they'd been spotted – then off into the night. Lights flickered in the distance, swimming in and out of view. Farms, houses, it didn't matter. As long as it wasn't here.

He gritted his teeth and lifted the wee girl in the pink dungarees over the fence. Hissed out a lungful of broken glass, then did the same with Stephen MacGuire. Had to pause for a couple of deep breaths as fire raged through his stomach. It was Ellie Morton's turn next, who, let's be honest, looked utterly ridiculous in her primary-school-nativity angel costume. It had developed a big smear of red by the time he lowered her on the other side of the fence.

He bent double, panting, left hand braced against his knee to keep him upright, right hand pressed against the stab wound to keep everything in.

God...

Come on. Only one more to lift over. Then you can go get yourself killed. At least then the pain would go away.

Right.

He straightened up in time to see Rebecca throw her teddy bear over the barbed wire, then climb the nearest fence post and jump down the other side.

She reclaimed the bear, adjusted her oversized hat and nodded at him.

He pointed over the wire, towards the furthest set of lights in the distance. 'I want you to run all the way over there. Can you do that?'

They all stared at him. Nobody moved.

'Look, I'm not abandoning you, I'm... I have to go back and make sure the other little boy or girl is OK. OK?'

Still nothing.

'Please. Just stick to the shadows and don't talk to *anyone* until you get there. If you see someone, *hide*.'

For God's sake, why wouldn't they go?

He winced down in front of Rebecca, smiling at her through the fence as he unbuttoned one of the epaulettes from his T-shirt. 'You're an official deputy police officer, remember?'

'I can arrest people tomorrow.'

'But today, you get these kids to safety and you call the police and you read them the number on this thing.' He handed the epaulette between the strands of barbed wire. 'You read them the number and you tell them "officer down", OK?'

'Officer down.'

'Good girl. Now go. *Run.*'

Please.

Don't stand there like a bunch of bloody garden gnomes in the rain.

Run.

Go.

PLEASE.

The tiny girl in the pink dungarees burst into tears.

Rebecca's scowl deepened, then she stomped over and thrust the teddy bear into her arms. 'Orgalorg will look after you.'

She blinked up at Rebecca, bottom lip trembling, then gave the bear a big squishy hug.

Rebecca grabbed her hand, then turned and did the same with Stephen's. 'Come on, you tits!' She ran and the others ran with her – Ellie catching up to make the crocodile whole again. By the time they'd reached the drystane dyke they were almost invisible in the dark, only Ellie Morton's bloodstained angel costume gave their position away.

Then they scrambled over the wall and were gone.

Thank you...

He sagged against the fence post, and breathed – great ragged plumes of fog that drifted away in the rain. In and out. In and out. Until the fire scorching its way through him had faded to glowing embers again.

Cold water trickled down the nape of his neck. Wasn't a single inch of him that was still dry. Or warm.

He turned, teeth chattering as a wave of cold shivered its way through him. 'Smart move, Logan. Sending five wee kids off to get help. On their own. In the dark. And the rain. When the place is crawling with paedophiles. *Really* smart.'

He limped onto the concrete between the buildings again, sticking up two fingers as he passed the barking dog in its four-by-four. 'Well what was I supposed to do, leave the sixth one behind? No. Of course not. So shut up and leave me alone.'

His feet scuffed through puddles, making for the machine shed. 'Assuming I don't bleed to death first.'

Logan hauled open the door and staggered inside. Lurched around the combine harvester to where Number Five lay. Spat. Bared his teeth. 'Why did you have to have a bloody knife?'

One more kick in the ribs for luck.

Pff...

'OK, I'm going to need your jacket, your mask, and your hoodie.'

Only there was no way they were coming off with Number Five's hands cable-tied together. Should have got his clothes off *before* tying him up. And while we're picking holes, it *might* have been better not to leave the packet of cable ties back at the Clio, unless the idea was to let the guy go free.

'Oh yes, thank you, Captain Hindsight. Very helpful.'

Logan lumbered back to Danielle's car, stuffed the packet into his pocket, grabbed the duct tape for good luck, and returned to the machine shed. Swearing all the way.

He unfolded the butterfly knife, squatted down and heaved Number Five over onto his side. Sawed through the plastic strip. Stole his gloves. Then struggled him out of his jacket and hoodie, leaving him in a Stereophonics T-shirt.

Good. He could freeze *his* nipples off for a change.

It took a bit of doing, but Logan got one of the guy's arms up behind the combine harvester's bottom step, then out through the gap between the treads. Hauled the other arm up the front and zipped a new cable tie tight around both wrists. Number Five was going nowhere.

And then, just to be petty, he wrapped a strip of duct tape around the guy's head, making sure it was nice and stuck in his eyebrows and hair. 'Serves you right.'

The hoodie made Logan's T-shirt stick to his torso like a clammy claggy hug. The jacket was too tight across the shoulders, but good enough. Now all he needed was the mask.

Back outside.

He inched down and felt under Danielle's Clio. Had to be somewhere around here... Aha! It was lurking behind the passenger-side rear wheel.

Logan picked it up.

Sod.

The plastic face was cracked down the middle, probably due to all the punching, and the strap was broken on one side so it wouldn't stay on. Not even duct tape was going to fix that.

Well, it'd have to do.

He limped across the concrete and into the equipment shed.

Someone had filled his boots with lead as well as rainwater – that's why they were so heavy. Number Five's jacket must've been lined with it too, because the weight of it made his arms droop at his sides. Pushed his shoulders down.

Come on, at least he was warming up a bit. That was something, right?

'I need a sodding holiday…'

OK, to-do list.

Empty crates: check.

Body wrapped in plastic sheeting: not check.

He stumbled over there, unfolded the butterfly knife again – not easy with gloves on – and slit the plastic from head to chest. A man. Dressed in black. With a black fabric bag covering his face. It probably wasn't him that put it on, though.

Logan took hold of the bag's top and pulled it free. Stared down at the battered and bruised head it'd been covering. Was that…?

He got closer. It was. Angela Parks – the journalist from Ellie Morton's house. The one Russell Morton called a 'skinny munter cow'. The one desperate to know if the Livestock Mart was real. The one who now looked as if she'd been run over by a minibus. Repeatedly.

'Great…'

He laid the bag over her face like a veil and hauled himself upright again. 'Come on, Logan: how do we do this? How do we do this?'

One old tractor. Six empty crates.

'I know: I'll ask them nicely to surrender or I'll *bleed* on them.'

What else?

'Need a weapon.'

He held up the butterfly knife. 'And you're sod-all use, there's hundreds of them.' He folded it shut and stuffed it in his 'borrowed' jacket's pocket. Needed something a bit more heavy-duty than that.

How about the racks of ancient equipment?

Logan hefted a rusty crowbar from a collection of clamps, shovels, and fencing tools. Substantial. Solid. Nearly as long as his arm. 'Not perfect, but you'll do.'

He slapped it into the palm of his other hand, smacking it against the leather. 'And stop talking to yourself. You sound like a mad person.' Then he pulled up the hoodie's hood, held the mask over his face, opened the door through to the cattle court and slipped inside.

46

The circle of animal masks had widened. Now, a little boy in shorts, sandals, and a Paddington Bear T-shirt was clearly visible – standing between a woman in a sort of crocodile mask and the woman in the snake mask. The boy looked a bit older than he had in *Cold Blood and Dark Ganite*, but it was definitely him: Aiden MacAuley.

Up on the walkway, the guy in the grey mask leaned on the handrail. 'Well, Dragon? The bidding now stands at fifty-three thousand pounds.'

The woman in the sort-of-crocodile mask nodded. 'Fifty-four thousand.'

Snake put her head on one side. 'Fifty-*five* thousand.'

'Sixty!'

Gasps from the other Animals.

Now, while they were all busy, where was Danielle Smith?

There – the woman in the Number Six mask, standing by a stack of wooden pallets. Logan waved at her.

Grey Mask clapped his hands. 'We have sixty thousand pounds! Do I hear any advance on sixty thousand pounds?'

Silence.

Logan pointed at Number Six, then at himself, then hooked a thumb over his shoulder towards the equipment shed.

She didn't move.

Why could nobody do what they were told?

'Sixty thousand going once. Going—'

Snake nodded. 'Sixty-two thousand.'

Logan had another go. She'd definitely seen him – she was looking right *at* him, for God's sake – so why wouldn't she... Finally. Number Six gave a small shake of the head, then scuffed across the straw-covered floor towards him.

'Dragon, Snake bids sixty-two—'

'Sixty-three thousand, three hundred and seventy-five pounds!'

Come on, come on, hurry up.

Number Six stopped right in front of him. 'What?'

Logan jerked his thumb at the door again, turned, and walked into the equipment shed.

Grey Mask's voice echoed through from the cattle court. *'Snake?'*

'I'd like to contact my client for guidance.'

'You know that's not possible.'

Number Six followed Logan into the room and shut the door behind her.

She stood, staring at the open crates. 'What the—'

And that's when he cracked her over the head with his crowbar. Not a full-on baseball bat swing, but a firm enough *clunk* to make her knees buckle and send her crumpling to the floor. And keep her there.

Logan dropped Number Five's broken mask. 'Not so funny when someone does it to *you*, is it?'

He peeled her mask off – yup definitely Danielle Smith. Checked for a pulse – still alive. Gritted his teeth, took a couple of deep breaths, then dragged her behind the crates in the far corner. Stopped for a grimace and some panting as the fires reignited. Braced himself against the wall while the world pulsed and hissed like waves on a stony beach.

Do not pass out. Do NOT pass out...

OK.

Come on. Not finished yet.

The gloves were too thick to work the cable ties, so he stripped them off and struggled one set around her wrists and another around her ankles, the plastic tacky in his sticky red fingers.

431

A strip of duct tape across her mouth, and she was done.

Meaning Logan could go rummaging through her pockets.

'Where are you, you little...' A hard, L-shape weighed down the left side of her leather jacket. Logan slipped the semi-automatic pistol free. 'Ah, *there* you are.'

It was an ugly black slab of a thing. Heavy. But it would do.

Now, did she have a phone?

Sod. No, she didn't. And, like Number Five, no wallet or ID either.

So much for Plan A: call for help. Time for Plan B: the gun.

The magazine slid out into his palm with a quick push of the release. Ten bullets. He pulled the slide back and checked the breech: empty. Right. He slapped the magazine in again and racked a bullet into the chamber. Clicked off the safety.

Here we go.

Logan put on Danielle's Number Six mask and flipped up his borrowed hood.

Too late to chicken out now.

Deep breath.

He opened the door and stepped into the cattle court.

Snake and Dragon were still facing off, the pair of them looming over Aiden MacAuley. Poor little sod. *Paedophiles* fighting over him.

Grey Mask had his arms out, preacher style. 'I'm going to have to press you, Snake. I have sixty-three—'

'Sixty ... five thousand.'

One of the Animals whistled. 'Bloody hell.'

Logan limped his way along the wall, gun arm tucked behind him.

Dragon turned towards the man on the walkway. 'I've got more money in my account: the twenty-eight thousand that Horse owes me for Rebecca Oliver.'

The Animals shuffled their feet and looked away. Some hissing breaths. A couple shaking their heads. Clearly uncomfortable.

Grey Mask shrugged. 'Ah... No. Firstly there's a twenty percent sales commission, and secondly those funds can't be released until the end of the evening.'

432

She stomped her foot. 'This *is* the end of the bloody evening!'

'I don't make the rules, Dragon. I just enforce them.'

Him: Grey Mask. He was the one to take down. Break him and the whole twisted organisation would collapse, begging to be arrested.

Yup.

Logan limped on, towards the walkway.

You keep telling yourself that.

Dragon turned to Snake, voice cracking. 'Please. Please, let me have Aiden! I have to have him. You don't know how important it is. *Please.*'

Snake held up a hand. 'I'm sorry, but the people I represent were very *insistent* about his ownership.' Then in a softer tone, 'There are plenty of other children out there you could have.'

'You don't understand! It's...' Looking around for support. Getting none. 'How about I buy Aiden from *you*? After this, when they give me the twenty-eight thousand?'

Grey Mask held up a hand. 'Less sales commission.'

'That's...' Dragon twitched the fingers on one hand. 'Eighty-six thousand pounds in total!'

Snake shook her head. 'Eighty-five thousand seven hundred and seventy-five.'

'Please: you go home with a huge profit and you don't even have to *do* anything!'

'It's one thing to be beaten, honourably, at auction. It's another entirely to accept *bribes*. No. It's out of the question.'

The plus side to all this haggling was that no one paid any attention to Logan as he scuffed his way through the straw along the edge of the walkway.

Dragon dragged in a ragged breath, her voice choked. '*Please!* You have to!' She threw back her hood and ripped off her mask. Dropped it to the ground. Followed it up with a blonde curly wig.

Oh ... *fuck*. Dragon was Sally MacAuley.

The other Animals retreated a couple of steps, putting a bit of distance between them and what was clearly an inexcusable breach of the paedophiles' sacred code of anonymity.

'He's my *son*!' Sally fell to her knees and held her arms out. Sobbing. 'Aiden … Aiden it's me! It's … it's Mummy. I'm so … I'm so sorry…'

Aiden stood there, face slack, as if there was nothing behind his eyes.

Grey Mask climbed down from the walkway. 'Well, well, well…' Getting closer as Snake slithered off to join the other animals. 'You know, in all the years I've been doing this, I've only ever *once* had a family member try to buy their own child back. A fisherman. Didn't end well for him.'

'Aiden? Aiden it's me! Don't you remember Mummy?'

'You lied on your application form, Dragon, and that's a disciplinary offence.' He stopped, six foot away. 'We take discretion very seriously at the Livestock Mart. Can't have you waltzing out of here with Aiden then clyping to the authorities, can we?'

'Aiden!' She stretched towards him, all tears and snot.

Grey Mask dipped into a pocket and produced a semiautomatic – completely wrapped in what looked like clingfilm. He gestured at the Animals. 'You see the things I do for you? You should—'

'ARMED POLICE!' Logan stepped out onto the straw, holding Danielle's gun in one hand and clutching his side with the other. 'DROP THE WEAPON AND MOVE OVER THERE! AWAY FROM THE OTHERS! SLOWLY!'

'Gah!' Grey Mask stared at the ceiling for a moment. 'You see?' He pointed his gun at Sally MacAuley's chest. 'This is what happens when people don't follow the *rules*!'

'Don't.' Logan took off his mask, the air cold against his skin. A dribble of sweat itched its way down his cheek. 'I'm having a really crappy day and I *will* shoot you.'

'Even if you do, then what? There are … seventeen of us – not counting this lying bitch – are you going to shoot everyone?'

'I'll shoot *you*.'

Sally was still on her knees in front of Aiden, only a few feet between them, but it might as well have been miles.

Grey Mask turned to face Logan. Stared at him for a while, head on one side. 'Is that *blood* I see?'

'Sally: take Aiden and get out of here.'

She didn't move.

'Looks nasty. Let me guess, Number Five introduced you to his knife? He's *very* fond of it.'

The world washed in and out again, hissing against the stones.

Logan blinked. Shook his head. 'Sally: take Aiden!'

She stared at him, bit her bottom lip, then shuffled forward on her knees and wrapped her son in her arms. Buried her face in his neck and breathed him in.

'Sometime today would be *spectacular*!'

Grey Mask took a step towards Logan. 'I think you've lost a lot of blood already. Feeling weak? A bit light-headed?'

'SALLY!'

She flinched. Seemed to remember what the hell was actually going on, and scooped Aiden up, holding him there.

'How long before you pass out, Officer?'

She wiped a hand across her eyes. 'Sorry, I—'

'Sally: focus!' Logan tightened his grip on the gun. 'I need you to go out the back door, pick a direction, and *run*. Get Aiden to safety.'

She just stood there.

'MOVE!'

Finally.

She half stumbled, half ran through the straw towards the equipment shed door.

Grey Mask raised his voice, watching her go. 'We'll find you, Sally MacAuley. We'll find you and you'll *both* be disciplined.'

She shoved through the door, thumping it shut behind her.

And now everyone turned to stare at Logan.

'Well, well, well, Officer. Alone at last.'

A large woman with the number two on her mask inched closer.

'Stand still!' Logan gestured with the gun. 'Everybody on the floor. Now!'

Grey Mask lowered his weapon. 'It's sad really. Kind of pathetic.'

'I SAID: ON THE BLOODY FLOOR!'

A fat man in a chicken mask lowered himself towards the straw.

'*Don't.*' A gloved finger. 'Think about it, Rooster: he's a police officer. What's he going to do, shoot unarmed men and women? Really?'

Rooster stood up again. 'Sorry.'

Danielle's gun was getting heavier. 'It's over. The kids are miles away from here by now. They go home to their families and you … you go to jail.'

'Their families?' A laugh. 'God, you cops are so *naïve*, aren't you?' He pointed at Captain Chicken Mask. 'Who do you think sold Ellie Morton to Rooster in the first place? Her stepdad. You think she'll be safer with *him*?'

Great. The old man with the stinky dog had been right.

'Face it: you've lost.' He stepped closer. 'All sales are final, Officer. So we'll … acquire Aiden again and make his mother *pay* for bringing you here. Then we'll recapture the rest of tonight's stock and deliver them to their rightful owners. No child left behind.' Another step. 'But first we'll take care of you.'

Logan backed up. 'You said it yourself: I'm a *police officer*. They'll hunt you down like…' He looked at Snake and Horse and Rat and Goat and Monkey and all of the other freaks. 'Animals.'

'Really? Because I don't remember them hunting me down when I forced all those pills and booze into Detective Sergeant Chalmers, then tied a noose around her throat. Don't remember that at all.'

'*You* killed her?'

'And now it's your turn.' Grey Mask snapped his gun up.

Too slow.

Logan's semiautomatic roared out across the cattle court, echoing around the metal roof and breeze-block walls. Roaring and bouncing and roaring and bouncing until it finally faded away.

Grey Mask stared down at the fresh hole in his hoodie. A dark-red patch spread out across the fabric. He dropped the gun. Looked up at his Animals. 'I don't...' Then crumpled to the ground. 'Oh Jesus! Aaaaaaaaaargh! AAAAAAAAARGH!' Curling around his stomach, *screaming*.

Everyone froze as Logan limped forward and picked up the fallen semiautomatic.

He used both guns to gesture towards the corner of the byre, away from the equipment shed door. 'All of you, over there where I can see you.'

'AAAAAAAAAAAAARGH!'

They shuffled through the straw, hands up, someone repeating, 'Oh God, oh God, oh God,' over and over to themselves.

If one gun weighed a ton, two weighed about eight times as much. Could barely keep them pointed at the inhabitants of the world's worst petting zoo and the numbers one to four. And seven. 'Keep moving.'

'AAAAAAAAAAAAARGH! OH CHRIST, THAT—'

Logan kicked him. 'You want me to take your pain away? Because I've got a *lot* more bullets!'

The screams faded to a sobbing whimper instead.

'Better.' Logan limped backwards, till the walkway stopped him. 'Listen up, people: here's how this is going to work. You're all going to lie facedown on the ground.'

Nobody moved.

Then Number One stepped forward. 'You heard the Auctioneer: he's not going to shoot us.'

Dog shuffled behind Rooster. 'He shot the Auctioneer!'

'All we've got to do is wait till he passes out and—'

Logan put a bullet in the wall above Number One's head. The boom reverberated around the shed as Numbers and Animals all scrambled for the ground. 'Hands on your heads!'

They didn't need a second telling this time.

'Anyone who moves gets a free bullet, are we clear?'

No reply.

'ARE WE CLEAR?'

A ragged chorus of 'yes's, partially muffled by them all having their faces buried in the straw.

'Good.' He slumped against the wall, sliding down it till his backside hit the deck. Sweat trickled between his shoulder blades. More stinging his eyes – he wiped it away with his sleeve. Glanced down at the glistening dark stain that reached out across his stomach and down his left leg.

The world did its waves-on-a-beach trick again.

Deep breaths. Deep breaths.

Why was it so cold?

Could kill for a pint of beer as well. Mouth was dry as a litter tray.

Logan rested Danielle's gun against his knee, propping it up. 'Now we're all going to sit here quietly till the police come...'

47

Oh, this was bad. This was very, very, *very* bad. Stan sneaked a look, keeping his blue mask touching the damp straw, trying not to draw attention. Or a bullet.

Everyone on this side of the cattle court lay on their fronts, the guys working the auction and the perverts as well. Nobody moving. Probably all trying to figure out how the hell they were going to escape before the cops descended.

And the only thing stopping them getting up and just walking out of here was slouched against the walkway, with that big red smear – where he'd slid down the brickwork – glistening behind him. Face pale as suet. The gun limp in his lap.

The one silver lining to this total shitstorm was that the bitch, Dragon, didn't have any car keys. She'd have to walk to the nearest farm, call it ten minutes away? After that, the cops would be here in what, fifteen, twenty minutes tops? So they had half an hour, *max*.

One of the kiddy fiddlers, Monkey, raised his head and stared at the copper. 'Is he...?'

'You!' The copper raised the gun in one shaky hand. 'Get your head down before I blow it off!'

Yeah: they were all completely and utterly screwed.

This was all the Auctioneer's fault. A journalist *and* a cop? One turning up would've been bad enough, but both? How could security be that lax?

Stan risked another peek.

The copper was still slumped against the concrete, but he'd tilted over to the left a bit. Arms limp at his sides. Eyes closed. Was he even still breathing?

The Auctioneer wasn't moving either. Good. Served him right.

Someone shifted on Stan's left: Rabbit. Raising himself up off the straw a couple of inches, mask fixed towards the copper. Then further. And further. And finally he was sitting up, the long white ears wobbling.

Nothing happened. No threat. No gunshot. Nothing.

Rabbit eased himself to his feet and crept towards the main door, pausing to nudge Snake with his foot on the way past. She got up and sneaked out too, followed by Tiger and Ox and Rat and Horse, and soon *everyone* was tiptoeing their way to freedom.

Stan picked himself up and crept across the cattle court, following Number One through the door and into the night.

Rain misted down, glowing in the farm lights. Making everything look slick and yellow, like it was infected.

They gathered in a clump by the door.

Number Two poked his head back into the cattle court, then out again. 'I think they're dead. Do you think they're dead?'

'Doesn't matter.' Number One paced away a couple of steps. 'If they're not now, they soon will be.' He pulled a Zippo lighter from his pocket. Flicked the lid open and thumbed the wheel, setting up a wee shower of sparks that turned into a wobbly flame. 'Going to be DNA and all sorts in there.'

Snake marched over and poked him in the chest. Voice all hoity-toity, and sharp. 'I want my clients' money back, this auction has been a *farce*!'

'Calm, OK?' Number Three shook his masked head. 'Nobody's getting their money back till we're out of here.'

'Excuse me?' Pig put his hand up. 'Can I have my car keys, please? I'd really like to go home now.'

Snake squared off with Number One. 'Do I need to remind you that the people I work for—'

Number One's left hook caught Snake right across the jaw, sending her sprawling. He stood over her, flexing his fist. 'You want to hang around counting silver till the police get here? Be my guest. The rest of us are torching this place and *leaving.*'

Pig put his hand up again. 'So: car keys?'

'You want some too?' Number One shook his fist under Pig's snout.

'I wasn't... Sorry.' Backing away.

'Didn't think so.' He pointed at Number Two. 'Two: give everyone their car keys and phones. Three: there's a can of petrol in the boot of the Range Rover, you and Seven...' He did a quick three-sixty where he stood. 'Where's Seven? SEVEN!'

Rat shuddered. 'Leaving the sinking ship...'

'Fine. Three and Four: get the petrol splashed around. I want this place up in flames *now*!'

Stan checked his watch. How long was that, twenty minutes? 'We've *really* got to get out of here. The cops'll be on their way.'

'Then get your finger out and do as you're told!'

Stan followed the long line of cars, lurching their way down the track. A dense cluster of tail-lights, glowing red into the distance. Still no sign of flashing blue-and-white coming over the hills to cart them all away. Not *yet* anyway.

His eyes flicked to the rear-view mirror.

Flames danced in the open doorway of the cattle court as the damp straw smouldered, then caught. Spreading. The cottage was burning too – and a damn sight faster than the cattle court – sending gouts of orange and yellow roaring up into the drizzly sky. Illuminating the Auctioneer's Range Rover and Number Five's filthy four-by-four with the big dog going mental in the boot.

The line of cars reached the junction, each one turning off in the opposite direction to the last: under strict instructions to do the same thing at every junction they came to – one left, one right – dispersing out into the night, to go home and wait for a text about the money.

To wait for a text and hope the cops didn't come knocking.

Stan tightened his grip on the steering wheel, the pear-drops-and-vinegar scent of unleaded wafting up from his gloved hands. They *wouldn't* come. He was safe. That was the point of all the

441

masks and anonymous texts and never using your real name. Even if the cops *did* manage to pick someone up, they couldn't inform on anyone else. The only person who knew who they all were was lying dead on the cattle-court floor, with a bullet in his guts. Burning away right now in their DIY crematorium as the flames got rid of the evidence.

And, yes, it was a shame about the dead police officer, but it was too late to worry about that now.

'Mmmnnnph...' Warm. Really lovely and warm. For a change.

The world strobed into life, between his heavy eyelids. Cattle court. Yes. He was in a cattle court on a farm somewhere out in the middle of nowhere.

Tired, though. Really, really tired.

Logan frowned.

The floor smouldered, dancing wisps of steam and smoke swirling around each other as they waltzed towards the metal roof.

Over by the main door a stack of hay and a pile of pallets was surrounded by flames. Then a *whoomp* as one of the wrapped bales went up.

Oh.

Great.

And all the scumbags in the masks were gone too.

Come on: up. On your feet.

Logan dug his heels into the damp straw underneath him ... and toppled sideways, in a slow arc, until he was lying on it.

Closed his eyes.

At least he wasn't cold any more.

Gah! Roberta stumbled on, torch held out in front of her, the other hand clasping a slightly scabby hanky over her nose and mouth. The air in here was *solid* with smoke. Bitter, dark, greasy smoke that reeked of burning straw, wood, and plastic.

Her torch barely slid through it, making sod-all difference to the complete lack of visibility. All it did was light up more bloody smoke.

A voice bellowed from somewhere outside. *'GET OUT OF THERE! IT'S NOT SAFE!'*

Aye, right.

She kept going, coughing and hacking. What was the point of giving up fags? Probably inhaled about six months' worth in the last three minutes.

The vast yellow bulk of a combine harvester loomed out of the smoke, its big rotating spiky bits the only things in focus, the rest of it hiding in the billowing darkness.

She hacked up half a lung and staggered around the side.

'SERGEANT STEEL, DON'T BE AN IDIOT!'

Blah, blah, blah.

Bit late to stop now, wasn't it? Habit of a lifetime and all that. Where the goat-buggering hell was—

'Aaaargh!' Something tripped her up and Roberta went sprawling, needles slashing at her palms as she hit the concrete. The torch skittered away, spinning across the ground, getting smaller as its beam lighthoused around and around.

She struggled to her knees and crawled after it. Grabbed the thing. Hacked and rattled the other half-lung up.

Great. She'd dropped her hanky.

'CAN YOU HEAR ME? GET OUT BEFORE YOU KILL YOURSELF!'

Aye, maybe he had a point.

She raised her other arm, burying her nose and mouth in the bend of her elbow. Swung the torch round to see what she'd tripped over...

Bloody hell.

It was a leg. A *human* leg. And it was attached to an ugly wee man – all trussed up and unconscious. Cable tied to the combine's steps. Broken nose. The bottom half of his face stained dark red. A strip of duct tape wrapped about his bonce.

Roberta shuffled over and felt for a pulse...

Yup: still alive. For now.

She swung the torch through the smoke again.

A line of scarlet, about two-hands wide, stretched across the concrete floor. Definitely drag marks. And the smaller red splotches running along the left side of it looked suspiciously like a single handprint, repeated over and over again. And the prints didn't start or end with the broken-nosed man. They kept going right past him.

She scuffed forward on her hand and knees, following the trail...

Then stopped and *stared*.

A man lay at the end of it, slumped back, arms and legs splayed, grey hoodie stained with blood, face the colour of antique ivory. And behind him, one arm still wrapped around the guy's chest, was Logan.

That's why there was the one handprint, over and over again on the concrete floor. Logan must have dragged this guy in here.

She scrambled over, grabbed a fistful of bloody hoodie and hauled him off Logan. 'No, no, no, no, no...' Smoke burned its way down into her lungs making her hack and cough and splutter.

'Logan!' Roberta took hold of his shoulders. Shook him.

Nothing.

This was no' the way today was meant to end. 'IN HERE! HE'S IN HERE!'

Three huge fire engines sat in the gap between the two agricultural buildings, pumping water onto the cattle court. Diesel engines growling. Their lights spun blue and white through the smoke, their warning chevrons fluorescing in the headlights of the ambulances.

Rain hissed on the cattle court's roof, adding to the massive plumes of steam and rolling smoke.

'Get off me.' Roberta slapped Rennie's hands away as she paced up and down the length of Logan's ambulance. Coughing – dry and rattling, burning up through her sandpaper throat.

'You've probably got smoke inhalation.'

'You'll probably get a shoe-leather hernia if you don't sod off and leave me alone!' Another trip up and down the concrete.

'At least drink some water.'

'I mean it, Rennie – the whole bastarding shoe!'

They had the ambulance doors shut, muttered voices and

444

barked instructions coming from inside. What the hell was taking them so long?

Tufty lurched over, hands and face smudged a dirty grey-black. He pointed at the closed doors. 'Any news?'

Moron.

'Does it sodding look like it?'

Rennie shook his head. 'He's lost a lot of blood. And I mean a *lot*.'

'It's all my fault...' Tufty shuffled his feet. Obviously waiting for someone to tell him that it wasn't. Well tough. He nodded, cleared his throat, and spat out a dark-brown glob. Then pointed at the other ambulance. 'We've got an anonymous I-C-One male suffering from breathing in too much smoke and probably concussion. And another one who's been shot in the stomach. Paramedics *think* they've got him stabilised. No sign of anyone else.' He spat again. 'Well, you know, other than the body wrapped in plastic.'

At that, the other ambulance *bleep-bleep-bleeped* as it reversed through a gap between the fire engines. Did a three-point turn, and raced away down the driveway – siren on full tilt, all lights blazing. Getting smaller and smaller. Disappearing into the rainy night.

You know what? Sod this.

Roberta stormed up the remaining ambulance's rear steps and flung the door open.

Logan was laid out on the stretcher trolley. They'd cut off his jacket, his hoodie, and his T-shirt, exposing skin pale as moonlight ... at least the bits not *covered* in blood. A couple of IV lines snaked into one arm, wires hooked his chest up to a monitor.

She banged on the open door. 'What the bloody hell is going on?'

One of the paramedics hurried over to shut it again.

Behind him, the other one stuck defibrillator lines onto Logan's bloody skin. 'Charged. Clear!'

The door slammed shut, and they were gone.

445

48

'Shh...' Susan wrapped an arm around Robbie and gave her a squeeze. 'He'll be OK, you'll see.' Because, let's face it, Susan hadn't made it this far through life by not being Princess of the Glass Half-Full People. Queen of the Silver Lining. Empress of Looking on the Bright Side.

The blinds were partially drawn, shutting out the storm, quivering in the air that whistled through the vents. Rain crackled against the window. Machinery bleeped and whirred. The ventilator hissed and squealed with every artificial breath.

And at the centre of it all: Logan. Still and so painfully, painfully pale. Hollows beneath his eyes. Tubes, wires, drips...

Susan gave Robbie another squeeze, then dug out a hanky and wiped away her tears.

Robbie blinked at her, all bloodshot and wobbly. 'What if he doesn't—'

'Roberta Steel, you listen to me: Logan isn't going *anywhere*. He wouldn't dare.' Susan kissed her on the forehead – still a bit smoky even after three showers. 'This is nothing more than a tiny setback. I promise.'

'Three hundred. Charging...' The defibrillator screen filled with the wobbly yellow scrawl of ventricular fibrillation. A shrill bleep sounded and the shock light turned red. Khadija looked up from the machine. 'Everyone stand clear!'

The whole team skipped away from the bed, like a lumpen ballet in pale-blue scrubs, and she pressed the button.

The patient stiffened, arms and legs rigid, then sagged back onto the sheets. Pale and naked, with a chunk of stained wadding over his side.

Khadija checked the monitor again: *still* in ventricular fibrillation. 'Damn it...' She thumbed the button up to five hundred joules and glowered at him. 'You are *not* breaking my winning streak. Charging!'

The Rolling Stones rocked out of Danielle's noise-cancelling headphones: 'Sympathy for the Devil'. Perfect accompaniment to putting up a chunk of stud partitioning.

Danielle positioned the length of CLS in the compound mitre saw and pulled the handle down – timing the blade's shriek to the music. Then dabbed the cut ends with preservative and carried it over to what was going to be the kitchen wall. Wedged it into place and hammered the bottom edge till it sat flush with its neighbour. Nice and tight.

She grabbed the nail gun and whacked a couple in down there, bracketing them, then did the same at the top and twice more in between for good measure.

Right – next stud.

She turned and...

Ah.

A police Transit and a couple of patrol cars scrunched to a halt on the track in front of her house-to-be. Their doors flew open and about a dozen officers burst out of them, some in uniform, some in plainclothes, and some *really* big ones in riot gear.

They swarmed up onto the concrete foundations, circling her, batons at the ready.

A goofy-looking one with bleached blond hair and a righteous expression on his stupid pink face strode through the ranks. He pointed a tin of pepper spray at her. 'YOU! DROP THE WEAPON! HANDS UP!'

She switched Mick off and removed her headphones. Raised an eyebrow at Blondie. 'Rennie, isn't it?'

447

'DROP THE WEAPON!'

Weapon?

Danielle's eyes drifted down to the nail gun in her other hand. It'd be a challenge, but she could probably take three or four of them down before the rest got her.

Then again...

She shrugged, lowered the nail gun, and put her hands in the air.

'Urgh...' Logan peered out at a strange room that smelled of disinfectant. Small. Blinds closed, thin slivers of sunlight chiselling their way in through the gaps to gouge holes in his eyes.

The air tasted ... horrible. Like someone had rubbed a toilet brush around the inside of his mouth.

Everything weighed a ton: arms, legs, head, the starchy sheet and pale-blue crocheted blanket thing covering him.

Machinery whirred, beeped, and snored?

He let his head roll over towards the window. It looked as if the place had been dive-bombed by the Get-Well-Soon Fairy. Mylar balloons, cards, a couple of over-sized teddy bears, grapes... And slumped in a big blue vinyl visitors' chair, head back and gob open: Detective Sergeant Roberta Steel. Snorting, gurgling, and droning away like bagpipes full of custard.

Logan closed his eyes and let the darkness swallow him again.

The *thump*, *thump*, *thump* of R&B blared out through the open window as Roberta and Tufty stormed up the path to Ellie Morton's house.

Sun was out. Almost made the street look pretty. But no' quite.

She clicked her fingers, then pointed. 'Better give it laldy.'

Tufty did, hammering on the red door with his fist, making the whole thing boom and shake. Even managed to do it so he wasn't in time with the music, so it was extra irritating.

A voice yelled out from inside. *'BUGGER OFF!'*

Tufty kept hammering.

The same voice again: getting louder. *'ALL RIGHT, I'M GETTING IT. ... I SAID I'M GETTING IT, YOU STUPID COW!'*

Then the door flew open and Russell Morton blinked out at them, both eyelids working independently of one another. Pupils big and black in a sea of pink. The thick sweaty reek of marijuana rolled off him like fog, accompanied by stale beer and whisky.

He grabbed onto the door frame and wobbled a bit, squinting as the music *thump*, *thump*, *thump*ed out behind him. 'The hell do you want?'

Roberta gave him a big happy smile. 'Well, well, well, if it isn't my old pal Russell Morton.' She clapped her hands, as if she was encouraging Naomi to go potty. 'Guess what, Russy-boy: you're *nicked*.'

The magic words seemed to cut through the fog of booze and dope, because those big black eyes went wide and Morton turned to run off into the house.

Tufty leapt inside, grabbed the lanky wee scumbag and wrestled him to the hall carpet. 'Hold still! HOLD STILL!' Struggling the cuffs into place.

Roberta pulled out her e-cigarette, inhaled a big cloud of black cherry and puffed it out in a satisfied sigh. 'Ahh... I enjoyed that.'

'You *still* no' up and about?' Steel plonked herself down in his high-backed visitor's chair and swung her feet up onto the bedclothes. 'Five days slobbing about in bed: that's malingering, that is.' Today, her hair looked as if she'd had a fight with a tumble drier. And lost. 'You're a proper sight, by the way. Can you no' have a shave or something?'

Logan shifted beneath his crinkly sheet, voice barely a whisper. 'Thirsty...'

She tossed a folded newspaper onto his bed. 'Present for you.'

His hands trembled a bit as he picked it up, the IV line jiggling about on the end of its cannula. 'Tributes Paid To Dead Homeless Man' sat above a picture of a young bloke with a long brown beard and sunken eyes, singing away outside the Greggs on Union Street – one hand on his chest, the other in the air. 'Oh no... Sammy Show-Tunes died?'

'No' that, you idiot, *other* side.'

Ah.

Logan turned the paper over. It was that morning's *Aberdeen Examiner*, with the headline, 'EVIL STEPDAD SOLD ELLIE TO PAEDOPHILE RING' stretched across its front page. A nice big photo of Russell Morton being bundled away in handcuffs.

Aw, diddums. He looked *very* upset.

A smile pulled at Logan's cheeks, making the layers of stubble itch.

Steel dug a hand into her armpit and had a good scratch. 'Don't say I never do anything nice for you.'

'Do you want to make it *two* nice things?'

She pulled in her chin. 'It's no' a bed bath, is it? Cos there's limits.'

God, there was an image.

'No: my mobile phone's got photos on it. One of the paedophiles from the Mart – I got his face and number plate.'

'Now you're talking!' She stuck out her hand. 'Well, where is it?'

Ah...

'Look! Look!' Stephen MacGuire stood on his tiptoes and placed a big squashed box of chocolates on the bed. 'We got you chocolates, but Ellie sat on them.'

Ellie stuck out her bottom lip. 'Did not!'

'Did too!'

The five of them surrounded his hospital bed: Stephen, Ellie, Rebecca, Vernon, and little Lucy Hawkins in her pink dungarees – hugging Rebecca's teddy bear, with one thumb wedged firmly in her mouth. The only kid *not* staring at him like he was a two-headed goat in a petting zoo was Vernon. He stood in the corner not making eye contact, a long-sleeve top pulled down over his fingertips to hide the small circular scars that covered his arms. All the kids from the Livestock Mart, except for Aiden MacAuley.

450

Their parents stood out in the hallway, looking in through the observation window, every one of them teary and smiling.

Good job he'd taken Steel's advice yesterday and had a shave.

Ellie stomped her foot. 'Did not!'

'Did too!'

Rebecca scowled at the pair of them. 'Shut up, or I'll arrest you both.' She pulled out a big folded sheet of paper and slapped it down on top of the chocolates, still wearing her serious face as she frowned at Logan. 'I drew you a picture.'

'Thank you.' He leaned closer to her, dropped his voice to a whisper, and nodded towards Lucy. The teddy bear in her arms was about three hundred percent tattier than it had been out at Boodiehill Farm, one of the ears barely hanging on. 'What happened to Onion-log? Organ-log?'

'Orgalorg.' Rebecca shrugged, matching his whisper. 'He's looking after her cos she's only little and she gets horrid dreams about the Grey Man catching her and feeding her to a big *pig* monster.' A wistful look crept across Rebecca's face as she looked at her tatty bear. 'She needs him more.'

Logan ruffled Rebecca's hair. 'You're a very brave girl, you know that, don't you?'

'Get off me.' She pushed his hand away. 'Not a puppy.'

'Right: let's see this lovely picture.' He unfolded the sheet of paper to reveal a felt-pen drawing of two lumpy figures – one bigger than the other – shooting about a dozen bad guys. And it was obvious they were bad guys, because she'd written 'BAD GUYS!!!' above them in green with a bunch of arrows pointing at their lumpy pink heads. Many of which had bright red felt-tip gushing out of them. 'OK...' Well, *that* wasn't disturbing at all.

She stuck one foot on the bedframe, so she could lever herself up – pointing at the felt-pen bloodbath. 'That's you and that's me. They're all tits.'

He tried for a smile. 'Thank you, that's very ... nice.'

And, for the first time ever, she smiled back.

Logan shuffled along the institution-green corridor, in his pyjamas and hospital slippers, one hand on the wall, the other wheeling his IV drip on a stand. It was like moving in slow motion – other patients, staff, and visitors wheeching past him at about nine times the speed.

Still, at least it gave him plenty of time to enjoy the paintings, collages, needlework, and murals that adorned the walls. Even if some of them were pretty terrible.

He paused for a breather in front of a series of screen prints: puffins and seagulls in muted shades. His own face reflected back at him: bags under the eyes, hollow cheeks covered with two days' stubble. Looking bent and broken and about ten years older than he had a week and a bit ago.

Yay...

He shuffled on, past the puffins, past a sort of Fuzzy-Felt-meets-Freddy-Krueger thing, past a huge oil painting of a tattooed woman's face, and over to the lifts. A walk of about two minutes that had taken quarter of an hour.

Still, at least it was a change of scene.

He pressed the up button and waited. And waited. And waited.

Ding. The lift doors slid open revealing a gloomy metal box, with duct tape holding sections of the floor-covering down. An old man stood in the corner, his back to the lift, one hand over his eyes, a bouquet of flowers dangling from the fingers of the other as he cried.

Logan stepped inside. Selected the floor number from the list of wards printed onto strips of masking tape with permanent marker. Stood there in silence as the lift juddered and groaned its way up through the building.

Ding.

He wheeled his drip stand into another off-green corridor lined with variable artwork.

Better view out the windows though. Looking across the rest of Aberdeen Royal Infirmary, down Westburn Road, and off to the North Sea. All of it shining in the afternoon sun.

He shuffled his way to a set of double doors, next to a green button, beneath a sign marked 'SECURE WARD ~ Ring For Entrance'. So he did.

Then stood and watched two seagulls fighting over what was

probably half a battered mealie pudding, until a nurse appeared and let him in.

'Thanks. You haven't seen a police officer kicking about, have you?'

She pointed. 'Down there, on your left. Can't miss her – she's like a black hole for bourbon biscuits.'

Logan put his best slipper forward and followed the directions.

PC Baker was right where she was prophesied to be, sitting on a plastic chair, outside a private room. Short and stocky, with one arm in a bright-pink fibreglass cast. Nose buried in a J.C. Williams book: 'PC Munro And The Hangman's Lament' according to the cover. She looked up as he shuffled over. Gave him a pained smile. Stood. 'Inspector McRae! I didn't know you were... Should you be up and about? You look like—'

'Is he awake?'

The smile got even more pained. 'Yeah, but maybe...'

Logan pushed through into the room anyway.

'OK, then.' She followed him inside.

It was a bigger room than his, sunlight streaming in through the open curtains, framing an even better view than the one from the corridor. The whole sweep of Aberdeen beach was on display, a crescent of gold and green, from the links all the way to Footdee and out to the hazy horizon.

Of course, Lee Docherty wasn't in much of a position to enjoy it. He was slumped in his bed, skin as pale as boiled milk, with drips and tubes and wires connecting him up to machines and various pouches – both ingoing and outgoing. The latter hanging from the bedframe like horrible fruit.

He scowled at Logan, breathing in short jagged gasps. 'Going to ... sue ... the arse ... off you.' Each word sounding as if it cost him a slice of his soul. And let's face it, there couldn't be much of it left.

'Good luck with that.' Logan leaned on the end of the bed, taking the weight off a bit. 'Lee Jonathan Docherty; forty-five years old; currently residing at three Forest Crescent, Udny Station; form for criminal damage and assault.'

'No ... comment.'

'You know we're going to break your nasty wee paedophile ring into tiny pieces, don't you, Lee? You and the rest of the kiddy fiddlers are all going to jail.'

Docherty's chin came up an inch. 'That's slander. I … am *not* a … kiddy fiddler! … My role is … strictly procurement, … inventory management, … and sales.'

'That's a shame, because fiddling with kiddies is *exactly* what we're going to put you away for. And you know what they do to people like you in prison…?'

A small growl. Then he raised a wobbly hand, the middle finger barely making it upright. 'No comment.'

'Then there's the murders of DS Lorna Chalmers and Angela Parks. *And* the attempted murder of Sally MacAuley. Oh, and trying to kill me too.' Logan winked. 'Let's not forget that.'

Docherty's hand fell back onto the covers and he panted for a bit. Then, 'No … comment.'

'Or you can make things easier on yourself and help us out? All those guys in the animal masks, do you think they'd take the fall to protect you?'

'No comment.'

Logan poked one of Docherty's legs through the blanket. 'We've got one of your crew, Lee. Ian Stratmann, your "Number Five". He's looking at a looooong stretch, so what do you think he's doing right now? Other than trying to grow his eyebrows back.'

More glowering.

'I'll give you a clue: it involves an interview room and telling us everything he can about you, your operation, your staff, and your customers.' A grin. 'Isn't that *fun*?'

Docherty closed his eyes and sank into his pillows, voice barely audible in the sunny room. 'No … bastarding … comment.'

'Thought so.' Logan turned and shuffled from the room, whistling a happy tune.

Outside the window, the sky was a swathe of dark violet with a thin smear of light blue at the bottom, fringed with gold as twilight turned into night.

Sally MacAuley shifted in the big visitor's chair, staring down at her hands clasped in her lap. 'I'm sorry we didn't come earlier.'

'It's OK.' Logan shook his head. 'I get out soon anyway. Which is nice. Ten days of hospital food is worse than being stabbed.'

Aiden sat in the other chair, next to his mother. Not fidgeting. Not moving at all. Staring off into space, like a mannequin. Not even interested in the huge collection of kids' drawings that plastered the room's walls – everything from Rebecca Oliver's violent fantasies and Ellie Morton's vampire mice, to Jasmine and Naomi's pirates and unicorns and zombies and dinosaurs.

Sally managed a moment's eye contact, before concentrating on her hands again. 'I... I wanted to tell you how grateful I am to you for saving Aiden.'

Aiden didn't even react to the sound of his name.

'How is he?'

'He's fine!' Sounding brittle, but *trying*. 'Aren't you, Aiden?'

Still nothing.

She shrugged. 'He's just a bit ... shy now.' Sally cleared her throat. 'That man in the grey mask, the Auctioneer, he would've killed me, wouldn't he?'

Of course he would.

'Best not to think about it.'

A nod. A long, uncomfortable pause. Then, 'My lawyer says I'll probably get community service. It was the stress made me do it. I only ... *borrowed* Rebecca because I was so desperate to save Aiden. I wasn't thinking straight.' She wiped away a tear. 'I'm sorry...'

Aiden just sat there.

49

Ten o'clock on a Friday morning and Divisional Headquarters should have been a buzzing hive of police work. Logan limped along the corridor without even the sound of a distant floor polisher for company.

Maybe everyone was out catching criminals for a change?

His crutch was one of those metal poles with a sticky-out handle and a plastic bit that your forearm fitted into. And it made an irritating *clunk-scuff, clunk-scuff* noise all the way down the grey terrazzo flooring.

Walking through the empty station was like something out of the *Twilight Zone*. Where the hell had everyone—

'Logan! What are you doing here? Aren't you still meant to be in hospital?'

He turned and there was Superintendent Doig, smiling at him, folder under one arm. Logan nodded. 'Guv.'

'You look terrible, by the way. And where's your uniform? Anyone would think you're auditioning for a Westlife tribute band in that outfit.'

'I'm not even on duty!' Logan frowned down at his jeans, shirt, and jacket. 'And what's wrong with my clothes? This is a perfectly good shirt, thank you very much.'

'Listen, while I've got you.' Doig held up his folder. 'I had a meeting with the Police Investigations and Review Commissioner about you shooting that Lee Docherty scumbag.'

Really?

'I didn't have any choice, he was going to—'

'Shoot you. I know.' A smile. 'And he would've killed Sally MacAuley too, if you hadn't intervened. Her statement tallies with your version of events one hundred percent.' He thumped a hand down on Logan's shoulder and gave it a squeeze. 'So I'm pleased to tell you that you're officially off the hook. There's even talk of a Queen's Medal!'

'A *medal*?' Wow. An actual Queen's Medal.

'Possibly. Maybe.' Doig glanced left and right, then dropped his voice and leaned in close. 'You know how these things go. Best not to put too much—'

The Pet Shop Boys' 'Go West' belted out of the Superintendent's pocket and he hauled out his iPhone. Smiled at the screen, then grimaced at Logan. 'Sorry, got to take this. Good to see you up and about. Don't forget your uniform next time, though!' Then he turned and marched away, back straight, chest out, phone clamped to his ear. 'Andy? ... Of course I do, been looking forward to it all day. ... Ha! ... Put the Tanqueray in the freezer and we'll celebrate when I get home.' Doig disappeared through the double doors at the end, launching into a laugh that sort of simmered, then bubbled, then was cut off as the doors closed.

All right for some.

Logan limped over to his temporary office and stopped outside. Took a deep breath. Then let himself in.

Blinked.

Maybe he'd taken more of those painkillers than he'd thought, because not only were Rennie, Steel, and Tufty all in there, they were actually *working*. There were fresh notes written up on the whiteboard – some of which had been spelled correctly – and a sense of ... well, *purpose* to the place. As if they'd gelled into a team in his absence.

Tufty was hunched over a laptop, frowning at the screen; Steel two-fingered-typing at a computer of her own – a pair of small square glasses perched on the end of her nose for squinting through.

And Rennie was on the phone: 'Are you sure? … No, run it *again*. … Because you've screwed something up, that's why.'

Logan knocked on the door frame. 'Don't tell me DI Vine's actually managed to mould you lot into an effective unit?'

They all swivelled their office chairs around.

Steel wheeched her glasses off. 'Laz!'

Tufty beamed. 'Sarge!'

Rennie mugged a grin and pointed at the phone he had to his ear, mouthing the word 'Phone', presumably in case Logan had forgotten what one looked like.

'Thought you were no' getting out till Monday!' She stood. 'I was going to pick you up.'

'Only so much grey cauliflower-cheese one man can eat.' He indicated the room with a sweep of his crutch. 'Figured I'd pop by and say hello on the way home. See how you all were.'

'Well, du-uh.' Rennie rolled his eyes. 'Because it's *obvious*, isn't it? Someone's mixed the samples up.'

Tufty bounced in his chair like a wee boy. 'Perfect timing, Sarge: I has had a genius of supermassive proportions!' He spun around and hunched over the laptop again, clacking away at the keys. 'Come see, come see!'

Logan limped over, Steel scuffing along behind.

She poked him. 'You had us all worried there. Well, this pair of big girls' blouses were worried. I'm made of sterner stuff.'

Tufty fiddled with the mouse. 'See I've been having hella difficulty getting into DI Bell's laptop and then my brain went "ping!"'

'No need to worry: I'm fine. Only got stabbed once this time, barely counts. *Might* even be getting a medal.'

'Aye, that'll be shining.'

'So,' Tufty pointed at the screen – the default Windows login page, 'I'd been trying all these combinations of Aberdeen Football Club dates and stats and stuff like that, but nothing ever worked. Then I "pinged": he's been living in Spain, so what if he speaks *Spanish*?'

Steel poked Logan again. 'Look … can you … next time someone offers to stab you with a knife, just say no, eh? Susan's barely eaten since she found out you died again. It's no' the same when she loses weight – I like a good handful when I go a-groping.'

'And then I tried "the Dons" in Spanish: "*los dones*", which is technically "the gifts", but when I typed it in...' His fingers clacked across the keyboard and the login page was replaced by a picture of Pittodrie Stadium, from the Richard Donald Stand, with a superimposed AFC logo. Subtle.

'What happened with Danielle Smith?'

Steel shrugged. 'Had to let her go. No evidence.'

'No evidence?' Logan banged his crutch on the carpet tiles. 'She nearly caved my skull in! Tied me up! I had to escape from the boot of her sodding *car*!'

'Aye, but you try proving that.'

'She stole my phone! The one with the photos on it.' Logan sagged. 'I got the fat sod's number plate...'

Tufty turned around in his seat again. 'Do you lot want to know what I found or not?'

'How could there not be any evidence?'

Rennie gave a loud performance groan. 'All right, all right: I'll hold.' He put a hand over the mouthpiece and pulled a face at Logan. 'You had Steel in tears, you rotten—'

She kicked him.

'Ow!'

Tufty folded his arms. 'I don't know why I bother, I really don't.'

'Well, what about DNA? Her boot must've been full of it.'

'DNA's sod-all use when you douse everything in bleach.'

Logan slapped a hand over his eyes. 'Oh for God's sake...'

A sniff from Tufty. 'I might as well not even be here.'

He sighed. Sagged. 'All right, Tufty, what have you found?'

The wee sod bounced up and down in his chair again. 'This!' He clicked his mouse and a QuickTime window filled the screen. Not professional footage – the lighting was too bad for that, the picture a bit grainy, the colours slightly wonky from a poorly set white balance.

'It was lurking in the system recycling bin.'

The video showed the inside of a shed, devoid of the usual tins of paint and lawnmowers and shovels and gardening odds and sods. The only things in here were a waist-height shelf along one wall with various cordless DIY tools on it, and a young man tied to a dining room chair. Fully dressed with a gag in his mouth.

Logan moved closer. 'Isn't that Fred Marshall?'

A figure appeared at the edge of the frame, too out of focus to be recognisable, but there was no mistaking her voice. Even though the words were a bit slurred and mushy. *'What's your name? Say your name.'*

Marshall mumbled something behind his gag.

Sally MacAuley stepped into shot and slapped him hard enough to make the whole chair rock. And when he straightened up again, streaks of scarlet dribbled from his nose.

She ripped out the gag. Wobbling slightly. Drunk. *'State your name for the record.'*

He glared at her, blood turning his teeth pink. *'I'm gonna kill you, bitch! I'm gonna carve you up like a—'*

She slapped him again, even harder. Then turned to the shelf while Marshall sagged against the ropes, shaking his head. Drops of red splattering down across his grey sweatshirt.

He sat upright. *'You think you're scaring me? You think I'm—'*

Sally smashed a hammer into his shoulder – a proper overhead all-her-weight-behind-it swing.

'AAAAAAAAAAAAAAAAAARGH!'

She grabbed his collar, leaning in close: *'WHERE'S MY SON? WHERE'S AIDEN?'*

'You're crazy, bitch! You're crazy!'

Then she grabbed a cordless drill from the shelf. Pressed the button. It *vwipped* and *buzzed*. Eager.

'Gah...' Logan recoiled from the screen as screaming belted out of the laptop's speakers.

Steel puffed out her cheeks. 'Jesus...'

'It wasn't DI Bell...'

Tufty nodded, a big smile on his face. 'And in case you're interested: the whole thing lasts forty-three minutes and fifty-two seconds.' He pointed at the numbers on the bottom right of the screen. 'I'm betting it gets a lot worse before the end.'

Marshall screamed and sobbed as Sally went in for another go.

'Where's my son? Tell me where he is and this can all stop. *Just tell me. TELL ME!'*

'I don't know! I don't know…' More sobbing. *'I never touched him. It wasn't me! I didn't—'* Then more screaming.

Rennie licked his lips. 'Yeah, we *might* owe the labs a bit of an apology.'

Steel jabbed him with a finger. 'What did you do?'

'TELL ME WHAT TO SAY! PLEASE TELL ME WHAT TO SAY!'

'It wasn't my—' Rennie's eyes bugged and he turned away from the laptop, phone up to his ear again. 'Professor Ferdinand, how lovely to speak to— … No, I appreciate that. … Yes.'

Logan reached forward and clicked pause. Sally MacAuley froze in the act of pulling the drillbit out of from Fred Marshall's blood-soaked knee. 'Does anyone else appear on this at *any* time?'

Tufty shrugged. 'No idea, I only found it a minute ago. But I can have a look?' He fiddled with the mouse and the picture lurched into fast forward, the figures blurring.

'No, Professor, you're quite right: professional courtesy costs nothing. … Yes. … I totally and utterly apologise. *Unreservedly.* … I—' Another groan. 'No, that's definitely your right, Professor. … Thank you.' Rennie hung up. Shuddered. Took a deep breath. Then turned, face and ears an uncomfortable shade of hot pink. 'That was Professor Ferdinand. He says they've found Sally MacAuley's DNA on DI Bell's body. They only got a match because she had to give a sample when we arrested her for abducting Rebecca Oliver.' He pulled on a sickly smile. 'He *might* get in touch because, somehow, someone at the labs thinks I *may* have implied that they're an incompetent bunch of arse-monkeys who couldn't find yuck on a jobbie… Sorry.'

On the screen, the video whizzed all the way through to the end, freezing at the final frame – Fred Marshall, sagging in the chair, covered in blood, face a ruined mess of flesh and bone. Sally MacAuley standing beside him, weeping.

Tufty shook his head. 'Looks like it's a one-woman show. Well, one woman, one victim, but you know what I mean.'

Logan thumped him on the shoulder. 'Get the car.'

Sally sat at the kitchen table, hands curled around her mug, face turned to the patio doors. She didn't look around as Logan levered himself into the chair opposite.

Through the patio doors, the garden was a riot of green and orange – the pale fingers of beech leaves falling in one corner. In the other, Aiden was sitting on the playset's swing. Not playing, not smiling, not laughing: sitting there. Motionless.

Sally wiped at her glistening eyes. 'It's like he's dead.'

Logan put his notebook on the table. 'It wasn't kids who burned down the shed, was it? It was you.'

'It's like they took him away and killed my baby boy. And all I got back was this lifeless husk.'

'After you tortured and *murdered* Fred Marshall, you needed to get rid of all that blood. So you burned it down.'

She bit her bottom lip. 'He's my son. But he's dead.' Wiped at her face again. 'All this time I've been telling people I know he's alive … and he's not.'

'Only DI Bell found out, didn't he?'

She tore her eyes from the motionless child outside. 'He was the only one who ever cared, so I called him up. I told him: "I've done something terrible…"' A bitter laugh rattled free. 'I only wanted Marshall to confess. To tell me what he'd done with Aiden, but he *wouldn't*. And I got angrier and angrier and then…' Deep breath. 'And Duncan came round and he was horrified, of course he was, but he *understood*. He made it all better. Made the body disappear.'

'Then why did you kill him?'

The wind picked up outside, tumbling fallen leaves across the lawn, setting Aiden swinging – but not much. As if the ghost of his father was trying to push him, but couldn't quite manage it.

Sally stared into her coffee. 'Have you ever done something you can't … undo? That it doesn't matter how good you try to be from that moment on, you've got this horrible dark *stain* that goes right to your core?'

Of course he had.

'You stabbed him.'

'It doesn't matter if I scrub myself till I bleed. I'll never be clean again. No wonder Aiden hates me.'

'Bell heard there was going to be a new slip road going right through the pig farm where he buried Fred Marshall, so he came all the way back from Spain, back from the *dead*, to dig Fred up and rebury him somewhere he'd never be found. To protect *you*. And you killed him.'

A small shrug. 'He'd found out about the plan to buy Aiden from the Livestock Mart. He wanted to go to the police.' Her bitter laugh got colder and harder. 'The *police*. All this time you've done *nothing*! And he wanted to hand the whole thing over to you. Let you ruin it. After everything I'd done to get that invitation.' She shook her head. 'I don't think so.'

Rennie put his hand on top of Sally's head, making sure she didn't bash it off the roof as she got into the pool car – both hands cuffed in front of her.

The other pool car sat between the horsebox and her four-by-four, blocking it in.

Steel took a long drag on her fake pipe thing, the words coming out in a huge cloud of strawberry steam. 'So Ding-Dong didn't kill anyone.'

Logan leaned on his crutch. 'Except maybe Rod Lawson. Assuming the body we exhumed is actually him.'

'Hairy Roddy Lawson? Pfff... I'd lay even money on the furry sod overdosing on bargain-basement heroin and supermarket vodka. That boy was a walking corpse at the best of times.'

Rennie buckled Sally in, clunked the door shut, and waved at them, grinning away like an idiot. Because what was the point of being one if you didn't advertise the fact? One last flourish, then he climbed in behind the wheel, and drove off.

Don't see what *he* had to be so happy about. It wasn't as if anyone got a happy ending out of this one.

Logan limped across to the other pool car. 'Only thing we can be certain of is that Fred Marshall didn't kill Kenneth MacAuley. What she did to the poor sod... He would've confessed, no way he wouldn't.'

'Guvs?' Tufty appeared around the corner of the woodshed, with Aiden in tow. The wee boy held his hand, but there was no *connection* to it. Tufty might as well have been pulling a wheelie suitcase behind him. 'Well, technically Guv and Sarge, but "Guvs" was quicker. Anyway: update from the Children and Families team: they're sending out a Margaret McCready? Says she knows you?'

'Fred Marshall's social worker.' Logan nodded. 'Suppose there's a symmetry in that.'

Tufty squatted down in front of Aiden and smiled. 'You're going on an adventure! Isn't that great?'

Aiden just looked at him.

'Come on, Laz, get a shift on, eh?' Steel leaned on the steering wheel, vaping out huge clouds of strawberry steam as Logan winced his way into the passenger seat.

He sat there, panting. Teeth gritted. It wasn't so much a raging inferno as one of those underground coal fires. Smouldering deep in his innards.

That's what he got for ignoring his consultant's advice and discharging himself from hospital.

A deep breath. Then another one. Damping down the embers.

Steel reached across the car and put a hand on his arm. 'Let's get you home.'

Not yet.

Logan struggled the seatbelt into its clip. 'Not till we've paid Danielle Smith a visit.'

Steel puffed out her cheeks. Shook her head. 'You're an idiot. You know that, don't you?'

'Yeah.' A smile. 'But right now, I'm your superior idiot. So drive.'

50

The pool car bumped into the wee industrial estate in Northfield. It was a lot more picturesque in the sunshine – OK, the Granite Hill transmitter still loomed in the middle distance, but it wasn't *quite* so angry Dalek-ish.

Logan pointed past the metal warehouses towards the Portakabins. 'That one, down the end.'

'And then we're taking you home.' She parked outside the AberRAD offices.

A big sign hung in the window, 'CLOSED Until Further Notice'.

So much for that.

Steel sniffed. 'What now, oh great Superior Idiot?'

'We try her home.'

Fields drifted past the car windows. They'd lost their lakes, and recovered a bit – the swathes of barley not quite so battered and bent, straightening out in the sun.

Steel frowned at him. 'Are you sure you're OK? Cos I've scraped healthier-looking things out of Mr Rumpole's litter tray.'

'How are you finding working for DI Vine?'

'I'm serious, Laz. From his *litter tray*.'

'Everyone seems to have really gelled as a team.'

A snort. 'Aye, because that's all down to Johnny "the Vampire" Vine. Man's got the people skills of a drunk pit bull.' She slowed for the limits at Drumoak, the fields giving way to bungalows and teeny semidetached houses. 'See, the key to dealing with motherfunkers like Vine is: you've got to keep them busy. Load them down with stuff to review and meetings to attend. Leaving *you* free to get on with the job.'

Logan nodded. 'Wish I'd known that when I was working for you.'

'Wouldn't work on me.' She turned into a housing estate of cut-and-paste bungalows. 'I'm no' a motherfunker. I'm spanktastic.'

'You keep telling yourself that.'

She took a left, then another right, past a row of homes that looked as if they'd been modelled on bird boxes. 'I'm a damn sight more spanktastic than you.'

'Blah, blah, blah.'

Steel smiled across the car at him. 'Have to admit, I've kinda missed this.'

He smiled back. 'Big softy.'

Danielle Smith's building plot sat at the end of the bird boxes, sealed away behind its border wall of temporary fencing. It looked as if she had company – two other cars had joined her white Clio on the driveway.

Steel parked across the entrance, blocking them in. 'Try no' to get stabbed this time, OK?'

'Do my best.' He clambered from the car, grabbed his crutch from the rear footwell, and limped up the driveway.

Danielle had been busy – the ground floor was laid out in stud partitioning, most of it wrapped in dark-blue builder's paper. No sign of anyone, but the smell of hot coals and barbecuing meat wafted towards him in stomach-rumbling coils of smoky goodness.

Logan hobbled up the makeshift wooden ramp and in through a gap in the woodwork.

Danielle, Raymond Hacker, and Andy Harris occupied a large skeletal room in the far corner. It was a proper suntrap, sheltered from the wind, and the two men lounged in their shirt sleeves and folding picnic chairs, drinking bottled beer from a large plastic cooler. Danielle wore a vintage Rolling Stones T-shirt, showing off a red floral tattoo that covered most of one forearm, grilling sausages on a kettle barbecue. Tongs in one hand, what looked like a G-and-T in the other.

She looked over her shoulder at Logan and Steel. Groaned. 'What is it with cops and sausages? I swear you lot have a special built-in radar.'

Steel puffed out a cloud of strawberry vape. 'Well would you look at that – the whole gang of tossers is here!'

Hacker curled his lip. 'Oh grow up. You were a pain in the arse when I was a DS and you're twice as bad now.'

'Aye.' Andy Harris grinned. 'Only we don't have to put up with it no more!' He and Hacker clinked their bottles together in a toast. As if this was all some sort of joke. As if *nothing* had happened.

Really?

Logan hurpled through the maze of stud partitions towards Danielle. 'You attacked me. You threatened me with an illegal firearm. You tied me up and stuck me in your bloody boot!'

Andy Harris's grin got wider. 'Some people would pay good money for that.'

She turned, tongs in hand. 'You attacked me from *behind*, tied me up, and left me to burn to death! If Andy hadn't found me, I'd be a Bacon Frazzle by now.'

'So you admit being there?'

Danielle glowered. 'You nearly ruined *everything*, you moron!'

Hacker sat forward, voice low and warning. 'Danners...'

'No, you know what? Time for some home truths.' She jabbed the tongs at Logan. 'You have any idea how long we spent getting in with those guys? Two years! Working weddings and events and charity dinners and concerts till they trusted us enough to do the Livestock Mart!' She grabbed a sausage with her tongs and waved it at him. 'And you swan in like a halfwit and come *this close* to screwing it all up.' She slammed the sausage down again. 'Should be ashamed of yourselves.'

Logan stared. 'You were there to...?'

'TO RESCUE AIDEN, YOU MORON!' Face red, little flecks of spittle glowing in the sunlight.

Andy Harris shook his head. 'Much good it did us. Never saw a penny of the reward.' He thumped Hacker on the arm. 'And has she answered any of your calls? No. Not a word. Didn't even return your savings.'

'That's not fair. She's—'

'Oh grow up, Ray!' Danielle hurled the tongs into the cool box. 'All that lovey-dovey stuff was just so you'd help find her son. Soon as she got him home: nothing. She *used* us.'

Andy saluted her with his beer. 'A sad truth, but a truth nonetheless. The female of the species, etc.'

Steel licked her lips, nostrils flaring as she sniffed. 'Any chance of a sausage?'

'See? Told you. It's like built-in radar. And they're *vegetarian*.'

'Oh...' Steel shrugged. 'Ah well, I'm prepared to risk it.'

Logan frowned. 'Hold on: you said it took years getting in with "them". I thought you told us you joined that agency to get dirt on Fred Marshall? He worked for the same...' Oh, bloody hell. Logan screwed his eyes closed. Idiot. 'It's Whytedug Facilitation whatnots, isn't it? They're the ones who organise the Livestock Mart!'

There was a low whistle. 'Got to hand it to you, Danners: you said he was slow on the uptake.'

Logan stared at Danielle. 'Why didn't you report it?'

'Because you lot wouldn't have done anything without evidence. And now, thanks to us, you've got some.'

'And you'll testify to all this in court?'

'To put a whole bunch of paedos away?' She took a sip from her gin and tonic. Smiled. 'You try stopping me.'

'Good.' Logan stuck his hand out. 'Now give me back my phone.'

'All I'm saying is it'd no' kill us to stop off for twenty minutes and get some lunch.'

A burger van, parked by the side of the road, went by on the right.

'I'm no' talking about a three-course sit-down with wine and petit sodding fours. A baked tattie, a double bacon cheeseburger.

468

Hell, even a Styrofoam thing of lukewarm stovies would be better than nothing!'

Logan checked his phone again. The battery was *still* showing a red line. 'Are you sure this charger works?'

'And before you say anything: no, two vegetarian sausages in a gluten-free bap doesn't count.' She shuddered. 'Who in their right mind barbecues vegetarian sausages? No wonder she got kicked off the force.'

He pulled the plug from the pool car's cigarette lighter and jammed it in again.

Maybe all that rain had buggered the wiring? Tufty could fix that, couldn't he? Or rip the data off the memory card and onto a laptop? Something.

Steel pulled into the Whytedug car park. 'You're a slave driver, you know that, don't you?'

'Oh stop wheengeing.'

'You're no' even meant to be on duty.'

'Look, I'll … buy you a fish supper afterwards, OK? Now can we go do this?'

She climbed out and waited for him. 'A *proper* fish supper.' Following him as he limped across the tarmac. 'And I want onion rings too, as compensation for my emotional distress.'

A police Transit growled into the car park, stopping right outside the front doors.

Logan paused on the way past and knocked on the passenger window.

It buzzed down and he leaned on the sill. 'Are we all set?'

Sergeant Mitchell grinned and offered him a printout. 'You want us to go first and Big-Red-Door-Key it?'

'No, let's go for the Pop-Up Surprise. I want to be there when it happens.'

'You're the boss, Boss.'

Logan slipped the warrant into his pocket then hobbled through the doors and up the stairs into the reception area.

Jerry Whyte's assistant stepped out from behind his desk with a broad smile, shark's-fin haircut perfectly lacquered. 'Inspector McRae, how lovely to see you! I read all about your adventures in the paper last week.' He put a hand against his Breton-topped chest. 'What an ordeal! I'm so glad...'

Logan limped straight past him to the doors.

'No, hold on, I have to buzz you in or—'

'"Or" what?' Steel poked a finger in his chest, blocking his way. 'That a threat, sunshine?'

Logan shoved the doors open and lumbered inside.

Jerry Whyte was on her leather couch, phone to her ear, bare feet up on the coffee table. Haggis the terrier draped across her lap – snoring as she stroked his yellowy fur. 'No, you tell the ambassador it's nothing but a tiny setback. My people...' She looked up. Pulled on an annoyed smile. 'Sorry, Claus, I have to go. ... No, something's come up. Nothing to worry your pretty little head about.' A throaty laugh. 'Yes. ... OK, bye.'

She put the phone down as Mr Sharksfin finally managed to work his way past Steel.

'I'm sorry, Jerry, they barged in!'

A shrug. 'It's OK, Harvey. Why don't you get us some coffee? Flat whites all round? Great.'

He slipped from the room, leaving the three of them alone.

Haggis woke up, stretched. Gazed around the room with rheum-crusted eyes.

She ruffled the fur between his ears. 'Now, Inspector, what can I do for you this lovely October morning?'

'We're here to—'

'Before we begin,' she lowered Haggis to the carpet and stood, 'first I want to say a *huge* thank you for bringing Ellie Morton home safe and sound. And not just her, but all those other children too!' Whyte launched into a one-woman round of applause. 'Absolutely astonishing. I saw it on the news. Stirring stuff. Well done!'

Haggis shuffled his way over and had a good sniff at Logan's trousers.

She held up a hand. 'And I know: I promised you guys a case of Glenlivet. Don't worry, I'm a woman of my word. And we've got to think about the *reward money*. Yes, it was meant to be for "information leading to", but I think it's only fair to let you guys nominate a charity for that. OK? OK. Great.' She raised her voice at the open office door. 'Harvey? Get my chequebook!'

Whyte settled into the couch again, arms draped along the back. Winked at Logan. 'Don't mention it. Happy to help.'

Steel looked at him, raised an eyebrow. 'Go on then.'

'Actually, Miss Whyte, *we've* got a present for *you*.' He reached into his pocket and pulled out Sergeant Mitchell's sheet of paper. 'Jerry Whyte, I have a warrant here to search these premises and seize all electronic items for forensic analysis.' He made a rising gesture. 'Up we get.'

She stood, frowning. 'But this is some sort of mistake, right?'

'Jerry Whyte: I am arresting you under Section One of the Criminal Justice, Scotland, Act 2016 for organising events where children are bought and sold for the purposes of sexual exploitation.'

Her face hardened. 'Harvey? HARVEY, GET MY LAWYER HERE! GET HIM HERE NOW!'

Deep breath: 'The reason for your arrest is that I suspect you have committed an offence and I believe that keeping you in custody is necessary and proportionate for the purposes of bringing you before a court or otherwise dealing with you in accordance with the law. Do you understand?'

'HARVEY!'

'You are not obliged to say anything, but anything you do say will be noted and may be used in evidence. Do you understand?'

Haggis stopped sniffing Logan's trousers and started barking at him instead.

Steel stuck two fingers in her mouth and belted out a deafening whistle. 'In your own time, boys!'

The 'boys' – Sergeant Mitchell and his team – trooped into the room, each one the size of a Rwandan silverback, dressed in combat trousers and big bovver boots.

Haggis squared up to them, barking and growling.

'I do require you to give me your name, date of birth, place of birth, nationality, and address.' Logan pulled out his handcuffs. 'You have the right to have a solicitor informed of your arrest and to have access to a solicitor.'

'This is *not* happening.' Jerry Whyte backed up, till she was stopped by her desk.

'These rights will be explained to you further on arrival at a police station.'

'HARVEY!'

Logan shifted in his chair. Didn't matter how much he wriggled, nothing made it ache any less. He wiped his greasy fingers on another napkin. No point getting it all over DI Bell's laptop.

He moved the mouse till the pointer hovered over the video of Sally MacAuley torturing Fred Marshall. Clicked it open again.

The shed. Marshall tied to a chair. Gag in his mouth.

Sally, sounding drunk: *'What's your name? Say your name.'*

Marshall mumbling something behind his gag.

She slapped him, ripped out the gag. *'State your name for the record.'* As if she was taking a deposition. As if this would have *ever* been admissible in court.

'I'm gonna kill you, bitch! I'm gonna carve you up like—'

Logan switched the video off before the screaming started. Slumped a bit further, rubbed his face with his hands.

Still no sign of anyone.

Should've headed home after arresting Jerry Whyte. It wasn't as if Whyte was going to confess, was it? Nope: it'd be an expensive lawyer, followed by about two hours of 'no comment' and, if they were *extremely* lucky, remanded without bail.

Yes, but there was no point going home till Steel and Rennie returned with Rooster, AKA: Lionel Beaconsfield. The greasy, child-molesting lump would absolutely brick himself when they dragged him in. That would be worth a watch.

Till then. Pfff...

He had a look in DI Bell's documents folder. All of which seemed to be in Spanish. So someone else would have to go through that.

How about the pictures?

The directory was full of folders, the folders full of happy family snaps. Bell and his new wife and their wee boy, grinning away in the Mediterranean sunshine. At a market. At the beach. In the mountains. Eating ice cream. A first birthday party. A romantic candlelit dinner for two...

And now he was dead. Because he tried to save Sally MacAuley from herself.

Logan swivelled his seat. 'Tufty, has anyone delivered the death message to...'

Ah. Right. He was the only one here. 'Talking to yourself again, Logan. Told you: it's not a good sign.'

He frowned at the laptop.

'I wonder...'

It only took a couple of seconds to track down the Skype logo and click on it. The sign-in box popped up, the username 'CARLOS-PRIETO1903' already loaded up as the account name. Logan clicked on 'NEXT' for the password screen.

What was it Tufty had come up with: 'The Dons' in Spanish?

Logan tried, '*los dones*' but that threw an error.

How about with capitals? 'LOS DONES' – still no.

'OK, all one word...'

Aha! The computer made its weird backwards-sigh noise and up came Skype, with all of Bell's contacts listed on the left.

He clicked on the 'RECENT' tab.

Top of the list was 'TERESA CASCAJO LUCIANA'. The avatar next the her name was the same happy woman from the family snaps. But second from the top was 'ROSE SAVAGE'.

Clicking on her name brought up a big list of interactions – the most recent being a call on Thursday, the day before they found Bell's body, lasting forty-nine minutes and eighteen seconds.

The office door bumped open and Tufty reversed in, carrying a tray with teas and biscuits on it. He clunked a mug down in front of Logan. 'Got an update on the Sally MacAuley interview. She's now denying she had anything to do with stabbing DI Bell. Says he was like that when he turned up at her door, and she tried to help him.'

She lied to them. Sergeant Rose Savage, *lied*.

Tufty wiggled a packet of Jammie Dodgers at him. 'You want a biscuit?'

The rotten, dirty, scheming—

'Are you OK, Sarge?'

Logan curled his hands into fists. 'I want you to go find Sergeant Rose Savage and I want you to bring her here. Right *now*.'

51

Sergeant Savage sat on the other side of the table, dressed in her civvies, hair hanging down around her shoulders. Arms crossed. Big Gary hulked next to her in all his porky glory – chest, shoulders, and belly straining his Police Scotland T-shirt to near bursting point. The sergeant's epaulettes on his shoulders looked tiny in comparison. And, for once, he wasn't smiling.

Tufty had his notepad out, the little red light on the recording apparatus winking away next to him. Pen wriggling as he wrote down Logan's question.

Savage shook her head. 'I don't know what you're talking about.'

'It's over, OK?' Logan shifted in his seat, but the burning embers wouldn't settle. They wanted to ignite.

She turned to Big Gary. 'Do *you* know what he's talking about?'

'Don't look at me.'

Logan tapped the tabletop. 'When I spoke to you at the Mastrick station, you told me you hadn't seen DI Duncan Bell since you identified his body two years ago. Would you like to amend that statement?'

Her expression didn't change. 'I haven't seen him.'

'Well, that *is* odd. Constable Quirrel?'

Tufty produced his phone and poked at the screen.

The Skype ringtone binged and booped out from Savage's pocket.

Logan pointed. 'It's OK, you can go ahead and answer that.'

She did. 'Hello?'

Her voice crackled from Tufty's phone. *'Hello?'*

Big Gary shook his head, setting his jowls wobbling. 'So she's on Skype. There a point to this?'

'I wanted to make sure that the Skype address we had was actually yours, Sergeant Savage. Would you like to know where we found it?'

'You're my Federation rep, Gary, do I have to put up with this, or can I leave?'

A huge rolling shrug. 'Wouldn't advise it at this stage.'

'We found your address on DI Bell's laptop. You spent forty-nine minutes and eighteen seconds on Skype with him on Thursday evening.'

Tufty checked his notes. 'Call started at twenty-five past seven and ended at eight fourteen.'

She stared. 'I don't...'

'So,' Logan spread his hands out on the tabletop, 'I'm going to ask you again: would you like to change your statement?'

'Bloody...' She took a deep breath. 'So, the thing is—'

'Before you launch into another lie, Sergeant, bear in mind we'll find out the truth anyway. And it'll look a lot better for you if you cooperate.'

She covered her face with her hands and screamed at the tabletop. Then sagged. Sat back. Let her hands fall. And stared at Logan. 'Ding-Dong wasn't a bad cop, he just...' She shook her head. 'The MacAuley woman had him wrapped so tight he was about to pop. He was talking about leaving Barbara for her. Thought she was this noble warrior queen...'

The only sounds were Tufty's pen scratching at his notepad and the distant-thunder growl of Big Gary's stomach.

'So he's all guilty that we can't get anything to stick on Fred Marshall and he goes round there and he blubs the *whole thing* out to her. What we knew, what we suspected. And two days later he gets this call from her – she's drunk and she's sorry and she needs his help. And what does Ding-Dong find when he rushes over there like a lovesick spaniel?'

Tufty glanced up from his pad. 'Fred Marshall?'

'Frederick Albert Marshall, looking like something out of *The Texas Chainsaw Massacre*. So Ding-Dong takes care of it. Buries the body on some pig farm he knows about, where it'll never be found. To protect her.'

Logan sat forward. 'What about Rod Lawson?'

'Ah.' She bit her lip. Frowned at the tabletop. 'Ding-Dong was *consumed* with guilt. After all: if he'd kept his big mouth shut she wouldn't have killed Fred Marshall. He bottles it up for weeks and weeks, but he's getting worse, you know? Calls me in the middle of the night and he's talking about ending it all.' Savage huffed out a breath. 'Eight days later he's following up a lead on a batch of heroin that's been cut with scouring powder, and there's Rod Lawson – lying on his back in this manky squat, all on his own, dead as a breeze block. Hadn't been dead for long – rigor mortis not even set in yet – but it's too late to save him. So Ding-Dong decides to fake his own death using Rod Lawson's body, then slips away to start a new life in Spain.'

'And DI Bell did this all on his own, did he?'

The car lurches and bumps into the clearing, its headlights catching a manky old caravan. Rusty, and forgotten. Which is what makes this the ideal spot.

Ding-Dong's Volkswagen Passat is already sitting there, parked opposite, the engine running.

Rose pulls up next to it.

He's behind the Passat's wheel, wiping the heel of his hand across his eyes. As if *now* was the time to start getting squeamish. Nope. Too late for that.

She hauls on the handbrake, gets out, and walks over to the Passat. Opens the driver's door. 'Ready?'

Ding-Dong just nods. Probably doesn't trust himself to speak without blubbing.

Typical.

'Leave your wallet and the suicide notes on the passenger seat.'

He bites his bottom lip and does what he's told.

'Come on, Guv: best get it over and done with.' She snaps on a double pair of blue nitrile gloves and leads him around to the boot of her car. Well, not *her* car. The car she 'borrowed' from outside Rod Lawson's house. The one that's going straight to the dismantlers, soon as they're done here.

Rose pops the boot open and frowns down at the star of the show: Rod Lawson, groaning and grunting away. Ugly, hairy sod that he is, all dressed up in Ding-Dong's Tuesday best. Hands cuffed behind his back, high-viz limb restraints securing his knees together. Well: no point taking any risks, is there?

'Grab his legs.'

Ding-Dong doesn't move.

'I'm not doing this all myself. It's *your* arse I'm saving here!'

Finally, he nods, and together they wrestle Lawson out of the boot, across the litter-strewn clearing, and into the caravan.

The car's headlights ooze through the grimy windows. Not enough light to read by, but enough for what they need. Inside, the caravan's filthy: most of the units twisted and broken, graffiti and stains on the walls, the door torn off the chemical toilet. The burnt stubs of roaches and scraps of scorched tinfoil make it pretty clear what this place has been used for.

Rose kicks an empty two-litre of supermarket-brand cider out of the way, sending it skittering and booming its hollow plastic song under the table, where it bounces off the pile of firewood stacked there.

Between them, they get Lawson propped up on the table. He wobbles a bit, but he stays there. It's OK: doesn't have to be for long.

She marches over to the car, grabs two of the green plastic petrol cans from the Passat's boot, then makes another trip for two more.

Ding-Dong still hasn't moved – standing there with his bottom lip trembling. Staring at Lawson.

Rose gives him a shove. 'Get the shotgun.' And *finally*, he stumbles out.

478

Poor old Hairy Roddy Lawson. The Sandilands Sasquatch. Wobbling away on a manky table, in a manky caravan, parked in a manky clearing. The huge egg growing on his left temple is all red around the edges – not yet darkened into a proper bruise.

'I got...' Ding-Dong climbs into the caravan, clutching the shotgun against his chest in his ungloved hands. He clears his throat and tries again: 'It's...' He fidgets with the gun, staring at it, avoiding the drug dealer in the room. 'It was my dad's.'

Why do men have to be such babies?

Rose arranges the petrol cans around the caravan. No point opening them yet – want the thing to burn, not explode.

Ding-Dong is still standing there.

'Sooner the better, Guv.'

A thick greasy tear fights its way over the bags under his eyes, rolls down his cheek and into his beard. 'I *can't.*'

Babies, the lot of them.

'Fine. We'll go arrest Sally MacAuley for murder instead. That what you want?'

'I never ...' full-on sobbing now, 'I never wanted ... any ... of this!'

She sighs. Puts her hand out. 'God's sake, give it here.'

The shotgun is cold and heavy in her hands as she swings it around and pulls the trigger. No hesitation. No sodding about.

BOOOOOOOOM! It makes the whole caravan vibrate as most of Rod Lawson's head disappears. Like popping a water balloon full of tomato soup. The air reeks of butchers' shops and fireworks, a high-pitched whistling screech in her ears.

Ding-Dong's mouth falls open. Eyes wide. Tears pouring down his cheeks.

She shoves him towards the door. 'Come on, out. Get out of here, *now*!'

Have to admit, without the head, Lawson looks a lot more like Ding-Dong. The clothes help, of course. Now: time for the finishing touches. She uncuffs his hands, opens the ziplock bag of jewellery and dresses him up in Ding-Dong's rings, watch, and bracelet. Double checks everything is where it should be as bits of skull and teeth and scalp and brains drip down the rear window.

Done.

She has one last look at him. Shrugs. 'Nothing personal.'

Then Rose unscrews the caps from all the petrol cans, tips three of them over, and hurries outside with the fourth – leaving a trail of unleaded behind her. As soon as she's at a safe distance, she stops. Takes out a book of matches, cups her hand to shield one as she lights it, then holds it to the puddle at her feet.

Blue and yellow flames race towards the caravan, leap the steps and WHOOMP! The skylight and windows blow out, spinning away into the darkness. Then the fire takes hold and Rod Lawson's funeral pyre pops and crackles as flesh and plastic and fibreboard go up.

She tosses the empty petrol can in through the door. Turns.

Ding-Dong is on his knees, arms wrapped around his head, sobbing.

Poor old sod. And all because he couldn't say no to Sally MacAuley...

Rose walks over and pats his shoulder. 'Come on, let's get you on that boat.'

The recording light blinked as Sergeant Savage frowned. 'I only found out what Ding-Dong had done when he Skyped me on Thursday. Completely out of the blue. He didn't mention anything about an accomplice, but ... I don't know. *Maybe*? Be impossible to prove, though. After all this time.'

Logan stared at her. 'Really.'

'I *genuinely* thought he was dead. When I identified his remains, I thought *that was him* on the mortuary slab.' She sighed. Shook her head. Pity poor me. 'I was going to come forward, after he called, but it's all been such a shock...'

Of course it had. And it was about to get much worse.

Logan pulled a sheet of paper from his folder and placed it on the table. 'If you hadn't heard from him, then why is there a big list of calls between your Skype account and his over the last two years?'

She pursed her lips and sat back in her chair. Crossed her arms again. 'I think I'm going to want to speak to my lawyer before I answer any more questions.'

'What a surprise.'

Tufty followed Logan out into the corridor and clunked the interview room door shut behind him. 'What do you think? Do you think she was in on it? I think she was in on it.'

Logan grunted, turned, and limped off down the corridor, his crutch making its irritating *clunk-scuff, clunk-scuff* noise all the way to the stairwell.

Tufty strolled along beside him. 'Bet she's guilty as a hedgehog in a condom factory.'

'I don't care. I'm tired, I'm sore, and I'm going *home*.'

52

Steel's MX-5 scrunched up onto Logan's driveway with a completely unnecessary roar. Roof down, stereo thumping out Frightened Rabbit's 'The Modern Leper'. Very cheerful.

He unfastened his seatbelt. 'I could've made my own way home, you know.'

'Aye, right.' She got out and produced her e-cigarette. Puffed herself a watermelon-scented fog bank. 'Anyway, got sod-all to do till your mate Beaconsfield's brief turns up. Fiver says I can get him to roll on Russell Morton *and* Jerry Whyte.' She jerked her chin at Logan. 'You needing a hand?'

'No.' Bloody MX-Bloody-5. Why couldn't they have made the thing easier to get in and out of for people suffering from a massive stab wound? Of course, if she'd left the roof on, he could've used it to lever himself up, but nooo...

He struggled out, using his crutch and the car door for leverage. Stood there, grimacing as fire burned its way across his stomach and up into his lungs.

She walked around the car and put a hand on his arm. 'You sure you don't want me to come in? Make you a cup of hot sweet tea, or something?'

'Go away. I'll see you tomorrow.'

She puffed a lungful of watermelon at him. 'You know, me being nice to you is a limited-time offer?'

'Go! Give Susan an inappropriate hug from me.' He turned and limped towards the house.

'OK. But I'm going nowhere till you've made it inside without collapsing or dying.'

He hobbled up the step, unlocked the front door, and scruffed inside. Turned and made shooing gestures until she rolled her eyes, climbed into her car, and vroomed off in a buckshot-spray of flying gravel and a blast of music.

'Oh thank God for that.'

He thumped the door shut and leaned against it as the fires raged.

Deep breaths. Deep breaths.

Aaaargh... Maybe checking out of the hospital three days early wasn't such a good idea after all? Grey cauliflower cheese or not.

He straightened up. 'Cthulhu? Where's Daddy's girl? Where's you, Cthulhu?'

No reply.

Logan limped through into the living room. Still no cat.

She wasn't in the kitchen either. But there *was* a massive pile of dirty pots and dishes in the sink. None of which were his. 'Great...'

Well, they could wait.

Right now it was time for a couple of antipsychotics and a whole heap of industrial-strength painkillers.

He hobbled out into the hall, and ditched his coat on the end of the stairs. Kicked off his shoes. 'Where are you, you daft cat?'

The stairs were a bit of a challenge, so he got both feet onto one before starting on the next. Paused two thirds of the way up for a breather. Then one last push from base camp to the landing.

'Cthulhu?'

So much for the big welcome home. Oh, I missed you, Daddy.

He stopped by the bathroom for pills and a pee, then clumped his way along the landing floorboards. *Clunk-scuff, clunk-scuff.* Unbuttoning his shirt with his free hand on the way.

'Westlife tribute band' indeed. Superintendent Doig was a cheeky sod.

The bandages around his stomach were pristine white, except for the faint yellow stain over the hole Number Five made. Still: could've been worse – Lee Docherty had an exit wound to deal with as well. And hopefully it *really* hurt.

Finally – the bedroom.

He opened the door and froze.

Sunlight streamed in through the windows. A solid bar of it lay across the bed, catching Tara's hair and making it glow like Lucozade. She was spreadeagled on top of the duvet, fully clothed in joggy bottoms and a tartan T-shirt, one leg hanging over the edge of the bed. Mouth open, making snuffling snorey noises.

At least that solved the mystery of the missing cat – Cthulhu was curled up on her chest. A fuzzy yawn and Cthulhu stood, back arched as she launched into her stretching routine, tail fuzzy as a feather duster.

'Well, it wasn't my fault I had to stay in hospital for a week, was it? Somebody *stabbed* me. Again.'

She padded over and he rubbed her ears, smiling as she closed her eyes and leaned into it, purring.

'Oh ha, ha. "That's just careless." You're a laugh riot, aren't you?'

More purring.

Tara screwed up her face, making little smacking noises with her mouth. Then peered up at him, blinking. Scrubbed at her eyes. 'Whtimisit?'

'Thought you were in Birmingham on a course?'

'Urgh.' She yawned. Shuddered. 'Time off for good behaviour.'

He peeled off his shirt, undid his trousers, and collapsed onto the bed. Winced. 'Ow...'

'And before you complain, I was going to tidy up before you got home tomorrow.' Tara rolled over and draped an arm across him. 'You're—'

'Ow! Get off, get off!' God, it was like being thumped with a crowbar.

She squinted at him. 'And if this is *your* idea of foreplay, it leaves a lot to be desired too.'

Ahhh...

'Are you sure this is a good idea?'

'Positive.' Logan settled in amongst the bubbles, mug of tea in one hand, the other making lazy ripples bob through the water. Warm. Comforting. Wet. 'My surgeon says I'm allowed baths.'

'Hmm...' Tara sat on the toilet lid, with a large glass of red wine. She held the shiraz out. 'I don't mind sharing, you know.'

'Can't: pills.'

Cthulhu hopped up onto the bath surround and sat there, watching him, head on one side, prooping and meeping.

Logan groaned. 'All right, all right, quit nagging. I'm doing it.' He turned to Tara. 'Thanks for looking after the furry monster here for me. It was a massive help and I really, *really* appreciate it.'

'That's the only reason you gave me a key, isn't it? So I'd look after your cat if you got stabbed and hospitalised.'

'Yeah ... *something* like that.' He rested his head against the tiles and closed his eyes.

'So, did it all turn out well in the end?'

Good question.

'Well, Sally MacAuley got her son back for a whole ten days – he's in care now and she's off to prison. DI Bell ruined his life for her and got killed for it. We still don't know who all the paedophiles in the animal masks were. A journalist got kicked to death. And I'm lying here with yet another stab wound to join the collection. So, on the whole? Not really.'

She dipped a couple of fingers in the water. 'God, you're cheery, aren't you?'

'There's one consolation: Mrs Irene Marshall isn't too happy about Crowbar Craig Simpson trying to pin Kenneth MacAuley's murder on her beloved dead husband. So she's been telling DI Fraser *all sorts* of interesting stories about what Crowbar's been up to since he moved in with her: extortion, drugs, punishment beatings, that smash-and-grab at Finnies in July... You know what they say: "Heav'n has no rage, like love to hatred turn'd, Nor Hell a fury, like a woman scorn'd."'

'Hark at you with the poetry.'

'And while we're doing him for all that, it'll give us plenty of time to prove he was the one who murdered Kenneth MacAuley and abducted Aiden. He'll get at *least* twenty years.'

Tara raised her glass. 'Then here's to Craig Simpson spending the rest of his life in prison.'

Logan clinked his mug against it and smiled. 'I'll drink to that.'

Marky scuffed his way down B wing.

The sound of what could almost pass for singing boomed out across the Second Flat as the newly formed HMP Grampian Male Voice Choir committed attempted murder on an acapella version of 'Bohemian Rhapsody'.

He stopped outside Crowbar Craig Simpson's cell. Peered in through the open door.

A small room, identical to all the others in this place: one corner walled off for the tiny en suite shower and toilet, a narrow desk with a kettle and a cheap TV on it, a barred window looking out to sea, walls covered in film posters and photos of a curly-haired woman with big glasses, a toddler, and an ugly dog. The inoffensive scent of lemon floor polish...

Crowbar was on his bunk, dressed in the standard prison-issue navy jogging bottoms and blue sweatshirt, one hand behind his head, the other mangling a paperback – the spine bent so far back it was broken.

Now that made Marky's gums itch. There were killers in here, people who'd strangled their wives, or battered a drug rival to death with a sledgehammer, or drowned their own brother, or slit a stranger's throat because they supported the wrong football team.

But to do *that* to a book?

Marky knocked on the door frame and Crowbar tore his eyes from *PC Munro and the Cheesemaker's Curse* for all of two seconds, before returning to his tortured paperback.

'What do you want, Marky?'

See, that was the trouble with your criminal element today: no respect. Someone like Crowbar looked at someone like Marky and all they saw was a little old man, his joggy bottoms and polo shirt faded almost grey after years of washing in the prison laundry. White hair going a bit thin on top. Arthritis-swollen hands. A back that would never be straight again.

Marky shuffled inside. 'You busy?'

'What's it look like?' Lying there with his stupid handlebar moustache and, what was it they called it these days, a 'soul patch'? A barbed-wire tattoo around your throat didn't make you a hard man. Not in here.

Didn't even have the decency to put his book down when someone visited him.

Very rude.

Marky made a come-hither gesture and Ripcord and Charlie Bing slipped into the cell. Huge men, but they could move like ballet dancers when they wanted to. Charlie Bing: almost totally covered in DIY tattoos. Ripcord: face like the back end of an articulated lorry. Both wrapped in the kind of muscles you only got by spending eight-to-life in a prison gym.

The cell wasn't big to start with, but now it was positively claustrophobic.

Marky put his hands in his pockets. 'No need to be like that, Crowbar, not when I've got a present for you.'

Crowbar turned the page. 'Not interested.'

He *still* hadn't looked up from his book. How could anyone be so completely self-absorbed and unaware?

'That's a shame.' Marky nodded at Ripcord and the big man eased the door closed without so much as a single squeak, muting the choir's crimes. Another nod.

Ripcord and Charlie Bing lunged forward, silent as cats, pinning the disrespectful sod to the bed – one of Ripcord's huge hands clamped down over Crowbar's mouth.

His eyes went wide, tearing across the three of them. Then the struggling started: bucking and writhing, accompanied by what were probably meant to be threats. It was difficult to tell with Ripcord's hand in the way.

487

But it was nice to see Crowbar paying attention at last.

Marky gave him a smile. 'Sally MacAuley wants you to have this.'

It was a lovely piece of cell-made craft – a half-razor-blade embedded in a toothbrush. And you could tell it was quality, because the guy who'd made it had melted the plastic in the toothbrush's head first, so the blade would stay in there nice and tight. Had to admire craftsmanship like that.

Unfortunately, Crowbar didn't seem too keen: he went absolutely berserk on the bed. But Ripcord and Charlie Bing held firm.

'Don't be ungrateful, Crowbar, she's spent a *lot* of money on your present. The least you can do is try and enjoy it.' Marky held the blade against the skin beneath Crowbar's left eye. 'And I know you'll be worried, but we've got *plenty* of time. At least a couple of hours till they fix the CCTV. Be lights out before they find what's left of you. And the choir will drown out any screams, so we won't even disturb anyone.' He let his smile spread, showing off as much of his dentures as he could. 'That's nice, isn't it?'

Marky eased the blade upwards, pulling a trickle of blood from Crowbar's eyelid.

'Now, this might nip a bit...'